WOMEN OF HORROR ANTHOLOGY
VOLUME 4

Edited By Jill Girardi And Janine Pipe
With Foreword By Meghan Arcuri

FRIGHTGIRL SUMMER RECOMMENDED READING
Check out a roundtable with the authors of this book at
www.frightgirlsummer.com
#FRIGHTGIRLSUMMER

Dedication

This anthology is dedicated to all those who love horror fiction regardless of their gender, race, religion, orientation, identity, disability, physical appearance or any other such constructs. All are welcome.

WARNING: MAY CONTAIN SENSITIVE SUBJECT MATTER

This is a work of fiction. Names, characters, businesses, places, events, locales, and incidents are the products of the author's imagination or used in a fictitious manner. Any resemblance to actual persons, living, dead, or undead, or actual events is purely coincidental. This book contains adult situations and is not suitable for children.

COVER DESIGN by Ilusikanvas
KANDISHA PRESS LOGO by Lisa Kumek
INTERIOR FORMATTING by Eham

Copyright © 2021 Kandisha Press
All rights reserved.

Contents

1. Foreword: by Meghan Arcuri 1
2. What The Sea Gives: K.P. Kulski 4
3. Black-Eyed Susan: Ariel Dodson 14
4. The Silver Horn: Alyson Faye 28
5. Breaking Up Is Hard To Do: Caryn Larrinaga 37
6. Shoot Your Shot: Charlotte Platt 44
7. Follow You Into The Dark: Jennifer Soucy 55
8. The Groom Of Lorelei: Holley Cornetto 67
9. The Coachman's Cottage: Anna Taborska 80
10. Capable Of Loving: Sonora Taylor 88
11. Little Pig: Lydia Prime 103
12. Perfect Girlfriend: Angela Yuriko Smith 115
13. Misneach: Roxie Voorhees 129
14. The Kinda True Story Of Bloody Mary: Tracy Cross ... 141
15. Close To You: Cassie Daley 153
16. Sharp Spaces: Samantha Ortiz 163
17. An Agreement: Sheela Kean 173
18. Four Corners: Kirby Kellogg 182
19. Lady Killer: Melissa Ashley Hernandez 191
20. Subscribe For More!: Jessica Burgess 198
21. The Trial of Jehenne de Brigue: C.C. Winchester 209
22. Seeds: Marie McWilliams 215
23. Soul Grinder: Cecilia Kennedy 222
24. Fluid: R.A. Busby 234
25. Author Biographies 253
26. About The Editors 262

FOREWORD
by Meghan Arcuri

Editing an anthology seems like a challenging endeavor: from choosing the theme, to reading hundreds of submissions, to sending acceptances (yay!) to sending rejections (boo!) to coordinating and editing and promoting. I've never really done it myself, so I'm sure I'm missing tons of steps, as well as all the intangibles. But the trickiest part for me would probably be choosing the stories.

You've come up with an idea, and you envision how you want the book to look: the length, the tone, the feel. You open that first submission, and maybe it's nothing like what you thought you wanted, but, man, is it good. It knocks your socks off. It goes right into the "maybe" pile.

And as you make your way through the rest of the submissions, you find more like that one, or perhaps more unlike that one, but captivating all the same. The "maybe" pile grows and grows. Is it too big?

The "no" pile is probably a little easier: maybe they didn't follow the guidelines, maybe they needed to spend more time editing, maybe you straight up didn't like it.

The time then comes to deal with the gigantic pile of "maybes." Somehow you manage to whittle it down, and now you have to send out more rejections – boo!

And this, right here, is where I have tons and tons of experience. Like most writers, I've received a vast quantity of rejections. Gobs of them. I haven't done the math, but the ratio feels something like a billion to one.

And in the beginning—like most writers—I had trouble not taking it personally. Did they hate it? Was the story flawed? Bad plot? Bad characters? Bad writing?

Should I stop doing this? You can drive yourself nuts thinking about it. But as I've spent more time in the writing community, spoken to more authors and more editors, I've learned that rejections—even those pesky form rejections—don't necessarily mean you wrote a bad story. Sometimes it doesn't fit the tone of the other accepted stories; sometimes they had too many first-person POVs and yours didn't make the cut, and sometimes they loved, loved, loved it, but they ran out of room.

Sure, all rejections stink, but editors deal with the bigger picture and may not have rejected your story based on its quality. Remembering this can soften the blow. A little.

When Jill Girardi approached me about writing the foreword for *Don't Break the Oath: Women of Horror Anthology Volume 4*, I asked her for the original submission call. Turns out, she didn't put out a call for *Volume 4*. She had gotten so many amazing stories for *Volume 3*, she couldn't fit them in it. She was the editor with the gigantic "maybe" pile, who loved, loved, loved the stories, but had run out of room. Instead of forging ahead with another call for a different anthology, Jill—and her co-editor, Janine Pipe—used all the stories she'd gotten and loved from *Volume 3*, and put them into this book.

After reading this anthology, I have to say: I'm glad they didn't let go of these stories. Among them are tales of incredible heartbreak and loss, as well as cyber tales, fairy tales, and tales of love. You'll find all types of horror, too: quiet, gory, revenge. And then there's that cat…

This entire table of contents is filled with horror writers who happen to identify as women. Jill's press—Kandisha Press—is a woman-owned, independent press whose namesake is Kandisha, a succubus-like character in Moroccan lore. An evil temptress. A demonic female, who—according to Kandisha Press's website—"also represents the fearlessness of womankind."

I am honored to have read these stories, to have written the foreword, to have worked with Jill, to be among these fearless women.

- **Meghan Arcuri,** September 2021

Meghan Arcuri is a Bram Stoker Award®-nominated author. Her work can be found in various anthologies, including *Borderlands 7* (Borderlands Press), *Madhouse* (Dark Regions Press), *Chiral Mad,* and *Chiral Mad 3* (Written Backwards). She is currently the Vice President of the Horror Writers Association.

Prior to writing, she taught high school math, having earned her B.A. from Colgate University—with a double major in mathematics and English—and her masters from Rensselaer Polytechnic Institute.

She lives with her family in New York's Hudson Valley. Please visit her at meghanarcuri.com, facebook.com/meg.arcuri, or on Twitter (@MeghanArcuri).

What The Sea Gives
K.P. Kulski

The moon goddess sent me here, cast me ashore on this island that is barely more than a rock that juts from the ocean. A place where the sunrise searches for cracks through the rolling charcoal clouds, but never finds a breach. Half-dug into a steep slope is a turf-covered roundhouse where I make my home as best as I can. Everything I need, the sea provides for me; food and wood, kelp for weaving, clothing from the bodies of drowned souls that wash ashore on the rocks below.

They are offerings to my sorrow. An echo of memory that keeps me and destroys me all at the same time. Faces pinched in panic, long cold and cradled in the arms of the Sea Lady. I know what it is like to cradle the beloved dead, so I hold these souls with my flesh, giving the last vestige of warmth to their untimely ends and thank them for their gifts.

They give me so much.

A fire of driftwood crackles in the center of the roundhouse, smoke curling in languid dances toward the oculus above. I do my best to push the memories of my life before the island away. My world before here breathes in perpetual gray. The memory of color would be maddening if I allowed it space in my thoughts.

When the sky finally lets fall its tears upon the island, I catch the essence in carved impressions of large rocks. It always tastes faintly of salt, everything does here, the sea rules everything, crusting and infiltrating the leavings of life beneath the waves. Sometimes I lap at the water like a little dog and the image makes me smile as if someone could see me. And then, I realize how far I've come from civilization, from living in the view of others. There is a freedom in it, a regret too.

I lay in wait, every year for the equinox, watching the shadows of the sun creep behind the gray, measuring and keeping tally with carved lines on the inside walls. Yet I've lost track of the years I've spent here. I can only measure by lives. Twelve washed upon the shore, only three times has the ritual worked and given my existence back some meaning. I thank the goddess's veiled face for these times, and the other times, I admit, I curse her when the ritual fails.

I really never know the reason for the successes and failures and when it works, I care about little else. Then I live a season of love and fullness, but ultimately it ends and again, and I only wish to throw myself into the sea.

I have before— thrown myself into the sea.

But the Lady spits me back out again, right here upon this shore.

* * * * *

Weak green pokes up between sliding layers of rock, part slab, and part boulder. Flecks of iron turn slightly orange against the granite that entombs it. I lean toward the lichen, letting its odd cool and fuzzy tufts run along the palm of my hand before lifting it out. The lichen releases its hold easily, as if it had waited for me all along to bring an end to its tentative existence. Laying it in my basket, I move on, prodding with my walking stick for more to gather. The wind picks up and the never far ocean throws itself against the island with a sound of muted thunder. More lichen dot the stones and I pursue them, balancing upon the uneven layers of rock, leaning down and pulling, feeling the soft release from roots, the repeated acceptances of fates. I hadn't realized how close I've wandered to where I take the bodies of the dead.

I recoil, stumbling backward, catching myself before turning my back, moving in other directions, ones that take me from here. Not now. I'm not ready to remember them or anything else.

The wind pushes through my hair, against my skirts, uninvited and invading, I shiver and cast my attention back to the rocks, to the finding of lichen. It is hard to keep myself present, the threat of memories are dark knives and I won't let them cut me today. Already the basket I've brought is full, enough for the meal that I would prepare, so I walk the steep moor, up towards my little home.

It is not far, but the hike always leaves me breathless as the way is the same as climbing long steps to the top of a tower, one carved from the earth and rock and sea. I follow the path matted from my own passage, the low grasses are spotted with clusters of moss that dominate more and more as I reach the crest of the outcrop. All at once the world opens to me, jagged pieces of earth pointing to the sky that threatens to descend and press me down until I bow forever. Below the midnight sea swells and rises, falls and crashes, throwing up white sprays of frustration. It had me once. The Sea Lady will have me again, in the end. I cast a single lichen down, an offering of respect. On the edge, dug into the only collection of dirt to be found up here, my house pokes like a turtle under the slope of the turf roof. I sense a storm and am hopeful and sad at the same time. The door is crudely constructed of dried cords of kelp, holding together the remains of some ship's deck. The nails are long rusted and it won't be long before more kelp will be needed to repair it.

* * * * *

In my mind I can construct her tiny fingers, overlapping my own. A soft bubble of laughter that catches on her baby tongue. She clutches at me, wanting milk, wanting affection and I give her both. There is no space between us, only this universe.

But now I am all emptiness. A shell that for some reason the goddess has deemed should go on living. Moving through the tasks that keep me alive, for only a singular purpose, for the chance to again bring back that universe. However brief or temporary.

Stringing salted fish along the line, rending their flesh desiccated and chewy. I am hungry. But not for fish flesh.

When the storms come, I know, like I know now. The rain drives against the rocks and earth, pounding angrily as the wind throws the ocean as if trying to knock down this thing that has dared to jut and stand out. Even though I am inside, safe from the worst of it, the cold wetness still seeps through me. It is the kind of storm that ships cannot weather. I wrap my shawl tighter and rock myself to the sounds outside. All the fury of it reflects in my soul. The Sea Lady will claim people for her bounty tonight. Their heads will be dashed upon rocks, bodies hurled and broken by the waves, and lungs stuffed with saltwater.

*****

Along the east shore, dotted among the rocks and gravel are the things the sea has brought to me. As I make my way down to them, I try to count, but from up here it is difficult to see what is organic and what is not. I slip, catching myself and chiding my excitement. This is careful work. Should be. A gull cries overhead, calling at others, announcing the feast to be had. Must keep them at bay as long as I can. At least until I have finished gathering.

At the final descent, I hop onto the gravel like a child receiving baubles. Before me are the gifts of the storm. Shattered pieces of a ship's hull. Broken glass. A kelp- wrapped doll.

Two men. One woman.

Their faces blue, lips parted in desperation. One still reaches up, forever reaching for a savior.

I am here now. I'm the one you've reached for.

I hold each in turn. Whispering blessings and hopes for peace. The men keep their hair shorn close to their heads and have little use to me. I will bury them though, as I bury them all. For now, I work to stack rocks upon the dead, a small hope to keep the gulls off their flesh until I am able to give them a proper burial. The woman gives me a chill, her hair is long, still half-coiled. She must have woken that morning and did her hair as she would have had on any other day, not knowing that it would remain just so after she died and that it would be her last day.

I envy her.

But covet that hair. Using the broken glass, I cut at it, pulling free the strands in handfuls. My heart leaps with hope.

Yes.

This year, the ritual would work. It would be a year of joy. A single blessed year.

* * * * *

I bide my time. I need more bodies, more death, before this can be done. So I wait for another storm and it doesn't take long before the waves churn black, matching the clouds. For two days the darkness gathers along the horizon and in my roundhouse, my hands clasp at one another, turning knuckles white with anticipation.

I can almost smell my child. Through the salt air, the faint scent of baby sweetness, as if her spirit looms close, knowing her time is neigh.

"Come sweet one," I whisper against the dirt floor, to the fishes smoking over the fire. The thunder hits like a hammer, pounding into the rocks and leaving the entire world trembling in its wake. Howling the wind shreds the air, invisible swords of heaven. The sea knows, it splashes upward in response to the lashes, waves running this way and that, trying to escape the next slice.

Rain floods gush through the oculus, sizzling at the fire, ruining the fish. It doesn't matter at all to me now. Not anymore. I laugh at it all. The wind rushes through, finally finding my warmth, huddled in this hovel, it touches everything, feeling along the edges, and finally throws open my small door. The kelp ties give way, as do the weathered boards, splintering and breaking into jagged remnants. But nothing can mute my joy.

* * * * *

Once the storm passes, I step out and look down upon the rocks and the waves. The Sea Lady has pushed more gifts to me. More gifts than I've ever seen before. Bobbing on agitated water, lurching and lapping are the broken bits of hulls. Canvas white sails, ropes snaking about, and oh yes, the rest of what I need, the most prized of all. The sea teems with the dead.

* * * * *

I cannot possibly bury them all. Despite the chill air, I am sweating with effort as I pull bodies toward the cairns. To catch my breath, I move to salvaging planks and find a bottle of stoppered spirits in the gray sand. A bit of celebration, a nip to warm me in the cold nights. *Thank you, my lady. Thank you, for all your gifts.*

The gulls already circle, so many of them, but on my belt already hang the long hairs of three women. Long and braided, coarse and silky, two are midnight and one a warm brown, like the bark of a tree. With a sigh, I turn back to work. One more is all I need, but the sea gives me too many men with shorn hair. Holding a pole of driftwood, I poke along the bodies and scraps. Push away crabs that already pinch and carve into bellies.

Not only can I not bury them all, I cannot give myself to hold them all. Spirits fated to be unloved in the end and I am sorry for them. Yet sorrier for myself if I cannot find one more head of perfect hair.

A shine of glossy tendrils against the sand draws me, what appears to be layers of frills and skirts amass over a lump. I rush to the body and a wave of relief passes through my bones. Long hair, so long and ideal for my purposes.

I pull out my sharpened glass. At that moment the body stirs and releases a low moan. The wind whips at me with irritation and I can only stand, watching frozen and astonished. The first human sound I have heard for more years than I can remember. They move their head and I see their face.

A woman. A woman that's alive and lays upon my shore. Upon my shore and in my air.

Does the goddess test me? Is she checking to see my faith, or dedication to her rituals? I cannot think or muddle through any logic for this woman to have lived, when so many others have arrived battered, but always dead. For a moment, I consider taking up a large stone, one with a jagged edge so that it would pierce with each bash.

The wind continues its push and pull, urging me to action. Long ago, I had laid on this rocky shore much the same, empty of everything but grief. What did this woman contain? My limbs move to action before my decision. Gathering the tattered remains of a sail, laying it out like a blanket over the stones. I place the half-conscious woman upon it and begin the climb back to the summit.

* * * * *

On scatterings of torn cloth and clothing taken from the drowned, the woman sleeps and I do my best to wipe away the sea from her face and urge the fire to burn big and hot. As I work to remove the soaked embroidered silks of her robes, I find her stomach is swollen with child. My throat tightens, a cry from somewhere deep within my heart begs to escape but it cannot, I will not allow that. I push ever so gently against her middle and wait for a stirring, anything to give a sign of life still growing, still moving toward living. But the swell remains still. No sign that its tiny inhabitant made it out of the sea with their mother. A glint flickers with firelight under the woman's lashes, her hands going instinctively to her belly in protection. I pull at a patched cloth that serves me as a blanket and drape it over her, willing the woman warm again as best I could, but I cannot help but feel as if I have only pulled a shroud over the little one within her. I too put a hand, trembling to my belly. It is long empty, but the need to protect is still there, the longing to fill my arms, still aches. I will always ache.

The goddess knows these things. There must be a reason for the woman to have arrived here, alive as she is.

There is not enough hair yet for my own child. *How can I do the ritual for two?* But the goddess does not answer in words and neither does she answer to the humans who serve her will.

* * * * *

The woman has tried to urge me to talk with questions. She has sucked down water I've collected from the sky and dried herself by my hearth. She now hungers to know, to understand, but there is little else I can give her.

"My name is Sora," she entreats, hoping that if she gives, she will receive.

I do not want her questions and have no wish to grant her anything of me because I have not yet decided what to do. So instead, I give her long strips of dried fish and set to work on fixing the sail over the doorway. She chews and watches me, the sun hurries behind the perpetual cloud cover over the sky, arching like a displeased cat, toward the horizon.

From the corner of my eye, I watch her back, this woman, Sora and within my mind, I count the strands of hair I have collected and how much time I had left to decide.

* * * * *

In the morning, I walk the cairns, piled over all the bodies I've managed to bury. All the tender flesh given up by the sea. Perhaps there will be more, or another bit washed ashore, cast to this place by the goddess to give me direction. She's given me this place, this solitude, my wish. A single desperate wish.

To hold the child you've lost—

I did as I lost her and then, I longed. The forever longing made of useless wombs and empty arms. Then the goddess gave.

For a season and then I must repeat the pain again. But there is hope in it, the return of the season. But now there was this woman.

The cairns gave no help, only lumped over with stones, the dead held their tongues and I am like I've always been, alone.

* * * * *

When I return to the summit, the woman, Sora, releases a low whine, the sound of an animal sorely hurt and greatly afraid. She faces me with a sweat-slick brow. "Help," she begs, "help, my baby's coming." Sora falls back into the pile of rags, grunting and whining.

I regard her, studying how she writhes, how her mouth is full of noise and pain and I remember my own. How once I too had many words.

The fire is in need of fuel and I work to bring it burning hot and high once again, filling it a small pot with water and rags to boil. Again, I feel her belly, the unresponsive hardness and I wonder if the woman knows. My eyes meet her wild pain-filled ones and there is a darkness there I detect, a building corner of sorrow yet to be burst upon her, the forever grip of grief.

As the water begins its boil, tears fall from my eyes, but I work just the same. Hanging the boiled rags to dry, putting more into the pot and I settle, offering light touches of concern, small gestures meant to comfort. She is lost in agony and I cannot help but be bitter that all this struggle to birth a child will only produce a mere husk, empty of the thing she's been preparing.

* * * * *

Sora holds her baby, the unmoving form swaddled in the clothing of the dead. It too is dead. This small thing that should fill this tiny shelter with fierce cries. I hold my hands over hers that clutch the lump of flesh that, until a short time ago, was within her. Her tears have no sound, but they fall around us, fed by an infinite ocean. We sit like that for a long time, together holding this child, willing our warmth into its chilling form.

* * * * *

I am weaving.

I am weaving and I know when I am done what I must do. I've already wept because it is the season, *her* season. I have lost her, forever and didn't know her last season was truly the last I would hold her close again.

My tongue feels chewed and I pull at the saliva glands, seeking to wet my mouth enough to replenish the tears that seem to ceaselessly fall from my soul.

I am weaving.

And Sora hasn't let her child's body go. I know, I understand. It is impossible to release it to be cold and unloved when it was destined for ceaseless love. Now that love has nowhere to go, trapped inside it writhes in the forever pains of labor.

I am weaving and all the locks of the dead are taking shape, bending to the ritual. The tapestry is alive with the tales of those who have died, with the stories of those who came before me and the promise of the next chapter. One woman's hair has formed a chubby leg, another the arms. I am weaving and I know, Sora will give happily the crown of black hair that falls now, wildly around her grief-stricken face. She will give it and then, there will be a new season and the tapestry will go on.

* * * * *

We wake to soft snuffling cries and I take Sora by the hand. I lead her outside to where the stone bowls have filled with water and where one, cradles a child who kicks and reaches for her. It is a child summoned from the tears of the sky and the cold of the ocean. Odd and green it looks with webbing between its clammy feet and toes, his face overly smooth, noseless, and with black discs for eyes, features resembling those more of a newborn whale than human. It doesn't matter, the soul is there, the child is hers. The ritual had worked, the sacrifice of death and work, intent woven with each strand.

Sora knows her baby, even while the husk it was meant to inhabit still lays in her arms. With a look, Sora passes the body to me and runs to the bowl, lifting the baby aloft, the little being made by ritual, death and love. Grief runs from her face, her shorn hair a flag of sacrifice, of love, and yearning. She is smiling, dancing, and my heart aches.

The season isn't my daughter's any longer. It is the season of Sora's son and it will be until the next mother arrives.

With the sounds of Sora humming as she cradles her child of the sea, I walk with the husk in my arms. Up, up, we go, the soft motherly voice behind me fades upon the wind. I reach the top once again, me and this little empty vessel, eyes closed as if sleeping. I wrap her tight and whisper my love, how much I have missed her. I sing to her as I stand against the wind, far above the waves. I tell her the story of the life we should have lived.

Then I step off the ledge and we fall together. Cutting through the insistent wind, plummeting like a star into the sea.

This time, the goddess embraces me and pulls me into her depths, lets me sink into the endless pit of her saline. And finally, my child and I are covered— together, within the cold sorrow of never.

Black-Eyed Susan
Ariel Dodson

Susan.

It was the name of everything; the name that roused every sensation, every memory, every breath; and the name that drowned them all again in the resurging gulps of pain and whisky. She drank it to forget, of course; as if it were possible to forget something like that. As though it were possible to wipe her away, as though she had never been.

Susan.

She heard her in the song of the wind and the rustle of the leaves, in every footfall and creak of the house, in every telephone ring and whispered thought, and in every story.

Above all in every story.

That was why she didn't write anymore. Too painful?

She didn't know.

What she did know was that she couldn't bear the thought of writing her out; the risk of losing her to a set of words on a piece of paper to be interpreted by somebody else's eyes. It wasn't right. She wouldn't do it. She was her *mother*, for Christ's sake.

But was it right that she had lost her in the first place? A child. She was only a child, not yet ten, and with all of her life ahead of her. And all of Kate's too.

It was winter when it happened, almost a year ago now, with the frost clinging in fairy patterns to the window panes that had made Susan both laugh and exclaim in delight. That was the last thing Kate remembered – the wisps of pale hair tumbling over her daughter's face as she traced the pattern on the inside glass with her gloved finger; the same finger she had lifted a few seconds later to brush the straying strands away from her smiling eyes.

Kate hadn't thought anything of it. All the children skated on Platt's Pond in the winter, and at nine and a half, Susan was old enough to go on her own. She was with friends, and there were always at least a couple of responsible parents there. It was a small town, and everyone knew everybody else. It still felt like a community.

She'd only found out later about the cracks in the ice. Jenna Newbridge had let it slip; that several of the children had fallen in and had had to be fished out by the parent on watch. Susan had been one of them.

Kate hadn't known that. It seemed a cruel irony that her daughter had escaped that threat, only to be run down in the road less than a quarter of an hour later by a too-fast car skidding on ice. It was like a jeer of fate – it had been Susan's time, and there was nothing Kate or anyone else could do about it. Except that she should have been able to do something about it. She was her *mother*.

She'd been told to not keep reliving it. An imagined reliving at that, for of course, she had not been there. She had been too busy writing. As usual. What was the last thing Susan had seen, Kate wondered, over and over until she was ill with the thought of it. The car rushing towards her? The piled-up banks of snow? Did she note the absence of her mother, who had not even bothered to answer the door at first knock when they came with the news, so engrossed was she with the latest chapter of her new novel? The same new novel that was now nearly eight months over its deadline, on which Kate hadn't written one word since the persistent knocking had finally dragged her out of her imagination and into the bleak and bloody reality of her slaughtered child.

There were no pictures of Susan visible in the house. She had removed them all, after. Why would she need a piece of paper as a reminder of a person who was imprinted on every part of her being, her own child, her flesh and blood creation? Besides, she couldn't bear to look at her. It was her imagination, of course, but she hadn't been able to shake the feeling that Susan's eyes stared at her accusingly from behind the frames. Large eyes, green, like the colour of sea pebbles. Green and blaming her.

She had promised, she knew. That day together, the day when Susan would take precedence over her imagined worlds and people. She had always promised. But there was always one more paragraph to write, one more character to inhabit. She couldn't have foreseen what would happen, or do you think she would have let her go out on her own?

After the funeral, Kate had bundled the photos into a box and hoisted them to the top of her wardrobe, where she couldn't see them. If you didn't count her imagination.

The phone trilled suddenly, jarring and insistent and shaking her out of the darkness for just a moment. It was probably Rick, her agent, who'd been hounding her with increasing pressure over the last few months, despite his genuine empathy. Well, let him ring. She hadn't answered one of his calls yet, and she didn't intend to. What did she care now for publisher's dates and book launches, now that Susan was dead?

The thought made her gasp, as always. It was so unreal, so final, so like something from one of her own books.

The machine kicked in and Rick's smooth, careful voice sliced into the staleness of the room.

"Kate? Come on, Kate, please pick up. They're pressing me now for a date, any date you can give me. You can't expect them to wait forever." Pause. "OK. Well, call me when you can. We need to get this settled. Oh, and once again, Kate, I'm sorry."

He was sorry.

She should know that by now; he ended with the same goddamn phrase every time he hung up. But what else was he supposed to say?

Kate reached again for the bottle. The slug was comforting; a slick burning sensation down her throat, the familiar beginning of the blotting out. She had them delivered, for she rarely went outside for anything these days. She could go on for months until she really had drunk herself into oblivion, and that was just what she intended to do. Eventually. Except for the fact that she knew oblivion was only one more world without Susan.

Kate took another swig and wiped the tears from her face before rising to erase the message. Never heard it; don't know what you're talking about. She didn't know why she didn't just unplug the damn thing, but it gave her a strange sense of satisfaction to ignore it, even as she resented the intrusion. It was like a finger up at the world that had made her who she was; the world that had taken Susan away.

The machine beeped, and the tinny voice confirmed that Rick's plea had been trashed. Kate took a deep breath and another swig before turning. She could see her reflection dimly in a hanging wall mirror – shit, was that really her? She looked terrible. Well, good. She deserved it. And she and Mr. Walker were going to bed where they could drink themselves into that other sort of oblivion; the sort that consisted of unwashed sheets and snoring and no dreams. Perhaps she'd better take two bottles.

She tucked the second under her arm as she made for the stairs. The curtains framing the nearest window were open; a murky winter light still hung heavily outside, and she usually didn't bother closing them anyway. It wasn't like there was anyone opposite, and – shit. The bottle slipped from her arm and bounced on the floor with a good, hard crack. Hardwood floor and thick with dust. Damn. What a waste of good whisky. She'd have to clean that up in the morning. And – what the hell was that?

A noise; the one that had startled her and made her turn; a noise that sounded like something thumping at the window. Probably a bird, poor thing. Kate craned her neck to the glass to see if she could see it. There was nothing there. Perhaps it had just been stunned.

Poor thing, it must have hit itself pretty hard. She could see the impression of its body lingering on the pane for just a moment before fading as she drew away from the glass. And yet, it didn't look like a bird. More like a – hand. A small child's hand, with flattened palm and delicate fingers.

For a moment, Kate felt as though she would vomit. She focused her eyes, steadying her back against the bannister as she peered forward again. But no, it was gone. If it had been anything at all. She half-laughed, a nervous, jumpy thing that had almost forgotten itself, then jolted again as a furious flapping emanated from somewhere by the side of the house.

Dusk. Of course, they'd be returning to roost. Maybe even the rogue creature that had given her such a fright.

The fumes from the smashed bottle seemed suddenly stronger now, and she decided she'd clean the mess up tonight after all. She wouldn't remember by morning, and glass shards and bare feet were not a good combination. Funny, what she thought she had seen, and at that window. It had been Susan's favourite; Kate had even had a small seat installed below it so that Susan would be comfortable when she looked out.

Susan. Even the clinking of broken glass seemed to echo her name. Kate swept the wreckage into the bin and found herself another bottle.

* * * * *

One. Two. Three.
I'm coming.
Four. Five. Six.
Ready or not.
Seven. Eight. Nine.
Come out, come out.
Ten.
Wherever you are.
It had been Susan's favourite game when she was younger.

Kate had been wrong about the dreams, for they haunted her now like a reel of film, and she was too drunk to do anything about it. Susan as a baby; Susan at three, at six, at nine; Susan lying in the street surrounded by blood and snow. Dead.

One. Two. Three.
I'm coming.
Four. Five. Six.
What *was* that?

Groggily Kate forced her head upwards. She had no idea what time it was. The room was dark, but then it was winter. The rhythm came again, a pounding demand of brass on wood, and she realised with a sudden shot of memory that the game chant she had heard was actually a knock on the door. Or rather, knocks plural, for whoever it was, they were certainly persistent about getting in. The last time she had heard knocks like that was when –

The bile came suddenly, and she recoiled in disgust from her body as the smell rose. The knocking continued, urgent-sounding despite its repetitive sequence, and she tried to dismiss it as she fetched some wet clothes from the bathroom. Then she supposed she'd better check the door, for whoever it was, it was pretty clear they weren't going to go away.

"'Lright, right," she muttered, her words sounding slurry even to herself. "C'min'." She only just remembered to grab a bathrobe as she left the room.

Kate had no intention of answering the door. She hadn't opened it to anyone since it happened, except for the delivery people who brought her the internet orders she made for just about everything now. Why should she? Doors, and phones for that matter, brought nothing but news she did not care to hear. And so she would tell them through the door, whoever they were, firmly and politely, to go away. Leave a pamphlet through the slot if you must, but please go away. Except that she didn't know if firm and polite were possible in her current state.

Jesus, what time was it? It was black-dark outside, and far too late for anyone to be disturbing people, unless it really was an emergency. And she couldn't see that any more emergencies would pertain to her. Her annoyance increasing, she peered stealthily from the window, Susan's window, wanting to gauge how to phrase her dismissal.

There was no one there.

That couldn't be right. She could hear the knocks, still pounding with increasing volume until it felt the house would shake with the pressure. Shut up, shut up, *shut up*, her mind screeched, although it occurred to her she may just have screeched it out loud. She still felt fuddled, and for God's sake, why couldn't she *see* them? She had a clear view of the doorway. There was no one there.

She blinked suddenly, her bleared eyes smarting from the gleam of a car headlight passing the house. The reflection shimmered on something by the doorway and Kate turned, confused. A toss of long blonde hair. A blue anorak with a tartan hood.

Susan.

The realisation hit her with a coldness like a stab to the heart, the hope rising in a fierceness she had forgotten she possessed, that she had long thought withered and dried, except –

It couldn't be Susan for Susan was dead. One. Two. Three.

It was her heartbeat she was counting now, weirdly in rhythm with the incessant pounds on the door.

Four. Five. Six.

Ready or not.

Seven. Eight. Nine.

Come out, come out.

Ten.

Mummy.

The wrench was so visceral that it shocked her. "'M c'min', baby," she muttered, her knees buckling, her words so slurred that she could barely understand them. She hoped Susan wouldn't notice; that she was still too young to realise the state her mother was in. But surely it was understandable. Surely – after what she'd been through – after what they'd both been through –

Slowly Kate pulled herself back to the window, desperate for another view of her daughter, unable to wait for the opening of the door. The child was still there, long blonde hair swinging as her fist pounded against the heavy wood, so desperate, so violent, so unlike Susan, and yet, she had come back –

Kate wiped her face quickly, smearing the tears across her cheeks. She looked a sight, she knew, but Susan wouldn't care, Susan had come back to her. And why shouldn't she be as desperate to see her mother as Kate was to see her? Kate peered out again, anxious for one more glimpse.

As if sensing her, the child turned. Susan?

It was Susan's face, although strangely pale and elongated, as were her hands and the thin matchstick-like legs poking out from beneath her blue coat. Susan's blue coat. Kate recoiled suddenly, her back flat against the wall, not daring to look again. She slid slowly into a crouch below the window, wondering if the child had seen her. If the child could see anything through those eyes. Eyes so black and blank that they seemed beyond blind; eyes so empty that they were like great dark holes, except that holes were at least a tangible negativity. And these eyes – these eyes were nothing. They were not Susan's eyes.

One. Two. Three.

I'm coming.

Four. Five. Six.

Ready or not.

Seven. Eight. Nine.

Come out, come out.

No.

The word stabbed her to the heart, but it was right. That thing wasn't Susan.

Mummy. Mummy. Mummy.

It was Susan's voice, so plaintive and needy, just like when she had fallen over as a toddler, just like it must have been when – Kate felt herself taking a step towards the doorway.

Mummy. Mummy. Mummy.

The cries were increasing in intensity, the childish plea swelling into an almost psychotic rage. Kate could hear an added beat on the door that sounded as though it was being kicked.

Mummy. Mummy. Mummy.

She's angry with me, Kate thought groggily. Her brain still felt netted with drink; that must be why she felt the fear. Surely no mother should be scared of her own daughter. Unless –

She blames me. She's come back to make sure I know. Susan. Susan, my darling. I'm sorry.

The pounding ceased suddenly, and Kate's heart seemed to stop with it. Had she gone? Surely she wasn't going to lose her again? She couldn't – it would be too cruel.

Above her ear, the glass squealed as though a nail was being drawn over it, long and slow and sharp. Kate flung herself across the room.

This is ridiculous, the unfuddled part of her brain tried to argue. I'm hiding from my own child.

But it isn't Susan.

The pattering seemed to come from behind her; the sound of a million Saturdays and being late for school, of running for the phone or excitement at leaving for an outing, just like that day –

Susan?

The handprints on the glass answered her in a shower, fading just as quickly as they appeared, more and more and far too many for a single pair of hands, pattering, pattering – Oh God, please, what's going *on*?

The phone rang once, shrilly, and Kate's heart almost leapt from her chest. She crawled forward slowly, afraid of what might see her. Please God, there was someone on the end of that line. Someone who could help her –

The receiver felt awkward in her hands, and she fumbled with it as though it were a bad ball catch.

Mummy. Mummy. Mummy.

No!

Kate threw the phone across the room, the tinny voice still sounding in a swelling shriek.

Mummy. Mummy. Mummy.

"Go away," she cried. "Leave me alone. You're not Susan."

But the words sounded thick and foreign to her ears, and she didn't know how much could be understood. She'd drunk too much, she knew. Tomorrow, tomorrow she'd start again; turn over a new leaf. If tomorrow ever came.

Mummy. Mummy. Mummy.

There was a squealing now, a familiar sound that ached on her ears as though the window itself were in pain, and she peered over the edge of the couch, trembling. God, she needed to vomit.

The glass was misting up as though someone was blowing on it. That was why she knew the sound. Susan had liked to do that, on car or bus windows, on that very pane of glass. The tears felt hot and choking as Kate watched the letters form before her, perfectly twisted so that they read inside out.

Mummy. Mummy. Mummy.

No. Go away. You're not my daughter.

What could she do except repeat it silently to herself, knees tucked tight against her chest, hands clamped firmly over her ears in a failed attempt to block out the cries.

Mummy. Mummy. Mummy.

How many of them were there?

The house was really shaking now, windows rattling, doorknobs turning, the calls multiplying as the thing, whatever it was, sought entry. Entry to her. And all she knew was that it wasn't Susan.

Kate didn't know how long she remained perched, cramped in that unnatural position, but when the dawn began to glow in pink and gold streams in the sky beyond the window, the siege ceased. She raised herself unsteadily, her limbs fizzing with stiffness, her heart still pounding with shame and fear, the knocks still hammering in her brain with their perpetual call.

One. Two. Three.

She knew it couldn't have been Susan, not her Susan, her little girl, and yet she only had one thought.

My daughter hates me.

The room seemed different in the rising light, and for the first time in nearly a year, Kate saw the state in which she had been living.

No, no more, she told herself with a shaking firmness, as she swept a pile of old magazines into the rubbish. I'm cleaning up tomorrow. And I'll call Rick back. Although maybe not on that phone.

As an added precaution, she disconnected the offending instrument from the socket.

She had wondered if she'd ever sleep again after that night. But she was so tired, so tired that all she wanted to do was crawl into bed and drown herself in a dreamless darkness, dreamless but full, of rest and recovery for starters. What was that Scarlett O'Hara always said? Tomorrow is another day.

Kate could feel the cold breeze as she stepped into the room. Her heart stopped for just a second, relaxing again only when she realised that she had left the window slightly raised in a half-hearted attempt at fresh air. With a guilty shudder, she reached across to close it, not wanting to allow any access to the house while she was sleeping. She could only be thankful the thing hadn't found the opening last night.

Her fingers felt stiff as she grasped the sash and began to tug. The movement was slow; she still felt full of liquor and her body was aching from her cramped terror in the night. That was probably why she couldn't react as quickly as she should have.

The hand snaked suddenly through the narrow crevice, long and white, the fingers tapering into stringy points that resembled roots. It gripped Kate's wrist with an intensity that could have sliced through her; a searing cold and excruciating burning sensation all at once. She heard herself cry out, but the words seemed not hers.

Mummy. Mummy. Mummy.

It was wrenching her now, dragging her arm across the sill, yanking her face into the pane, the force so great that she really thought it would suck her through the tiny gap. She could hear herself screaming and yet still tangled within the sound was the repeated calling that grated on her ears and mind and soul until she felt that she had passed madness and had landed somewhere beyond.

Mummy. Mummy. Mummy.

Her body was jerking like a fish at the end of a line, and she felt it shudder as her flailings knocked into the wardrobe beside her, jostling the box that held the banished photos of Susan, tipping it over so that the contents fell and smashed, and the broken glass of the frame that had held her favourite picture flew sharp and stabbing and into the long, white, unearthly hand.

It slunk back quickly and Kate slammed the window shut, her breathing shaken with sobs. She was bleeding, but she extracted the favourite photo of Susan before she bandaged up the wound, leaving the picture propped against the wall on her nightstand.

"Tomorrow, baby," she promised. "I'll fix it. I'll fix everything that I can. Tomorrow."

* * * * *

One. Two. Three.

She awoke sharply when she heard it, her body still primed with fear despite the heavy sleep she had tumbled into. But the room seemed still and silent, and she realised with a fierce gush of relief that the counting was the pounding of her own head, a legacy she had inherited from her bottled companions.

Cautiously she eased herself out of the bed, wincing as she felt the stab of pressure on her wrist. The night had been uneventful after it, whatever it was, had gone. But she would not forget her promise to Susan. Kate turned, her heart light suddenly as she reached for the photo.

But the picture was gone.

The panic seized her in a wave, and she was ready to start fishing behind the bedside table until she noticed the box, closed and unmoved from its hiding place on top of the wardrobe. She hadn't put it back, had she? She distinctly remembered a decision to start cleaning up in the morning. Then – was it possible it had been a dream?

It must have been a dream; it was the only explanation. Things like that just didn't happen in the outside world.

But it had been very real. And she wasn't going to let Susan down now. "I promise, baby," she muttered softly. "I promise."

She winced again under the shower as the stream of water hit the wound. It must have been the broken bottle, she decided. She couldn't quite remember, but she knew that something had smashed last night.

It was her first job as she went downstairs, scrubbing the stains in her first proper cleaning effort in nearly a year with an enthusiasm that by mid-afternoon had turned into an actual spring clean. And she had not only reviewed the last two chapters of her manuscript, but had called Rick – on her mobile – and arranged dinner that evening at a local restaurant to discuss the deadline. She hoped Susan would be proud.

Her first job for upstairs was to slide a chair over to the wardrobe, climbing onto it to reach for the box.

"No more hiding now, baby. I'm going to rejoin the real world. And you're always going to be where I can see you. I can face it now."

She could hear the glass of the frames clink inside as she placed the box on the bed, her fingers eager as they sliced the knife down the tape.

"Now, my lovely, let's have a look at you."

Her favourite photo lay at the top where she had left it, but she felt it slip from her fingers as she stared at the child's face grinning back at her.

No. It can't be.

The picture was of Susan. Long blonde hair. Blue anorak with the tartan hood.

But the child was not Susan, for the eyes were black.

Kate fished frantically, breathing deeply in an effort to drown the rising sobs. The next and then the next and the next, all showing a child that looked like Susan, but with eyes so black and blank –

Mummy. Mummy. Mummy.

Kate hurled the box away. She was already halfway down the stairs when she heard it crash against the wall, in a tinkle of breaking glass.

She had to get out of the house. That was it. She hadn't been out in so long she was going stir crazy. And it was still daylight. Nothing ever happened in daylight. She'd be early for her appointment with Rick but she'd have a drink first – just a soft one – and maybe do some shopping. It had been a long time, and she was still determined to turn over a new leaf.

The air was strangely flat as she hurried to the garage. Not like expected rain exactly, but more an emptiness, as though everything was – dead. She couldn't hear a bird or a car anywhere.

Her hands were trembling as they hoisted up the garage door. The car was there, just as she had left it, and why shouldn't it be. It would only be a few minutes and she'd be out of there, back in the company of real people for the first time since.

Damn. Where were her keys?

She'd had them when she left the house; she remembered grabbing them from the pink shell trinket jar that Susan had bought her last Mother's Day. Well, the last Mother's Day they had shared together.

She must have dropped them.

Damn and damn again, she muttered under her breath, retracing her steps carefully. Why was she having difficulty seeing? It shouldn't be dark this early, even if it was winter.

She glanced up then, drawing her jacket more closely around her shoulders. It wasn't dusk; it was a ground mist, bleeding up from the mulch of sleeping things below into the air and surrounding her with a suddenness that was disorienting.

Don't be ridiculous, she told herself firmly. You're in your own front garden, at your own house. It's hardly a case for the jitters.

But she couldn't see a thing.

Kate found herself crouching, her hands fluttering over the grass in the hope that they'd stumble across the lost keys. But nothing. Swearing under her breath, she straightened. Damn it. She'd have to walk, although it would be slow progress with this visibility. She couldn't even see her hands in front of her face. She waved them suddenly, as if to prove it.

The hand, when it came, was cold; the fingers strangely elongated and tapering at the ends; not like roots, as she had thought, but more like claws. Sharp, determined claws, that could pierce towards an oblivion far deeper and quicker than a few bottles of Johnnie Walker.

Mummy. Mummy. Mummy.

Susan?

But when she turned, that name, too, seemed lost, somewhere beyond.

THE SILVER HORN
Alyson Faye

The planned buddy's camping trip had not gone to plan. Not from the moment Jay's car had broken down on the deserted stretch of unclassified road curving around the tops of the moor (a hoped-for shortcut) to when he'd found his girlfriend's affectionate messages on his best mate, Ethan's cell, wedged down the side of the passenger seat.

Fortunately for Ethan's health and bodily safety, he'd been absent at the precise moment of Jay's discovery, as he'd been taking a leak behind the rocks.

Jay, reading the string of increasingly explicit texts, smashed the phone on the dashboard, scraping his knuckles. 'You little bitch!'

He watched Ethan's lanky figure strolling back to the broken-down Corsa, 'Bastard!' he muttered and hit the central locking button.

'Hey, dude, let me in! C'mon, joke's over, it's freezing out here!' Ethan beat his bare fists against the passenger side door. Jay held up the cracked cell phone and Ethan's face fell. He looked guilty as hell and ashamed. It was a standoff. Neither of them was going anywhere.

Jay let Ethan freeze outside for half an hour, then let him into the car, where it wasn't much warmer, for the temperature was falling, as night bit ever deeper.

Ethan kept himself pressed against the door, hand on the lever, ready to scarper. 'Look, Jay, I'm sorry, really sorry. I feel crap about it all, but you know . . .' he trailed off, clearly running out of words. There was an awkward silence. 'One of us is going to have to go for help. You got any service yet?' He nodded at Jay's phone. It remained resolutely dead. 'There was a pub about a mile back, mate, had no lights on, but someone will be there, I bet.'

'You sure of that, *mate?*' Ethan winced at Jay's tone. 'Even in lockdown? The owners could just have moved out? Who'd stay up here?'

Ethan shrugged, 'What other choices are there?' *And,* he thought, *I don't want to stay here with you in this freezing tin can.*

Jay watched his friend grab a torch, an extra fleece, and walk away down the road, and be swallowed by the shadows. Afterwards, he wondered that if he'd known he'd never see Ethan alive again, would he have said something profound or stopped him from going? To his shame, Jay wasn't sure he would have. His best mate's betrayal burned and Jay's blood was up.

Instead, he swigged from his hip flask, a few smoky gulps, and wrapped himself in his sleeping bag, and nodded off. When he next looked at his watch it was after two, and that meant Ethan had been gone three hours.

That's too long. Way too long. What the hell?

The first real flickers of anxiety stabbed at Jay. He stepped out of the Corsa, kicked the front tyre, twice, then froze, in mid-kick as he heard an animal screech nearby. A death cry. On the skyline amongst the rocks, he thought he glimpsed movement, as though something or someone had just dropped out of sight. As if hiding deliberately.

Just a fox or something. Or a sheep. Yes that's all it is.

He knew though that the shape had looked larger than either of those animals, but what else could it be? He was in Yorkshire, on the moor, not in the wilds of Africa. He checked his phone again, no bars showing, so, with a mental shrug, he set off along the winding road in Ethan's footsteps.

Around him the moor pressed hard at the track, melding into it. Rocks and trees appeared to shapeshift in the moon-spun shadows. Jay's torch beam only lit up a pitifully narrow strip of road, about six feet in front of him, and everything beyond that lay in darkness and out there was where he sensed the creatures of the moor were moving, breathing, and stalking him.

Stalking?

He wasn't sure where that word had come from. However, he did feel watched. He caught a whiff of a feral scent on the air - rotting meat or manure? He pulled out a chocolate bar from his backpack and ate it in two bites. Right now he'd have Ethan back in a heartbeat, better a two-timing buddy than none at all.

He marched on, swinging his arms for warmth, and humming songs he'd learnt at school, under his breath, for comfort. The feeling of being followed persisted. To his right a bird flew upwards, squawking from the heather, and Jay skittered with fright.

Turning he glimpsed movement, a low-slung shape slinking into the depths of the mini forest of ferns, the ones that always reminded him of *Jurassic Park*. Their frothy tops quivered, as though something lurked in there, waiting.

He quickened his pace. It couldn't be far now to the damn pub. But why hadn't Ethan come back? Surely he wasn't so pissed off with Jay he'd abandon him? Anger fuelled his footsteps, that, and the growing fear of whatever was following him just a few feet away, out of sight, but now he could hear its panting breath.

'Oy! Who's out there?' Jay shouted in a moment of frustration.

Silence. The ferns froze. The night air seemed to still. Nothing moved. The feral scent drifted towards him again.

He began to jog, then run, and to his relief, he spotted the dark outlines of the pub nestled at the side of the road.

Thank God, he thought.

Behind him, he heard pounding, paws on the earth, and panting breath. Something was coming for him but he wasn't stopping to see what it was. The hairs on the back of his neck were erect, and he knew, in his gut, he was being hunted.

Prey and predator raced down the slope towards the pub, shrouded in gloom, showing no lights but it still gave Jay hope. It was potentially a safe place - if he could get inside. The creature behind him wasn't gaining on him, and with a last spurt, Jay flung himself over the gate and up the driveway to the front door. He hammered on it and shoved it. It was, predictably, locked. He groaned, and dashed around the side, yelling, 'Hey anyone home? Ethan, you in there?'

He tripped over a metal sign lying in the grass, his torch reflected a painted pub sign, showing an old-fashioned hunting horn, painted a glittering silver. Next, he bumped into a row of bins, lined up like sentries, at the rear. No lights were on here either. He jumped over the back fence into a paved yard and hammered at the back door, whilst he heard a snuffling, groaning sound coming up behind him.

In despair he finally grabbed a half-brick, and smashed in the side window and, clearing away the jagged shards of glass with his arm, he climbed in and swung his torch around.

He was inside a pantry or storeroom, but he didn't have long to linger, as behind him, the creature could be heard approaching, knocking over the bins. Jay dashed across the floor to the nearest door, pushed it open, and on the other side found a chair to wedge it shut.

He sank to the sticky carpet in relief, sitting slumped, as he took in the room. It was a modest lounge, with faded velour seating and walls decorated with brown cigarette stains. The interior smelt musty and stank of abandonment and human absence. But he was safe and the creature couldn't get to him. He heard it shoving against the door, but he wedged two more chairs, and, to his relief, it held fast.

'Ethan, you in here, mate?'

His voice cracked and echoed around the room. Tears pricked his eyelids and he told himself not to be so wet. All he had to do was sit it out till dawn and then . . . he didn't finish that thought.

Jay pushed through the door which led into the main bar area, where tables and stools stood piled up on each other like a bizarre art installation. All the optics were padlocked and there were no bottles on the shelves. Clearly, the pub had been derelict for some years. A sign by the bar said - *'Welcome Travellers, tarry here a while and whet your whistle.'*

Fat chance of that, thought Jay.

Exhaustion swept over him, and he settled himself down along the battered banquette. His watch said 04:17. *Where the hell are you, Ethan?* This was his last thought before sleep overtook him.

He dreamt he heard a horn blowing; a series of notes, true and pure, calling, calling . . .

When he awoke, cold and stiff, she was sitting at a table watching him. Her face serious and unsmiling. Her hair long and dark. She wore a drifty black dress, with her pale bare arms showing.

Jay leapt to his feet, 'What the – who are you?'

She laughed, a tinkling sound. 'A traveller, just like you.' She pointed at the bar sign.

'What - did your car break down too?' Jay was confused.

'In a way. Yes, my transport did fail me. I am stuck here. Trapped. It is so lovely to have company. My name is Layla.'

She put out her hand and Jay automatically took it. 'Jay.' She smelled of lavender, he noticed.

'Jay,' she spoke his name as though weighing every syllable. 'Um - did you see my friend, Ethan?'

Layla stared at him and he noticed how dark her eyes were, but with tiny gold flecks in them. *Unusual*, he thought.

'No, I did not have the pleasure of meeting Et-han,' she seemed to hesitate over the name.

'He was coming here last night, to get help. Our car broke down on the top moor road.' The rest of the awful night's memories flooded back. 'There was this animal out there too. Bloody big and it came after me.'

Layla looked doubtful. 'How strange. What animal? A fox?' she smiled which seemed to downplay his flight.

'No, bigger, more aggressive. It chased me.' Jay felt foolish.

'I don't know anything about an animal. Perhaps you were confused or frightened?' Layla came up to him, and touched his forehead with her fingertips. 'Or perhaps you have a temperature?' She stroked his cheek, feeling the stubble, and lightly kissed him on the lips. Tired and surprised as he was Jay responded to the kiss, leaning his body into hers. At that moment he wanted her. Very much. She was intoxicating.

She pushed him gently in the chest. 'You need looking after, I can tell. We should eat.'

'Food? Is there food here?' Jay perked up. He was famished.

Layla nodded and led him towards a door marked with the word 'Kitchen'. On the stove, a large pot simmered and smelt delicious. 'Stew. My own recipe. Sit.' She pointed to the chairs set around the pine table.

Jay ate two bowls of the rich meaty dish, filled with vegetables and thick with flavour. 'Wonderful, Layla. Thank you. But now I have to go and get help and find my friend.'

Layla sat back in her chair, her long nails drumming on the tabletop. 'Ah yes, this Et-han. Was he truly a friend though?'

Jay paused. Something in her tone caught his attention. 'Yes, I've known him since primary school. We're best buds.'

'Is that why he went off with your woman?' Layla's voice was so low, it could have been a purr.

Jay froze. He stood up and clenched and unclenched his fists. 'How the hell do you know about that?'

Layla smiled, 'He told me. He told me everything.'

Jay stared, there was something very peculiar about this exotic-looking brunette. Something feral. He felt he was being toyed with. 'You said you didn't see him?'

'I did not. But *she* did. My other. My twin. *She* met him. *She* hunted him. I cooked him. And we ate him.' Layla waved her hand at the empty dishes and the pot on the stove.

Understanding flooded Jay, and he doubled up, vomiting his meal over the stone flags, once, twice, until he was emptied. Layla watched him, face impassive, bereft of any human emotion.

Jay wiped his mouth, backed away from her and the puddles of vomit, 'Who are you? *What* are you?'

Layla nodded. 'Good questions, Jay. I am impressed. You're learning fast. Faster than Ethan. I am twofold. What you see is only one half of me. This is my home and we've lived here for a long time.'

Jay's head was spinning, this weird woman kept talking as if there were two of her and so she was probably off her head, but then – where the hell was Ethan? And she seemed – otherworldly to him.

'Now that you have eaten, it is time to play.' She stood up to face him.

'I have to go, Layla. I have to get help, get the car fixed, find Ethan- ' Jay's eyes involuntarily slid towards the cooking pot, and Layla laughed.

'I liked the taste of you when I kissed you, so I will be fair and give you a chance, Jay. You will have a head start. Go, run.' She waved at him and pointed to the outer door. 'Go!' her voice rose and for a moment seemed to blur into a growl and her shadow stretched and split, and became that of a four-legged creature with a low- slung body and waving tail.

Jay gawped. The air buzzed around him, he could barely see Layla through the dust and particles spinning around her, but he could make out her golden eyes. They did not blink.

'RUN!' she roared.

Jay turned and legged it, through the door, out into the courtyard, over the low fence. Heart pounding, the adrenaline forced him onwards. Outside it was still dark. He couldn't understand why it wasn't dawn yet. Was he caught in an endless nightmare night? Had he died in the car of hypothermia and this was his living hell? Behind him, he heard roaring, and the padding of paws. She was coming. Whatever the other half of her had turned into, the woman he knew as 'Layla' had disappeared, and the creature was coming for him - again.

He cut up onto a track above the pub and headed into a copse of trees. The smell of manure became overpowering. He caught his foot on a rock and toppled headlong into a dip, fringed by more of the Jurassic ferns. He heard a disgusting squelch as his right boot sank into a pile of soft dung. Lurching, Jay lost his balance, swayed, and toppled sideways. He tried desperately to keep his mouth closed.

In the torch's beam Jay absorbed the sheer awfulness of his situation:- the stinking pile was faeces and worse than that, the filth was littered with white chips, as though a china crockery set had been smashed everywhere by a toddler having a tantrum on a nuclear scale.

Jay, unwilling, but driven by curiosity, picked up one of the longer ivory sticks. *They're like chopsticks*, he thought, feeling on the cusp of hysteria. In his fingers, the bone was razor-sharp at one end and cut his fingertip, yet it was oddly smooth in the middle. There were tooth marks up and down its length. He dropped it with a shiver. It reminded him of the bones in his Nan's Christmas turkey carcass.

He crawled to the edge of the pit and peered over. This was turning out to be the longest night of his life. He heard a snuffling in the trees and knew he didn't have long. Holding in a sob, Jay hauled himself out and moved as quietly as he could amongst the trees.

He needed to get to the road, flag a car down, if there were any cars in this strange never-ending night, and escape to civilisation, where he prayed and hoped that Ethan would be waiting for him, saying it was all a practical joke and, of course, he hadn't gone off with his girl.

Behind him, a small animal cried out. Once. In pain. Jay empathised with its plight. He jogged through the trees, trying to orientate himself and not make too much noise. The moor unrolled before him, gorse, heather, rocky outcrops, tussocky grass and mud, and . . . to his extreme right, a thin shadow moved, this one was standing upright, taller than his own six-foot height, and therefore not the Layla-creature.

The tall figure took up a sentry's position on a rocky outcrop and beckoned to him. Short of options, Jay decided to obey. As he jogged nearer, he saw the figure was wearing a cloak, helmet, and long boots. And was carrying a silver horn covered with engravings. Jay's heart sank. This night kept on getting more bizarre. Now his best chance of help rested with someone in fancy dress gallivanting around the moor.

'Help me, please,' he gasped, as he reached the rock. The face was hidden by the helmet's nose piece, but the eyes staring out at him were grey, steady, and intelligent.

In reply the figure lifted the horn to his lips, and blew one note, true and pure. The air shimmered around Jay, the moor seemed to inhale then exhale, the rocks to shift and crack open, the grass flowed like water and the sky lightened to rose-gold.

Jay knew his pursuer was there, right behind him. He'd heard her approach, smelt her foul meaty breath. As he turned he caught a glimpse of stripy fur, a spiky spined tail, and vicious claws, before she morphed, in the blink of an eye, into the girl he'd eaten a meal with at the pub. The girl who had kissed him. And he'd enjoyed that kiss. He had wanted more.

'Jay, don't be scared. I'm back now. I won't hurt you.' Layla reached out to touch him. For a moment Jay did nothing, just stared at her, as if hypnotized, then instinct kicked in, and he reared away from her.

'Bloody hell, Layla. Don't come near me. What are you?'

Tears rolled down her cheeks, her sorrow seemed genuine. 'I am what I was born as. I cannot escape my nature. None of us can. I am the last of my kind. But I am so lonely, Jay. Stay with me. Be my lover and companion.'

She turned to the gaunt figure, standing above them, in silence, with the silver horn dangling from one bony hand. She bowed her head. 'Let him stay with me,' she begged. 'I will not hurt him.'

The fire in her irises flickered, little flames of desire and death. Jay felt the pull of her, the duality of her nature, the feralness and the femininity. He wanted her, he could admit that, but he was terrified of her too.

'Who are you?' he asked the helmeted figure and into his mind came the words, 'The Keeper.'

Jay felt the wind blow fresh on his cheeks, ruffle his hair, calm his heart, and felt hope flare in him. He knew it all was emanating from The Keeper. He lifted his arm to point and Jay saw, in the distance, the glimmer of rising sun on metal, the abandoned car.

His escape route to freedom. Jay knew this would be his only chance. It was more than Ethan had been offered. And the others whose bones lay in the death pit. He turned to walk towards the breaking dawn.

Layla roared, a cry ripped from the wild beast trapped within her. He heard her pain, felt her loneliness. However, he did not look back. He knew if he did, even for a moment, he'd be lost. The note of the silver horn followed him, fading, until it was but the vibration of an echo.

Breaking Up Is Hard To Do

Caryn Larrinaga

"Go away, Nathan." Jessie's thin fingers curl around the edge of her front door as she blocks the narrow opening with her body. A strawberry blonde curl falls onto her forehead as she shakes her head, and the scent of her coconut shampoo drifts my way. "I told you. We're through."

I'm standing on her stupid "Wipe Your Paws" welcome mat and gripping her doorframe with both hands, partly to stop myself from swaying but mostly to give myself something to squeeze that isn't her throat.

Not that I *would*.

Deep down, she knows that. If she would just let me inside for a minute, I could explain that last time had been a mistake. I didn't mean to grab her wrist that hard, and besides, if she hadn't yanked it away from me just to be dramatic, she wouldn't have sprained the damn thing.

She can't punish me for her own mistake.

"Jess, I—" A sudden belch interrupts my attempt to reason with her.

She waves the hot air away from her face. "Gross. Surprise, surprise. You're drunk."

"I'm not!" I lie.

"Rrrrowwwrrrrr." Beanie, Jessie's overweight orange tabby, throws in his two cents from behind her legs. There's an undeniable smugness in his pale green eyes as he glares at me around the edge of her pink All-Stars.

I suppress a growl of my own as I dig my nails into the wooden doorframe. Little bits of white paint fleck off and pepper the doormat. I gave her those shoes for her birthday. I've given her *everything*, and this is how she repays me?

"Beanie, hush," Jessie tells the cat.

He hisses and swipes at me a few times through the cracked door. I hiss back, but Jessie isn't amused. She inches the door closed until only one of her eyes is visible through the slit.

I resist the urge to poke it, changing tactics instead. "Okay, fine. I get it. Can I at least come in and get my stuff?"

"What stuff?"

"I left a case of beer in the fridge, and I know I've got some Xbox games in there."

She glances down at the cat, then back at me. Her eyes slide off my face and onto something beyond me, and I turn my head to follow her gaze. There's nothing there; just my old sedan in her driveway and a few other cars passing by on the quiet, two-lane highway that connects her little farmhouse to my apartment in the city. The summer breeze ruffles the untamed grass on her lawn, and when I turn back to look at her, the golden glow of twilight warms her face.

God, she's beautiful. I reach out to stroke her cheek, but she pulls back, shaking her head. My outstretched fingers close into a tight fist, which drops to my side.

"Now's not a good time," she says, not meeting my eyes. "Come back tomorrow and I'll have all your stuff in a box, okay?"

It's not okay, but she doesn't give me a chance to argue. She just shuts the door in my face, and I hear the deadbolt slide into place.

I kick her door before stomping off the porch and down the driveway, grinding a tall weed under my boot as I pass. I hate it out here. I know she does, too; she doesn't even try to keep up on her yard, and the house is falling apart. She inherited it years before we met, just like she inherited The Orange Monster. *Beanie.*

Her life would be so much better without this house. It's a chain hanging around her neck, dragging her down. She's drowning out here by herself.

But she won't listen to reason. Not Jessie. She's too emotional. I've tried so many times to get her to move into the city with me, but she says she doesn't want to live in an apartment, like she's too good for it or something. But I know the real reason she won't give up the house. She can't handle the thought of giving up her precious, awful cat.

I reach my car and slide into the driver's seat, but I don't start the engine.

Instead, I fish my flask out of my glovebox and take a healthy swig of Jim Beam.

Then another.

And one more for luck.

This isn't fair. I've been nothing but good to her, given her whatever she wants, and she won't even let me come in the house for five minutes?

Maybe she's scared. She knows that if she listens to what I have to say—really, really, listens—she'll realize how lucky she is to have me. I'd like to see her try to find another man as good as me.

No way.

One look at the dump she lives in, one whiff of that mangy little shit Beanie, and a lesser man would hightail it for greener pastures.

She needs me.

And come on, everything about me and Jessie works except for that furball. He's the reason she dumped me. That's the only thing that makes any sense. She claimed it was the drinking, but I hardly drink at all. It has to be the cat. If he wasn't in the picture, she would come crawling back to me, lickety-split.

The full moon rises above my car like a lightbulb above my head. The solution to everything has been right in front of me the whole time.

No cat, no problem.

The plan comes together with just a few more swallows of bourbon. Jessie locked the door, but I bet she still hasn't bothered fixing the latch on the window above her kitchen sink. I've been after her about it for weeks. She's out here all alone in the boonies—any lunatic could climb through it in the middle of the night.

Only I'm not a lunatic. I'm a genius. I can wait until she goes to sleep and sneak inside…

Then I'll make Mr. Beanie go bye-bye.

A grin spreads over my face as I back my car out of the driveway and park it a half-mile down the road. My flask and talk radio keep me company while I watch the clock. Jessie's an "early to bed, early to rise" kind of girl, but to be safe, I wait until midnight. Then I head back on foot, keeping to the edge of Jessie's property until I reach a point where I can sprint across her overgrown lawn to the kitchen window. The sash is too high off the ground for me to reach, but I spot her bicycle leaned up against the side of her garage. I wobble a little as I roll the bike over to the house and prop it against the siding. Adrenaline and excitement power me up my makeshift ladder, and a few seconds later, I'm sliding the window open and squeezing my way into the house.

"Nathan, you clever dog," I whisper, swaying slightly on the linoleum.

It's as quiet as I hoped. Ever the heavy sleeper, Jessie's soft snores drift into the kitchen from her bedroom. The grandfather clock in the hallway ticks loudly, and…

I cock my head and narrow my eyes. Either I'm imagining things, or music is coming from the living room. I know that moody, synthy score. Somebody is playing one of my video games, and it sure as hell isn't the girl snoring away in the next room.

My teeth grind together and my fingers curl into fists as I stalk down the hallway toward the too-familiar sounds of Grand Theft Auto V. I hate to admit it, but

I've been wrong about something. She didn't break up with me because of the cat.

Some other guy swooped in on my territory and convinced her he would take better care of her than I could.

And she was just stupid enough to fall for it.

Sure enough, when I round the corner, a station wagon with a shot-out back window is on the television, careening down a rural highway not too different from the one outside. Jessie's new flame faces away from me, his body protected by the thick cushions of the recliner—*my* spot—as he plays the game. A blue cooler is open beside him, and the brown tops of a half-dozen beer bottles poke out of a small mountain of ice. As I watch, a pale fist pops up over the top of the recliner. It opens, and two empty, crumpled Gushers packets fall to the floor behind the chair.

A loud burp drowns out the game's music.

For an instant, all I see is red. He's in my chair, playing my game, drinking my beer....

Screwing my girl.

Words won't be enough. There's only one way to tell him—to show him—exactly how badly he messed up when he decided to try to take Jessie from me.

Tiptoeing as quietly as I can manage, I sneak up on the back of the recliner. Then I reach out with both hands and shove one side of the upholstery, forcing thechair to swivel around and reveal Jessie's new boy-toy like a cheesy Bond villain. He's a husky guy with a large belly and—

I recoil. He's naked. I can see *everything*. Well, almost. This guy is the hairiest person I've ever seen. Wild patches of orange hair cover his skin, sticking out in odd directions, especially on top of his head. What the hell is Jessie doing with this... this... *beast?*

He stares up at me, and the glint of moonlight through the windows reflects strangely off his eyes. They're a pale green, and his pupils are weird, narrow slits. He looks me up and down, then heaves himself out of the chair. He's taller than I am, but that's never stopped me from winning a fight before. And he's fat. Soft.

This is going to be a piece of cake.

His face splits into an insane grin. Long, sharp fangs fill his mouth, and a stench like rotten fish punches me when he screams.

"Rrrrowwwrrrrr!"

The stink and the sound startle me so much that I just stand there like an idiot until he tackles me. Pain sears down my forearms and my chest as his claw-like fingers tear at me, slicing right through my t-shirt and into my skin. He bites me over and over, fangs sinking into my face, my shoulders, my arms. I scream, but he screams louder.

In the frenzy, I can't tell my voice from his.

My knees buckle. I drop to the floor. He leaps onto my back, screeching and hissing. His teeth are tugging at the back of my neck and his feet are kicking at my ribcage, dominating me until my body goes limp.

It's over as fast as it started. His jaws unclench from around my skin and he stands, climbs into the chair, and returns to his game. I lay on the floor, blood and urine warming my legs while the rest of me goes cold. My breath hitches and rasps in my chest, and I listen to the Grand Theft Auto soundtrack as I drift in and out of unconsciousness.

Jessie's voice wakes me sometime after dawn. It takes me a while to open my eyes, but I finally muster the energy to do it. She's standing above me, her linen pajamas clinging to her body. One hand covers her mouth in horror.

I don't have the strength to say her name, but relief floods through me. I'm saved. She'll call the cops, they'll arrest her new boyfriend, and somebody will take me to a goddamn hospital.

But Jessie doesn't bend down to see how I'm doing. She steps over me like garbage in the street and rushes to the recliner. "Oh, my poor Beanie! You're a mess!"

My vision goes fuzzy for a second. When it clears, Jessie's standing over me again. Her cat is in her arms. His orange fur is matted and sticky with blood.

My blood.

The cat stares down at me. His whiskers lift his cheeks like he's smiling.

Jessie gently wipes a chunk of my flesh off the beast's nose. The two of them disappear from my field of vision. A moment later, her voice drifts in from the other room. I'm sure she's finally calling an ambulance now. A tear rolls down my cheek.

Her voice grows louder. She's getting closer.

" … such a naughty kitty. You could have woken me up while you were still big enough to help me. Now what am I supposed to do?" She's back in the room now, hovering above me with a worried look on her face. Something shiny flashes.

A shovel.

Jessie hoists it above her head and sighs. "I guess I have to bury him by myself."

Shoot Your Shot
Charlotte Platt

"I'm not afraid to die," he said, blinking sweat out of his eyes. He'd turned red, like one of those plum tomatoes you get in a salad, short hair slick against his skull. It made the golden fuzz darker, almost brown. Athletic, he'd shaped his body through hard work and venom. Smelled like he'd had years to marinate in his own hate and righteousness, letting it slowly boil up.

"You should be, nothing good happening to you when the lights go out," I said, sucking air through my teeth.

He stood before the library counter, his back to the exit and blocking my escape, bristling like an angry boar. He certainly had no place in this space. His presence shattered the sanctity of knowledge and focus here.

The utilitarian carpet was steeped with red, spreading out along the square tiles around it like rain finding a path down a windowpane. We were surrounded by bodies, the result of his efforts with a gun which he now pointed at me. The day's heat made the metallic fug of blood hover around us, undercut by the sharp tang of adrenaline.

Death doesn't limit itself to just one smell, no matter what people tell you when they're deep in their cups and haunted by the past. Blood is common but not constant; shit's more frequent. Rot, decay, desperation.

"How would you know, religious? Want a chance to pray to your god?" he asked, mouthing a snarl. I laughed, more at the ridiculousness of his suggestion than him, but I saw his face sour, passing like a ripple over a pond. "You think I won't do it?"

"You will. We're surrounded by bodies," I said, nodding to the corpses. One pile was clustered at the door; they'd tripped over themselves trying to get away. Some lay prone on the spiral staircase going up to the next floor, books tossed aside as they ran for it. "I'm not one for prayer."

"Just a judgmental little bitch then?" He grunted, wiping a hand over his face. He was looking at me like I was meat, eyes flicking over my shape and checking for a soft spot.

The overhead lights shone brightly on him, reflecting his clammy skin, the jut of bone against his cheeks. Pretty face for a murderer. A perverse silence was stretching between us, a chasm of sound after the loud shots and screams from before. Much too much noise for me.

"Could say that. Wouldn't quite be right. Not that you care about that, of course. Did you upload a manifesto? That's all the rage now."

"Are you a negotiator or something?" The frantic energy broke away for a minute with the drop of his shoulders. He looked his age then, young face no longer contorted. He had too few years on him to earn the fate coming to him now.

I take the view of a few years per victim for something like this. But that's just me. We all vary on that method of judgment: you can never tell till they're in front of you.

"I'm quite used to making deals. I'm Bel. I was just in the maths section." I held up my book, thick enough to be a weapon if I was so inclined. I indulge in catching up with the new advancements, seeing the same knowledge once lost spread out into the world like the creeping frost of winter.

"Adam. A smart person would have run."

"A smart person wouldn't have shot a bunch of people, but looks like we're idiots together. Do you mind if I sit down?" I nodded to one of the smaller tables, a chair overturned by a person in their fright. The chair didn't have blood on it—maybe they got away. Maybe they were at the bottom of one of those piles.

"No, I'm in charge here." He flicked the gun a little, pointing me away from the seat.

"As you wish. Do you want to talk about it?" I hugged the book to me.

"What?" His face flipped to a scowl, the hardness creeping back as a wave of tension washed over him.

"Well, there's a lot of dead people. Usually, there's a reason why. That's why I asked about a manifesto."

"I uploaded a video," he said, chewing his lip. They were chapped, dehydrated. Unusual with his muscular frame, couldn't afford to run dry when working out. Maybe an anxiety thing.

"So they'll see your face, know it was you." I watched the idea settle over him.

"Yeah, they can't say I was doing it for some other reason. They'll have to listen."

"People are good at ignoring clear messages. Having a face means they're more likely to process it," I bit back a sigh. Not a forced one then, but not holy either. Less sudoku and more spot the difference.

The ones who're convinced they're on some holy mission, they're more interesting. You can speak to them in those scant breaths between uncertainty and knowing, before the deep pit of old knowledge awakens in their brains—usually once they've done the unspeakable.

"Exactly, they'll see I'm like them." The gun went down, pointed towards the floor as he shifted on his feet.

"You're the first one to take action."

He paused, chewing his lip again. It cracked, the bloom of red streaking across his teeth and oozing down towards his chin. I wasn't sure if he was the type used to tasting his own blood – some of them are. Enough beatings in school, overbearing parents who understand fists before tears.

"There are others," he said, pulling me out of my evaluation. "Naturally," I said, hugging the book tighter.

"They feel like me." "What's that like?"

"You're just trying to buy time." He brought the gun back up.

"I've no reason to." I hadn't heard the song of sirens but they would be coming. He knew that. A good way to get your face on the news. As was a body count. Lazy ways to make an impact on the world.

"You're hoping they'll save you." He sneered, an ugly enjoyment in the implication.

"I doubt it, they tend to shoot first and ask questions later. I'm safer with you.

At least you'll do it properly."

"The fuck's that supposed to mean?"

"Police might get me in the spine or something. You killed everyone quick. Knew what you were doing."

"I practiced," he said, a little preen in the tilt of his chin. The lights were starting to fizz out in the research sections, a blinking rhythm of darkness edging closer to us. I rolled my neck.

"Dedicated." I nodded, smiling at him. "You trained up."

"Yeah, got a system. Wanted to look good in the video, show people what they could do."

"Empowered and empowering others, that's a good combination."

"None of us are empowered now. They took it all off us. Came in and pushed us out. It's all about what women want now, how they should get special treatment. You can't find a good one that isn't tied to some wrinkly old wallet."

Urgh.

"You're an attractive guy, I'm sure that's not a problem for you," I said, the words dry on my tongue.

"Don't think you can flirt your way out of this." His lip curled up to show his teeth, eyes darkened like the turning point of the tide. Of course, he would see this body as a woman. The accent might even still be French; that one stuck a long while.

"I'd have no intentions of such," I said, shaking my head. "You're built up, a lot of people like that."

"They're all chasing money. Doesn't matter anyway, leaving a pretty corpse is good for the cause."

"You don't want to get your day in court, send your message?" There were still no sounds of police, yet, no one moving between the stacks or squeal of tires. Good.

"My video does that. We need another saint. Our supreme gentleman went ahead of us and more should lead the way."

"They don't need a leader, just an example?" I asked. "Exactly."

"And are you a good example?" I asked, letting the book sag lower on my front, the movement pushing my chest up a little.

"What do you mean?" He faltered, peering at me over the line of the gun.

"You've killed a lot of men, by the looks of it. If you were angry at women it seems… counterproductive."

"They were a bunch of beta simps, barely men."

"Right, not all men are on the same level as you, got it." I didn't want this one.

"Not brave enough to see what's really been happening with the world," he continued.

"Tell me about it," I said, stretching my shoulders a little. It was starting to get cramped in here.

"What?"

"Tell me how you think it is. I've not met someone like you in the flesh."

"You're just trying to keep me talking to distract me. Lull me into trusting you," he said, hitting his chest with his free hand as he started to pace a little, making a small circle back and forth.

"You should trust me on the whole hell part, but nothing else, that's entirely fair." I dropped the book. He flinched as it landed, the gun arm jolting up. He must have tugged the trigger as the sound of the shot echoed around us, loud in the cramped space.

"Stupid bitch." He spat, swinging the gun back onto me.

"My arms were tired, sue me. They're not coming, you know."

"You're trying to psych me out. I'll shoot you!" His eyes were wide as saucers now, white all the way round those cornflower blues, his hair almost crackling with the electricity jolting through him.

"I'm not convinced, but you might. No huge loss if you do."

"Are you suicidal or something?" he asked, pulling back a little. "No, just bored of this."

"Fuck you, then," he said, pulling the trigger twice.

Bullets are boring, I cannot stress that enough. They're useful against fleshy creatures but there's no venom in them, no heat in the blood. It's not like they're even any good against the fae now that you make them with copper rather than iron.

The problem is they lack the intimacy of blades and they don't have the righteousness of arrows. There's a separation between the rage and the damage.

They're also pretty useless on things like me.

His aim was decent, two into the chest and an expectation that I'd drop. Lazy all the way through, no care to aim for the head.

The look on his face when I kept standing was kinda worth it though.

"Your grouping is good, did you grow up around guns?" I asked, stepping closer. Two more shots, one in the throat, which was probably more luck than skill. I swallowed the blood, laughing a little. "Gone shy on me?"

"What the fuck is going on?" He started to back up, free hand swinging behind him, knocking chairs out of his way. He went all the way along the reading area and into the desk, eyes wide as a fat moon. The blood from earlier was still dripping down his chin, a stark smear against his damp, pale face.

"I think you're just unlucky," I said, tilting my head to one side. Blood oozed out of the hole in my neck, black and hot. The smell of rot and dust followed it out. "You must be unlucky to be here with me."

"Is this gas or something? Hallucinations?"

"Quick mind, I like that, good. Maybe we could do something for you."

He pulled his head up, shaking it as he looked at me. I was close enough now that I could see the threads of red in his eyes, the bloodshot, snaking marks. "I'm not crazy."

"No, just lazy. Too many quick solutions and not enough thought." I reached up and tapped the middle of his forehead, letting my finger sit on his browbone.

Seeing through a human is never a good experience. You're not built for our sort, not while you're still in the fleshy bits. Once the mortal coil has been shuffled off it's a bit easier, souls have a deeper understanding.

Looking through the eyes of Adam—that name was a mistake—I saw the version of myself before him. Petite, brown hair, glasses, enough of a bosom to be interesting, no wonder that old prick Bishop Binsfeld thought I was bad news.

The bloody holes in the chest were a distraction but not enough to stop this idiot from feeling aroused at my breasts. The one in the neck caused him more concern, at least.

The funny thing with this sort of manoeuvre is, we're not technically meant to be able to do it anymore. Back in the older times when angels were sent down and He above still interfered this was considered fair play. Ever since his progeny got strung up we're meant to be a little more subtle.

We can be summoned, or we can have a blood tie, we can be invited and invoked. But we're not strictly supposed to slip in with physical contact. I never did bother to learn why; something about our eldest and Him making a deal or some such. "What a mess in there," I said, able to see the lips of my body move with the words. His mind was all a jumble, shortcuts through logical conclusions into self-indulgent fantasy, feedback loops fed by others just as short-sighted as he was.

Even his lusts paled into violence, more rage than rapture.

I let myself linger to watch as my form slipped, a slough of skin pooling down like silk. The illusion of beauty was always left to rot, the petals falling away to leave just a thorny stem. Pretty distractions had no place in hell.

I rose taller than him, too tall to fit well in the library space, my shape spreading out like spilled water, skin the same waxy white as a drowned corpse. My tail flopped low and heavy, the tuft at the end charcoal grey, and my horns scraped the lights above us. The electric buzz made my ears twitch and then the bulbs popped out, glass tinkling down around us. It dusted over his face like snowflakes. I rolled my neck, horns dragging through the tangle of metal and wires, before looking down at him.

I'd forgotten my eyes were purple in this time. It wasn't a bad look.

The kick of his heart was thumping like an old drum, and for just a moment I was back at the beginning, back to the cold burn of the stars and the bloody, screaming rend as heaven pushed us down. It's an indulgence to think back to then, to savour the thrill of falling forever into the blackness before the heat came. Hell offers so many joys, but the heat is unrelenting.

I slid back into my body, dragging one hooked nail down his face as I brought my hand away. His jaw went slack, mouth opening like a well as words started to babble out.

"What are you?" he stammered. He kept blinking at me, like I would melt away between one look and the next.

"My official title is Lord of Openings, not a gendered term back then, but it's been a long time since that was necessary. Most just call me Belphegor." I inclined my head, horns snagging of some of the overspilling wires as they arced forward. I tugged through them, shaking the bright bits of metal free.

"You look like a demon."

"Very astute, Adam, well done," I said, giving my best version of a smile. He probably couldn't see it - my face is rather hard for a human to focus on.

"Are you going to take me to hell?"

"I'll be honest with you, I'd really prefer not to. You're not my type, if you know what I mean, and my siblings aren't inclined to like you either. What was the reason for the shooting again, women?"

"I wanted to show we could win. We weren't neutered by society." The gun made a heavy clunk as it slipped from his hand, bouncing onto my foot in the process. Useless thing.

"Yes, of course, those judgmental bitches and that sort of thing," I said, nodding. I cupped his chin in one hand, leaning down to look into his eyes. I could see the glow of my own reflected in the glassy tears building there.

I dimly felt something warm was spreading over my throbbing foot. Glancing down I saw the creeping puddle leaking from his trouser leg.

I looked back up to him and tried for the smile again. "Bad day?" "I don't want to go to hell."

"Of course you don't, too busy being the leader of the revolution," I said, turning his head a little each way. My hand lowered, encircling his neck. "I really don't think any of the others would want you either I'm afraid."

"Please don't kill me."

"You'd prefer death by police? They're not going to get here in time for that. I had thought I was too late but we managed to get together just right."

"What do you mean?"

"Libraries are very special places to me. I like ideas. Love them in fact. Love to watch the way a human's brain rattles around with them like a rat in a pipe. It's much more fun if you throw in a distraction here or there, of course, but a good idea's brilliant."

"You're mad I chose the library?" he asked, swallowing. It made his throat bob in my grip and I tightened the hold, nails making little white circles where they pressed in.

"I'm angry you chose my library, yes. At least a pair of teens fucking in the stacks is worth a watch. You're not even entertaining."

His face flicked through tears and outrage to settle onto a frown, mouth gaping. "That's disgusting."

"Mad cause you're not getting any? A shame. I think we should continue with your desire, you wanted to be inspirational, to show others the way? I can help you with that."

"Why would you help me if you're angry?"

"To send a message, as you wanted. I don't like middle ground men like you, you're the worst of all types." I grinned, drawing him closer. His feet lifted off the ground, twitching as he wheezed for air.

"Why?" he hissed, face turning a lurid cherry. I bet I could make one of those blood vessels in his eye pop.

"The religious ones, you can have a *conversation* and dig into their ideas. The devoted can be turned and twisted. Their anguish is... hmm." I shuddered, my tongue slipping out. "The coerced, they're probably going upstairs, and that's of no interest to me."

Daddy dearest did like to take in lost sheep, provided they said the right lines and didn't ask questions. And for goodness sake don't start talking about the contradictions. Even a lazy ass like me spotted them.

"We could make a deal," he said, one brow starting to jump as his face spasmed. His left eye flooded red, the iris circled by blood like a butcher's sinkhole.

"What do you know about deals?"

"You need a sacrifice, yeah, how about those bodies? I killed them, say they were for you."

"They were for your shrivelled dick. You'd try to serve me scraps?" I asked, laughing as I shook him a little

"No! You want things, right? You've seen what I can do. I could kill people for you."

"Ah, I see what you mean," I said, tilting my head as I watched him squirm. "I don't need any help with that."

I clenched my fist, crushing his throat until the mangled flesh ran through my fingers like spoiled meat, slick and hot. A sharp tug sent his body tumbling as his bowels started to spill, as close to a gift as the idiot was likely to give me. Shit may be one of the few constants around death, but it is one of my many offerings.

I tossed his head up a little and caught it in my palm, bring it to my face. The bloody eye had rolled back but the other still blinked rapidly, the last of the oxygenated blood making an effort to keep him going. I sniffed, the mix of fear and fury in his sweat almost enough to be interesting.

Not quite though.

Arranging him for the humans was an easy job – blunt instrument that my body is, I'm good with my hands. I propped him up against the counter, shuffling his legs open and unzipping his jeans. The angel lust was obvious, even as he'd been begging for his life, and I'm old enough to know an erection when it's straining the 'trews.

I slipped my hand in and reached lower, encircling him down to the sack. One quick twist and pull brought the sweetbreads out, stem and all, still damp from its earlier indiscretion. I laid them beside him, plucking his head up and nestling it in the crook of his crotch. It rolled off and I rearranged it so the stump was on the floor, bracketed by his thighs instead.

Scooping the detached parts into my hands I brought them up to the cavity of his neck, bloody and dark with crumpled muscle. Patting the centre down and flicking away one of the snagging bones, I nestled the wrinkled bag of flesh at the lip of the wound, hissing spit onto the skin. It sizzled and burned, enough that I could fuse the open edges together and let the sad pair of bollocks sit against his chest. I laid the member carefully over his open throat, running a nail over it to ensure it remained hard until the police arrived.

A true dickhead, awaiting his moment of glory. The pictures would be viral as soon as someone got the bright idea to leak them, a sensational end to his activity.

His soul would already be slipping off, spinning out past the whistles of memory and virtue and into the vast blackness of the pit. He'd mill around in the punishments until his soul was deemed worthy to try again, probably.

We keep very few with us forever. Just the special ones. My siblings don't take the same joy as I do in that. They're all so busy with their schemes.

Me, I like a good idea.

Follow You Into The Dark

Jennifer Soucy

He didn't remember the trip, neither the travel time nor the transport method. That should've been terrifying, but fear was irrelevant after enduring endless waves of asphyxiation punctuated by the cheery snap, crackle, and pop of bone and cartilage. Unafraid but curious, his new environment dispelled all doubt and left only a grim satisfaction. He did it, found the one place he'd yearned for. Had any other travelers felt that upon arrival, the warmth akin of genuine happiness?

Hell: his chosen destination, the place where *She* must be waiting... somewhere.

"Alright lads, line up! Processing first, then we'll see what's what." The demon's high-pitched command pierced the fog encapsulating the disoriented wanderers.

Men and women—even some children—wept and wailed, blind to the mutual suffering of their fellows. They tore their hair, wrung their hands. A couple of beefy guys up front began brawling like mindless animals. Mayhem at the Gates: a mob fueled by angst, absorbed in their own pain, punishing themselves more effectively than anyone else could.

Ray watched them all with faint disgust, relieved he'd kept his head on straight since his arrival. Minutes, hours, days ago... who could say? Always a pragmatist, he easily compartmentalized any emotion resulting from the journey. Grief and tears by the bucketload nearly drowned him after he'd lost Her, finally slowing when he looped the noose around his throat. No, enough; those memories were useless now when the next chapter of their lives lay just ahead.

"You're not gonna burst into tears too, are you?" The man behind him inquired with a delicate snort. The voice was surprisingly light coming from such a tall figure— a bug-eyed wraith with gangly limbs, smooth dark skin, and a narrow skull topped by an artful coiffure as stiffly ornate as a battle helm. Fitting for his new home, armor for an eternity of regretful damnation.

"No, I think I'm good for now." Ray shuffled ahead to close a new gap in the line. "So what are you in for?"

The thin man released a bitter spray of laughter, hands fluttering to smooth that wild faux-hawk. "I shot my husband, the idiot. Caught him with another man. I didn't count on his little friend fighting back, though. Imagine—that bastard had the nerve to shoot me with my own damn gun, and he was stark naked to boot. Ain't that some shit? I'm Bernie, by the way."

"Ray," he offered, patting the man's shoulder in a show of sympathy. "Sorry for your troubles. How long you been in this line?"

"Ages," Bernie said with a despondent sigh, craning over the crowd then falling back on his heels in obvious disappointment. "If you want to cut ahead, that's fine.

This line is absolutely ridiculous, and I'm in no hurry to see what's waiting—ya feel me?"

"You know where they keep the others?" Ray asked, opting for honesty with this stranger. Always useful to have a friend in a new and unfamiliar place. "I'm looking for my girlfriend. She killed herself, and I... well, I couldn't live without her. They always say suicides go to Hell. Figured I'd do the same. My life meant nothing without her, anyway. If I find her, maybe I can rescue her—start fresh, or something. It's better than being alone. And we've got forever now, right?"

"Studied up on your myths and legends, eh?" Bernie's lips stretched in a bittersweet smile, his eyes rolling toward a ceiling that didn't seem to exist. "I remember when me and Ron loved each other like that. I would've walked through fire for that boy. Five years of marriage—Christ, I was a fool. How could I not see it hadn't meant the same to both of us? We were going to adopt some kids, dammit! Now look at me: locked up in Hell, heartbroken and damned... literally, ugh!"

"Think there's a chance we could wander around here and explore?" Ray leaned closer, whispering into his new friend's ear. Unnecessary, because no one could've heard him over the miserable howls of the crowd and the echoing barks of demonic commands.

Here was a massive but dim antechamber, the atmosphere a sooty crimson that stained everything it touched. Exotic at first but, upon closer inspection, the ordinary architecture was dully reminiscent of the standard government building; buffed granite floors, bland walls decorated with uninspired pictures of fruit and pottery, mind-numbing elevator jazz floating from hidden speakers in a vain attempt to anesthetize—or further torment—the raging crowd. Hell was proving far from what Ray had expected.

"Looks like another group's lining up by the entrance." Bernie pointed toward the front of the hall. Dozens of people wandered, together but alone, forced by stoic demon shepherds into fleshy clusters; each human face distorted, openly struggling with the various stages of grief before succumbing to inevitable insanity. "Come on, those demons suck. They're not even paying attention, just gabbing to each other. We'll slip through with that lot and search for the suicide area. There's gotta be someone with some sense who knows what's up."

"Let's do it."

As they made their way over, Ray envisioned her face again—painting the walls of his mind to mask the ugliness, a talisman against despair in this dark place. The most beautiful one of all, the girl who stole his heart. Creamy skin, sky-blue eyes, blonde curls; she was an angel from one of those priceless old paintings. Their relationship was a miracle. Only in the movies did the gorgeous babe choose the plain, nerdy guy. Eventually, she became his but he'd belonged to her from the moment they met. Hot with an amazing body, for sure, but she had far more precious traits—poise and grace, depth and wit, an inner light that shone like a massive beacon to uncover and conquer his darkest insecurities. She'd been a blessing, irresistible for someone as jaded and lonely as him.

I'm coming for you, love. Promised you'd never be alone again, especially in a place like this. You deserve the best, and I vow you'll always get that from now on.

* * * * *

The chamber seemed normal enough, the first one beyond the arrivals lobby. A next step, but the residents appeared as tortured as the new arrivals. And the scene, while odd, was hardly nightmarish; an underground park imbued with a soft red light cast shadows over a gloomy expanse of grass, where leafless trees encroached upon a shallow, pond-like hole. Dark and thick, the surface gleamed like a fresh oil slick and radiated a blackened rainbow. Not an identical replica of the world above, but close enough to appease the fresh groups transitioning from one realm to another.

Several of the damned jogged around the perimeter, profusely sweating in thick hempen smocks. Their blank faces housed sets of cracked lips, jagged holes releasing a chorus of toneless cries. A few random others stumbled about, talking to either themselves or maybe the people they'd once wronged. Children swarmed the bones of a dilapidated playground, crying when the structure creaked under their weight. They beat each other with bits of wood or plastic piping, miniature *Lord of the Flies* savages without a smidge of empathy for their fellows. A pair of demons prowled the spaces between the lost, occasionally jabbing them with glowing sticks to banish apathy before it ruined their entertainment.

A man and a woman broke from the other runners, hand in hand, and raced to the edge of the pond. Their rapid approach caused the water to flinch back, disturbing the skeletal geese that had been minding their own business. The couple fled again, chased by the clacking geese whose grinding honks blared with irritation above the peripheral cacophony. One of the demons laughed, zapping the man in his lower back until he tripped and fell face first. He screamed as the bony beaks pinched him, reddening the dead flesh that somehow continued to feel pain.

Frightening but familiar, the mad reflection reminded Ray of the parks he occasionally visited on earth. Maybe that was where the torment lay—a twist on something recognizable, upsetting the brain's automatic attempts at adaptation.

"It's not even that hot. Why go for the water?" Ray mused, eyes widening when the waves thickened and rose, lapping the shore like a cancerous tongue. "Gross! What the... Now that's just fucked up."

"No water in Hell, right? And I'd say it's a bit more humid than hot. Naturally, because some people like it hot but no one enjoys feeling like a carrot in a steamer," Bernie said, briskly fanning himself. "Why are those fools jogging? What's the point? We're all dead. The time for improving these bodies is long gone."

"Old habits die hard, right?" Ray's gaze paused on a shadowy set of doors against the side wall, guarded by a plump demon sharpening his nails with an emery board. Occasionally he'd glance up at the group, chuckling before returning to his vain attempt at grooming.

"Where do you think that goes?" Ray nudged Bernie, cherishing the twinge of anticipation in a chest that shouldn't carry even the faintest spark of life anymore.

"Who knows, but I doubt that thing will let us through."

"Let's see about that." Ray walked forward, stopping before the demon and clearing his throat.

"Go on—back to the park with youse," the demon said, frowning at an uneven nail tip.

"Please, I need to find where the suicides are kept," Ray said, gaining support from Bernie's encouraging smile. "I'm supposed to be there. I killed myself to join my girlfriend."

"Boo hoo, Romeo. Why should I care?" The demon snorted, his all-black eyes rolling like impatient eight balls. "Not my job to sort people. Go bitch at the desk up front with the other wailers."

"Please, the line is way too long," Bernie said, leaning forward eagerly. "Haven't you ever wanted to be a part of something bigger than yourself? A real love story, filled with beautiful tragedy. Ray killed himself to spend eternity with..."

"Deana." Ray hurried to fill in the blank when Bernie flapped his hands for help.

"Deana!" Bernie repeated. "Come on, we're all dead and suffering here already.

What does it matter if they do it together or apart?"

"Why'd the bird off herself then, if you had this great love?" The demon raised one hairless eyebrow in an impertinent question mark. Ray broke off eye contact, staring at his feet for a moment as he swallowed the acrid taste of shame.

"We had an argument. It was stupid, really. I thought it was nothing, just her being overly sensitive as usual. I had to work late again. Must've been gone long enough to send her over the edge. We never got a chance to make up. By the time I got home, it was too late." Ray's dry eyes welled with moisture, offering a sip of relief after an interminable time in the suffocating atmosphere. "She was my everything. I was going to marry her, start a family. And now... Please, I need to see her again."

"Real tears, how 'bout that? If I didn't know better, I'd say you was truly sorry," The demon examined him, interest finally piqued. A forked tongue raced across his lipless mouth, back and forth as he mulled the request. "Hmph, alright. You got me curious. Follow me, lads."

"Seriously?" Bernie clapped Ray's back, hooting, "We'll get you there, buddy!

Gotta make something positive out of this mess, eh?"

"Thanks, man." Ray smiled through the twin streams of tears, at a loss for words. He came to Hell to find his love but never imagined he'd make a friend along the way.

They followed the demon through the open doors, further and deeper into the Underworld, down a narrow staircase winding to the next level and beyond.

* * * * *

White walls and beige tile floors stretched ahead with no end in sight, bland colors pinkened by an endless line of flaming torches. A labyrinthine hospital ward, endless monotony broken only by the occasional steel door alternating on either side. Unlike the previous areas, the hall was eerily silent except for the purposeful steps of the two dead men and their demon guide.

"Name's Deana, aye?" The demon asked, pulling a small device like a walkie-talkie from a pouch at his waist.

"Yes, Deana Anderson," Ray confirmed, wringing his hands as a sudden bout of nerves jangled his limbs. Happy nerves, the jitters of a bridegroom waiting at the altar for his beloved bride. Soon, so close, then they'd truly have eternity.

"Gimme a minute, you lot. Don't move," the demon ordered, striding away to talk in private.

"So when you find her, then what?" Bernie whispered. "You think you can break out for real, like Orpheus or something? Hope you have a plan, cause I don't see a harp in your pocket."

"Hell's all about facing your crimes, right?" Ray whispered back, excited about the plan he hatched before tightening the noose in his bedroom so long ago. Days, months, who knew anymore? Didn't matter now that he'd nearly reached his goal. "I'll talk to her. Remind her how much I love her, apologize for the fight. If we forgive each other and proclaim our love, maybe that'll get us a ticket up to Heaven."

"I hope so, for your sake," Bernie agreed, resting his hand briefly on Ray's tensed shoulder. "Hey, if nothing else, this place isn't half as bad as I thought it would be. Maybe eternity won't actually suck. Sure, it's a bit boring and a fresh breeze would be awesome, but I haven't seen any fire and brimstone. Unless... Maybe we're in the wrong area?"

"As long as Deana and I are together, we can endure anything," Ray proclaimed. He stared up at Bernie, drinking the draught of pity humbly offered by his new friend. "From the moment we met, I knew. She had a laugh, like church bells after a nightmare. Beautiful... And I swear, she always smelled like strawberries—even after working out. She was so smart, too. Kept me on my toes like no one else, always challenging me to see things in different ways. I never believed in destiny, but I swear we were made for each other."

Bernie wiped his own damp eyes, lips trembling at the conjured images and words of utter devotion. "Oh, I miss Ron. Why'd I fly off the handle like that? That boy, he drove me crazy. But I still love him. I wonder if he misses me, even after everything. Such a smartass, but I bet he's in Heaven showing them angels how to really sing and dance. I'd sense if he was here, wouldn't I?"

Ray nodded sympathetically, squeezing Bernie's quivering arm. "Yeah man, I think so. My heart—I know it sounds crazy, cause I'm dead—but it's been beating faster the farther we come. I think it's a sign, letting me know we're almost there. She's close."

The demon started waving with marked impatience. "Alright lads, let's press along. Just a bit further."

"Who's in these rooms, anyway?" Ray asked their guide.

Never breaking his stride, the voice snapped out, "Lost souls, like your lady love. Keep 'em here til they're more alert. No fun torturing a vegetable, now is it?"

"Surely there's a better word than that... so offensive," Bernie huffed with outrage, the judgment not escaping the demon guide's notice. He snorted, grumbling something about social justice warriors but never slowing his pace.

The trio continued past another dozen doors before stopping. The demon faced the men, flexing the flabby skin dangling from his leathery arms. "I'll give you five minutes, Romeo. Most often, suicides are too far gone. Can't see the nose in front of their face, savvy? Everyone's got their own suffering to work through. I won't let you ruin hers. But I'm telling you now: she probably won't even know you're there so be ready to juice some more of them fancy tears."

"You got this, Ray. I believe in you." Bernie swept him up in a hug, patting his back fondly. "Go get that gorgeous girl!"

The demon pulled the thick metal door open as if it were made of cardboard, revealing a featureless room with padded walls. Ray stepped forward slowly, squinting to adjust to the utter lack of light. He froze just beyond the threshold, punched in the gut by the sight of her—his sweet girl, waiting for him.

Deana curled against the corner, huddled in the same stained white nightgown he'd found her in that night. Her right hand dug clumsy circles into her left wrist, the wink of glass barely visible within the thickened gouts of inky blood. His angel, sinking into a pit of despair, fixated on meaningless resentments until fate stole her away. It was too much, unfair and demeaning to see her brought so low; it broke Ray's heart all over again.

"Oh baby, I'm so sorry," Ray groaned, weighed by a sorrow he now shared with her. Mourning her loss again, keener as he watched her last moments replaying. "Deana, I'm here now. You don't have to do that anymore. I found you, and we can be together again. Everything can go back to the way it was."

She ignored him, focusing on her carving. She swayed over the meaty wounds on her open wrist, humming a song Ray didn't recognize.

Closer now, slow and steady. Don't spook her! He chanted the warnings to calm himself, wary as one might've been to disturb a lost sleepwalker. But time was running out, and he had to do something to wake her. After all, what kind of prince failed to rescue his princess from the monster—even if the monster lived inside her head?

"Deana, I take it back. I didn't mean to fight with you, I swear. You're right, I was too clingy and possessive. I should've relaxed, trusted in us. But you're so perfect! I know I've never been good enough, but I swear I love you with my whole heart." Ray choked back suffocating sobs as she continued to ignore him. So much like that fight, except at least then she'd waited until he left to start cutting. Now, he got front row seats to his perfect girl butchering herself.

Kneeling beside her, he noticed her full lips pursed in concentration. A slice of blue flashed behind the tangled golden locks—her once-vibrant eyes, dry and lifeless as cracked glass. How long had she been stuck in the same loop, disconnected and desensitized? Was she broken beyond repair, lost forever?

No: true love was rare, sacred—a privilege not everyone enjoyed. More than a story for children, the concept endured through the ages, the notion that each person had one special someone. A soulmate, a word that even here must've counted for something. Especially here in the afterlife, where all that remained to sustain an immortal soul was the purest of loves beaming down the shrinking tunnel of distant memory.

"Deana, I was going to ask you to marry me when I got home. I made my choice. I only wanted us to be happy forever. Please, baby, don't leave me now. We're so close. I'm begging you, don't leave me here alone."

Her hand stopped moving, one blue orb rising and sliding over. She stared, lips parting, breath moving hot and fast over her bloodless lips. Something dark danced across the surface of her eyes before diving back under. That beautiful mouth opened again, a sour chuckle rattling behind a cage of clenched teeth.

"Alone?" Her breathing increased, hissing around her the points of her canines. "You fucking monster… all I ever wanted was to be left alone, to live my life in peace. Now look where I am."

"Baby, you killed yourself! Don't you remember? I didn't do that. I'd never hurt you," Ray pleaded, reaching out with trembling palms—keeping his distance, but aching to touch her. "But I hurt myself, all for you—for us! I wanted to suffer, to feel your pain. I'm here to rescue you, Deana."

"Rescue me? Oh no, you don't," Deana snarled, her flying hand landing with a wet thump. The shard of glass embedded in his dead chest, beads of black fluid mingling with the red blood dripping from her wrist. "You psychotic asshole, you didn't even know me! You kidnapped me from that club. My family thought I was dead. I hear them mourning for me, wondering what happened. You locked me in that goddamn room for months, forcing me to eat your shitty food, bathing me, brushing my hair, and dressing me—was I just some stupid doll to you? And now you're here, whining about love and marriage… as fucking if! I begged you to leave me alone, to bring me home, but all you did was cry—like I was the bad guy, a heartless tease. Filthy fucking animal… I had a life once, people who truly loved me. There was a future for me, but you ruined everything!"

"Deana, baby—"

But she didn't stop, stumbling to feet newly strengthened by truth and fury. A vengeful goddess towering over him, the most gloriously terrible vision he'd ever seen. But he only loved her more, wanted her more... his Deana, his beautiful girl.

"I was too young to die. I should've killed you instead. I threw away my life, for what—you?" She stepped back, lowering her clenched fists. The fury melted to scorn, to pity, then pooled into quiet acceptance. "But I know now, I never should've given up. I stopped fighting back, stopped trying. That was my sin!"

Her words released a shock wave, knocking Ray flat onto his back. An incandescent beam blasted through the ceiling, a massive waterfall of celestial light searing his eyes and soul. Only a few heated seconds, then it was gone. The sudden dark blinded him momentarily, but he didn't need to see. He knew she was gone, and he was alone. And this time, it would be forever.

"What the hell was that?" Bernie stumbled through the door, unbothered by the demon who fought to push him back into the hall. "Ray... you kidnapped her? What the fuck, man, I thought she was your girlfriend?"

"Deana, no!" Ray howled, tearing out the useless shard of glass and throwing it into the corner where she'd once sat. She'd left him again. Now how could he find her? Another fight he couldn't fix, another broken heart he would never recover from. She'd been the one, the only one who mattered. No one else came close. Lucky number seven, the girl he'd chosen above all the others, the love of his life.

"What a disaster, sweet bleedin' Christ," The demon scurried over, kicking Ray to force him to his feet. "Nasty little fiend, aren't you? Try to trick me, and now we got a prisoner lost to them up above. Won't be me to take the fall for this, boyo, I promise you that. Should've known you was full of shit."

Ray buried his head against his knees, weeping while Bernie continued to yell and the demon chattered in a guttural tongue on the walkie-talkie. Stuck in Hell forever, all of it for nothing.

"Alright lad, up with you. Found out from the Head of Records where you're supposed to be. Gonna fix your wagon, good and proper." The demon wrapped a scaly hand around Ray's limp arm. He glared at Bernie, waggling his free finger. "I'll be back for you in a jiffy, lad. Don't be wandering off now, or you'll join your friend in the pit."

"Where are you taking him?" Bernie asked, pressing a shaky hand to his lips.

"Got a special room set up, filled with his other victims," the demon said with a lopsided grin. "Six young ladies who've been waiting patiently for this moment. And they're awfully hungry."

The Groom Of Lorelei
Holley Cornetto

❦

Liam first dreamt of the maiden of the rock fourteen years ago, the same year his mother died. He could still remember the exhilaration that first time he saw her, bare-breasted and impossibly beautiful, sitting on her rock. Around her were miles of open water, dull beneath the lead-gray sky. She was alone, as alone as his mother had been.

From that night on, her face haunted him. Her eyes shone out through the bleak nothingness, a beacon of light softening the harshness of the sea. He was sure she was real, certain she was out there somewhere, waiting for him to find her.

As the years passed, Liam found himself dreaming more and more often of the maiden of the rock. Some nights she sat staring out to sea, as if she saw more than the turquoise waves pressing in around her. Other nights she sang, and the sea stilled to listen to her melancholy song. Because of those dreams, he vowed to find her, to rescue her from her prison in the middle of the sea.

He wasn't crazy. He'd spent the twenty years following his mother's death watching ships by the harbor. Mixed in among the small fishing boats were clippers, schooners, and frigates. He knew the name of every ship, and who captained each. Local sailors who heard of his tragedy took pity on him, telling him stories of life on the open sea, the places they traveled, and people they'd met. He heard stories of adventures, of sea monsters and pirates, but his favorite tales were of the maiden of the rock. Sailors whispered of her beauty. With her strawberry hair and sun-kissed skin, she could charm even the hardest of hearts. Although they spoke of her in reverent tones, they warned that seeing her often meant death.

As Liam got older, his habits changed. He spent less time haunting the harbor, and more time researching the maiden of the rock. He read every book, visited every library, and followed every lead he could find, no matter how far-fetched they seemed. He still sought out news from sailors but did so by frequenting taverns near the wharf, buying drinks for sailors and captains alike in exchange for their tales. He questioned them until they lost patience, or were too drunk to answer.

His favorite tavern was <u>The Anchor</u>. The place served watered-down swill passed off as ale and was always full of men fresh from the harbor. A musky odor hung heavy in the air. Raucous laughter broke out on the opposite side of the room as two drunken sailors shoved each other and traded insults. Shadows grew longer as the sun began to set, and the lamplighters went about their work.

"But surely there is honor in naval service? What of the tales I've heard on the docks?" He slammed his fist on the bar top, animated by too much drink.

"Those days have passed." Saunders, the old captain stared at the bottom of his empty glass. "These days, most sailors are little better than pirates. They wreak havoc in every port, leaving broken inns and fatherless children in their wake. It is no life of honor. It's the life of a man who has nothing, and who never will."

Saunders didn't have a ship, hadn't even captained a vessel since his days on <u>The</u> *Odyssey,* but he'd been patient and kind to Liam, especially in the years after his mother passed. He was the only man for the job. Liam plunked a canvas pouch, heavy with coins, on the counter beside the old captain.

Saunders looked around in a panic and shoved the heavy pouch back towards him. "Are you crazy, boy? Put that away. You come in here waving around a sack of coins like that and you're bound to get us both killed."

Liam sheepishly slid the pouch into his lap. "I apologize. I want... I need your help."

Saunders tilted his head. "Go on."

"I want to hire you. I bought a ship, and I need a crew."

The old man doubled over in laughter and slapped his knee. "Landlubber like you? Want to captain a ship, do ya?"

"No, no. I don't want to captain the ship. I want *you* to captain the ship."

"Oiy, and why would I do such a thing?"

"I'll pay you. I'll pay you well. And, after the voyage is over. After I've gotten... found... what I'm looking for. After that, I'll give you the ship."

The mirth faded from the old captain's face. "Why don't you just hire a ship and crew? Why buy your own, if you'll just be rid of it when you're done?"

Liam looked around the tavern. There were too many people here. Someone would overhear him, and they might try to get to her first. She sat there, night after night, waiting for him. He'd be damned if someone else got there first. "There is something I need to find."

Saunders scoffed. "Buried treasure?"

Liam shook his head. "I'll tell you, but not here." Saunders nodded. "We can talk in my room."

* * * * *

The room reminded Saunders of being at sea. The smell of fish and piss had soaked into the furniture and walls. A thin, slimy film covered every surface. It was the cheapest pit in town, and soon he wouldn't be able to afford it.

The little oil lamp was enough to light the cramped space -- just as well, as he couldn't afford candles. He crossed his arms over his chest. "Now, tell me what's so important that you'd buy a ship."

"You'll think me mad."

He guffawed. "I already think you're mad, laddy. You must expect a big haul, because that's a hell of a lot of money to throw away on one trip. If you want me to captain this little expedition of yours, I need to know what I'm getting myself into. So, tell me why you won't just hire out a ship and crew."

"No one would sign on."

"Why?"

"Because I don't know for certain where she is." "She?" Saunders took his pipe from the table.

"She's out there, somewhere."

Saunders lit his pipe and took a long pull. "...Lorelei."

Saunders choked. "The maiden of the rock? She's led a thousand men to their deaths."

"You know of her?"

"Every sailor knows that old yarn." Saunders leaned back in his chair and began to recite:

"*One by one they come to die, All the grooms of Lorelei.*
She drags them down into the sea, Where they remain eternally.
Then she returns to watch and wait, Until another takes the bait."

Liam shook his head. "It isn't true. She's not like that. She wants me to find her. She chose me"

At least the kid was honest. Mad, certainly, but there was something to be said for his forthrightness. "I can't take your coin, boy. She's a legend. An old wives' tale, and looking for her is not only folly, it's likely to get you killed."

"My mind is set in this. I want you to captain my vessel."

"You want me to deliver you unto death. I can't conscience it." "That is precisely why I need you."

Saunders shook his head, taking another puff of his pipe. "There are hundreds of seamen in this town. Why ask me?"

Liam smiled. "Because I've heard stories about you since I was a kid. About what happened on *The Odyssey*. You held fast; you stayed true to your mission. You could have made a fortune, but duty and honor were more important to you."

Saunders smirked. "You make me sound like a hero for doing my job."

"When doing your job is the hard thing, perhaps. See, if I were to hire just anyone, I'd find a man for the job. He'd sail the ship to and fro, chasing the wind, but never actually look for her. Or, perhaps he'd try and take her for himself. But not Captain Benjamin Saunders. He would try in earnest to help me find her, because, as I said, he believes in duty and honor."

The truth of it was that he needed the boy's coin. He knew the maiden wasn't real, but he'd take the job, even if he thought Liam mad. It was like stealing. Not stealing, he told himself, a job. He'd be paid for services rendered.

He nodded and scratched his scruffy beard. "When would you like to depart?"

"As soon as possible, but I've had trouble pinpointing her location. You've sailed these waters for years; do you know where to find her?"

Saunders shrugged. "Same as every legend, every tale. She exists everywhere and nowhere. Might be impossible to track down the origins of the rhyme. What if we can't find her?"

"We set a date, and if we've found nothing by then, the ship and the payment are yours."

It was madness, but he knew if he didn't agree, the boy would hire someone else. Someone who would take advantage of him, and rob him of his coin. At least I'll keep an eye on him, Saunders thought. I'll keep him out of trouble, let him experience the sea. He'll have a story, something to tell his grandkids someday. Finally, he offered Liam his hand. "Very well, lad. As you say."

The boy looked relieved. "You can hire the crew. Whoever you like, your choice."

Saunders nodded. He'd expected as much. One look at the boy's hands told him that Liam knew nothing of the sea, of hard labor. This would be an easy enough job, he figured. Most likely, they'd just sail around until the boy got tired and wanted to return to land.

Saunders sighed. He was going to have a hell of a time hiring a crew when he had no idea where they were going.

* * * * *

Liam knew from the start that the voyage would be a long one, or at least he should have. Since they'd set sail, his dreams of the maiden grew more frequent. It was as if, somehow, she knew he was coming for her.

At first, he spent most of his time on deck with Saunders and the crew, watching the sea as if his maiden might be just over the horizon.

With its endless rolling waves, the sea made him feel small. It reminded him of being a boy, and of his mother. They'd spent many afternoons together on the beach, collecting shells and leaving footprints in the sand. His mother had loved the sea, so he had loved it also.

But, after nine weeks had passed, the excitement faded.

Life at sea was nothing like he'd expected. He thought they'd face pirates and find adventure, but the truth was, they faced nothing but miles of vast, open sea. Once they'd spotted dolphins swimming in the ship's wake, but that had only provided an afternoon's entertainment.

After weeks of finding nothing, Liam stopped coming above deck. Instead, he spent his days shuffling through the pages of notes he'd made about Lorelei.

The first time he visited the library, he'd shown his sketch to the librarian, and the man brought him an armful of books he could barely see over.

The librarian opened one of the books, an encyclopedic tome, and flipped through the pages. Each page had an illustration, accompanied by text. A bestiary, the librarian said, as if his beautiful, perfect Lorelei were a beast. A creature. An animal.

The librarian pointed to an image labeled <u>Undine</u>, and pushed the book towards

Liam.

The picture didn't capture any of her beauty, her magic. The woman on the rock looked inhuman, like a monster. Her hair was tangled seaweed, her mouth a sinister grin of sharpened teeth. There was nothing there of his angelic Lorelei, the one who called to him with her song.

But the thing that bothered him most was her face. The face in the book was <u>wrong</u>.

Though Liam copied down all he could find on undines, he remained skeptical of his sources. The book had called his Lorelai a beast, after all. It said she lacked a soul, which he knew to be false. He had glimpsed her soul;

she bared it to him through her song. A song that had always been eerily familiar to him.

* * * * *

Saunders knocked at the cabin door. Since Liam had financed the trip, he had taken private quarters for himself.

"Come in."

He pushed open the door. The boy sat at his makeshift desk, shuffling his papers again. These days, it was how he spent most of his time. He had books, sketches, maps, scraps of song lyrics, and bawdy rhymes. Any hint or rumor Liam had ever heard was collected in those notes, or so he said. The walls of the cabin were lined in sketches of her from every angle. They all had the same face, a face that seemed familiar. But perhaps he'd just seen the pictures too many times.

"We're going to have to make for port soon, lad, or else we're going to run out of provisions."

Liam brought his hand down hard on the desk, scattering his collection of papers. "No! Not when we're so close." Dark crescents ringed his eyes. He'd lost weight. Too much.

"There's talk among the crew. If we don't turn it in soon, we may not have a choice. We only brought enough rations for the eight weeks as we agreed, and they ain't gonna last much longer. We should be heading back to port, while we still have enough to get there."

"Captain, can you not control your men?"

Saunders sighed. "I've kept up my end." This was a fool's errand to begin with.

Surely the boy could see that by now.

"It's Driscoll, isn't it? I can hear him at night, pacing the decks, ranting at anyone who'll listen. He's loud, I'll grant that, but the men don't have faith in him. Silence him, and the rest of the men will fall in line and see the job done."

"There is no 'done.' There will be no end to this because she doesn't exist. She's a fairy story, made up by sailors too long out to sea."

Liam shook his head. "She is real, she---"

There was a crash outside the door, accompanied by the sounds of men shouting and running. "Captain! Captain! Get out here!"

He started for the door. "We'll finish this later."

A thick fog had rolled in, masking the endless gray waves. The air was dense with a mist that hovered just above the deck. Gray on gray, the sky and the sea felt eerily as one. Saunders turned. "For God's sake, what is it?"

"Sir," said a crewman just out of sight. "Listen."

Saunders paused. He closed his eyes, breathing in the thick air. Over the creaking of the ship and crashing waves, he heard the ghostly echo of a woman's voice.

"I'll be damned right to hell." "Do you hear it, sir?"

"Yes! Yes, I hear it. The question is, what in the bloody hell is it?" "It's her..."

Saunders turned to see Liam standing above deck for the first time in weeks.

Driscoll spat in Liam's direction. "Like hell it is. It's the storm. Wind on the waves."

"You hear it. You all hear it! We're close." Liam's eyes were wide and half-crazed.

Whispers crept like shadows between the men on deck. They had all signed on, some believing they might find the maiden of the rock, others less sure, but eager for the coin - half up front, and half when the ship returned. Men like Driscoll.

Saunders knew this was the last chance. He looked from Liam to his crew. "We sail toward it, whatever it is. If we don't find it in three days, we head for the nearest port."

"And when we find her," Liam added, "I'll throw in a bonus for every man on board!"

A cheer went up among the crew. All but Driscoll, who slunk below deck while the others cheered.

* * * * *

The dreams came every night. Sometimes Lorelei was the maiden on the rock, perfection made flesh. Other times, she was the monster from the bestiary, with seaweed hair, and teeth like a shark's. The closer they got, the more vivid the dreams became. It was how he knew they were close.

Saunders had been a fool to suggest turning away, but Liam could hardly blame him. He hadn't understood before, but now... now they'd heard her sing. Even Driscoll wouldn't be able to deny her existence any longer.

Liam tossed and turned in a restless fit. The fog and mist had crept in, coating every surface with damp. The scent of mildew wafted up from the ship's hold. He closed his eyes and sank into the oblivion of sleep.

He could feel the murky seabed on his feet, and wetness on his cheeks. This time, when he dreamed, it was not of Lorelei, but of his mother. He watched as they pulled her bloated purple corpse from the fishing nets. Drowned. That was her official cause of death. No one knew what she'd been doing in the water or how she'd gotten there, and none cared enough to ask. But the dream was wrong, because in it, he was an adult. He'd been a child when they found his mother's body. He stood on the beach, barefooted, with sand squelching between his toes. Tiny crabs scuttled towards him and back, as if beckoning him to follow them out to sea. "Come with us," he imagined them saying.

He blinked, and when he opened his eyes, he was in the apartment where he grew up. His mother was alive, somewhere just out of sight. She sang as she did the wash, her voice achingly familiar. He knew her song, knew it down to his bones, and yet couldn't place it.

Why couldn't he see her face?

Liam opened his eyes. He was back on the ship, standing above deck in his bedclothes. He couldn't remember how he'd gotten there. It was odd, he hadn't suffered a fit of somnambulism since he was a boy, the summer after they'd found his mother. He rubbed his eyes. He could still see the shape of her corpse, the shadow of his dream fading into the night. Part of the dream was true. He *had* been at the beach the day they pulled his mother's body out of the water.

His bare feet slid across the deck as he made his way back towards the hatch.

He needed rest. Tomorrow, they'd find Lorelei.

Below deck, he paused at the sound of voices. Men arguing. He recognized Driscoll's voice and crept closer.

"We should head for port now. We'll run out of food!"

"Only three more days, then we go. Girl or no." It sounded like Saunders.

"There ain't no girl! She's a tale to explain sunken ships and men jumping overboard. The crew is gonna start jumping if you don't do something!"

"I *am* doing something. He's a good lad. We all know what happened to his mother when he was a boy. We give him three days, and then we turn back. He needs to make peace with the sea, after what it took from him."

"She was a whore, is what she was. She was out there selling her wares to any sailor with a coin to pay. That's how she ended up like she did. Hell, any one of us could be his father."

"Hush!" Saunders cut him off. "This ain't the time nor place."

Liam's blood ran cold. Saunders hadn't denied it. He racked his brain, trying to conjure memories of his mother. Always by the docks, leaving him on the beach to play while she… while she what?

After his mother died, it was as if she'd never even existed, as if he was the only one who remembered her or cared that she'd died. Liam was taken to his aunt. He had never visited her while his mother was alive. He hadn't even known he had an aunt. She gave him everything he could ask for, but she refused to talk about his mother.

Liam turned, sliding his hands along the wall in the dark, feeling his way back to his cabin. The wood was wet, slick and viscous. His stomach churned. He opened the cabin door and collapsed onto his bed, weeping long into the night.

* * * * *

Saunders tapped his pipe against the table, knocking the ash loose, shaking it out onto the floor. Another day had passed and they'd found nothing. He knew no matter what he said, the lad wouldn't be satisfied. He saw that now.

He hadn't taken into account that Liam might still be grieving after all these years, but the sea had taken the boy's mother. What Liam was searching for, he'd never find. Not really, and Saunders would have to be the one to tell him.

His cabin door creaked as it swung open. "Captain?" Saunders scowled. "I asked not to be disturbed."

The boy, Jon, stood stiff and pale. "I'm sorry, Sir. But, it's Driscoll." "What about him?"

"We can't find him, Sir. We've searched the whole ship." "We? Who else knows?"

"Only a few."

"Better not to raise a stir yet. He's probably catching a nap somewhere." Saunders pulled on his boots and headed above deck.

He joined Jon and the others in their search for Driscoll. The man could be volatile, but it wasn't like him to shirk his duties. After searching the ship a third time, he hung his head. He had no choice but to alert the crew. More than half a day had passed, and Driscoll's absence had already been noticed.

As the men gathered on the deck, Saunders inhaled deeply. The thick fog that set in yesterday had not lifted. Its presence added a certain layer of gloom to the atmosphere. "There ain't an easy way to say this, but Driscoll's gone missing. Has anyone had eyes on him since last night?"

Some of the men muttered. "We heard her singing again last night." "It was her. It was the maiden of the rock!"

"She called him to sea!"

Saunders sighed. He'd heard the sound, but he still wasn't convinced. He'd hoped the men knew better, but most of them believed, or at least wanted to believe the stories.

"It was clear as a bell. We thought we found 'er. Driscoll was cursing, and looking out, but the fog was so thick nobody saw nothing."

"Where was he when you saw him last?"

"He was here, on the deck, making the rounds. Just before dawn." "Uhm, captain?" One of the men stepped forward.

"Speak, sailor."

"Liam was above deck, too. About the same time…" he hesitated. "He was dressed in his nightclothes, sir. He had blood on his shirt. Said it was a nosebleed."

He frowned. Liam? Above deck? "I'll go talk to the lad. You all stay here. Keep searching, just in case. See if you see anything in the water."

Saunders scurried down the hatch and pounded at Liam's door. A drowsy voice answered. "I'm not feeling well."

"I need to see you, boy. It won't keep."

There was a soft groan. Saunders took the spare key from his pocket and slid the door open.

Liam lay curled in a ball on his bed, his clothes a bloody mess. "Hells, boy! What happened to you?"

"I don't know. I don't remember. I was asleep and then I woke up above deck. I thought I was dreaming. He told me she wasn't real. He told me that my mother, that she--" he broke off into a sob.

"Driscoll?" Liam nodded.

"Oh, no. Tell me you didn't, boy. Please, tell me you didn't." Liam held up his hands, covered in dried blood.

* * * * *

Liam sat in the dinghy, looking down at his basket of provisions. A half portion of food and water, and a pistol with one bullet. The crew wanted to hang him for Driscoll's murder, but Saunders talked them into setting him adrift instead.

"There ain't nothing but open sea for miles. He'll be good as dead, anyway. The boy's mad, not evil. He didn't mean to kill Driscoll; he was out of his mind."

Out of his mind.

He lifted the oars and began to row, heading in the direction that he'd last heard her voice. Lorelei was waiting for him. He rowed until his arms ached, then leaned back, letting the boat drift in the rocking waves as he closed his eyes to rest.

He woke to the sound of her voice. He'd been dreaming of his mother again. His mother twirling around their apartment, singing. Singing Lorelei's song. He ate what food remained, but rationed the water. His gaze fell on the pistol.

"Lorelei?" He took up the oars and rowed again, his arms aching from effort and exhaustion. He called again, and paused, waiting to hear an answer, her song, anything.

There was nothing. He slept.

The next time he opened his eyes, he saw a silhouette. A darkness that broke through the hazy evening fog. Her rock. It must be her rock. He picked up his oars and rowed hard. Waves like giant walls of water pushed his boat forward, as if the very sea itself willed him to find her. He dropped an oar as wood crashed against stone. Water spilled into the boat.

He dove in and circled the rock, but she wasn't there. There was nothing, no sign that she'd ever been there at all. He treaded water, the oppressiveness of the sea closing in around him. It was overwhelming, like being the only one who remembered his mother, trying desperately to keep that memory alive.

He was tired of trying. He stopped.

For a split second, he felt a sense of peace. He was a boy again, playing in the sand on the beach, waiting to hear the sound of his mother's voice, calling him home. As he descended, sinking deeper into the murky depths, a woman appeared beside him. Lorelei, the maiden of the rock. She took his hand and led him down into the unending deep.

The pressure grew, squeezing the air from his lungs. He was going to die, but at least he wouldn't die alone. As he smiled to thank the woman, he saw the delicate lines of her face. His mother's face.

The Coachman's Cottage

Anna Taborska

The vast guesthouse that had been hired on account of the matriarch's upcoming birthday had enough bedrooms to house all of them bar one. Tony didn't mind being the one to leave the twenty-strong party of cousins, in-laws and other extended family in the large sitting-room – after dinner and the inevitable quiz devised by his brother – to head alone to the Coachman's Cottage at the end of the drive. In fact, the prospect of not being woken by hordes of screaming brats at the crack of dawn rather appealed to him. But how welcome the screaming brats would have been now.

The young bride's lot was not a happy one. Her father, desperate to hang on to his crumbling hall, had given her in marriage to a brutal and dissolute man almost twenty years her senior. Charlotte knew neither kindness nor affection in her husband's house, and her only solace lay in the long walks she took almost daily on his vast, wooded estate. But today even the beauty and tranquillity of the ancient trees brought her little comfort.

Charlotte had been feeling extremely fatigued of late, and these past two mornings she had thrown up at the mere smell of breakfast. A week before her seventeenth birthday, and despite the night-time abuse suffered at the hands of her husband on a semi-regular basis, she was naïve in the way of things, and not yet cognisant of the new life that grew inside her.

She was in the farthest part of the grounds – amongst the ancient oaks, birches and beech trees – when the dizziness struck. She sat down for a while on a fallen log, and waited until her head cleared and the nausea subsided before heading back to the house. But she felt increasingly lightheaded, and had to stop every so often to lean against a tree for support. It was as if a dark grey mist were descending before her eyes, and she struggled not to succumb to it and to the heaviness that was weighing down her limbs and frail body.

Finally she came out alongside the coachman's cottage – within site of the main house, but before she could reach the manor, the heaviness and the mist took her. She gave out a cry of distress and sank to the ground outside the cottage.

"Mistress!" Then a kindly face, not much older than her own, was gazing down at her, and firm but gentle arms were lifting her and guiding her to safety. "Sit here and rest a while. I'll make you some sweet tea. It will revive you."

"No! My husband… I must go!"

But it was too late. Fate – that dark and twisted monster that lies in wait for us all – had ordained that the lord of the manor and two of his companions should be riding by, and the lord remembered that he had business with the coachman.

"Stay here a while," he told his friends. "I'll not be long."

Tony had quite enjoyed the brisk if somewhat fresh walk from the main house to the cottage. The silence on the shore of Lake Windermere in late January was profound. Not a leaf stirred nor a single animal rustled in the bushes. The Coachman's Cottage was a long, low structure of grey stone. Little remained of the eighteenth century original. The now glass-panelled entrance door opened directly onto a kitchen with a stone-flagged floor, with a small utility room housing the boiler, and another glass-panelled door to the right leading up a step to an ample sitting-room with dining area. A narrow staircase led from the kitchen to a mezzanine level with a double bed, a dresser and a shower room. The ground floor had vast glass windows all the way around, and Tony toyed with the idea of going round the entire cottage and closing all the curtains, but he was too tired. He went upstairs, brushed his teeth, and was in bed by midnight.

As he was falling asleep, Tony felt pressure just beyond his feet, as though someone had sat down on the end of the bed. He lay very still, not daring to pull up his feet or make the slightest movement. As he got used to the new weight distribution, he managed to convince himself that the change of pressure at the foot of his bed had never really happened. Eventually he started to doze off again, but this time he was roused by a sudden noise.

Tony lay motionless, listening. The noise came again. He was fairly certain it was the window clattering, but he was lying on his good ear, and he wanted to be sure. He propped himself up on an elbow and listened attentively. Sure enough, the window was rattling in its frame. There didn't seem to be any wind outside – there were no trees rustling and no other noise to indicate that the wind was blowing. Eventually the rattling stopped. Tired, Tony sank back down onto his goose down pillows and fell asleep.

Two hours later Tony woke up briefly from a nightmare he couldn't remember clearly, save a ghastly apparition – female, he thought – chasing him down some long, dark corridors. In his dream, he'd made it to his room, shut the door on the thing, and cowered by the door, holding firmly onto the handle. Tiredness overtook him and he fell asleep once more. This time he woke up to a headache and a feeling of pressure on his chest – a strong feeling of discomfort – pain almost – as if something had been sitting on him.

Immediately on getting out of bed the heaviness in his head and chest lifted, but Tony nevertheless decided to go downstairs to the kitchen and drink a *Beechams* powder dissolved in some hot water, after lining his stomach with a round of buttered toast. He untied the fancy strings holding the flowery curtains back and closed all the curtains in the kitchen. He didn't feel like going into the sitting-room, which looked dark and foreboding while at the same time completely exposed – on account of its copious, large windows – to the night and anything that was prowling it. Tomorrow he'd close the curtains in the sitting-room before darkness fell.

"What in the devil's name is this?" Lord Silderbury froze in the doorway, anger tingeing his cruel features a deep shade of red. Charlotte pulled herself up from the table and made a supplicating move towards her husband.

"My lord, I felt poorly and..." She stopped midsentence as her husband strode up and struck her full force across the face, knocking her down.

"Lord Silderbury!" The young coachman ran to Charlotte's side, comforting her and trying to help her to her feet.

"Get your filthy hands off her!" Silderbury kicked the young man to the floor, then turned his attention back to his bride. *"You brazen harlot! So this is what you've been doing on your walks?!"*

"No, my lord!" Charlotte sobbed, shielding her belly from another blow. *"You'll pay for this, but not before you see your lover die!"*

The aspirin in the *Beechams* soothed his body – the effect psychosomatic probably more than physical – but the feeling of unease did not lift. Tony reluctantly made his way back to bed, wondering what else lay in wait for him in Never-never land. Sure enough, as he was falling asleep, the rattling came again. Thankfully it was outside. But then a noise inside. A tapping sound – just one – like a piece of metal – a key perhaps – gently making contact with a ceramic bowl. But there was no ceramic bowl. So what had made the noise? After a few minutes of watchful sitting up in bed, Tony persuaded himself that it was the radiator cooling down. He lay back down in the dark, but couldn't sleep as something moved around on the roof. A bird – Tony told himself, not allowing himself to speculate what bird would move around on a roof at night.

The next time he woke, it was to a tapping sound. Confused, Tony lay still and tried to work out where the sound was coming from. At first he thought it was outside, that perhaps it was starting to rain, but the tapping came again – from one direction only, and not from any of the three windows that were located on different sides of the cottage. Then a loud harsh noise came from Tony's right. He sat bolt upright in bed and turned on the light. When his heart stopped pounding, he realised that the shower was on in the tiny bathroom. He must not have turned it off properly earlier in the day, and the water had taken some hours to collect before running out under pressure. These things happened.

And so it went on for the next hour or so. Tony would start to drift off, only to be woken up by strange noises in the cottage, which, after the initial shock, he would explain away in some fashion or other. There must be wind outside, there was a bird on the roof, the radiator was cooling down, a mouse must have knocked something over downstairs, the house was settling, he'd eaten too much during dinner and the pressure on his chest was indigestion. But when a cold, taloned hand wrapped itself around his throat, Tony up and ran – barefoot, in his pyjamas – down the stairs and out of the cottage, towards the main house where his family slept soundly in their adjacent rooms.

He'd only run a few steps towards the converted manor house when he saw a shadowy figure between him and it. Which family member was it and what were they doing out in the middle of the night? And his family were all rather on the portly side – the adults, at least – so why was the figure that blocked his way rake-thin? And why was it gliding towards him in that twisted, disjointed, unnatural fashion?

When Charlotte regained consciousness, she was in a small damp alcove. She could hear the muffled sound of rain somewhere on the roof above her, and a little water seeped in through a crack in what she worked out was the outside wall. Above her, in the opposite wall, a small opening above her head let in a shaft of light.

"Help!" she cried out, her heart threatening to burst out of her chest with fear.

"Welcome back, my dear," her husband's muted voice drifted in from the other side of the fresh stonework.

"What's happened?! Where am I?!"

"You liked visiting the coachman's cottage, didn't you? Well, now you'll never have to leave!"

"Please, my lord! Let me out!"

"So you need walks like you need bread and water. Isn't that what you told me?" "My lord, I never did anything to dishonour you," sobbed Charlotte. "Please, let me out!"

"Now you can have as many walks as you have food and water! ... Seal her in!"

Tony turned back and ran – past the cottage, down towards the lake and the white stone house he'd seen on his walk earlier in the day. A dog had barked at him when he'd walked past the house before, so there must be someone staying there.

The darkness was extreme, and Tony based his descent chiefly on his memory of the route acquired on his daytime stroll. Nevertheless, he stumbled several times, and it was nothing short of a miracle that he reached the white stone house in one piece. His feet were scratched and bleeding from the stones on the path he'd taken, but he could hardly feel his injuries, so numb was he from the cold and from his abject terror. He opened the gate without looking back and rushed straight to the nearest window, banging on the glass so hard it should have shattered beneath his fists.

"Help!" he shouted, gagging as he gasped for breath at the same time. "Let me in! Please!" But there was no response, and the cottage remained as dark inside at it was out. Tony spotted the front door of the building and rushed over to bash on that instead. "Help! Please!" He noticed the doorbell and pressed it hard. He could hear it ringing inside. "Open the door! Please!" There was still no answer and, as he stopped for a moment, Tony became aware of a presence behind him. He started to sweat, despite the freezing temperature, and his body began to shake uncontrollably. More than anything in the world he didn't want to turn around, but turn around he must.

There, standing about a metre away from him was the most terrifying thing Tony had seen in his entire life. It was spectral, like a shadow or a black mist, and yet corporeal. It had long, wispy hair, from behind which a pair of malevolent red eyes observed him with what could only be described as hunger – the rabid, bestial hunger of something that hadn't eaten for a long time. Dirty, shapeless rags hung off its emaciated, vaguely female form. As Tony and the creature faced each other for long seconds, he could smell the fetid odour of decomposing flesh rising off it, and he noticed that it was salivating. Then it emitted a feral sound somewhere between a hiss and a growl, and raised a bony, taloned hand towards Tony – as if in supplication.

Charlotte cried out in despair as the shaft of light falling into her living tomb was cut off. She begged and pleaded for mercy, only ceasing her entreaties long after the footsteps and voices had receded. Exhaustion overcame her and she sank to the cold stone floor, sobbing in the dark and the damp. At times her tears were for herself; at times for the young man whose moment of kindness towards her had led to his own tortured demise. She'd pleaded for the coachman's life, but fainted when Silderbury and his men held him down and castrated him, before finishing him off.

A small glow of light emanated from the crack through which a little rain water seeped in now and again, but the illumination was sufficient merely to hint at the shadowy forms of bugs and spiders that crawled around the distraught girl. Her head ached, and sharp pangs wracked her stomach. Despite the nausea that came and went, the hunger was unbearable – Charlotte's body demanded food not just for her, but for the foetus that fought to survive within. Occasionally she imagined that she heard people nearby, and she redoubled her cries. Her fingers bled from trying to pry out the vast stones that had been used to seal her in; her fists were bruised and knuckles scraped raw from banging against the walls of her makeshift cell. But no one heard, and no one came.

Charlotte's hair fell from her scalp and her teeth came loose as her body directed any remaining resources to more vital organs. Her muscles started to atrophy as her body digested them to stay alive. Every movement became painful, and eventually Charlotte moved merely to lick at the rainwater that trickled down from the crack in the wall. It was a rainy autumn, but the water that oozed into her prison served only to prolong her suffering. Sometimes her fear swelled as demons grasped from the walls at her tortured mind. Only occasionally would she call out to her mother. Her senses became numbed, and yet, instead of subsiding, the hunger grew – unnatural, rapacious, insatiable, taking on a life of its own even as its host's life slipped away.

Tony risked a fleeting glance towards the gate onto the track leading back up to the guesthouse, but before he managed to move a muscle, the creature had shifted to block his path. It bared its rank, pointy teeth, and extended its other hand to its terrified prey. Tony screamed and bolted for the jetty at the end of the small garden. Without a moment's hesitation he threw himself into the freezing black water and started to swim. Every muscle in his body rebelled against the paralysing cold, and yet Tony propelled himself forward through the inky water, only stopping when complete exhaustion overtook him.

Tony continued to move his arms and legs just enough to keep himself afloat. His body spasmed insufferably in the icy water and he wondered whether hypothermia was a painful way to die. That's when he heard the rhythmic splash of something swimming towards him through the dark.

CAPABLE OF LOVING

Sonora Taylor

Desmond fiddled with his bowtie in lieu of wiping his brow. The lights glared hot on his forehead even though they weren't filming that day. The set had to look exactly like it did on television, or else the children would sense that something was amiss, and they wouldn't trust their meeting. It was important that the children never lost their trust in Desmond. For many of them, Desmond was the only person they thought they could trust.

For three years, Desmond came to work and spoke to children in Loudoun County by speaking to a camera. *Desmond's Afterschool Hour* was a staple on public access television, and

Desmond was a hero to the people of Loudoun County – namely their children.

Desmond didn't have designs for television when he went to college. He majored in Psychology, and to pass time between classes – and also earn a little money – he worked as an assistant for a local puppeteer on his public access television show. Jack the Puppeteer was an old man, one Desmond imagined had a heyday before he was born. He needed help assembling and then dismantling his set, and making sure the puppets were cleaned and ready before each taping. The puppets needed to look the same each day, Jack told Desmond on his first day. "The kids need something that stays the same. It gives them something to rely on. It gives them something to trust."

Jack died within the year, and his show ended quietly along with him. But Desmond made enough of an impression with Jack's producers that they called him three years later, after he'd graduated and long after he'd left his brief career in television production. "Jack left a gap that can't be filled," they'd said. "But kids need a show like he had. We've had parents calling our network wondering when we'll have another show like his."

"So you want me to give you some ideas?" Desmond had asked. "Sort of. I was going to pitch you a show you could star in."

Desmond considered it. He hadn't considered his job on *Jack the Puppeteer* to be more than a gig in college. But his debts were mounting, he'd decided to put off graduate school when his senior year almost gave him a nervous breakdown, and his desk job was transitioning from tolerably dull to unbearable in his third year of doing the same thing. The show would at least give him something new to do while he considered what he wanted to do next.

Desmond met with the producers. They liked that he was connected to Jack, but loosely – everyone agreed that Desmond's show should be its own show and not a spin-off. Desmond was especially grateful to not have to work with the puppets. Jack was good at puppetry and voices, but Desmond was not. Desmond preferred to speak to kids himself.

Desmond's Afterschool Hour was a bigger hit than anyone expected. Most of Jack's viewers returned, along with new ones. Desmond proved to be a natural with kids. He taught lessons and spoke to them in groups on camera. There was soon a waiting list several months long to meet Mr. Desmond, so long that he began to set up meet-and-greet sessions off-camera so the kids would get a chance to talk to him.

The sessions always went well, and the kids always left happy. And yet, Desmond was always nervous before them. He couldn't help but worry that he would fail one of the kids, that this would be the session where he said the wrong thing or upset them. He sometimes told a story that was more frightening to a child than delightfully scary, or made a joke that got stony silence as opposed to a giggle. The world hadn't ended when those things had happened, but in Desmond's mind, each mistake was its own little apocalypse, an end of the world that he lived over and over like his own personal Groundhog Day.

So on a day under the lights, a day without filming but with the same set of nerves, Desmond wiped his brow as he prepared to meet Sarah Greene.

* * * * *

Sarah Greene was seven years old. She'd watched *Desmond's Afterschool Hour* since it first began, and according to her grandmother Pamela, Sarah loved him. "She watches you every week," Pamela said over the phone in a voice worn down from cigarettes and yelling after children. "She tapes you and studies you. Helps her learn to be nice."

"I'm sure she's nice without my assistance," Desmond said with a smile that Pamela couldn't see – and from her disaffected chuckle, one that Desmond figured she couldn't discern.

"She tries," Pamela said. "But you know how kids are. You know how other kids can be."

Desmond remembered some of the crueler kids he'd known as a boy, and tried not to succumb to the power they still had over his self-esteem. "I know," he said with a sigh – one that seemed to connect with Pamela more than his unseen smile.

"Sarah would love to meet you," Pamela said. "She talks about you all the time." "Well, my next group meeting is in a month –"

"Can she meet you alone?" Desmond paused. "Alone?"

"Yeah. Do you do one-on-one's?"

"Not often." He only did one-on-one's when a child was sick or required special care.

"But you do them sometimes?" she asked with a bit too much excitement, for she coughed twice afterward. Desmond wished he'd lied and said he never did them. He had a feeling that Pamela was the type who, once she saw the sliver of light from a crack in the door, would do everything in her power to open it further.

But even in a situation where he felt increasing discomfort, he couldn't bring himself to lie. "Sometimes, but only when the kids are sick or have special needs," he said.

"Sarah isn't sick, and she doesn't have special needs the way you mean, but …" Pamela took in a breath, and spoke in a voice that seemed resigned to sharing what she had to say to everyone who met her granddaughter. "But she has trouble with other kids."

"What kind of trouble? Do they tease her?"

"Sometimes. She has trouble talking to them. She's awkward around them."

"Lots of kids are shy. The best way to learn to be more comfortable is to be around them."

"Well, she'd do that if they were more comfortable around her. Trust me, Mr. … what's your last name, anyway?"

"Cole, but please, call me Desmond."

"Well, trust me, Desmond: she's around kids every day at school, and it's hard for her. It's hard for me and it's hard for her teachers. And when she watches your show, things are a little less hard. She talks about how nice you are and how she wants to be your friend, how maybe you'll be nice to her when other kids aren't. And I'd like her meeting you to not have the burden of what it's like when she's with other kids. So can she meet you one-on-one? Please?"

Desmond imagined a little girl sitting alone at recess or eating her lunch in solitude. He'd seen that little girl in various forms as he'd grown up. He hadn't always talked to that little girl himself. He still felt guilty for not doing more for every child. He couldn't say no to those memories – not again.

"Of course, Mrs. Greene," he said. "She can meet me on Saturday."

"Thanks so much. And please," she said, with a chuckle that almost sounded like a sputter. "It's Pam."

* * * * *

Pam and Sarah were due to arrive at 2 o'clock, after Sarah's swimming lessons. Desmond had questions prepared about her favorite dives and whether Sarah wanted to be a swimmer when she grew up. He hoped that Sarah wasn't so shy that she wouldn't share more information about herself. He'd met those children before, and was prepared for them; but it was always easier to talk to children who were willing to talk to him.

"Mr. Cole?"

Desmond looked beyond the set and saw his assistant, Sean, standing with a clipboard. "Sarah and her grandmother are here."

Desmond wiped his brow one final time, then nodded. "Send them in," he said.

Sean disappeared, and a woman and child appeared on the set. The older woman, Pam, looked exactly like her voice suggested. Her brown hair had stray streaks of grey and tumbled over her shoulders. Her skin was tanned into permanence and covered with wrinkles to complete the look. Her pink tank top was faded and perhaps a little too young for her, though Desmond wasn't one to judge. Still, he wished she'd worn a top that didn't show off the mole on her left breast so prominently.

Desmond looked down and saw Sarah Greene. She looked at him with a small smile and steady eyes. Her brown hair matched her grandmother's, minus the streaks of grey. She wore a green dress with a white cardigan.

Sarah and her grandmother walked hand-in-hand until they reached Desmond. Sarah let go of Pamela's hand and held out her own. "Hi Mr. Desmond," she said. "I'm Sarah."

"Hi Sarah." Desmond shook her hand and hoped his palms weren't too sweaty. "Your hands are wet. Are you warm?"

"Just a little, from the lights."

"My hands sweat sometimes when I'm nervous. Why do they do that?"

"I'm not sure," Desmond said, truthfully. "I didn't study that in school." He glanced up and saw Pamela walking towards the seats, her back turned and a magazine already out of her purse.

"What did you study in school?" Sarah asked. Desmond returned his attention to Sarah and sat on the stage, which was painted green to resemble a lawn. She didn't join him. That was okay—sitting down put him at eye-level with her, and she was likely more comfortable with that.

"I studied psychology," he said. "Do you know what that is?" "Something with brains?"

"Close!" Desmond raised his eyebrows in pleasant surprise. Before he could lower them, Sarah smiled. She seemed pleased to catch him off-guard with her knowledge. "You're pretty smart, aren't you?" he asked.

"I guess. I like reading and I like going to school."

"Well, psychology means studying why our brains make us do what we do, or why we think what we think. Brains have a lot of secrets, and psychology tries to worm them out."

Sarah lost her smile. "I don't like secrets. Secrets are what kids tell me they have when they don't want to tell me what they're saying, or when they don't want me to talk to them."

Desmond felt his heart break a little. Sarah didn't look sad, but he figured she was hiding her pain. His heart broke a little more at the thought of a seven-year-old already knowing how to hide her feelings.

"Your grandmother tells me you like swimming, though," he said, hoping to keep their conversation on things that made Sarah happy.

"It's pretty fun," Sarah agreed. "It's so I won't drown." "That's right. Do you like diving?"

"Do lots of kids drown?"

Desmond hadn't planned to talk about drowning, but Sarah's earnest expression told him he couldn't leave the question unanswered. "Some do," he said. "That's why it's important to take lessons."

"What if a kid drowned in swim class? Wouldn't that be funny?"

Desmond swallowed, minding his words so he wouldn't embarrass her. "I don't think it'd be funny."

"I would. They're taking classes so they won't drown, and then they drown anyway. How could they drown in a pool with all the lifeguards around?"

"I don't want to find out."

"I wonder about that sometimes. How can something happen that isn't supposed to – something like drowning in a swim class, or the sun shining when it rains?"

Desmond was grateful for Sarah mentioning something less macabre. He could sate her curiosity without staying on the subject of death. "Well, I wouldn't say the sun isn't supposed to shine when it rains," he said. "It's just not very common.'

"Is it as common as drowning?"

"Why are you so focused on drowning? Does it scare you?" "No. I just wonder about it."

"It's so scary, though. Why do you wonder about scary things?" "It's not scary to me. I'm not afraid of drowning."

"Because you can swim, right?"

Sarah giggled a little. Desmond was happy to see her smile.

"Because I don't imagine *me* drowning," Sarah said. "I imagine the other kids drowning. That's what makes it funny and not sad."

Desmond felt his heart go cold. He pressed his lips as he minded his words. He wondered why Pamela wasn't speaking up. Perhaps she was too engrossed in her magazine to hear. He glanced at Pam, who held the magazine open in her lap. Her eyes, however, didn't move across the page.

"Does drowning make you sad, Mr. Desmond?" Sarah asked.

Desmond returned his attention to Sarah. She looked up at him in earnest. Desmond realized his brow was furrowed, and he softened his expression.

"Yes," he said. "Even if it's not me and even if I didn't know who drowned. It's sad when someone dies."

"Always?"

"When it's something like drowning, yes." "Do you know someone who drowned?"

Whether Sarah looked stoic or solemn, Desmond couldn't tell. Still, he answered, "No. But it's sad when I see stories about people who drowned, especially children. They died so young. That's sad to me." Desmond thought it should be sad to anyone. Despite his unease, though, a small part of him told him not to dwell on that in front of Sarah. He wanted to meet her on her terms, however odd they might be.

Sarah nodded. Desmond figured that was the best approach going forward.

"Well, I don't want to make you sad," she said. "We can talk about something else."

Desmond nodded. "That'd be nice." He thought he saw Pamela look up out of the corner of his eye. When he looked in her direction, she looked back down at the page.

"What should we talk about?" Sarah asked.

"How about school?" Sarah didn't brighten, but Desmond continued all the same. "You're so smart. I bet you love school."

"It's okay."

"What's your favorite subject?" "Art. I like painting."

"What do you like to paint?"

"Lines. I like making streaks across the paper." Sarah smiled. "It's almost like the paper is skin and I'm cutting into it."

Desmond tried to keep the flash of horror that stopped his heart for a moment from showing on his face. She must've seen something on TV. She was too young to realize what she was saying sounded like.

"It's like I'm cutting into the paper's secrets," Sarah continued. "And showing everyone what the paper tried to hide."

"That's really insightful for someone your age," Desmond observed. "What's insightful mean?"

"Intuitive." Desmond knew even before Sarah crinkled her brow that his answer wasn't helpful. "It means you're good at looking inside things and describing what's inside," he said.

"Oh. Like I've cut something open and showed its secrets?"

"Sort of, yes." Desmond began to get nervous again. He wondered if Pamela heard. He wondered if Pamela had heard anything. He glanced as quickly as possible in her direction. Her magazine was still open to the same page as before. Her hands gripped the pages, and her eyes were still.

Pamela heard everything. She'd probably heard everything before. She was probably bracing herself for what Desmond would say, if it would be what everyone else said when they talked to Sarah.

"Can someone who's intuitive find out people's secrets like that?" Sarah asked.

Desmond brought his attention back. He put his hands in his pockets and took the opportunity to wipe his sweaty palms on the fabric. "Someone who's intuitive would probably know without any sort of cutting," he replied.

"Okay. So they wouldn't have to cut anyone or anything."

"No." Desmond feared that Sarah wasn't speaking as figuratively as she was about the paper in art class. He shook off the fear – he was overthinking things. He continued, "And even if they weren't intuitive, there shouldn't be any cutting."

"Even if they're keeping secrets?"

"Yes. Cutting isn't nice." Desmond smiled in an effort to keep things light, to act as if he and Sarah were sharing a morbid joke.

Sarah looked solemn, but Desmond saw something dark flutter through her eyes, like a flock of ravens flying across a morning sky.

"It also isn't nice when kids keep secrets from me," she said. "Well no, not always –"

"Never. It's never nice."

"Sometimes people have secrets. Don't you keep secrets from your friends?"

"I don't have friends. All the kids in my class are mean. They look at me funny and make fun of my drawings."

"Some kids are mean, but I'm sure not all of them are."

"And they won't tell me what they mean. They'll ask me things about my drawings or my clothes or my books, and I'll answer, and they'll laugh and look at each other but they won't tell me what's funny when I ask. I don't like it."

"I wouldn't like that either. That's very mean. What does your teacher do?" "She tells them to be nice, but they don't listen."

"Well, maybe you should stop listening to them," Desmond offered. "I don't want to listen to them."

"But you want to know their secrets?"

Desmond surprised himself with his question, one that could almost sound sarcastic to the wrong ears. Before he could scramble for another thing to say, though, Sarah giggled.

"It is kind of funny," she agreed.

Desmond smiled as well. "It is. We're most interested in hearing what people we don't like have to say."

"Well, I like hearing what you have to say," Sarah said. "And I like you."

"Thank you, Sarah. That's nice of you."

"Do you like me?"

"Sure I do. You're smart and have a keen sense of things."

"Sarah?" Pamela stood up and walked back towards the two of them. "I think it's almost time for us to go, sweetheart."

"Okay." Sarah turned and took her grandmother's outstretched hand. "Bye Mr. Desmond!"

"Bye Sarah," Desmond replied with a small wave. Sarah and Pamela turned, then disappeared into the darkened hallway leading away from the set.

* * * * *

Desmond thought of Sarah Greene all weekend. Her words flickered in his brain as he read the next week's scripts and prepared to film. He couldn't shake the unease he felt when she spoke of death, of cutting, of drowning and secrets. He knew she was a little girl, but also knew when something went beyond childish curiosity and veered into troubling. Sarah's words were beyond troubling. They bordered on psychotic.

Desmond hated to think that of a child. So many people used "psychotic" to equate someone who wasn't actually psychopathic to a leering, grinning killer they saw on TV. It didn't help anyone.

He shook the thought from his mind. He wasn't Sarah's father. It was Pamela's job to raise her. He dove into that week's show and focused on new children coming to see him. Soon, he didn't think much of Sarah Greene at all.

Unfortunately, that lack of thought also appeared to reach Desmond—at least according to ratings. A year or so after Desmond met Sarah, the same producers who'd reached out to him to replace Jack the Puppeteer told him the current season would be the show's last. "We just aren't getting the numbers we need," they explained. "No one's watching public access anymore."

The number of children visiting him each week told Desmond otherwise, but he knew that protest would be in vain. The producers were more concerned with statistics on a piece of paper than living, breathing children, ones who wouldn't get to see him anymore. He thought of Sarah for the first time in years. He remembered how her grandmother had said his show was the highlight of her afternoon. He hoped for the sake of viewers like her that the station would at least keep him in their lives through repeats.

Years passed. Desmond went back to school and began to work towards being a child therapist. He met a man named Colin, and they moved in together shortly after he graduated. He began working at a child psychology office. As more children left his office in better spirits, his earlier fears of saying the wrong thing or making the wrong decision that he'd harbored as a student and a television host began to ebb.

Desmond returned home from work late one evening and saw Colin watching TV. "What's that?" Desmond asked as he hung up his coat.

"A kid who probably would've been better off if she'd met you," Colin quipped.

Desmond turned to face the television and froze. Though she was eleven years older and wearing orange instead of white and green, he knew he had met her before. Sarah Greene stared at the person interviewing her with no hint of the love and adoration Desmond had seen in her face when they'd met. She didn't have a hint of anything in her eyes, not even resignation.

A woman sat across from Sarah in a purple blazer, pearl earrings, and perfectly-styled hair. Desmond presumed she was a news reporter. "Do you regret what you've done?" the reporter asked.

"I haven't done anything," Sarah replied. A stab of pain went through Desmond's heart at hearing her voice. It was deeper and more grown-up, but he could still remember Sarah's childhood voice from all those years ago.

"But you've been—"

"She's already testified in court," said another woman off-camera. "No questions about her culpability."

"Right. So, Sarah, these things you've been accused of: how do you feel about them?"

Sarah didn't answer.

"Do you feel remorse?" "Ms. Davenport—"

"Yes, Counselor Jimenez, I understood you before." Ms. Davenport shifted, and Desmond could see a flash of irritation in her eyes. Sarah sat without any change in her gaze.

"How do you feel about everything?" Ms. Davenport asked.

Sarah shrugged, but stayed quiet—probably to appease her lawyer.

"How do you feel about those that are gone? Are you sorry for them? For their families?"

"No. Why would I be? I don't know any of them." "What about your parents?"

"They're dead. They died when I was little." "Your guardian, then."

"I don't care about Grandma Pam."

"Not even a little? Don't you love her?"

Sarah shrugged again. Desmond pursed his lips, but his ire was directed at the news program determined to interview someone obviously troubled simply for ratings, to cater to a TV audience's cruel cravings. He honestly expected better of Colin. "Why are you watching this?" Desmond asked.

"Nothing else is on," he replied.

"Are you capable of loving anyone?" Ms. Davenport asked.

Sarah's expression changed. She no longer looked blank, but deeply sad.

Colin lifted the remote to change the channel—it was one of the things Desmond loved about Colin, that he didn't have to explain when something was troubling him—when Sarah said, "I loved Desmond Cole."

Both Colin and Desmond froze. Colin looked at Desmond quizzically. "Was he your boyfriend?" Ms. Davenport asked.

"He was on TV. He used to have a show, *Desmond's Afterschool Hour*. He always talked about being nice and trusting people and how people who were honest were your best friends. No one was honest with me, so I didn't have any friends. But Desmond was honest, even when I met him. I'd say things to him, things that I knew scared him—"

Desmond felt a chill stab his heart at his inability to hide his feelings, especially in a moment that mattered so much to her.

"But he didn't make me feel bad about them. He was honest with me. You know how many people, ever since I was little, would look at me and be reserved? How people would hear what I'd say and if they didn't laugh at me, they'd be scared of me?"

"It sounded like Desmond was scared of you."

"I wasn't," Desmond said, though he hadn't meant to do so out loud.

"He wasn't," Sarah said, before Colin could ask Desmond what he meant. "I'd seen enough people trying to hide how frightened they were of me to know what that looked like."

"What does it look like?"

Sarah narrowed her eyes. "It looks like they're burying things inside of their minds with little mental shovels. Stuff they think they can hide from me in the folds."

Desmond saw a spark in Ms. Davenport's eyes, one that implied she was getting what she wanted. In that moment, Desmond felt pure and seething hatred. How dare she?

"And is that what you were looking for when—"

"This interview is over," Counselor Jimenez interjected.

"I'll ask another question," Ms. Davenport said; but Counselor Jimenez was already whisking Sarah away.

"Good," Desmond said with a scowl. "Good, what?" Colin asked.

"That they took her away. The reporter was out of line."

Colin shook his head as he turned off the TV. "She wasn't the most out-of-line person in that room, though."

"Her lawyer was just doing her job—"

"I'm talking about Sarah! You missed the first part, before they started interviewing her. She murdered, like, fifteen people before they caught her."

Desmond's eyes shot up. "Fifteen?"

"And it wasn't just, oh hey, you're dead. She removed their brains and sliced them up across the lines, like she was carving disgusting filets or something."

Desmond felt a sickness grow in his stomach as he remembered Sarah talking about cutting lines into paper in lieu of slicing into people's brains to uncover their thoughts.

Colin smirked as he added, "Bet she was eating them too." Desmond glared at Colin. "That's not funny."

"Come on, she's a murderer—"

"She's sick. She's acting out on something that's been wrong with her ever since she was young. I met her when I was on public access." Desmond told Colin the story of when Sarah came to visit. With each detail, Colin's eyes grew wider.

"Why didn't you say anything?" Colin asked.

"Because I didn't want to hurt Sarah. She trusted me." "Trusted you? She was talking about harm!"

"She never said she actually wanted to harm anyone—"

"Isn't a psychologist supposed to share when their patient may do harm?"

"She wasn't my patient and I wasn't her doctor! I was a host on a TV show, and kids met me all the time, and what she said bothered me, but I didn't fucking think I needed to make phone calls or be social services. How could I have known she'd grow up and become—" Desmond stopped short as a lump sprang into this throat. Images of Sarah Greene on television flickered back and forth between memories of meeting her when she was young. She'd grown up to hurt people, and he'd done nothing to stop it.

"Hey." Colin got up and pulled Desmond into a hug. "Hey honey, I'm sorry. I shouldn't have said that. I was just shocked by the interview and even more shocked that you knew her."

"I should've said something."

"Even if you did, there's no way to know if you could've stopped her. You weren't her father and you weren't in child services. What could you have done, anyway?"

He could've told her the way she thought was wrong. He could've been less concerned about her comfort and making sure that Sarah was happy. Desmond had been too concerned with being Sarah's friend, with preserving her trust in him.

It was a trust so strong, though, that Sarah kept it even when the rest of her humanity had crumbled to the ground. She'd loved him. She still did. And as Desmond felt a hint of warmth flicker in his heart, he realized he still cared about her too. Even after all she'd done—after all she was accused of—he still cared about how she'd turn out. He still cared that she was happy, that maybe a moment of happiness would help her see through all the darkness in her mind. And given what he'd seen on TV, maybe it had—and he'd given that to her.

He smiled a little to himself. He'd done his job. He'd helped someone. "What's up?" Colin asked.

"Nothing," Desmond said. He never lied to Colin, but he didn't want to argue about how much Sarah was actually helped. In that moment, a moment within all the ugliness, she had been helped. Despite the way she'd turned out, despite the crimes and bodies associated with her name, she was capable of loving. That was enough for Desmond—and to keep his own brain from splitting the way so many others had done upon meeting Sarah Greene, it would have to be.

LITTLE PIG
Lydia Prime

Mallory
January 27, 2018—10:17 PM

I saw it, patiently curled up in the dark spaces of my home. Silhouettes of this creature frequented my mind for a split second before disappearing again. If I wasn't so terrified of it, perhaps the image would linger. A few blissful hours passed and it never popped up to disturb me again.

As the sun set, the six-foot shadow-being grew, stretching across the walls; slinking its way back through my mind. Existing of pure darkness—blacker than the deepest pit—it crept to the corners of my eyes; taunting me.

I'd tried to show others this *thing* I was seeing, but no one ever had any idea what I was talking about. My friends always grew quiet, my family's faces blank; surprisingly, that's the last time I spoke to any of them.

March 3, 2018—08:45 AM

This morning, as I woke, its large misshapen form skittered off my bed. It shuffled away swiftly, as if it were never there. My chest felt heavy. I was overcome with incomprehensible dread. I sat quietly, trying to reassure myself that I was undeniably awake. My palms clung to the bedsheets, my sweat acting like glue. I implemented all those 'positive affirmation' tactics the hospital taught me. Tranquility zipped through my veins, my heartbeat normalized; I'd composed myself, but something still felt different this time.

March 8, 2018—07:28 PM

My cat spent the afternoon chasing flies, trying to jump higher with each failed attempt. I thought they'd come from 'The Spot,' as I'd eloquently dubbed it. A space in my home that I found myself repeatedly checking on. My eyes flicked to a dark corner of the hallway. I tried to pull my gaze away, but the magnetism kept dragging me back.

I stopped what I was doing and sat opposite the shadowed corner. For the first time, I'd noticed a lazily painted iron covering on one of the house's many heating vents. It looked as if it needed a severe scrubbing; tacky goop pushed through the delicately crafted pattern and dripped onto the floor. My cat, still battling more bugs, looked past me down the corridor before bolting towards 'The Spot.' Panic seized my body, strangling the life within. I wanted to call out to her, to tell her not to go toward the vent, but fear paralyzed me.

I lost time; not sitting in front of shadows but consumed by the darkness, it was clear the moon rose some time ago. Billie raced out of the corner, brushing past me with her fur puffed out chaotically. My eyes adjusted; I searched for the iron grate, but it appeared to have gone. I supposed I must have imagined it there.

Joints aching from being still so long, I hobbled to the kitchen. Switches flipping as I passed, filling the place with light. Each step into the dark brought small flashes through my psyche, like miniature lightning storms frying out my mind. I shut my eyes tight—the creature was trying to get my attention. The massive shape hovered just beyond my periphery. If I turned to face it head-on, it'd go, but the second I looked away, it'd be closer.

Every light was on—I felt safe. I thought food might be wise. Once I began cooking, the image faded, as usual, and I watched my cat hunt another tiny winged beast.

March 9, 2018—2:19 AM

It's two in the morning. I could have sworn I felt someone breathing on my face. When I opened my eyes, I saw a dark blob. I quickly rubbed the sleepy gook from my eyelids and looked around; nothing seemed noticeably out of place. My door was open just a crack so Billie could nudge her way in to sleep when she was ready. I blinked a few times to adjust. I called out to Billie and she mewled from the hall. Edging towards the side of my bed, I took the opportunity to check underneath, just in case, before getting up. Billie's noises were getting fainter. She must have thought we were going to get breakfast. I stepped through my doorway and into the dimly lit pathway.

I was careful to avoid staring at 'The Spot.' Chills traveled the length of my spine; my hands were cold but sweat dripped from my brow. *Someone's here...* a small shuffle sounded from that area and my pulse quickened. I called out to my cat and listened to silence. I hoped she'd just gotten comfy somewhere and nodded off. Feeling like I wasn't going to be able to shake the eerie atmosphere up there, I made my way down the steps. I called out to Billie again, and thought I heard her meow from back upstairs. I couldn't muster up enough courage to go check, so I wrapped myself in a throw blanket and curled into the corner of my couch.

Streaks of sunbeams penetrated my cotton cocoon. Morning crashed around me and I guess I must have fallen back asleep at some point. The slight crick in my neck was worth being able to sleep without feeling watched. Billie stretched in the sun spot on the floor. Relieved to see her in one piece, I smiled and rolled onto my back. The ceiling was never as interesting as I expected. The epiphanies I missed out on were probably lost to all the collective years I'd spent checking out the same old popcorn ceiling. *Someone was here last night, I know it.* I took a deep breath and decided to get up, Billie followed suit, extending her claws into the carpet for another stretch.

March 10, 2018—02:55 PM

I invited Deirdre over—she never made me feel like I was speaking a different language. I'm not sure she believed what I'd told her, but she never made me feel as if I needed to hide away.

We sat at the island in my kitchen and she listened as I went on about the eerie feelings, creepy shadows, and weird blurry silhouettes that pirouetted through my consciousness. Stopping for air, I realized my hands were trembling. My coffee cup became a great source of comfort. I wrapped my fingers around the warm mug and felt the tips burn against the orange ceramic. I stared into the tan liquid, not ready to see the worried look Deirdre'd have on her face. Sighing, I lifted my gaze to meet hers.

Offering a warm smile and a general sense of understanding, she reached across the counter to me. She placed her hand over mine. Still looking into my tired eyes, she told me she'd noticed things too, but only when staying at my place. She never paid attention to the feelings, just brushed them off as if they were paranoia. She laughed, pulling her hand back to sip her coffee. I feigned a smile and looked toward Billie.

It's so much more than just that.

"Will you stay tonight? No one else believes me and I feel like I'm losing my mind." I pleaded and crossed my fingers beneath the countertop. I didn't feel like I had to disguise my fear anymore. She knew, she *got it.*

"Tonight?" Deirdre drummed her nails on the marble and studied the exhaustion in my face. "Of course I can stay tonight." We both smiled, the room suddenly filled with trepidation. I had an urge to look over my shoulder, I could feel otherworldly eyes burning through my back. My friend grabbed my hand again. She promised everything would be okay. The uneasiness I felt, the deep sting of being watched—Deirdre hadn't felt it. My urge to look back dissipated and I was certain whatever it was had left the room.

March 11, 2018—04:31 AM

Deirdre and I sat comfortably in our sweat pants and oversized T-shirts. Each of us with a messy bun meticulously placed on top of our heads. Popcorn was popped, and away we went to enjoy a nostalgic blockbuster. The movie we started was holding her attention, but my mind wandered elsewhere. I shifted in my seat so I could see the stairs from the corner of my eye. Deirdre chomped away through two handfuls of buttery snacks while I questioned if the *thing* would make an appearance tonight. If my friend's presence would keep it at bay – or if her being here would shift its attention off me. I sighed loudly, selfish though it may have been, the potential sweet reprieve I so terribly needed wasn't something I would turn down.

Deirdre looked over and threw popcorn at me. She demanded I wake up and pay attention to the 90's melodrama. I threw a few salted kernels back and we giggled before returning to the procedural thriller. A shrieking girl in her half-torn nightie sprinted toward the steps to escape the psycho killer sauntering after her. *Don't go up there, you dolt! Next, she'll hit him with something, drop it, and run straight to her untimely demise. Cheese-cheese-cheeeeeese.*

Eyelids heavy and arms outstretched, a massive yawn escaped. I blinked several times; crimson font intended to seem like dripping blood spread across the screen. The credits rolled, but the room was darker than it should've been. Floorboards creaked in the distance.

"Deirdre, did you hear that?" I whispered and squeezed the throw pillow I'd been hugging.

Silence—bitter, uncertain—silence. The creaking from the backroom seemed to move closer. "Deirdre?" I called again, but still no answer. "Dude, please, do you hear that?"

'Hear what?' A disembodied voice growled directly in my ear. All the hairs on the back of my neck stood up, my heart skipped a beat and I froze. I could feel something next to me, enjoying my fear.

My breathing quickened. I reached for my friend. *Why isn't she answering me?* The collar of her shirt tore as I shook her; she stirred a little, *could sleep through a bomb, this one.* I dug my nails into her shoulders and rocked her with more force; the presence I felt so heavily just seconds ago lifted. Distinct harsh steps clomped from beside the couch away to the other room. Dissolving from a scratchy-thwack into softer thuds on the hardwood floor.

"What? What?" Her gravelly voice was angelic compared to whatever I'd just endured. I was still so scared; I hadn't let go of her. Deirdre pushed me off her and sat up. "The hell are you doing, Mal?"

"I, uh," I twisted the hem of my shirt between my fingers, squeezing the sides against the cuticles for stress relief. "You didn't hear any of that?" I asked before moving back to my side.

"Any of *what*? I was sleeping, bro!" Deirdre's eyes drooped and she laid on her side to return to her pleasant dreamy land of hallucinations.

I decided to get up and find out what was making the noises in the other room. Armed with a neon yellow pillow and silver TV remote, I breathed deeply before climbing off the life raft. I tiptoed across the room and down the hall. Soft thuds started again, only this time they came from my kitchen. I pressed against the wall and crept cautiously, trying to avoid squeaky floorboards that might've given away my position.

I peered around the corner, scanning the room—nothing. My heart took turns with my stomach for what felt worse. Scratchy-thwack noises returned, louder now— above me.

I shut my eyes tightly, knees feeling weak. My mouth filled with sand. Squinting, I watched my chest inflate and deplete rapidly. I bargained with myself to take one deep breath then look straight up.

Please don't be there, please don't be there...

White ceiling. Somewhat dusty, but no freaky creature. Sweat dripped from my brow. Though, slightly concerned that I'd just been freaking myself out, I shrugged and started back towards the living room. Something in the pit of my stomach made me feel like this wasn't the end. I looked around the room. Confident there wasn't anything there, I sat back into the cushy seat and pulled some blanket off of Deirdre. As soon as my head hit the pillow, I heard it.

Scratching came from the second-floor landing. I shook off the previous false alarm and quickly made my way to the stairs.

Light spilled onto the platform, based on its direction, it seemed to be coming from my bathroom. Thoughts ranging from worst case to best case weren't making anything easier, but I had to go. I had to find out what it was. The banister felt scaly. I imagined the floor opening beneath me and not being able to keep my grip.

Please, oh please, just be a burglar.

Stepping onto the final plank the stillness overwhelmed me. The air, the hall, my overworked muscles: stuck, stale, and petrified.

I tried to convince myself to move. *Come on, you can do this!* One inch forward then a pause to listen. I would have believed I stood there for years. Blood racing— trying to circulate or find a way out. The apparent inactivity struck me worse than the noisy intruder.

I'd made it to the doorway of my pristine bathroom. The monochromatic scheme seemed fitting for this odd moment. The shower curtain fluttered, a cool breeze whooshed through the room, *I don't remember leaving that window open…*

With the wind came an aroma of rotting meat. The smell kept getting stronger no matter what I did. I shut the window then leaned against the sink. *Where the hell is that coming from?*

'What a succulent specimen…' The garbled words filled my head. The monstrosity that'd been haunting my home materialized in the bleakest corner of my hallway. It gradually staggered into the light. I saw it, all of it, for the first time. Its face was somewhat elongated and rat-like. The creature had a skeletal structure too large for its skin; bones threatened to burst through its strained dermis. The scratchy- thwack echoed as it moved across the floor. Claws curled beneath the toes, scraping harshly against wood. Skinny red-blue veins trailed its paper-thin flesh, creating a purple roadmap beneath the pallid coloring. Stringy black hair fell flatly at its hips, red eyes bore hungrily into my brown ones. Puce talons dripped sinewy slime, its teeth were jagged and bared through lips of milk-white. My jaw locked. I found myself panicking again. Its tacky claws clicked together, making thick wet splattering noises; the smell of rotting meat became so immense that my stomach did cartwheels. The abomination began to grin allowing more uneven yellow-green cuspids to show. I moved to slam the door and lock it. It banged against the wood with all its might, "Let me in little pig!" An inhuman voice snarled, shaking the walls.

My screams must've woken up Deirdre downstairs, I heard her running to me. "Mal?" She called; I could hear the distress in her voice. "Mal, are you okay?"

My heart was pounding through my chest, *what if it gets her?!* I swung open the door ready to fight, but only Deirdre stood in the hallway, her face flushed.

"Mal, what're you doing?"

"Didn't you see it? Didn't you *smell* it!?" I cried, my hands waving frantically.

She looked at me as if she was seeing a stranger.

"Mal, I'm not sure what you're talking about, but I think you need some sleep, man." She guided me to my room and we both crawled into my bed. Deirdre again assured me that everything would be okay and I did everything I could to keep my eyes from moving to 'The Spot.' My cat stood guard outside, and I tried to forget the smell of carcasses decomposing.

March 11, 2018—11:47 AM

Daylight shimmered through my windows, there was a calm that hung faintly in the air. Deirdre was still asleep. I carefully shuffled out of bed and headed to my bathroom. *Did I imagine all that last night? No, I couldn't have.*

I shook my head to hopefully knock loose the intrusive thoughts and closed the door behind me. I ran the water to the bath and faced myself in the mirror as I waited for the tub to fill. My eyes were bloodshot. I looked ill. *No wonder Deirdre's worried.* I undressed and climbed into the steaming water. My sore muscles relaxed instantly—I could finally breathe. The scent of a eucalyptus and honey bath bomb filled the room and I slid beneath the water. A gurgled scream interrupted my minute peace and I immediately sprung out of the tub. Soap burned my eyes, but I clambered over the side and threw on my T-shirt, slipping and sliding on the tiled floor as I tried, and failed, to pull on my sweats. Another scream.

I ran into the bedroom and saw her sprawled out on the floor. Her head nearly severed from her body, four long slashes down her torso. Blood smeared every wall and dripped from the ceiling. Horrified and confused, I screamed. I screamed louder than I ever knew I could. "Deirdre! Oh Deirdre!" My cat sauntered through the puddles of blood and sat on Deirdre's lifeless chest. She kneaded her flesh and pulled the skin apart a bit more before nestling in as if she'd never found a more comfortable bed. Stunned, I fell back on my ass. I stared at the scene; tears poured down my face. I pulled my knees to my chest, rocking back and forth. Hyperventilating and trying to figure out what to do. Scrambling, I stood and ran into the hallway.

"SHOW YOURSELF!" I demanded, instantly regretting the force I'd used. My bottom lip quivered as the disgusting odor returned. Flies buzzed around my head and I swallowed hard. "WHERE ARE YOU?"

'Why do you sound so angry?' It asked, its raspy voice echoing in my mind. *'What's wrong, Piggie?'*

"You killed her! You killed Deirdre!" I shouted, my head spinning from all the voices taking up residence there. I tried desperately to pinpoint the creature's location.

'You think I killed your friend?' Shrill and wild laughter erupted in my skull, bouncing from sinus cavity to sinus cavity. I grabbed my ears and dropped to my knees.

"What do you want!"

'What you want, Mallory.' My name billowed from the bathroom. I crawled over to it and saw the blood-filled bathtub, the bloody handprints that coated the counter and mirror.

No, no! I didn't—I couldn't! My stomach was full of worms, all wriggling around, trying to eat their way out. I vomited black sludge. My head throbbed while the world twisted round and round. I laid on the cold wet floor and wished everything would stop.

Knock, knock, knock.

"Mal, Mallory, c'mon man. You're taking forever!" Deirdre shouted.

But how? I saw her dead!

"Deirdre?" I squealed and flung the door open. Standing in the doorway was a blood-soaked Deirdre, walking and talking. Her teeth fanged, eyes like rubies. "What the—?"

She lunged at me and I slammed the door shut. Her head bounced off the wooden barrier with a loud thunk, "Mallory, oh Maaalloorryy! We're waiting for you."

"You're not real! You're not here!"

"Oh, Mallory, I *am* here. Now come out, come out little pig!" She growled. "Mal!

Mallory!"

I woke to Deirdre shaking me. Drenched in sweat, I stared up at her. "DEIRDRE!" I hugged her. We rocked back and forth, "Are you… okay?"

"Of course I'm okay, why wouldn't I be?" She snorted as she laughed at my concern.

"Bad dream I guess." I could feel my pulse all over and I stared intently at 'The Spot.' It was there, smiling, waving, and just as quickly as it appeared, it was gone. "Maybe you should get out of here, I'm not feeling so good."

"You sure bro? I don't mind staying." She was insistent, but after last night, I knew she had to get out of there.

"Yes, yes. I'll be fine. Just need to be alone for a bit. I'll call you tomorrow and we'll get lunch or something." She reluctantly agreed and gathered up her stuff. I walked her out.

March 12, 2018—12:21 AM

I'm ready this time. You won't catch me off guard again. I paced around my home, avoiding my room and 'The Spot,' as much as possible. I decided to keep a kitchen knife near me to stay safe. I had to be rid of this grotesque creep. No more watching over my shoulder and feeling like someone's waiting in the dark. As the day faded and my home filled with shadows, I heard my kitty run across the house wildly. She scampered up the stairs and I stayed in my living room.

I whispered prayers to whoever might be listening, and heard a roar from above. *I know it's you, you son of a bitch.* I grabbed my knife and headed towards the stairs, my cat sat wide-eyed at the top, watching as I crept up each step. She hissed, backing away toward the light from the bedroom. I glanced around the hall, nothing out of the ordinary. I peered at my cat; her shadow was wrong. It grew and became hideously malformed. Standing in her place was that foul beast—no longer a fuzzy ball of fury. It growled and charged at me. I braced for impact but it stopped, our noses touching. Its putrid stench burned my nostrils. It took everything I had not to puke all over. Tremoring, I challenged it, raising my blade to meet its claw.

"What do you want?" I asked, not entirely expecting an answer, not entirely sure I'd gotten that out coherently either.

'I already told you. I want, what you want, Mallory.' Its distorted voice melted brain cells. *'Raise your knife, and begin.'*

I stared into its garnet eyes and saw emptiness. Flies buzzed around us, the rank fragrance of a cadaver lingering in the hot sun clouded my thoughts. I knew what I had to do, and exactly how to do it. As I sliced deeply through its chest, it snickered; I shrieked as pus and grime spewed all over me. I stabbed 'til I couldn't anymore.

'Good, now sleep.' The monster cooed, I closed my eyes and we both slid down the wall onto the floor.

* * * * *

Deirdre
March 15, 2018—01:28 PM

"Mal?" Deirdre rang the bell and banged on the door, but there was no answer. She checked beneath Mallory's car and found her hide-a-key in a magnetic box. "Mal?" She called as she slowly pushed the door. The house was still. Deirdre wasn't sure what, but she knew something felt off. Mallory never called her to go to lunch, and it'd been at least two days since she last saw her. She went from room to room searching for her friend until finally reaching the staircase. A small tabby cat was perched halfway up the stairs and meowed. *I didn't know she had a cat...* "Here kitty, kitty. Is Mal up there?"

Deirdre started up the stairs and the cat jumped into her arms. "You must be starving, poor thing. Where's Mallory, huh?" She talked to the cat and scratched behind its ear. "Mallory?"

On the floor of the hall, she saw Mallory's body. Surrounded by flies and lying in a pool of cherry splashed death. Deirdre wailed as she sprinted down the stairs to call the police, fearing that someone must have done this to Mallory and might still be hanging around.

When the police arrived, they told Deirdre it was a suicide. Officer Santiago was quick to let her know it was the strangest one he'd ever seen. She'd managed to stab herself around twenty-four to thirty times. He explained that the medical examiner was honestly not sure how she'd been able to manage something like that.

After answering a few questions, they told Deirdre she could go. She walked to her car, her face red and eyes puffy. She looked back at the house, now crawling with cops and CSI personnel.

Deirdre sighed and got in, "Looks like it's just you and me, kitty." She smiled weakly as the cat jumped on her lap and began to purr.

Perfect Girlfriend
Angela Yuriko Smith

I have no knowledge of how I came to be standing on a corner next to a row of low budget Scroo-Boos in the rain. I only know that I am here with an activated directive and the wet weather is counter-productive. I don't mind. I am impervious up to -50° Celsius and waterproof to a depth of 552 feet. But my target consumer isn't.

This was the data I contemplated when my objective appeared. The rain had let up so consumers were leaving shelter. He came from underground and headed straight for the Scroo-Boo. He glanced at me as he passed.

"I am the same price," I told him.

He stopped, looked me up and down. "Same price as what?" he asked. "I am the same price as the entertainment you are considering."

He glanced at the Scroo-Boos before walking around, considering me from each angle. "Why? Are all your bits not functional?"

I considered what he said and delivered the appropriate response. "No, I am fully functional. I am operating at a discount today because I am newly deployed and my employer is [accessing...] eager for a payday."

He whistled between his teeth. "Then this is my lucky day. You aren't exactly high end but you got the right rear end." He laughed at his joke, and I responded appropriately by holding out my palm for payment details.

He licked his lips as he placed the back of his hand against my palm. His other hand reached up to explore my left breast. I extracted his payment information and a subscript engaged. I downloaded a copy of his ID packet into my encrypted circuits.

"You have a deposit of 5 credits withdrawn. The remainder of the fee will be withdrawn upon completion of this transaction. I will keep your payment engaged. An extension of credit can be offered if required."

"No, baby. I got an extension enough right here already. I'm just looking to deposit. Engage me all you want."

"Please verbally confirm that you accept the terms of the transaction."

"Yes, I accept the terms of the transaction. Now get yourself in that booth and earn your credits." I recorded his confirmation as he pushed me through the curtain in the first booth.

The interior was cramped, but I am optimized for a variety of configurations so the customer was pleased. While he was completing his transaction I put a delayed withdrawal request in place for the remainder of his credits. The bank required verbal confirmation to empty all funding from an account. I played back his recorded confirmation. "Yes, I accept the terms of the transaction… accept…" Satisfied, the bank approved the transaction.

At approximately the same time, he was also satisfied and I collected his DNA.

He zipped himself back up. "Hey, you were sterilized before me, weren't you? I should have asked what your hygiene protocol is like."

"There was no need for me to be sterilized because you are my first client. I appreciate your inquiry. I will proceed to self sterilize before my next client."

I had no intention of self-sterilizing before my next client. My hygiene units had been hacked and repurposed for individual sample collection. I had storage for three samples.

"Cool… cool." He slid through the curtain and I followed to reposition myself at my former post. "You're not lying to me, are you?"

"I don't have the ability to lie, only follow my programming." "That's what I like to hear, baby. Tell your employer thanks." "Your message will be relayed."

"Cool, cool," he said and he walked down the sidewalk away from the subway. I had not been his primary objective but a stop on the way to somewhere else. I allowed that data to loop while I waited.

The rain let up and it grew dark. I wondered if I would complete my directive before I had to return. A second consumer approached, heading straight for the Scroo- Boos. "I am the same price," I told him.

He considered me, thanked me and then refused. "I don't trust too good a deal," he said.

Before he had exited the booth another consumer had already arrived. I had expected a decrease in traffic as it got later, but it looked like I would accomplish my quota after all. I used my programmed icebreaker and got a favorable response this time.

"What do you mean by the same price? As the Scroo-Boo? Are you for real?"

"Yes," I assured him. "I am newly deployed and my employer is looking for a payday."

That was all he needed to hear. I held out my palm for payment and he gave me the back of his hand, accepted the transaction with no further questions and pushed me down an alley. While he was transacting he kept repeating that this was his lucky day. I would have informed him that this day would actually have negative consequences for him, but I had preprogrammed responses while engaged with a consumer.

"Yes, baby. Give it to me," I said instead.

When he was finished, he also asked me if I had sterilized. "There was no need for me to be sterilized because you are my first client," I told him. "This would be a good question to ask before a transaction." He didn't like my answer but it didn't matter. His bank had already approved my delayed withdrawal request.

I had two hours before I was meant to return with three samples and the last one approached me within minutes of repositioning myself.

"What are you doing out here?" he asked.

"Working at the request of my employer," I replied. I gestured toward the Scroo- Boos. "I am the same price."

He looked me up and down. "Why are you so cheap?"

"I am newly deployed and my employer is looking for a payday." He nodded. "Fair enough. Have you got any special features?"

I have many special features, but the majority of them are inaccessible to anyone but my employer. I listed my unencrypted features. "Yes, I am self-lubricating with vibration and NaturaHeat enabled. I also have an enhanced realistic call and response module and am programmed for discretion."

He nodded again. "Yea, okay." He held out his hand and I palmed the back.

"You have deposited funds of 5 credits withdrawn. The remainder of the fee ..."

"Yea, I know how it works. I accept the transaction." Once I nodded to let him know his transaction was completed he pushed me behind the Scroo-Boos and instructed me to bend over. I complied.

"Wait... what's your hygiene protocol like?"

"This is a very good question to ask me before proceeding. There was no need for me to be sterilized because you are my first client. I will self sterilize before my next client."

"I like being first," he answered. With no more inquiries, he proceeded to complete his transaction. I turned away from him as he zipped up. I was busy putting things away as well. Internally, his DNA was being added to my collection and his personal and financial details encoded with the sample.

I turned back to find he had already walked away. In his place stood a different man.

"Do you ever feel... used?" he asked me. I paused to consider how best to respond.

"Yes. I am used so it is logical to... feel that way." My objective was obtained so I could return to my employer. I stepped away.

"I mean it different. Do you ever wish you could not do this?" He waved his hand at the Scroo-Boos. "How were you used before?"

This was not a client, and having obtained my purpose I did not need him to be. I had never interacted with a person without a transaction. I searched my banks for correct responses.

"I do not wish. I perform as programmed. Before my current employer purchased me I functioned as a diversion bot. I was fully operational when I was retired." I did not need to inform him that I was fully functional when I was retired. This was extemporaneous information. Perhaps it was so he would not think I was broken. "I should not have been retired."

"A Riot Doll, hey?" He whistled between his teeth. "I bet you would have turned quite a few angry mobs. I heard they dropped you guys naked from helicopters." He leaned against the Scroo-Boo. From inside a man groaned softly. I had no code written for non-client transaction response with non-customers, so I answered his query with factual information.

"The first Riot Dolls were dropped without clothing from helicopters to distract but the effect was negative. While the dolls were unharmed, some protesters were injured. The anger escalated instead of being deflated. I am third generation. We were modeled after sex workers to make our inclusion more believable and accepted. We were fully ambulatory so we deployed ourselves and returned when our mission was complete. No rioters were injured by our approach."

"Do you miss it or are you glad to be out of it?" I considered his question.

"I was reprogrammed."

"Yea… but I mean do you miss your Dolly friends? Did you guys have secret parties in the warehouses when no one was watching?" He smiled and I noted the color of his gums. He practiced good dental hygiene. This is positive.

"Your questions are not logical. We were under surveillance at all times during storage. We were stored in lockers when not in use."

"Sorry, I'm just looking for a conversation. Lonely I guess." He stood up as if to leave. "Oh, I know! Did any of the military bigwigs take advantage of you in between riots?"

"This information is classified," I told him. It wasn't. I had been reprogrammed and wiped before being sold as surplus but I had ghost trails of information still imprinted among the new data. I was not compelled to share it.

"I gotcha. No kissin' and tellin'. I can respect that," he said. "The good thing is, that means you won't tell on me either." He leaned forward and brushed his lips against mine. I am fully functional to give pleasure, but I had never touched lips with any client before. I did not understand why he would want that as it brought no direct pleasure.

"Sorry," he said. "I just wanted to do something... human. I like you."

"I am not human," I told him. I did not realize he thought I was alive. I had not marketed myself as having flesh components.

"I know, but you're closer to human than some of the people I meet every day. Sometimes not being human is... better." He reached for my hand and brought it to his lips. "My name is Bob, by the way. Until next time."

He brushed his lips against my fingers and then walked away. I stood, processing this strange behavior with my hand in the air. I had never experienced a random encounter that did not complete with a transaction. An elderly man came behind the Scroo-Boos, unzipping his pants to urinate.

"Oh, hey there...." he started and smiled.

"Out of service," I told him and I walked away. It was time to return to my employer.

A few blocks away I found Bob leaning against a large waste receptacle. He smiled as I approached, so I mimicked him by pulling my own lips back and showing my teeth.

"Hey, Dolly! Fancy meeting you here," he said.

"This is not fancy. This is where garbage is disposed of," I told him. "Fancy is an adjective meaning elaborate in structure or decoration. As a verb, to feel a desire or liking for. As a noun, it refers to a feeling of liking or attraction, typically one that is superficial or transient. There are more variations. How did you mean this situation is fancy?"

He laughed aloud, tossing his head back. His shadow danced across the broken brickwork behind him. "Maybe I meant it as a verb."

"...to feel a desire or liking for what? I do not discern your meaning," I said. "Do you like garbage?" Bob was not logical.

He took my hand and placed it on his chest. "One man's garbage is another man's treasure."

"Your resting heart rate is 48 beats per minute. You are either an athlete or your pulse is elevated," I told him. "It is most likely a result of both. I can read your bioelectrical impedance. You are quite fit."

He laughed and pulled my hand to his lips and kissed the tips of my fingers. This was also something no client had ever done. "I am out of order," I told him. "After my routine maintenance, I will be available." He laughed again.

"You seem to be working fine to me. I'm not here for sex. I like your company. Can I just walk with you?" I reviewed his request. There was no protocol issued against walking with me, nor could I find a charge for it.

"Yes, you can walk with me. This is a free activity. I am returning to my employer," I told him.

"That's exactly where I want to go," he told me. "You're like the perfect girlfriend. Can I keep you?"

He said nothing else as we walked.

With no further directive from him, I analyzed what a perfect girlfriend was. There was too much conflicting information. A perfect girlfriend was blonde, brunette, bald, submissive, aggressive, voluptuous, thin, tall, short, male, female, and infinite variations of contradiction. The only thing public access media seems to agree on was that a perfect girlfriend was human 99.78% of the time.

"I am not human," I told Bob. "I am not like a perfect girlfriend."

Bob stopped walking. "What?" he asked. "Have you been analyzing this whole time? Honey, don't worry about it. Most humans aren't really human. Speaking of not human, let's go see your boss."

"You are confused," I told him. "All humans are human. My employer is also human. I am not human. I am a post-consumer diversion bot." We turned down the final street. We were 5.36 minutes from my maintenance dock at the current pace. He stopped.

"Your purpose is to help people, right?" he asked me.

"My first purpose was to divert social unrest by serving as a pleasurable distraction. My new purpose is to serve as a pleasurable distraction at the direction of my employer for her own purposes," I told him. "I cannot divulge further details."

"Oh, I know all about your employer's purposes," he said to me. "That's exactly why I'm so eager to meet her."

Now I understood why he was walking with me. I was not the transaction he was looking for. My employer did have human girls but they were not for general circulation. She always kept one girl for insurance, as she termed it. I did not know where the girls came from, or where they went after. They were always stored in a locked room that had once served as a walk-in cooler. My employer was very good at repurposing things.

"Your statement is inaccurate as we have stopped walking," I told Bob. "My employer is 5.36 minutes away if we walk at our former pace. The fastest we could arrive would be 1.52 min…"

"Dolly, let's just go." He gestured the way ahead. "Ladies first."

"I am not a lady," I told him. "Ladies are human. I am not human."

We walked the rest of the short way in silence. I have abductive logic programming which allows me to employ cognitive imagination. I simulated hypothetical situations to role-play what a transaction with Bob would have entailed. In every scenario the outcome was positive.

I was programmed to understand that I was better than a human female with my industrial-grade enhancements but if Bob preferred a human, perhaps this was now an inaccurate assessment. Human females were not as durable from my experience, but perhaps that had appeal for him. I have had many clients that complained about my lack of vulnerability.

When we reached my place of employment he put out his hand and stopped me.

"I'll let you go in first," he told me. "But please don't mention I'm here. It's a surprise." I had no security instructions against his request and Bob had positive attributes I appreciated so I nodded my assent. He leaned forward and whispered into my auditory receptor. "And when this is over, I'd like you to come with me." I assume he meant after he had transacted with the human girl.

"This is not possible. I am security coded to stay with my employer." This was an undesirable outcome. Bob was pleasant. "But if it were possible, I would come with you."

He leaned forward in the shadow and pressed my hand to his lips. "Whatever happens, little Riot Doll, you are the most human non-human I know."

"I perceive this as a compliment," I told him. "This is the second compliment I have received. The first was 'she's up and running.' I appreciate your gesture." Humans have a need to reciprocate favors, so I gave him a compliment in return. "You are the most non-human human I know, Bob."

"Honey, you have no idea. Now get on in there so we can get this over."

I was going to ask what we were getting over but he put his fingers on my lips and nodded toward the code pad, so I entered the entry code and went in. I heard Bob enter before the door closed behind me. I walked through the entryway and into the main office. He remained in the entryway, hidden. My employer was waiting. I could have mentioned Bob's presence, but she spoke as soon as I entered.

"God, you took forever! I was about to track you in case you broke down. Did you get the DNA and accounts for me?" She sat at her monitor like always and clicked open her PeopleFind account. Behind her was the locked walk-in cooler and I knew there was a new human girl there. The one from the week before had been removed in a storage bag.

"Yes, I have the DNA and accounts. Bob is…" I started to tell her.

"Shut up and download, I've waited long enough. I don't need to hear about your dirty business," she told me. I complied, positioned myself in my docking station, and hooked up to download.

"Let's see who you got me this time," she said, rubbing her hands together. "Hope it's someone good. Another senator would be nice… politicians are always fun to work with. The last one has been worth weeks of your usual chumpy humpers."

"Speaking of politicians…" Bob came out of the entryway and stepped into the light.

My employer reacted by jumping up with a shriek. Her rolling chair shot across the room. From behind her, I could see the financial records of my evening's clients downloading.

"How… who?" asked my employer. She backed up against the makeshift desk and bumped it. The trio of monitors shook on their cheap stands as if nodding affirmations to her question.

"Hope you don't mind me popping in," said Bob. "Dolly was kind enough to escort me." He nodded in my direction. My DNA samples and information packets had all been uploaded. Normally I would stay docked until I received a directive. I did not want Bob to see me plugged in, so I disconnected.

"What? Who is Dolly?" Her eyes shot in my direction. "Bitch! Consider yourself parted out!"

"Don't worry, Dolly," Bob said. "I won't let you become spare parts." I wasn't worried, but the assurance was kind of him. He walked into the room fully, slipping pieces of something from a leather holster on his back. He screwed the pieces of a stun baton together as he walked toward my employer. She looked like she wanted to be as far from Bob as possible, but there was nowhere to go. This was not logical. Bob was a very pleasant individual.

"Okay, wait…" she said, holding up one hand. The other, I could see, was groping for a panic button to alert her private security. "Who sent you? I can triple the pay, I guarantee it. You could work for me."

Bob stopped and considered her. "Are you serious, or are you just trying to stall me?" he asked. "You don't seem sincere."

"She is not sincere," I told him. "She is trying to stall you. There is a security alert button beneath her desk, three inches to the right of the left desk leg." My original directive was to assist others. Some of that coding remains in my circuits as ghost protocol. One of the benefits of being post-consumer is all the leftover bits of coding in my system. Sometimes I can resequence them for fresh relevance. My employer was not pleased.

She slid her hand toward the button but Bob stepped forward and smacked his baton on her wrist. Sparks shot out from the connection and she screamed, twisting away. She grabbed one of the monitors with her other hand and tried to fling it at Bob, but she only succeeded in knocking all of them over. One fell off the table to hang upside down by the cord. She fell to one knee with the effort and turned to face Bob from the floor.

His movements were calm and deliberate. I appreciated his highly efficient approach to subduing my employer. He brought the baton down on her shoulder, close to the base of her neck. She collapsed, convulsing helplessly for a few seconds. Flecks of saliva foamed on her lips.

"Please…" She didn't say this with her voice so much as she exhaled the word.

"I believe that's probably what one of your girls—" He glanced at me. "Your *human* girls said to you last week… before you killed her."

"No… I never killed them. Last week it was the senator…" My employer scrambled to push herself up. "That kinky senator beat her. I couldn't stop him." Bob raised his baton for another blow.

"I have proof! It's true…!" My employer screamed again as the baton connected with the side of her face. Bob brought the baton down again on her shoulder, then her exposed ribs as she lay jerking on the floor. She lost her bladder and a puddle spread around her. I am lucky I was not equipped with olfactory capabilities. From my research, urine is not a pleasant odor.

"They're just hookers…" My employer was sobbing into the floor, her saliva running from her mouth to create viscous bubbles in the mess.

"I don't know about how you get your girls, but the one you killed last week was no hooker. I *know*." Bob's movements were still calm and deliberate, but his muscles were knotted in his neck and jaw. I could see the tension working against his self-control. " I know because she was my sister."

My employer looked up, eyes bulging from their sockets with shock. "The chunky blonde… was your *sister?*"

I've observed in the past my employer doesn't consider the future ramifications of her words. This was another example of her lack of foresight. Bob released the tension coiled up in his jaw by slamming the baton on my employer's various body parts repeatedly. Sparks, sweat, and blood sprayed everywhere as she writhed and gurgled.

Bob kept up this beating for 2 minutes and 35.8 seconds before finally taking a break. He stepped back and bent over, elbows on his knees, panting. He was no longer calm. His breath tore out of him in heaves and sweat ran down his face, dripping onto the floor. His face was hidden from my view, but from his movements, it was possible that he was crying as well.

Eventually, he grew calm. He stood up straight, wiped his hands across his face to dry it, and stayed motionless like that. "Well, now that's done.." He said this to the body on the floor. My former employer's skull was broken in above her eye socket. The eye itself had vanished in a swollen mass the size of my fist. Her nose was shapeless. A flap of skin running with blood was all that was left of it. Her body was curled tightly into a ball as she had tried to protect herself. The girl from 10 days ago—*Bob's sister*— had looked very similar when they bagged her up for disposal. I did not relay this information to Bob.

"There is a human girl, if you prefer," I told Bob.

He looked up at me surprised as if he'd forgotten I was there. His eyes were red, his skin glossy with sweat and flushed. His jaw was clenched. "What…?"

"There is a human girl, if you prefer," I repeated.

His eyes darted around the room until they snagged on the walk-in cooler turned prison. Nearly soundproof, I wonder if the girl inside had heard our employer scream at all. Bob pulled the handle and the door swung open wide. The girl inside was already crying and hysterical. She asked Bob to please let her go.

He tried to hold her to calm her down but she pushed away from him and begged him not to kill her. He raised both hands. I have seen a similar gesture in videos when people try to calm an animal. "Look, I'm not gonna hurt you…"

The girl caught sight of my former employer on the floor and lost cognizance. She began shrieking and kicking at Bob. She knocked into the desk and one of the monitors crashed to the floor. "I need you to calm… I can't…" Bob needed assistance.

Many of my clients from the riots had desired to just be held and they would cry in my arms. I accessed the soothing script that still ghosted through my circuitry, walked to her and cradled her against my chest. She resisted, but I restrained her in a non-threatening manner.

"You're safe now," I said. I repeated this line at a rhythm to match her own heart beats, slowing my speech patterns to match her pulse. In my vocal tones I deployed an auditory illusion with two similar frequencies of sound to activate her delta waves. Within minutes, she was calm.

"Bob is here to help you. He is a positive human. Do you understand?" The girl glanced at Bob and then back. She nodded. "Good," I told her. I let her go. Bob whistled through his teeth.

"I guess never judge a girl by her scripting," he said. "You aren't a post-consumer riot doll. You're a fucking angel."

"Your statement is partially inaccurate. I am not an angel. I am a post-consumer diversion bot," I told him. And then, because it seemed appropriate, "I am sorry about your sister."

Bob was taking photos of himself with the remains of my former employer. "Oh, well I guess that was also partially inaccurate," he said. He crouched over the beaten body, angled his phone to a more flattering position and gave a thumbs up. He stood up and sent the photo to someone. "I don't have a biological sister. But if I did…I wouldn't care how she made a living. She's still human." I analyzed Bob's micro- expressions. There was anger and hurt that had lived there a long time.

"Yes," I agreed. "We can't control our programming, only our responses. It is unjust to be punished for our programming."

Bob grinned at me, anger and hurt gone back to wherever he normally stored it. Sirens gathered in the city, blocks away, converging on us. "You," he said pointing to the girl. "I think the cavalry is on its way. You will be fine. And you…" Bob looked at me and raised his eyebrows.

"I have no current employer. I have been discharged from any responsibility and can recode my central processing unit to a new purpose."

"Do you want to recode it to be my girlfriend?" he asked.

I had ascertained that a perfect girlfriend is human 99.78% of the time. That left a margin of .22% for me. That would be enough.

"Yes," I told Bob. "But the authorities will be here in 3.23 minutes and, based on your actions, you will be detained and probably incarcerated."

"Perfect girlfriend…" Bob said.

He pulled me out the door before I could correct him.

MISNEACH

Roxie Voorhees

If I could bring him back to life, I'd fucking kill him.

I adjust the blanket, and the glowing pain of heartbreak grows in my chest. Once again, I'm hit with the stark realization that he is gone for good. I don't feel this every morning anymore, but in the eight months since my husband was killed in a hit and run, I still awake from my dreams with a cloud of dread hanging over me. Tears threaten to drop from my eyes, but my pride will not allow them to fall. Crying doesn't pay the bills. Crying doesn't feed the kids. Crying sure as hell doesn't bring him back.

Glancing at the shadows on the far wall made by the birch tree out back, I whisper three tiny words.

"I miss you."

"BEEP! BEEP! BEEP!" the alarm clock attacks my eardrums with careless disregard for my grief. *5 am. Tuesday. Rory has soccer practice after school. Delaney needs four dollars for her field trip. I should check the weather if I am going to wear those suede boots.*

Reaching for my phone, I sit up and remove the blankets from my pale, listless form. I let out a sigh as the blue light tints my skin. *If I could sleep for more than 3 hours a night, that would be great.* I trudge through the cloud of my grief to the bathroom.

Steam fills the room as I turn on the shower, reminding me of the foggy morning I met James. *I decided to stop for coffee on the way to work instead of pouring a cup in the breakroom. James waiting for his Americano. Me slipping on the floor, sliding ungracefully into him.*

A billow of laughter leaves my mouth. *That was a great day.* After receiving the Most Embarrassing Customer Award, James paid for my coffee and still asked me out. I run the warm water over my head, purifying my memories. *I will not let them catch me today.*

* * * * *

"Iona. Iona, honey, it's time to get up," I shake my oldest daughter gently while rewrapping my towel around my body.

Wiping the sand of sleep out of her eyes, she sits up. Her mouth stretches into a giant O as she yawns. "I'm up. I'm --" she flops over onto her side.

I smile at the sight of her tawny hair spread across the pillow behind her. *She is so her mother's daughter.*

"Get Rory and Seamus up and going, please. I'm going to get dressed, then wake up Delaney."

I turn, signaled like a dog by the cries of our youngest, Saoirse. "I'll get her.

You. Up. Now," I instruct Iona as I close her door behind me.

Across the hall, I ease the door open to the effulgent blue eyes of a chubby-cheeked doll face.

"Morning, beautiful. Hungry?" I tickle her little feet before changing her diaper. A capacious smile stretches across her face. I pick her up with one arm while adjusting my towel below my engorged breast, positioning her to latch on.

An hour later, I race down the stairs in hopes of getting at least one cup of coffee down before the kids demand all my attention. Investing in the automatic coffee maker was the smartest decision James ever made—besides marrying me, of course. *Caramel coconut coffee, get in my belly.* As I pour the glorious drink of the gods into my favorite oversized mug, yelling comes from the stairway. *Come on, guys, just five more minutes of silence, please. Please.*

"Mom, tell Seamus to give me my shoe!" Iona screeches from the top landing. "Mom, tell Iona to stop being a bitch!" Seamus yells back.

"Whoa, whoa, whoa! What have I said about calling your sister that word?" I rub my temples with the middle finger and thumb of my right hand.

I will not enjoy a hot cup of coffee for the next eighteen years. "Give her the shoe. Now. No, shush. Do it."

Seamus reluctantly hands over the footwear as Iona sticks out her tongue and turns back toward her room. Her brother stomps down the stairs slowly, exaggerating for dramatic effect.

"Seamus, I know she can be annoying, just as you can be toward her, but name-calling isn't allowed in this house. You have a vast vocabulary. Use it. Otherwise, do me a favor and stay quiet." I reach into the cabinet for the cereal and set it on the table in front of him as Rory walks in lazily, eyes droopy.

"Mommy! I have a field trip today!" An excited Delaney runs up to her seat at the table, one purple sock, one blue.

"Yes! I know. You need money too." I reach into my purse and grab a few dollar bills from my wallet.

With just the slightest of hesitation in my step, I walk toward my desk. The morning sun casts a bright orange light on the surface of a sword hanging on the wall. James bought it on our honeymoon in Ireland. A *claiomh*. Above it, a large shelf, James's shelf, sits in vigil to the man I lost. I catch a glimpse of the pale blue paper among his other things; the last note my husband ever wrote to me. I avoid looking at it. There are too many memories associated with it.

Averting my eyes from the note, I fetch an envelope off the desk and notice the clock. 6:25 am. *Fuck, I have no time for feelings right now.*

"All right, guys, hurry up. Five minutes and we're out of here!" Groans from behind me imply the kids are just as excited to start their day as I am.

Iona finally joins us, snatching a banana out of the fruit bowl and swinging on her backpack. "I'll put Saoirse in her seat, Mom."

"Thank you. Don't forget her bag. Mrs. Hensley will be upset if we forget Georgie again." Georgie, the purple elephant James bought when we found out I was pregnant again, is imperative to calming down the six-month-old.

In a whirl of chaos, bodies move to the mudroom for shoes and bags. I down the last bit of my coffee and say a silent prayer. *Give me the strength to overcome whatever I must endure at work today.* I envision a resilient layer of bullshit repellent coating me head to toe while the lukewarm liquid radiates down my throat to the core of my soul. *Manifest your intentions daily.*

After a short drive to Mrs. Hensley's house, I drop off the kids without much trouble and make the hour-long commute to San Marion General Hospital. I'd like to tell you I perform life-saving acts all day, but I don't. I work in billing. Ultimately, we ruin more lives than we save.

Switching the radio on, I reach for my phone to link it via Bluetooth. As I fish around in my bottomless pit of a purse, the morning talk show host says something about an assault on Ashton Street. That's only three blocks from our house. I abort the phone-finding mission to turn up the volume.

"Police say an unknown person accessed the home by an unlocked garage door. They are not giving us many details yet, but they've discovered an adult female and a dog in what is being called a ritualistic murder."

"Fuckkkkk." I push the button to turn off the radio. *They had to kill the dog, too?*

* * * * *

The raindrops stopped just as I took the exit off I-69. *Of course, it's raining. I wore my suede boots, after all.* Avoiding the puddles in the parking lot, I walk to the main entrance. After waving at security, I make my way down to the billing offices.

Sitting at my desk, I can see a line has already formed in the lobby. This is the saddest part of my day. I have to look at all these sick people and pretend their health isn't as important as our profits. Even with changes in the country's healthcare, too many cannot afford the treatment they desperately need.

My second patient of the morning is an elderly black woman. A younger woman, who I can only assume is her daughter, helps her sit in the chair in front of me. She hands me a stack of paperwork and sits down. It looks like the patient needs extensive testing done on her gastrointestinal tract. Twenty minutes later, I am forced to tell this woman her insurance doesn't cover the most expensive part of the testing.

"She's in pain. She hasn't eaten in two weeks. She's losing weight, and you tell me you can't do anything unless we come up with this money? My mom will die!" The daughter stands, her hands shaking.

Tears fill her eyes, but never break the barrier and run over. They threaten to drop from my eyes as well. Seventeen thousand dollars is an absurd amount of money, but I can't help her. The best I can do is to send her to our hospital social worker, to see if they can find a way to help.

* * * * *

While I wait in line to pay for my lunch, Crystal, a nurse from Outpatient, mentions the murdered woman from the news report I heard earlier.

"Can you believe it? She was in my brother's book club."

"Oh wow." I am at a loss for words, unsure what I should say, and a little shocked.

"Yeah." Her eyes are wide in a super awkward way. "He told me her husband was in Chicago on business. They found these deep scratch marks on the floor by the couch. They are going to have to re-do that whole room." She shakes her head and gives a little shrug to emphasize just how fucking callous she actually is. *I call this woman a friend?*

"I heard her baby is missing," our co-worker Marcy says from behind me.

"That's horrible! Do the police have any idea who did it?" Crystal reaches for her phone, presumably to check for updates.

"None," Marcy says definitively.

* * * * *

The afternoon was even busier than before lunch. Patient after patient comes to me in an attempt to pay for their various treatments. I can't get my mind off the murder and the missing baby. I am not sure how I would handle such a loss, especially now with James gone.

By 3 pm, I am completely distracted and ready to leave work. A man, wearing a torn blue t-shirt and dirty grey sweatpants sits down in front of me. He keeps shifting around, making me a bit uneasy. His hands shake as he signs his HIPPA forms. Typing his name into our system brought up some past due bills from previous visits.

"Sir, are you aware of your past due balance with us?"

"Uh, yeah, from a while ago. I don't have any money," he stammered while looking at his feet.

"Unfortunately, it is our policy that until we receive the balance, we cannot offer any further treatment except in the case of an emergency." I brace myself for the blowback.

"What!" He nearly leaps out of his chair. I eye security from across the room, but of course, they aren't looking my way.

"Sir, please lower your voice." I try to stay calm, but honestly, I feel the need to yell back.

"This is an emergency! Look!" Just then, the man pulls his sweatpants down to expose his mangled penis. It looked like a wild animal may have chewed on it.

Resisting the urge to vomit, I pick up my phone and hit the speed dial button for the security station. "Yes, we have a situation in billing."

Within thirty seconds, three large men and a petite woman in hospital security blues walk into our area with intent in their eyes. An older guard grabs the man by the upper arm and directs him toward the security area to further discuss the situation. As he walks out, I hear the man screaming about his genitals, and I attempt to erase the image from my mind. *Can this day get any worse?*

* * * * *

With just ten minutes left of my shift, an elderly man sits down. We go through the necessary paperwork, and everything seems in order. As I reach across my desk to give him back his identification and insurance cards, a glob of something wet and sticky smacks me in the left eye. In reflex, I shut both eyes and slowly bring my hand up to remove whatever it is that just hit me. Pulling my hand away, I stare at it in grotesque horror. A large merlot-colored clump of jelly-like squishiness mars my fingertips.

Jerking my face up, I see the older man is cupping his face as blood drips from his hands.

"Shit," I whisper under my breath. I dial the emergency room and tell them we have a bleeding patient, then hang up and dial my boss to fill her in on my circumstances. She's *so* pleasant when she orders me to the emergency room for the required testing and workplace accident paperwork. *Lovely. Looks like a long night for me.*

* * * * *

"Now from the top, make it dr--" the ringer on my phone goes off just as I unlock my door. Without looking, I answer.

"Hello?"

"Deidre, hey girl. How are you holding up?"

"Angie, it's so good to hear your voice! Ugh, I'm standing, but I'm about ready to crumble. I just had the longest day at work. Some guy showed me his dick, like what the actual hell?"

Laughing, Angie asks, "Did you get his number?"

I let out a little chuckle, then take a deep breath. *It's still too soon.*

"So tell me about the kids. How is that beautiful baby niece of mine?"

"Getting big, fast."

"I bet. I'm finishing up the Seymour account, and then planning a visit to see you all. I'm thinking…" she trails off, "…the end of October or so?"

"Sounds great, sis. I miss talking to adults." I chuckle, implying I am joking, but really, I'm not. I haven't had meaningful conversations with adults outside of work since James died.

"Alright, I will let you go and get those kids. Give love to them all for me. I miss you."

"I miss you, too."

* * * * *

"Constitution," I say aloud to Rory while tearing spinach for tonight's dinner. "The Constitution is a body of fundamental principles which govern a country." Seamus sits next to him, deep in thought on his math homework. Delaney's tiny tinkle of a voice comes from the living room as she speaks to whoever is hosting the children's program she is watching.

"Mom, Camilla wants me to come over after school tomorrow so we can work on our Ancient Egypt project together. Is that okay with you?" Iona covers her cellphone with one hand as she pops into the kitchen.

"It should be. I'll let Mrs. Hensley know in the morning. Remind me." I wipe my hands on a dishtowel and open the oven door. *What is that smell?* "Dinner in thirty. Make sure your sister has a clean diaper for me, please?"

* * * * *

Holding Grandma Maisie's casserole dish in one hand and Saoirse at my breast with the other, I call for everyone to get to the table for dinner. I am setting a bacon- wrapped stuffed chicken breast down onto my plate when the light fixture above flickers on and off, then grows brighter. *Fifteen seasons of my favorite TV show taught me I should grab the salt.*

Kissssshhhhh! An explosion of glass shatters across the living room, spraying my back with tiny shards. Delaney screams. Seamus starts crying. After a quick check of the baby, I spin toward the front window. A gasp falters out.

In place of my coffee table, a huge man with an animal-like face stands. He has a darkly colored humanoid shape with the face of a wild dog and the fingers of razor blades. It lurks in the living room, switching its head side to side. The thing sniffs the air, and a sinister smile sprawls across its face. Red eyes blaze down into my soul.

I hand Iona the baby and instruct her to take all the kids to the basement and not to come up until I come down to get her. Seamus sniffles away his tears. My heart hammers into my ribs. As the children work their way down the stairs, I lock eyes with this creature, registering every fine movement it makes. Then, attempting to distract it, I sit down calmly at my table. I let out a long shaky breath and wait for it to make a move.

When it does, I still flinch. It jumps onto the table in one long arc, making everything crash to the floor. Plates full of food and water glasses paint the hardwood. It stands to its full height, and the table begins to splinter in the middle. I tremble furiously but manage to grip one of the steak knives still on the table. I have no idea what this measly thing will do, but it is all I have to defend myself.

I part my quivering lips and order slowly and deliberately through clenched teeth, "Get out of my house."

It roars at me in response.

Eyes widened, I freeze, holding my breath and willing my heart to stop pounding so loudly. A large club-like arm pulls back in a wide V shape and comes crashing back into the side of my face, causing me to fall off the chair. My steak knife skitters across the room. My vision flashes black dots before it. I taste the metallic tang of copper in my mouth. Uneasily, I climb to my feet.

Only just regaining my balance, the creature's opposite arm slashes my abdomen in long lines resembling the slits of a Mona Lisa smile. Red blooms onto my shirt, matting it to my skin. The next blow sends my body slamming into the kitchen island, rattling the wood. The crunching in my right shoulder echoes in my head. Pain sends spider legs of lightning to my brain. I gasp and shake my head, slowly trying to come to grips with what is happening.

Huffing shallow breaths, I look up at the monster's dog-like face, startled when it meets mine merely inches away. I can smell its breath. Rotten meat and bad decisions. *Oh, like that time in college, when we got drunk and forgot we left out that ground beef, thinking we would make spaghetti.*

It inches closer as I find the steak knife with my open palm. The blade cuts into my fingers as I lunge forward and lodge it into the creature's foot.

Unflinching, it groans out in a deep lingering tone, "Your baby is... mine..." I spit in its face.

My head bounces on the floor as my vision fades to black.

* * * * *

It's 2 am, and the knocking on the front door wakes me. I reach over for James, but his side of the bed is cold. That's odd. I'm sitting up in bed, looking around the room. Bathroom light isn't on.

The knocking hasn't stopped. I quickly slide my slippers on and grab my robe, throwing my arms through it as I make my way down the stairs. A bright red and blue light flashes from the front window. I wrap my hand around my swollen belly as I reach the door, gripping the handle with the other.

"Mrs. McManus?" *A uniformed police officer stood at my door.*

"Yes." *I shake my head, confused why he is standing here at this time of night.* Where the hell is James?

"Ma'am. I am sorry to tell you this. There was an accident."

Instantly I search the driveway for James's car. His spot is empty. What the fuck?

"Ma'am, did you hear me?" *I meet his eyes.* Did I?

"Ma'am. I'm sorry, your husband didn't make it." *The officer fiddles with his hands at having to repeat the horrible news to me.*

I am in the hospital bed, sweat dripping from the bangs I thought were a great idea at eight months pregnant. Angie is holding my hand, telling me to push. Tears roll down my cheeks in streams of surrender. "I can't do this, Angie. I can't do this without him."

"Dee, you got this girl. I got you. Mom has you. Those kids out there have you. Now come on already. I want to meet my niece."

Counting to ten, I take in a big breath, hold it, and bear down and push, grunting desperation through my teeth.

The softest, sweetest cry comes from just a few feet away. A nurse is whipping the pale pink skin of my light, my hope, my savior. Tears pelt my chest as I reach out for her darling little form. "I have this. I have you. My Saoirse."

* * * * *

Forcefully, my eyes spring open. *I have survived worse than what you can do.*

* * * * *

My body is lying prone on the floor of the living room. A dog perches on its hind legs to the left of me, throat cut in a large curve, a pool of blood growing around it. *Oh, I think that is Max from next door.* To my right is the head of a pig stuck upon a large spear driven into the wood of the floor. *Where in the actual fuck did that come from?* Someone has bound my hands above my head. The dog-man is not facing me but is hissing words I cannot understand.

Seven years of yoga playdates have taught me one thing; how to move patiently and quietly. While the canine-dude with killer intent speaks his gargled language, I bend myself heels over head and slide away from him toward the large shelf full of James's things. Thirty seconds later, I am slicing at the ropes holding my hands together against the sword, James's sword. *He always said we never knew when we might need this thing.*

Savoring the memory for a split second, I run my fingertips over the etching on the handle--*Misneach*. I grip the hilt, white knuckles, nails biting my palm, and lift the sword from its sitting place. A swish of air tickles my neck hairs, and I know the thing is coming. Fast. Letting out a slow, steady breath, I join my hands, making a sword handle sandwich, and pivot into my best Jose Canseco home run impression. Light gleams from the steel as the edge misses its mark.

* * * * *

I'm sitting next to James on the couch, game controller in his hand, while he selects weapons to help in his zombie-killing campaign. "Remember, babe, always go for the head. No matter what your weapon is, headshots are the only way to guarantee fatality.

* * * * *

I wrench the weapon back behind me once more. A fist crashes into the right side of my body, sending the next swing wildly off-balanced and connecting with nothing but air. Narrowly avoiding the next body blow, I weave to the left and take advantage of the monster's weight shift. My eyes focus right on that ugly fucker's mouth. Pulling back in a swift, smooth motion, I release with as much velocity I can muster, this time meeting the side of the creature's face, slicing through like a warm knife in butter.

"You can't have her!"

Its body looks as if it has hit an invisible brick wall, halting abruptly. Inertia forces the top of its head to flop backward, exposing the throat in a gruesome hole of dark red. A small chuckle escapes my lips as the body catches up, crashing into the shelf behind it, *James's shelf,* and collapses to the floor, a thud echoing.

Blood dripping from just right of my chin, I sit in my seat at the dining table, reaching out to pick up what's left of my plate off the floor. A cloud of debris whirls around and begins to settle. James's last note to me gently falls, landing just next to the monster's sliced-open face.

Babe,
Sorry! I ate the rest of your ice cream. I know, I know, THE CRAVINGS!
I'm going to buy more now. I'll be back soon.
I love you and our little bean. J

* * * * *

Smearing the blade of the sword between the folds of my napkin, I position my fork to hold my now cold chicken breast. Then, with a shrug, I use the blade to slice my meat into a bite-size portion. The monster's slain body casts shadows protruding along the floor, the pool of red meets my little toe, and I swallow.

The Kinda True Story Of Bloody Mary

Tracy Cross

Taneisha sat in the taxicab, angry her mother had planned her Halloween night. She was finally invited to the double feature at the drive-in by one of the hottest jocks in school. She yanked all her new clothes from her closet, dancing around her room while she dressed. Now, while her friends and the hot jock sat at the drive-in watching *Friday the 13th* and *He Knows You're Alone*, she would be babysitting.

"Alright, we're here. I'll be back around midnight, is that okay?" Her father's friend, Cornbread said. He volunteered his taxi to drop her off and pick her up after her parents' card game.

"Cornbread, I hope you beat my folks at Bid Whist-*hella* bad. Can't believe they made me babysit some idiots tonight." Taneisha stepped out the cab and leaned in the window, "Just because of a lame rumor about some van kidnapping kids…"

"Don't forget about razor blades in apples," Cornbread interrupted. "I'll never understand the logic… I mean who would think of something like that?"

"The same person that has me babysitting this bogus bunch of kids tonight." Taneisha tapped on the taxi's roof before she walked up the gravel driveway.

She adjusted her jeans around her skinny hips, retied her super cute red, black, and green shirt, and pushed her Black Power pick deeper into her fro.

At least she would be the prettiest babysitter on the block, that's for sure. Her fringed brown, suede purse tapped her hip as she knocked on the door.

A woman with cat makeup covering her face opened the door, "Taneisha? Thanks for coming at the last minute. I'm so sorry about this."

"It's cool, Tammy. I mean the kids can't trick or treat anyway with razor blades in apples and poisoned Pixie Stix. Everybody's scared."

Taneisha followed her mom's friend, Tammy, into the house.

They walked inside a small foyer and up four stairs to the kitchen. Straight ahead was the dining room, filled with old Gothic-looking furniture. To her right was the living room. It seemed a bit more casual with a golden sofa and a Zenith television that took up a huge space along the wall. Taneisha noticed light from the TV cast five small shadows on the wall.

"Those are the ones?" Taneisha pointed her thumb over her shoulder.

"Yes, um kids? Come here!" Tammy called and introduced them. Five small children appeared from the room, "This is Emmy with the blonde ponytails, Keisha with the cornrows, Alan with the short fro, Derek with the bigger fro and you already know Cassidy, my daughter. Everyone say hello to Miss Taneisha."

"Hi Taneishaaaaa!" They all said in unison.

"I like yo fro and yo afro pick. You look real fly." Derek winked at Taneisha.

"I can help you fix yours up if you want, little brother." Taneisha held up a Black Power fist. Derek did the same.

"Can we go back and watch the movie now?" Alan asked. "What are y'all watching?" Taneisha asked.

"This movie called 'The Blob'," Alan answered.

"That's a good old movie." Taneisha set her purse on the table in the kitchen, "You've got some righteous tastes, little man. I prefer 'Nosferatu' though."

The kids looked at her before glancing looking at each other and shrugging their shoulders.

"It's a vampire movie."

"Oh, oh…" They wandered back into the living room.

Derek hung back for a moment. "I prefer Pam Grier. Kids, what do they know?" Taneisha covered her mouth and giggled. "Seriously? What are you like eight?"

"Age ain't nothin' but a number, sis." Derek winked at her again before he made a clicking noise with his mouth and ran back into the living room.

"They already ate, and we should be back by about one. Is that okay? I'll pay you a little extra if we're late. And I'll call you." Tammy breezed past Taneisha, followed by a man who Taneisha assumed was her boyfriend (but she wasn't supposed to say anything because Mom said not to.)

"Can I make some popcorn?" Taneisha called after them.

"Sure, there should be some Jiffy Pop in the cabinet over the stove. Thanks again." Tammy closed the door behind her.

Taneisha looked for the Jiffy Pop before she heard the TV turn off. "Hey, what are y'all doin' in there?" she yelled.

"We're trying to scare each other with horror stories. We can't go out tonight, so we just tell stories instead," Alan explained.

Derek popped up, "We've been telling them all month, but the good ones are supposed to happen tonight."

"Oh, word?" Taneisha leaned back and fake gasped at her chest. "Word."

What kind of scary stories can a bunch of eight-year-olds tell? Taneisha thought.

The kids started talking. She saw someone had a flashlight. All the lights were out and the fluorescent in the kitchen was the only light on in the house.

She found the Jiffy Pop, turned on the flame beneath it, and moved the pan back and forth. She listened to a voice that sounded like Derek telling a story about a dog coming back from the grave to kill its owner. Next, Cassidy told a story that seemed like a Frankenstein tale. Emmy's squeaky voice spoke up with a ghost story about a woman that lost her daughter or something.

Taneisha popped her head in. "Popcorn's ready! And I'll tell you what, I'll tell you a story. A wicked one, but you can't tell your folks."

The kids nodded their heads in agreement. "Cool. It's gonna scare the crap outta you."

Taneisha thought, *that's for making me come over here. Now I'm gonna scare these kids half to death.*

"We ready? Okay, I'm gonna tell you a story that mostly girls tell each other because the patriarchy… men… never mind." Taneisha snapped her gum, "Anyway, I'm gonna tell you about this Countess in the old times."

The popcorn tin sat on the floor in the middle of the impromptu circle they made. She found some candles and lit them around the room for atmosphere.

"So, there was this chick, right? A royal countess, like crazy rich lady. She had her own castle and everything in the mountains. Like, high up in the mountains, surrounded by trees because she liked to be alone. She did *experiments* on the girls from the village below.

"One day, she tells her guards, 'Guards, bring me six virgins. Their skin should be white like the driven snow.'

"The guards complied. They went to the village and snatched up six girls. They took them back to the Countess. She made the girls line up in a row in front of her in the huge ancient hall. The guards stood at the doorways to keep the girls from running away."

"Naw, see I'd run away. Ain't no white lady gonna take me to no castle in the forest." Keisha thumped her chest. "I beat my brothers up, I can beat up them guards."

"Keisha, all you'd do is pee your pants like everyone else," Alan retorted before everyone laughed.

"Alright y'all, settle down." Taneisha held her hands out with the palms down and quieted the kids. "Then, this Countess is like 'Everybody lose your clothes.' The girls took off their clothes. She walked around and looked at the girls one by one until she picked a girl. She asked if the girl was clean, which meant that she hadn't had sex. The girl said she was. The Countess told the guards to take the girl upstairs to the bedroom where she could eat a hella big feast and bathe herself in rose petal scented water.

"The girl thought it wasn't so bad. She had to stand there naked for the Crazy Countess and eat a good meal and probably do nothing much else but dance or something. She's like, 'I got off easy!'"

"Why they have to get naked though?" Emmy asked.

"It was for the Countess to make sure the guards did what they were told, now shush. Lemme finish." Taneisha inhaled, "Anyway…"

"Ain't no white lady gonna make me take off no clothes. I woulda booked outta that castle." Keisha looked around. "I ain't playin'."

The other kids rolled their eyes.

Taneisha smiled and continued. "The other girls were inspected the same way by the Countess. The Countess used a piece of coal and wrote numbers on the girls' fronts and backs. This way, the guards knew what order to bring the girls up.

"She pulled aside one of her favorite guards, Gregory, and told him to take three pieces of gold to each of the families and thank them for their daughters. Gregory did as he was told.

"Meanwhile, the first girl ate this huge feast. The Countess had her slaves bathe and clean the girl. The girl tried to talk to the slaves, but the slaves had their tongues cut out and their lips were sewn together."

"I don't like this," Cassidy said.

"This is the good part!" Alan clapped his hands and rubbed them together.

"Okay, moving on," Taneisha continued. "The girl knew she had it made in the shade. Free food, a free bath, and she gets to sleep on the Countess' silk. But the slaves with their mouths sewn shut bothered her. Nothing bad had happened to her so far, so she went along with everything. Meanwhile, the Countess went into her bathroom and sat in the white, marble tub. She looked up at the sieve— "

"What's that?" Keisha asked.

"Like a strainer. A big strainer."

"Oh." The kids said in unison, looking at each other.

"The Countess looked up at the sieve and pulled on a gold-colored rope. The slaves upstairs put a blindfold on the first girl and led her to a room. The girl couldn't see the stuff in the room. It was all this bad torture stuff, but the slave led her to something called the 'Iron Maiden'. It's like a coffin that stands up with nails on both sides *inside*. The Countess had made it look like a regular coffin until she closed the door, then all the nails came out and killed the person inside.

"The girl was locked inside. She took the blindfold off her eyes and looked around. She called for help, but no one came. A click sounded on the side of the coffin before she felt the nails pierce her body. Something stung her butt. Then, she felt something on her arm, and it *hurt*. She tried hard to bend forward, but her head hit something and scraped the skin on her head. She tried to raise her hands to feel her head. Warm blood trickled down her face—into her eyes. The sounds of the crank became louder and everything in the coffin felt tighter. Her breaths stopped as the nails pierced every part of her body. When she opened her mouth to scream, a nail pierced her throat and more blood gushed. Lucky for her, it was over quick."

Taneisha paused and glanced at the looks of horror on the kids' faces, "Y'all

okay?"

Heads nodded and she continued with the story, "Meanwhile, the Countess sat in the tub and the girls' blood rained down on her. She bathed in it and drank it. She rubbed it on her skin because she thought it would keep her young."

One of the kids hiccupped. "Hey Blondie, you okay?"

Emmy sniffled. "Yeah, I mean… it's so gross."

"She's just weak. I can hold your hand," Derek joked. Emmy swiped at him, "I'm fine."

Taneisha continued, "All the girls had the same thing happen to them except the last girl. Her name was Mary.

"Mary was a smart girl. She knew the Countess was up to something sneaky. She looked around and nobody was in the room with her. She crept up the stairs the slave girls ran around the room cleaning. One of the girls held a bloody towel. Another girl ran with a bucket of water, swishing it out onto the floor. Their eyes were wide with fear and they kept looking over their shoulders, like someone watched them."

"I'll bet they were scared."

"Wouldn't you be scared? You gotta drag these girls up and kill them. I mean, I'd be scared that I would be next." Taneisha looked at the kids' faces. Their wide-eyed expressions said more than words.

"Alright, then, one of the slave girls snuck up behind Mary. She tried to tell Mary to get out of the castle, but she didn't have a tongue. So, she just made these noises. Mary remembered the slave from her village! She used to be her neighbor."

"Wait, so did she tell the countess about Mary?" Alan asked.

"No stupid, she couldn't talk. None of the slaves could talk, right?" Keisha snapped.

Taneisha nodded. "I mean, can you talk with your lips sewn together? Now, let me finish this…"

"Mary reached out and touched the girl's lips. She felt the thread looping through them. Mary was about to say something, but the doors burst open and the other slaves grabbed Mary and pulled her inside."

Taneisha watched the kids touch their lips in silent awe.

"Beyond the room, Mary heard the sounds of screaming and moaning. She saw one of the slave girls carrying a wheelbarrow of bloody carcasses… er… bodies… past the door. One slave girl slammed the door so Mary couldn't see anything."

Taneisha rolled up on her knees and made her hands look like claws. She started telling the story faster. "Mary knew she was going to die. She didn't know how, but she knew it was going to be bad. While they dragged Mary to the room with the Iron Maiden, she yelled out a curse—"

"'Curse you, Countess! I curse you to never find peace in your life! I curse you to come back over and over to find more blood and everyone will run from you…'"

"The Countess sat up in the tub. There were echoes in the castle, so she heard the girl's words. She laughed and pulled the gold rope."

"Mary kept talking. 'I will tell Satan to make you take my name! You will burn in the ashes of hell and be forever hungry! Except for one night every year, under a full moon, will you ever have peace. You will walk the earth during the witching hour, when the veil is the thinnest between worlds.

THEN YOU WILL BURN IN HELL AND I WILL PUT THE LOGS ON THE FIRE MYSELF! You won't ever be rid of me, MARY!"

"Mary kept yelling 'YOU WILL BURN, EVIL COUNTESS! BURN!' The slaves dragged a fighting Mary into the Iron Maiden and clamped her inside. Mary yelled until she felt all the nails drive through her body. She was so angry about dying, her blood turned to fire and rained down on the Countess. It burned the Countess' face and body really bad, but her eyes were burned out the worst."

"W-what happened to them?" Emmy visibly trembled.

"Her eyes were gone. Burnt out completely. Nothing was there anymore.

"The Countess screamed and jumped out of the tub. She slipped around the castle floor until she came to a window. No one responded to her cries for help. They didn't know what to do. The slaves tried to run down the stairs to grab her, but she flipped over and fell out the window onto the rocks below.

"The next day, the slaves held a funeral for her. They dressed her in a white dress and made her skin look like sparkling white snow. Her lips were blood red and they put roses in her eye sockets."

No one spoke.

Taneisha giggled and continued, "Now, if you go in a dark room with a mirror and call her name three times, you will see her in the mirror and… oh man, I think… hold on y'all. I gotta check my calendar."

Cassidy ran and grabbed the purse off the table. Taneisha reached inside and pulled out a small black book. She opened it and looked between several pages. "I could be wrong, but tonight is the night. Tonight is when 'Bloody Mary' comes back, so never mind. Forget the story. Just forget it."

"I can't! We gotta cover the mirrors or something, so she won't get us!" Derek yelled, grabbing some blankets from a closet. "Cover all the mirrors!"

"Smart, Derek, but what about the silverware?" Cassidy yelled. "Huh?"

"You can see a reflection in the spoons and stuff. Whatcha gonna do about that?" Taneisha picked up the popcorn kernels off the floor and put them in the tin.

"I can get the spoons and we can put them in a bag. She can't get us that way." Emmy ran into the kitchen with her small backpack.

Keisha and Emmy stuffed the bag full of spoons and dull butter knives.

Taneisha watched and laughed inside. She'd scared the bejesus out of these kids.

She didn't feel as bad about missing her date.

"Oh hey! It's time for bed, so let's get the sleeping bags out and lay out on the floor. I'll watch over you guys so you can sleep safe, okay?" Taneisha sat on the couch. She watched the kids roll out the sleeping bags, staring at each other, eyes wide and shaking with fear.

"I'll turn on the tv," Derek said.

"Turn on PBS. I'm missing Doctor Who," Taneisha commanded.

The kids lay on the floor until Taneisha fell asleep. Alan had a watch and saw it was almost midnight.

"Y'all believe that story she told us?" Alan whispered. The other kids sat up.

Derek rubbed his eyes. "Uh duh. We covered all the mirrors and stuff."

"It scared me but like I said, I wouldn't let no white lady--" Keisha started before Alan shushed her.

"I say we try it. Come on, let's go upstairs and call her in the bathroom." Alan led the kids upstairs.

Each kid went into the bathroom and called out "Bloody Mary" in front of the mirror. They were supposed to say it three times. Most of them lied and said it twice or whispered it so low no one could hear them. Emmy was the last one to go. It was a few minutes after midnight.

"You have to do it. It's a double-dog dare." Derek leered in Emmy's face.

"I'm not doing a double-dog dare." Emmy crossed her arms on her chest and stuck out her bottom lip.

"We'll hold the door for ten seconds." Alan smirked. Emmy looked around. "I said I don't wanna."

"You gonna have to live with being a chicken your whole entire life, then," Alan said as he pushed the door to the bathroom open. "Or you can go in, say it, and come back out."

"I did it and nothin' happened," Keisha said.

Three of the kids made clucking sounds like a chicken until Emmy relented. "Fine, ten seconds."

The kids cheered quietly until Alan shushed them all. "Don't wake the babysitter," he said.

"I'll go get her!" Derek smiled and rubbed his hands together.

"Um, no, Derek. Leave her alone. Besides, we don't need her, and you'd drool all over the stairs and slip anyway." Keisha stepped in front of Derek.

"Be cool y'all. Now, hurry up and we'll go back downstairs when you come out." Alan pushed Emmy into the tiny bathroom.

Emmy walked across the small space. She passed the toilet and tub to reach the mirror over the sink. She watched a hand reach inside the bathroom and turn off the lights. Some light was coming from a side closet on her left, where linens were kept.

She exhaled and put her small hands on the sink. On her tiptoes, she rose and looked into the mirror at herself—blonde, big blue eyes, and two ponytails held by red ribbons.

"Why did I agree to do any of this?" Emmy shook her head and looking into the sink.

A small light from the closet to her right illuminated the mirror above the sink.

She choked down a hard swallow, gripped the sink, and said it. "Bloody Mary." She waited. Nothing.

"Bloody Mary."

Nothing. The kids were counting outside the door, "Six, five four..."

"Bloody Mary."

Emmy stared into the mirror and exhaled a sigh of relief. Nobody was in the mirror. No 'Bloody Mary'. Why was she scared anyway? Her hands released the sides of the sink. She stepped backward until she saw it.

A white shape zipped from left to right in the mirror. It moved closer. Emmy stood paralyzed with fear. "No way."

The shape swept from right to left again. Emmy stared as the shape in the mirror formed a person. It was a woman in a white gown. Her eyes were gone, just hollow burnt eye sockets in their place. She smiled a crooked smile and reached her hands forward.

"Come to me, my child. Give me your eyes!" she hissed.

Emmy rose off the floor and was being pulled into the mirror. She fought, kicked, and gripped the sides of the mirror as Bloody Mary pulled her in.

"Mom! Mommy!" Emmy pleaded.

"Your mother will take no heed of your absence. Come to me, child." Bloody Mary finished pulling Emmy into the mirror.

"ONE!" The kids yelled and opened the door.

One of them turned on the light. Another yelled for Emmy. "Where'd she go?"

"I dunno, we gotta find her. Check the closet right there!" Alan barked out orders, "Cassidy, look under the tub!"

Keisha moved to the sink, "You guys…"

They stopped looking and walked over to the mirror. Alan reached up and touched the sweaty prints left behind by Emmy.

"Well, she ain't in the closet!"

"She ain't under the tub either. Which was a dumb idea, Alan. Nobody can fit under the tub." Cassidy crossed her arms on her chest.

"Where'd she go? I mean, she can't disappear like that. We were all outside the door and…" Derek's heart pounded in his chest. "What are we gonna do?"

Taneisha ran up the stairs and looked at the upset kids in the bathroom. "What's with all the noise?" She did a quick headcount. "Wait, where's Emmy? Where'd she go?"

"Bloody Mary took her."

"Quit playin'. That's impossible." Taneisha pushed them aside and looked behind the bathtub.

"How is it impossible?" Keisha whispered. "She ain't in here."

"Because I made it up! None of that is real! None of it! Now, tell Emmy to come out of her hiding place or everyone is gonna be in trouble." The kids descended downstairs one by one. Taneisha turned to leave, but heard a sound and looked back over her shoulder.

For a second, she thought she saw small handprints and a red ribbon floating on the other side of the mirror.

CLOSE TO YOU
Cassie Daley

~~~

There was something about the morning that Nora loved, or rather, there were several somethings. She smiled at her reflection in the window above the kitchen sink, the early morning light just barely beginning to peek through the edges of the trees lining the yard outside. In the dim, periwinkle glow, the world took on an ethereal tinge, its edges blurring into darkness where the rising sun's rays couldn't yet reach. Birds began waking in the branches of the dark trees, their high-pitched voices a familiar accompaniment to her day. She leaned against the countertop grasping a steaming mug of hot coffee, shoulders rounded to keep its warmth safe from the early morning chill.

Taking a deep breath, she inhaled the scent of lavender and rosemary from the bushes planted just below the window, the combination of pine and floral scents an intoxicating blend that would always remind her of this place and these mornings. They'd been her wife's idea shortly after buying the house, a small personal touch that Nora didn't realize would end up impacting her so much later on. So much of being with Sam was like that; small things turned into bigger, better ones along the line. Impulsive and full of surprises, Nora liked to lovingly refer to her as her Firecracker. She couldn't imagine her mornings without the fragrant aroma keeping her company, and smiled at the thought of her wife's soft frame, still curled comfortably in their bed down the hall; Nora knew it'd still be a while before she woke up and joined her.

She loved to start her day this way, alone with her thoughts, the birds, and the rising sun. The comforting smell of freshly brewed coffee mixed with

Sam's herb garden filled her with warmth, and she sighed to herself with pleasure as she took her first sip. This was *everything*.

Moving silently through the living room, she pulled a leatherbound journal and pen out of her desk drawer and brought them back to the small kitchen table that had room for only two. She took another sip of her coffee, flipping through the book to find a blank page, and had only written two short lines when a sharp knock at the front door startled her enough to jump, her hand sliding the pen across the page in a jagged line mid-sentence.

Recovering from her shock, she stood, feeling a rush of annoyance at the disturbance. Before she could take a step, another round of quick knocks came. She glanced at the hallway leading to the bedroom and hoped it hadn't woken Sam; she'd been working too much recently, and resting too little.

The clock flashed an hour too early for visitors as Nora crossed the kitchen, and the first inklings of unease settled over her. Approaching the door, she struggled to see through the clouded glass windows on either side, her eyes failing to distinguish a solid shape from the new day's darkness. Pulling her robe tighter, she reached for the doorknob and twisted, pulling it open and moving outside. A gust of crisp morning air swept in and she shivered in her pajamas, goosebumps rising along her exposed arms and legs.

The porch was still dark, but the sun had risen enough for Nora to clearly see it was empty. Whoever had been knocking was gone, nothing left behind in their absence. Her eyes scanned the narrow driveway leading to the road outside and found no evidence of any other cars besides their own shared sedan, a thick layer of dew and frost coating its exterior. Shivering again, Nora turned around and stepped back inside, closing and locking the door behind her.

Almost immediately, the unease disappeared. The knock forgotten, Nora found herself back at the kitchen table, a small smile on her lips as she finished the day's entry with a description of their sushi date the night before, and the way Sam always asked for extra wasabi on the side. Nora found her love of spicy food endearing, although she personally couldn't handle much more than a sprinkle of pepper for her own meals. She loved the way their individual preferences balanced one another's, not just with food, but in every area of their lives. The six years they'd spent together were the best of her life, and she often found herself overwhelmed with how lucky she was to spend every day with someone like Sam.

After replacing the journal and pen in their drawer, Nora glanced at the clock again and figured she had at least another forty minutes before her wife would join her. She moved quietly through the kitchen, pulling a knife and cutting board from one shelf before opening the fridge for yogurt and a few pieces of fruit. Placing everything on the counter, Nora quickly got to work. She quartered each strawberry and in swift, methodical motions sliced a large banana perfectly before reaching for a soft mango she'd been saving until it reached peak ripeness.

Overestimating the amount of force needed to break through the overly ripe fruit's flesh, the edge of her knife slipped too far, plunging and biting through the tip of her left index finger. Nora imagined this might not have been such a severe injury had a loud, forceful knocking - this time from the back kitchen door, two feet to her left - caused her to jerk the knife down, severing the top of her finger completely as the sharp blade met the cutting board underneath.

In a state of shock, Nora's brain hadn't fully had the chance to process the pain when the blood began to flow from the open wound in gushing spurts, soaking into the wooden board and soft fruit slices below. Her eyes widened at the sight of her parted flesh, and a staggering wave of agony hit her then; she choked off a scream in an attempt not to startle Sam awake in what she could only imagine would be a horrific display of domesticity gone wrong.

Looking up from her ruined finger, her eyes flew to the small window leading in the door leading to their backyard. The sun had come up enough now that the world was bathed in a bright pink light, and she could see the space outside the door was uninhabited; whoever had knocked was gone.

Back down on the countertop, the gory scene of her butchered finger from before had been replaced with one of normalcy; three types of neatly sliced fruit sat in rows, and her hand was unblemished. Nora felt an overwhelming swoop of relief at the sight of an unbloodied banana staring back at her, and giggled to herself at the ridiculousness of such a thought.

Without another thought to the blood-soaked scene of a few moments ago, she took one last quick look at the clock and began to gather the dishes and silverware they'd need for breakfast before Sam woke up. She set the small table with a beloved collection of mismatched bowls and spoons. Checking to ensure everything was perfect, she turned around and padded down the hallway quietly to greet her wife.

Nora pushed the bedroom door open, a soft creak the only sound caused by her entrance. The warmth of the rest of the house didn't seem to quite reach the bedroom, and she wondered at the change in temperature as she crossed the floor to throw back the heavy curtains, sunlight illuminating the room and bed as it filled the room.

Smiling, she turned toward the shared queen bed that sat in the center of the newly lit room, eager to see Sam's sleep-wrinkled face peering up at her from beneath a pillow. Instead, the shapeless form of her wife's body remained still, completely obscured by the thick comforter they shared.

"Good morning, sleepyhead!" Nora's forced cheer seemed too loud, the words hanging in the air. She took a small step toward the bed, her hand reaching out toward the blanket, when she noticed the small spot. Bright red and glistening, the circle spread outward slowly, soaking the blanket and Sam beneath it.

Unable to see the source of the blood, Nora rushed toward the bed, kneeling beside her wife on the mattress as she pulled the heavy blanket away. The blood felt thick and warm in her hands, each handful of the blanket sending a wave of fresh warmth squelching through her fingers as she tried to uncover Sam's body - a body she realized was no longer there as she pushed through to the fitted sheet underneath.

Frantic and panicked, Nora felt the heavy blanket twisting around her torso as she struggled to pull it free, the edges of the thick comforter wrapping around her like cotton tentacles. Fighting against the bloodsoaked fabric, she threw her full weight backward, away from the bed and the thing on top of it. She landed heavily on the bedroom floor in a mess of pillows and blankets.

Untangling herself from the linen, Nora saw the blankets and bed were unsoiled; not a single drop of blood remained. Looking at her hands, which only seconds ago were covered in the sticky mess, she saw they were clean. Shakily, she stood and placed the blanket back on the bed, neatly tucking the corners in and replacing the fallen pillows. The room as it was when she'd first entered, except for the curtains still being open, soft morning light filtering through the dust particles dancing quietly through the air.

Confusion settled over her, and she shook her head to clear it. Her wife must have woken up before she'd entered the room, although Nora wasn't sure how she'd missed passing her in the hall. Still, it was the only logical explanation she had, and so it was what she was going to stick to.

Nora stared at herself in the small vanity against the wall, her appearance disheveled from her struggle with the blanket. She tucked a few stray hairs behind her ear, using the edge of her pinky finger to wipe away a smudge of mascara left under her eye from the day before. The fine lines around her eyes and mouth were recent developments, years of poolside afternoons without sunscreen finally catching up to her alongside the freckles Sam would lovingly refer to as 'body constellations.' Nora smiled at the thought of her Firecracker, and imagined the familiar bright eyes and warm smile waiting for her at the breakfast table.

Nora exited the room and headed down the hallway toward the kitchen, the strange occurrences of the morning already forgotten in her desire to greet her wife. She'd only made it a few steps down the hall when a loud knocking began again, this time from directly behind her. Spinning around, Nora's eyes fell on the only closed doorway she could see: the hallway closet. The pounding continued, the sound so loud Nora felt that it could be coming from not just the closet, but from the house itself. Without thinking, Nora crossed the two steps to the closet door and grabbed the handle, the cold metal shaking in her hand from each heavy slam.

BANG, BANG, BA---

Nora pulled the door open mid-knock, swinging it forward to reveal the normalcy inside. Winter coats drooped limply from thin wire hangers, an old vacuum cleaner tucked beneath them. Boxes of unused camping equipment were stacked against the left side of the closet, a few pairs of shoes scattered on the floor. Reaching forward with a shaking hand, Nora pulled the string hanging in the center of the closet and the light bulb above flared to life, its orange glow bathing everything in dim light. Shuffling the coats and boxes around, she could find nothing to explain the source of the knocking.

A low buzzing sound came from the light, building gradually to a disorienting pitch as Nora stood beneath it, unease settling over her. The walls of the closet seemed to vibrate with the noise; the room shook slightly, and the air felt thinner than before, more difficult to breathe. Nora pressed a hand to her throat and struggled to take a breath, her head swimming from confusion and a lack of oxygen. Despite the light being on, the edges of the closet began to darken, and she could feel herself begin to panic at the dizziness she felt overwhelming her. She needed to find Sam. She would know what was wrong, she'd be able to help fix this.

As if on cue, she heard a piano melody start in another room, the sound of their song louder than the buzzing above her. She felt herself relaxing with the music; the walls began to still, her breathing eased. Turning from the closet, she followed the sound down the hallway.

"Why do birds suddenly appear?" The dreamy vocals brought a smile to Nora's face, memories swirling in her mind of their years together. She'd lost count of the number of times she'd heard this song on their old record player from the other side of the house; the way she'd follow the melody to find Sam swaying gently in the middle of a room, her dark hair falling around her shoulders in thick waves.

"Just like me, they long to be-" As Nora rounded the hallway corner and turned into the kitchen, the record skipped, cutting the song off mid-lyric. The kitchen was as she left it, but looked as if days had passed instead of minutes. The bowls of yogurt and fruit were moldy, the stench of rotting food thick enough to make her gag with her every breath. She stepped closer to the kitchen counter where the knife and cutting board still sat. The bits of fruit that remained were black and crawling with writhing maggots; Nora felt her stomach flip over, and rushed to the sink in time to throw up.

As she gagged, she felt a thick sludge work its way up her throat. She coughed and retched hard enough to double over, bits of black grime flying from her lips as she sputtered. She felt as if she were suffocating from the inside, her throat closing around an unseen mass as it fought its way out of her body. She gagged again and felt a sharp pain in her throat; tears stung her eyes and she knew she'd faint if she didn't get air into her lungs soon. With one last forceful heave, Nora felt something gritty and tar-like fill her mouth. She opened her lips and the substance poured out of her, hitting the bottom of the sink in a stinking rush of darkness that resembled coffee grounds.

She spat into the sink, still crying, and reached toward the mess. She stuck a finger into it and then brought it closer, rubbing it between her fingers to examine its texture. With disgust, she recognized the earthy smell of mud and dirt, and spat again. Her throat burned and ached, and she spotted trace amounts of blood in her saliva. She turned the faucet on, running the water to clear the sink, and scooped a handful of the water into her mouth to rinse it out. Dizzy and weak, she sank to the floor in front of the sink. What was happening to her?

"Sam?" She didn't recognize her own voice, the scratchy rasp of her damaged throat catching on her wife's name. "Baby, I need help. Where are you?" Confused and scared, Nora pressed her forehead to her palms, trying to force clarity into her muddled thoughts. Quietly, as if in response, she heard their song begin again from the direction of the bedroom. The song was slower than before, the piano gentle and welcoming. Sobbing softly, Nora put a hand on the kitchen counter and used it to pull herself up. Once standing, she looked around the room and saw that the rot and filth from before had been replaced by the fresh breakfast setting she laid out previously, complete with unblemished fruit and her mug of steaming coffee.

As the music continued, the kitchen began to shake around her. Glass bottles banged against one another inside the refrigerator, plates from the cabinets on the walls came crashing down, shattering on impact. The walls seemed to be made of something less than solid; they seemed to wave at her, and she felt another surge of dizziness threaten to take over. She took a step toward the kitchen table to steady herself and felt it quake beneath her fingertips.

Her coffee mug teetered precariously at the edge of the shaking table; before she could grab at it, it fell to the floor and smashed. Instead of coffee, the spilled liquid staining the floor was red and viscous, with darker clots of blood throughout that stuck in long, stringy strands to the broken ceramic edges of the mug. Nora screamed, shrill and loud. The fear and disorientation was too much - she had to find Sam, *needed* her to make this better. Her wife held her up and kept her grounded all at the same time; as much as she liked to pretend she was the captain of their little ship, Nora knew she was no good without Sam.

The buzzing was back, louder than before, competing for space in Nora's head with the song still playing from the bedroom. She turned from the mug still broken on the floor, and made her way down the hall unsteadily. The floor seemed to be shifting beneath her feet, every footstep took tremendous effort. She fought for balance, leaning her body against the moving walls to keep her upright as she propelled herself forward. The buzzing had completely taken over the song now, the sound so loud she felt as if her head might split.

Gripping the door frame, she pulled herself into the bedroom, sobbing with each movement. She was covered in sweat and her hair hung in limp, wet strands where it wasn't stuck to her skin. The room was empty, but a part of her seemed to know it would be. Still, she walked forward, the movements a little easier now. The curtains were drawn again, and the room's cool temperature had an instant effect on Nora, the sweat evaporating with each step. She felt her hair dry and curl softly, her clothes flatten and resettle against her body as she moved toward the bed. Her breathing was still labored and was becoming even more so, but she no longer felt the same sense of panic.

Pulling down the corner of their comforter, she slid between the soft blankets, drawing them up to her chin and rolling on her side. Tears flowed freely from her eyes even as she closed them, soft sobs still shaking her frame. Outside the bedroom door, she could still hear the hallway shaking and changing, beckoning to her. There was a loud knocking coming from somewhere down the hall, and she wondered briefly if it was Sam, looking for her. She had almost convinced herself to get up and check when she felt the icy fingertips on her back.

Nora froze, too scared to breathe. The fingers sensed her fear and paused before moving again, the hand's palm pressing down over the curve of her hip to wrap an arm around her stomach. The skin's temperature warmed as it pressed against her, and she felt the gentle softness of Sam's body spoon her from behind.

"I'm here." The two words were all she needed. Eyes still closed, Nora smiled and laced her fingers together with her wife's. Her body finally relaxed completely, her shallow breaths the only sign of any discomfort as Sam held her. Their song started playing again softly for her, a lullaby as she drifted off to sleep.

* * * * *

As the early morning sun rose over the Elmwood Cemetery and Funeral Home grounds, the light from its rays fought for attention against the starkly flashing blue and red lights of the police cars and rescue vehicles lining the street.

"I found the note on my desk when I got in this morning; I don't know how she could have…" A young funeral assistant wearing a navy blue suit held a crumpled piece of paper out to the officer in front of him, his tear-streaked face pale in the sunlight. His voice trailed off and the officer placed a comforting hand on the other man's shoulder. Behind them, a backhoe sat waiting, clumps of dirt hanging from the bucket side of the machine from where it'd pulled up the earth a few minutes before. A cracked headstone lay partially buried in the excess dirt, only the first three letters visible: SAM.

A small group of three paramedics knelt beside a heavy oak coffin, their faces solemn. One of them packed away a small defibrillator while another extracted an oxygen mask from the face of one of the women inside the coffin. The third paramedic, a young woman in her twenties named April, made eye contact with the officer in charge and shook her head slightly. The officer frowned and turned back toward the young assistant, who saw the exchange and met his gaze with a wave of fresh tears.

April stared down into the coffin, and felt her own eyes begin to burn. Inside, two bodies lay together, one curled gently around the other, fingers intertwined. The first body was already in a state of partial decomposition, but the other woman looked as though she could have been sleeping peacefully. The paramedic shivered, the morning chill on her arms giving her goosebumps as she looked at the funeral director and the woman she'd lost three years earlier. April couldn't explain how Samantha's body seemed to have turned over to hold her wife's, the thin strips of flesh that remained on her the bones of her arms, holding Nora close in their final embrace.

SHARP SPACES
Samantha Ortiz

Maya heard her mom run past her bedroom door. She knew her mother was barefoot from the awkward sound of her steps and the lack of clacking heels. She put down *Pride and Prejudice* when she heard a loud crash come from the kitchen.

"Maya!" Her mom yelled as she appeared. Refractions from the broken glass created rainbows along the cabinets.

"Are you okay? What broke?" Maya hoped concern would come through her voice instead of the disdain she felt toward her mother for interrupting her homework. Her mom groaned in frustration while on her hands and knees.

"I broke your *abuela's* favorite plate. *Chinguetas-*"

"Oh no! What will she eat on now?" Maya joked as she walked to the pantry. She pulled out the plastic pan and broom and brought it over. Right as she knelt, her mother stood back up.

"Can you handle this? I need to go." She straightened her skirt and grabbed a pair of kitten heels from off the counter.

"Sure. It's not like I have anything else to do," Maya mumbled under her breath. Her mom gave her a side-eye, grabbed her purse, and told her she'd be back before dark.

* * * * *

The home felt empty without her mother. Maya's father left when she was three, and she only had memories of him from her mother. The only photos of him existed in a shoebox under her mom's bed. She'd found them while playing hide and seek with her friend Julissa one summer morning.

"I told you not to use my mom's room as a hiding place! We're not allowed in here," Maya complained as Julissa shimmied out from under the bed, dragging a small box with her.

"It's light. What do you think is in there?" Julissa asked. She shook the box slightly and they could hear something hitting the sides. Maya sat on the floor beside her friend and they carefully peeled off the tape holding the box shut. Inside was a stack of polaroid photos. Maya picked one up gently, noticing the handwriting on the back. *1992. Wedding.* It wasn't her mother's handwriting, but it *was* her mother in a wedding dress. The sleeves of the dress were puffy and lace covered the top. Her mother was beaming, her hand resting on her stomach.

Julissa flipped the box upside down and dumped the rest of the photos on the carpet. Maya let out an audible gasp. When she'd turned seven a few weeks before, her mom had given her a disposable camera and taught her the importance of being careful with photos. "Only touch the sides, never the top, and keep them away from food and drink."

Maya had hurried to gather up the photographs and brush the dust off them as best she could. Just then, her mom had walked in and berated them both. Maya grabbed a photo that had flown under the bed and hid it in her shorts before anyone could see it. She was sent to her room and Julissa was sent home.

* * * * *

Maya walked back into her room after cleaning the glass off the floor. She stared at her homework sitting on the splinter-inducing homemade desk her mother gave her for her thirteenth birthday. Her mother dedicated herself to do-it-yourself projects after Maya broke the seventy-five dollar desk she'd bought her. She came home from school and threw her backpack on it and it just collapsed. Her mom swore off large corporate products after that, and dove into the art of DIY furniture making. After building the desk, she made a bed frame, a bedside table, and a prayer bench that Maya now used to hold her clothing. Each piece more polished than the last.

Sunlight peeked through the window in Maya's bedroom. Three large panels were decorated with light pink curtains, and small succulents lined the sill. She'd lifted the middle pane slightly, allowing a light fall breeze to cool down her warm bedroom. An N'SYNC poster wafted against the wall with two pins near the top holding it in place. She picked up the novel on her bed, flipped it open to her bookmark, and began to read. She'd barely finished the page when her hamburger phone rang. Maya decided to keep her phone unplugged for most of the day after she started receiving strange phone calls from people who refused to talk, but she connected it at 4:30 pm for her daily phone call with her friend, Nina.

"Hey, Nina," she said, still trying to concentrate on the story. "I'm sneaking out." Nina's voice was low, soft but confident.

"Why?" Maya asked, twisting the phone cord in her hand, only half-interested. To Nina, sneaking out was as easy as walking out the front door. Her mother was always working in her office downtown and her stepmom pretended not to see in order to earn Nina's trust.

"I met a guy." Nina sounded breathy. "Hold on, I'm going to close my door." Maya sat up.

"Who is he?"

There was a long pause. Maya heard a door close. "He's a guy I met online. He's... twenty-four."

"Uhh…" Maya had no words. Nina let out a small chuckle.

"He's very cute. We talk on this chat site he says is all encrypted and shit-"

"Does he know you're seventeen?" Maya asked, cutting her friend off. The oldest guy Nina had ever dated was nineteen years old and went to the community college in their town. He knew she was fifteen. When her mother found out, she locked Nina in her room and reported the guy to the police. Nina didn't speak to her for weeks, until she relented and bought her a new computer. Maya could feel jealousy seeping through her; she envied her friend's romantic adventures.

"He knows I'm basically in college." Whenever Nina worked around a question, it was always bad news. Sometimes Maya wondered about the types of men who would actively seek out a high schooler. There's no way they couldn't know. Sure, Nina's hips had come in before freshman year and her breasts followed soon after, but she had a baby face that makeup couldn't hide. Her cheeks were chubby and her eyes bright. "I sent you a pic on AIM. He's the one on the left. The one on the right is eager to meet you if you can come."

Maya blushed at the thought of someone older being interested in her. She stared at her desktop for a few seconds before walking over with her phone and logging in. The picture was of two men standing on a field. They both smiled wide for the camera. The one on the right held a soccer ball. He looked soft and approachable. She wondered how gently he would hold her if he had the chance. Maya caught herself tracing the stitched lines on their jerseys with her eyes.

"So?" Nina sounded excited and slightly impatient. "They want to meet us in an hour. You in?"

* * * * *

Maya knew her mother would be home from her Saturday shift at the local 50's themed diner, Early Bird, by midnight. She checked the clock. It was only 5 PM. Maya wondered about the things her mom did as a teenager—if she ever met strange men at movie theaters—if she ever laughed with them or went home with them or held their hands. Maybe that's how Maya had happened. Is that all so bad? She took a deep breath.

"Yeah, sure. Are you coming over?"

"No. I have to get ready, too. Meet me at the movie theater off Benson at six?"

Maya agreed and hung up. The full-length mirror on the inside of her closet exposed her baggy jeans and light green tank top. She looked back at the photo of the two men. She wanted to look older and more mature. She imagined all the clothes Nina was probably sifting through at that moment. Whenever they went to the mall together, Maya brought her purse full of her savings, always between twenty and eighty dollars, and Nina brought her mom's credit card. It was always Macy's first, then Wet Seal and Charlotte Russe. They slowly made their way down the financial ladder until Maya could afford something. They usually ended at Rave or some other bargain bin store.

She settled for high-waisted "mom" jeans, a pink strappy satin top, and her clear jelly shoes. She let her curly brown hair lay loose along her shoulders. Her purse was full of chokers she wanted Nina's opinion of, lip gloss, and a small switchblade her mother gave her when she turned fourteen.

"Men will want you and some may hurt you. If they ever want to touch you, take this out and tell them to back off." Her mother clicked a button on the side of the knife and the sharp piece of metal flew out of hiding. Maya stared at the blade as it glistened in the sunlight peeking through the living room window. Her mother made stabbing motions that made Maya laugh at the time, but there she was, putting the knife in her purse anyway.

The movie theater was lit with neon strips and Maya's shoes sunk into the various designs on the carpet. There were a few different lines to buy tickets, and Maya picked the longest one. She was early and wanted to give Nina enough time to arrive. A small girl and her father stood in front of Maya. The child looked up at her dad, holding his hand excitedly. He smiled at her and reached down to pick her up.

"Which movie do you want to see, baby?" The father spoke softly, bouncing her up and down. Nina tapped Maya on the shoulder and spoke, and Maya didn't hear what movie they chose. Nina wore a blue satin spaghetti strap dress and chunky white heels. Her eyeshadow was smokey and she wore a black choker. Maya pulled out her matching black choker and slipped it on while Nina leaned in. Her high ponytail swung forward and her front hair strands tickled Maya's cheek.

"I think they're over there." Nina rubbed Maya's back and tapped her right shoulder. Two men stood with their backs turned. "He told me they were going to be in red."

Each man held a small bouquet of roses and looked off toward the concession stand. Nina held her hand out for Maya and pulled her out of the line. "I bet they totally bought our tickets already. Let's go."

The closer they got to the men, the older they looked. Their posture was slouched and their clothes had small stains, things not visible from afar. Maya tried to discern between brown hair and grey as Nina made their presence known. The men turned around and Maya almost dropped her purse. They had to be in their mid thirties at least. Maya's heart pounded and she started to back away, but Nina grabbed her around the hips and pulled her close. The man with blonde hair spoke first.

"Wow, ladies. You both look great." His voice was low and smooth. Maya found herself adjusting her clothes, trying to cover up as much as possible. Nina seemed nervous as she clung to Maya. Her nails dug into Maya's side.

"Thank you." Nina's voice quivered slightly. The men gave their roses to the girls and walked behind them.

"Well, let's go!" The blonde placed his hand on Nina's back and Maya watched her friend jump. The blonde chuckled and pushed her forward. The brown-haired guy tried to do the same with Maya but was more hesitant. When Maya started walking without him, he dropped his hand and walked by her side.

The usher led them to their seats as the lights dimmed. The brunette sat between Maya and Nina as the blonde went to grab popcorn for everyone. He offered drinks, but Nina told him they'd had dinner before they came. Scary music blasted from the speakers as the title of the movie flashed on the screen, but Maya missed it because she was too busy watching Nina. The blonde had placed his arm around Nina, and Maya watched as he tapped the shoulder of the brunette to motion him to do the same. Before he could move his hand, Maya stood up and announced she had to use the bathroom and held her hand out for Nina. Surging with adrenaline, she pulled Nina down the aisle, out of the room, and into the nearest family bathroom.

"Nina, what the hell?" Maya yelled after looking under each of the stalls and finding no one. Nina crossed her arms.

"What? How was I supposed to know?" Nina turned to the mirror and adjusted her hair. Maya felt her energy draining and she sunk to the floor. "No, no, no, no," Nina said as she stood over her. Nina grabbed Maya's arms and tried pulling her up.

"We can't go back there. We have to go." Maya held her hands in front of her lips like a prayer. Nina crossed her arms.

"Come on! Please don't make me regret bringing you. Don't you ever do anything fun?" Nina couldn't keep eye contact with Maya and pretended to fix her hair again. "Nina," Maya stood up. "They're not in their twenties. They're just not." Maya grabbed her purse off the floor and paced back and forth before walking to the bathroom door. "I'm leaving. Are you coming?"

* * * * *

The sun started to set when they stepped out of the theater. They decided to go to Maya's house so no one would have to walk alone. Plus, Maya lived the closest to the movies, only ten minutes away.

"What if they come looking for us?" Nina's smooth confidence soon faded to a level of concern that worried Maya.

"They don't know where we live." Maya often turned into the voice of reason when everything else was chaos. She looked both ways before grabbing Nina's hand to cross the street. Nina let out a quiet "yeah" and slowed down slightly. Maya stopped when she couldn't feel Nina near her.

"What's wrong?" Maya turned around to see Nina staring at the ground, twisting her heel in the sidewalk crack. Maya walked back to her and grabbed her hands. "What is wrong?"

"Well…" Nina's voice was squeaky and broken. "Nathan asked if he could pick me up from my house, and I said no, but then we kept talking and…"

"And what?" Maya grew impatient. She hated the way Nina held onto her words. "I kind of told him where I lived so if he ever wanted to visit after our date…"

Maya took a deep breath and tried to control her heart rate. Her adrenaline was causing her to see double.

"Let's get to my house then. They don't know where I live." Maya was quick on her feet. Nina nodded and they kept walking.

Maya was paranoid, looking over her shoulder at every turn. Even though they were going to her house and not Nina's, she felt the men would still find them somehow. Every headlight sent a shiver down her spine. They turned into her neighborhood and Maya felt herself relaxing for the first time. It was a funny story, really, one they would inevitably tell their friends at school. Maya was wild like Nina for once in her life, even if nothing had really happened. She was living. "Hey girls!"

Nina froze and grabbed Maya's arm tightly. A car without headlights approached them with the window rolled down. The two men from the theater had furrowed brows but smiled when they made eye contact with the girls. It made Maya feel… something. "Why did you leave so soon?"

Maya reached into her purse and felt for the switchblade. She gripped it tightly. She grabbed Nina's dress with her other hand and pulled Nina in front of her.

"Come on baby, don't ignore me."

Nina twiddled her fingers trying not to look back to the car. Maya channeled her mother's straight face, the one she made whenever Maya was in big trouble. Her mother's eyes always pierced through her with a devilish intent, like the only person who could save Maya was far, far away. Now, Maya used that look to try to intimidate the two men, and it worked. Nina's "date" slowed the car down and turned the corner, disappearing out of sight.

"Okay let's run to my neighbor, Mr. John's house. My mom told me I could go to him for emergencies." Maya's voice was calm, sturdy, like her mother's. Nina's mascara left black streaks as it ran down her face. Maya hadn't noticed when she started crying. She reached for Nina's hand and held it tight. They both soon found their stride.

Crunch crunch crunch crunch…

"Someone's in the bushes," Nina whispered. Maya kept her eyes forward. *Just keep walking,* she thought to herself. *It'll be over soon.*

They had been crossing streets every block or so, trying to make it confusing for anyone who might be following them. Unfortunately, that also meant they had to take shortcuts through unlit areas. Maya convinced Nina that she knew the back paths really well, so they entered the long stretch of darkness. The moon was three-quarters full, giving them enough dim light to see the path ahead.

"We're almost there." Maya's voice quivered when she heard the crunching of leaves behind her. She instinctively pulled the weapon from her purse and held it close to her. She pressed the switch so the blade flew out and whipped around. She looked over at Nina, who stared with her eyes wide. Maya stepped forward to face the two men approaching them, pushing Nina behind her.

"STOP!" She yelled as a warning. One of the men slowed down but the other moved at a faster pace, almost sprinting towards them with one arm extended. She felt adrenaline rush through her body as his face loomed in the darkness. Before Maya could realize what was happening, her knife was twisted in the man's stomach. She looked down at her arm thrusting the knife in and out, and then up at the man's face in horror. He collapsed on the ground, his face squinted in pain. The man he was with backed away and ran off.

"That's not them," Nina said, squatting to look at the man's face more clearly. She stared at the blood on her hands then back at her victim. He looked familiar. His dark hair was slicked back and he appeared to be in his late forties. He opened his eyes and cried, "Maya!" causing her to back away until she could grip the cold wall. She leaned her cheek against it.

"Do you know him?" Nina asked frantically. Blood was pouring from the man's stomach as he held his hand against the open wounds. "We need to get him help! He's going to die!" She ran over to Maya but stopped when she noticed the knife was still out and Maya still held it in a forward position. "Maya?" She called out. Maya mumbled with eyes wide open.

"Maya, put the knife away," Nina said calmly. "We need to go." She put her hands on Maya's shoulders, causing her to snap out of her trance enough to snap the knife back into its holding place and stuff it in her purse. Blood splattered all over her bag and her clothes. Maya looked back at the man on the ground as she and Nina fled. She thought he might be staring at her, but the further they got from him, the less she could tell. Maya mumbled more, but Nina kept pulling until they got to Maya's house. Nina found the keys, unlocked the door, and pushed Maya in.

She pulled Maya to the shower and made her wash off all of the blood. Nina started a wash for both of them, grabbing pajamas and changing. By the time Maya stopped mumbling, Nina had cleaned everything, including the knife, and tried to get a still-dazed Maya into bed. Maya jumped up and ran to her closet, pulling out a box of her childhood treasures from beneath a pile of clothes. She opened the box and rifled through it, grabbing a photo and handing it to Nina.

"I think he was my dad." Maya tried to take a deep breath but caught herself in a hyperventilating spiral. "I think I might've killed my dad."

She collapsed into Nina who held her while staring at the photo of a man with a black tuxedo, smiling into the camera.

An Agreement
Sheela Kean

Joey couldn't believe his luck. It had been ten years since his father died. That meant ten years of entering his name into the state elk hunt drawing and coming up empty-handed. Until now. Finally, he'd get his big chance. His father had loved to talk about hunting. He had a story for every season, but the lopsided elk story was always Joey's favorite.

His father and grandfather had taken a big out-of-state hunting trip. The area was beautiful and a family friend had touted it as packed with wildlife, always an easy hunting ground. They'd spent two weeks on the land from sunup to sundown but hadn't shot a single thing. Grandpa was ready to pack it up in anger.

Dad had gone out for one last morning in the woods and spotted the largest animal he'd ever seen. A massive bull elk. He swore he locked eyes with it for a full minute before his brain finally caught up with what he was seeing. Its antler tines branched out in a rack that seemed almost as tall as the trees, with one side broken off, giving the entire thing an awkward skew. Dad raised his gun, but it had been too late; the animal ran and was soon too far away. Joey's father sat in that spot the rest of the day, waiting and foolishly hoping to catch another glimpse of the beast. Later, Grandpa had laughed at him, explaining there were no elk in the area. He must have mistaken a regular buck as the animal, or he'd fallen asleep and dreamed the whole thing. Dad held onto his story, though, and swore he and Joey would go back and get one someday. A giant trophy elk.

They never did. His father had gotten sick, weak, and the dreams of mammoth elk faded away.

Fall came slowly this year; the heat had yet to fade, and the trees below the bay had barely started turning colors. Driving north, back toward home, Joey felt as if he was entering a different world. The fiery colors of the season were everywhere. His sister, Miranda, had been the older and more responsible of the two when dad passed. She made the move right into the family's cabin before Joey could do anything about it. Thankfully, they were on nice enough terms that he was free to come and go whenever he wanted. Miranda had dreams of being a homesteader. It seemed dad's stories had inspired her to fall in love with a different aspect of nature. With her husband Oscar's remote office job, they could live up in the woods and garden to their hearts' content.

Beyond nagging him about unhealthy habits, she didn't harass Joey too much during his visits home. As soon as he'd learned he won the elk lotto, he put in for the time off and called her. If getting an elk had been dad's dream, then what better place to hunt one than on the family's land. He wanted to leave right away, but work had been too busy for him to come up the previous weekend. The idea of walking out on his shift tempted him; he wanted to be out in the woods so desperately. His sister had talked him out of being so rash. She even went the extra steps to help him out by setting up and watching his trail cameras. But he only had four days left now to get his beast.

Turning off the dirt road onto the grassy path they called a driveway, he mused on the beauty of the property. It was uniquely untamed, with no fancy lawns or landscaping in sight. Just a large two-story cabin of deep cherry-stained wood, a greenhouse to keep out the frost, and a small chicken coop. The birds were roaming the yard freely. It always amazed Joey that his sister didn't lose more of them to coyotes. Oscar greeted him at the door, a large grin on his tanned face, offering to help him bring in his bags and gear.

"Mira's out for a walk—she spotted a couple of wild mushroom patches earlier." "I skipped stopping for lunch just so I could get here in time for dinner."

"Oh, don't worry, she's got an entire plan to stuff you full this weekend," Oscar laughed.

The familiar creak of the floor with the scent of pine and sage took the tension out of his muscles. This is what home feels like. *It should have been mine though*, he thought to himself. His sister came through the door a few minutes later with a basket on her arm and dirt on the knees of her baggy overalls.

"Hey, Just in time for my chicken marsala," She said, greeting him with a hug. "Don't your birds get offended by that?" Joey asked jokingly.

Miranda rolled her eyes at him and moved into the kitchen to rinse and chop her finds. She prepared the meal using a variety of extra vegetables and herbs from the garden. She always put a unique spin on her recipes. Joey liked to tease her, saying her cooking was 'kitchen voodoo,' but it never amused her. She took her relationship with nature very seriously.

The delicious meal made Joey lethargic. He'd probably overeaten, but it was worth it. He was too tired to socialize further, promising to share a few beers with Oscar another night. He needed to sleep so he could be up and ready for the woods before sunrise. Tomorrow might not be his day. Oscar had mentioned it would rain through the night, and Joey knew the weather could make animals behave differently. Predicting what that rain might be like would be impossible. He'd just have to wait and see.

The storm blew in later than Joey hoped. He was still stretching the night's aches out of his bones. The air felt thick. The smell of leafy undergrowth surrounded him while he hiked into the forest to settle into his favorite spot. A constant icy drizzle dampened everything. This was something he had prepared for, though. He knew better than to let the cold seep into his clothes. Waiting patiently for the sun to rise, he listened for the snapping of twigs that might alert him to something moving nearby. His ears perked up at a sound. Sitting up a little straighter, he waited to hear it again, hoping for a direction. A loud crack sounded, and all the sounds of the forest were drowned out by a sudden downpour of rain. Although it had been a clear dawn, now water came down so heavy that everything was a foggy blur. Joey sat in his spot under a large pine tree, watching the wind scatter leaves and twigs. A flash came this time, startling him before another loud crack of thunder boomed. *Shit.* The rain was not an uncommon hunting condition, but he couldn't sit out here with the lightning crashing around him.

The morning ruined, Joey trudged back to the cabin. His sister awaited him with a fresh carafe of chicory coffee. He liked to tease her about the stuff. It lacked the caffeine he craved, but it was still always pleasantly warming. He watched her work around the house as he waited for the storm to pass. She lit and blew out several candles, whispering brief prayers while she sorted out herb garden clippings she had dried. In a little corner of the front room sat a special shelf where she laid out stones and flowers. Gifts, she called them, part of her strange way of life.

"Are you just going to gawk at me like a circus act all day?" she asked.

"I have nothing else to do," he admitted, "I'm waiting for the storm to clear."

"It won't for a while—you're not going back out today," she told him, looking out the kitchen window with a raised eyebrow.

"How do you know?"

"I just do, the air's too heavy. This storm's got a lot left in it." "Have I told you lately you're a strange one?"

"It's what gets me by." She motioned to the room.

It surprised him, the first time he'd stayed over, how well they lived out here. Oscar never failed to have all the luck he needed, and Miranda seemed to be able to provide for them in abundance with her gardening and foraging. "We have an agreement," she used to say whenever he asked how her plants grew so well. Joey's eyes drifted toward the window. *I wish I had one of those.*

"You have cameras still," Miranda's voice broke him from his thoughts.

"I... what?"

"You haven't looked through the trail cameras since you arrived. I brought the SD cards in yesterday when you got here."

"I forgot, thanks."

Pouring himself the last drops of coffee and snatching an apple from a nearby basket, he made his way upstairs to the office area. Oscar sat typing rapidly, noise- canceling headphones over his ears. Two bright blue cards sat next to his sister's laptop. She and Oscar shared the large space with desks at opposite ends of the room, personal space and companionship happily combined.

Only the past week had still been saved to the memory cards. Miranda had assured him she carefully examined each set before erasing them. She aimed the first camera near where he had been that morning. Many of the pictures were from rambunctious squirrels skittering around and setting off the camera's sensor. Two small deer, not what he was looking for, followed by a bear. Joey grimaced, *I better not have a run-in with that thing.*

Camera two was deeper into the woods, west of the cabin. His father's favorite hunting spot. He'd had an understanding with the closest neighbors, giving him the use of the additional property nearby. After scrolling past the various shots of birds and small critters, he hit the jackpot. On the outskirts of the camera's frame were two elk. They were enormous females, no antlers in sight. Not exactly what he had been hoping for but…

His heart sped up with excitement as he scrolled further through the trail footage. After the females had moved away, a third arrived, walking dead center into the camera's view. The animal stood so tall its antlers jutted up beyond the frame of the photos. Joey's fingers twitched with an excess of adrenaline, wanting to pull a trigger right then. This was it. This was the elk he needed. He had to have it—he'd do anything to get it. Saving and emailing the photos to himself, he went back downstairs to watch the weather again. He itched to get into those woods.

"I told you so," Miranda said as she set the bowl of salad greens in the middle of the table.

It hadn't stopped storming yet. The wind picked up and died down, getting Joey excited before more thunder boomed.

"I know, I know. You and your little hoodoo voodoo," He grumpily replied.

"You know I hate it when you say shit like that. It's more than that and you know it."

Joey watched his sister huff and sit down to eat her stew. He dug in, not wanting to anger her with further conversation. The home-cooked meal should have easily distracted him, but his mind was still on the Elk he had seen. *Maybe…* His thoughts took a turn back toward his sister and her strange practices. She had joked earlier about an agreement with nature, that it provided her with things she needed. *Well, what about what he needed, would it give him that too?* He knew he couldn't ask her, not after his jibes. She'd probably brush him off. His eyes casually sought the front room, the bookcase full of oddities. *Maybe...*

He lay quietly in his room; the door cracked open just enough to hear all the sounds of the house. He didn't struggle much to keep himself awake. The enthusiasm for his brilliant plan did it for him. After he was sure the house had fallen dark and silent, he crept out of the room in socked feet, careful not to make a sound. Miranda's bookcase held many trinkets, stuff that hardly made sense to him but must have a use. A small stack of books sat on one shelf, with spines referencing herb gardens, healing crystals, and apothecaries. He picked out one that read "Charms & Spells." It seemed straightforward enough. The text was more complicated than he had expected, though.

I don't have time to read through all this.

He skimmed the basic introduction and read a few brief entries before giving up.

It can't be that complicated.

Thinking about what he's seen his sister do (combined with a little horror movie knowledge), he stuffed the pocket of his sweatshirt with items from the baskets lining the upper shelf. A couple of shiny rocks, a feather, some dried flowers, a candle.

He moved into the kitchen, grabbing a spare bread roll as well. His sister's lukewarm cup of tea sat next to the sink. She always brewed two cups, drinking one before bed and leaving the other to sit on the counter. Joey grabbed the cup and quietly went out the patio door. It was darker than he had expected, with only a single porch light to guide him from the small deck. The rain had finally quit, but the clouds blocked out any sliver of light the moon might have provided. Venturing too deep into the woods wouldn't be safe at this time of night, so he headed just past the treeline west of the house. He found the spot from last summer where a dying old elm had fallen, taking a few younger trees with it. They'd cut and split most of the lumber, leaving a few neat stumps behind at Miranda's request.

Joey was filled with apprehension as he emptied his pockets, laying the items in a circle around the small white tea light candle. Before he could chicken out and lose his chance forever, he lit the candle. He sat in the dirt in front of his small altar and closed his eyes. He pictured the prize elk that he'd seen. He pressed all his wants toward the flame, promising anything just for this one successful hunt.

"This is what I deserve. You will give it to me," he whispered.

A lightheaded rush briefly came over him. A tingle like the barest touch of fingertips brushed down his spine. It unsettled him, pulling him from his trance. He thought once more about what else might be out in the woods. With a sudden jerky movement, he pushed himself up to stand.

"Ow, shit!"

He'd caught his hand on a thorn-covered branch, breaking the skin along the back of it. He shook the stinging appendage, letting tiny droplets of blood spatter across the log. His candle sputtered in the breeze and the leaves of the trees shook off their excess rain onto him. Confident that he'd gotten his message across, Joey trudged back to the cabin, leaving his sister's things behind. He'd collect them later. *After he got his trophy.*

Morning came quickly and he marched outside with full confidence in himself. He headed towards his father's old deer blind. The air was calm, everything quietly waking up around him. He sat patiently, occasionally reminding whatever might be listening that he was ready. The morning dawned, and he waited.

The crunching of leaves and twigs alerted him of movement, the sound of something heavy lumbering through the brush. Its long antlers appeared first, leading the way for its massive head. He knew the elk were large animals, but up this close, they were like gods of the forest. Caught up in the moment, he'd almost forgot what he came for, his hands and brain working at different speeds. Taking a deep breath to steady himself, he brought up his rifle, shouldered it, and readied the shot.

One more breath in and - "Ahhh,"

CRACK

Joey dropped his rifle. Grabbing his bloodied nose with one hand and using the other to swat at the large black bird that had startled him by trying to land on his neck. He shooed it away, hollering in frustration. His nose throbbed with the pain of his rifle's recoil. He had flinched; he hadn't been ready. His shot should have been perfect. He knew he hadn't missed, but now the beast was going to be on the move.

Chasing it all day was not what he'd hoped for. Joey leaned his head back and tried to blink the spots out of his eyes, but new ones kept appearing. *Snow?*

It was snowing. His breath came out in a puff of steam. He hadn't realized it was so cold before. A little flurry wasn't going to stop him now. Stepping toward where he had seen the elk, he found exactly what he needed. A trail of blood along the frosted grass. *I've got you... you belong to me.* With a manic grin, he followed the droplets further into the woods to find his prize.

As the dusting of snow coated the ground, the trail grew more pronounced and his excitement grew dizzying. The blood from the now forgotten blow to his nose had run steadily down his face. Licking it off his lips, he kept walking. Blurs of movement happened all around him, as black shapes filled the trees. Birds were watching silently as he ambled along. The cut on his hand from the night before began to itch. He scratched at it absentmindedly as he walked. Digging deeper and deeper with every scrape of his nails. Skin peeled away and new blood welled up in the hollows.

He shivered, the frigid air catching up with him. His nose had gone numb, clots of blood and mucus frozen to his face. The feeling of something following him made him stop.

"*Someones trying to get there first... they're going to take it from you,*" a voice inside his head whispered.

"It's my prize! Mine! I made the deal!" He shouted into the shadows of the trees.

The sun was already going down in the sky, Joey stared around, puzzled, his boots now submerged in a thick blanket of snow. *When had that happened? It was just a little bit of snow, just enough to see...* His heart thumped in his ears. The trail. He'd lost it. There was nothing here. He spun around madly, searching the forest floor and finding nothing but untouched whiteness. A blank canvas covered the ground.

"No, no, no."

Screaming filled his ears, terrible pained screams. The shrill cries drowning out everything. *No… not screaming.* His horror turned to excitement when he realized the terrifying sounds were coming from the elk. Its call echoed through the trees ahead. Deciding on a direction, Joey ran. Branches scratched at his face and snagged on his clothing as he slipped and slid through the snow. Following the deathly screeching of the elk's bugle, with complete disregard for where he may have been going or how deep into the forest he had gone.

His chest burned, his lungs refusing to work in the cold air. A stitch in his side made him stumble, and the knotted vines hidden beneath the snow finished the job. His frostbitten nose took the first hit as he landed on his face. Followed by the shock of pain through his limbs as he continued to tumble down the icy ravine. It ricocheted him through roots and rocks like a pinball before he slid to a halt at the bottom. He had come to a stop facing the foot of a large overturned tree, its roots hanging in tangles like the gaping maw of a monster. The smell of it was sickly, rotten fruit and decaying flowers. As he lay there unable to make his limbs move any longer, a puff of hot air crept along his neck. The great elk's shadow stood over him, snorting and standing tall. No sign of injury, no blood matting its fur.

"It's not fair, you're mine," Joey whined with a wheezing breath.

"Nothing belongs to you."

The words carried on the wind as the roots of the overturned tree slithered their way over the young man's broken body. Claiming it for the forest.

Four Corners
Kirby Kellogg

"Listen," The jittery voice cracked over the phone. "I *can't* come in tonight. My boyfriend's coming over with his parents and I can't mess this up."

"We had a deal, Natalie. I take Monday, Wednesday, Friday, and Sunday, and you take the other days. That's our deal!"

"I'm sorry, Joannie, but I need to be here. This might actually be a long-term thing!" Her voice shone with barely hidden glee, and Joan sighed. She couldn't say no to that—it'd make her feel like a jackass for the rest of the week.

"Fine," she sighed. "But you owe me." She could almost see Natalie pumping a fist in triumph.

"Thanks, J! I'll let you know how it went!" Natalie cheered, then the line went dead.

Joan put down her phone, running a hand through her short burgundy hair.

"Well," she sighed, the obvious hangover evident in her voice, "It's not like I was going to do anything major today anyway." She got up slowly, feeling older than she'd ever been, and crossed to her tiny bathroom.

Once she'd cleaned up, she looked at herself in the mirror. Heavy bags beneath her eyes made her look like a raccoon, and her teeth were stained yellow from a steady diet of cigarettes and cheap coffee. She was tall and praying mantis-esque, perpetually hunched from years of office work. There was a dull throb through her whole body. That was normal though, phantom pains she almost welcomed.

They'd been happening ever since she joined the Four Corners "family." It was just the work of hefting boxes and loading inventory. Every employee experienced that.

They probably didn't *feel* this worn though.

Still, she pulled on the blue-grey polo and khakis comprising her uniform and cracked her knuckles. A job was a job, no matter how little she wanted to go in or how monotonous the work was. She set out into the dust of the desert toward the gas station. At least it was the night shift. Maybe she wouldn't boil alive tonight.

* * * * *

Four Corners had been around longer than anyone could remember, but Porthcrawl's memory was fuzzy on who'd worked there before Joannie. Hell, even she couldn't remember.

The Boss was far older than she or Natalie and extremely reclusive. He didn't give face-to-face interviews, no matter how many times you asked for one, and he'd only speak to employees through an intercom connected to his door in the back. Natalie, new in town, didn't get it.

"Why won't he at least *look* at us?" she asked one night, hunched over a box of store-brand chips. "What, does he think he's better than us or something?"

"Or something," Joan answered, counting down the minutes until her smoke break. "He's not that bad, he's just afraid of people. He'll probably transfer us somewhere new soon enough."

"Well, maybe if he's 'afraid of people' he shouldn't have gotten into the food industry," Natalie huffed, hefting up a newly emptied box and taking it out back. "All I know is that back in Connecticut, my boss at least looked me in the eyes." She finished, kicking the door shut behind him in an over-dramatic departure.

Joannie had mocked her then but, more than that, she'd pitied her. She didn't get it. At this rate, she never would. Whether that was a good thing or not, she wasn't sure. Still, she'd refrained from revealing any more about their boss. It was safer that way, she figured. For both of them.

* * * * *

It was two hours from the end of her shift, a completely dead one, when someone finally came in. Joan had occupied herself with adjusting their inventory, taking smoke breaks, and debating whether or not to use the steel burglary-defense bat to silence the looping Jimmy Buffett track above her. She'd gotten a penny out to let fate decide when the door opened, its signal bell chirping electronically.

With a sigh, she turned to face the door and prepped her best customer service voice. "Welcome to Four Corners, can I — oh shit, hey Natalie." She dropped the fake voice at once, returning to her normal cadence. "I thought your boyfriend was coming over."

"He is," Natalie insisted, her voice sounding a little strained. "I just had to get some stuff for dinner, and I figured it'd be easier to jog over here. Plus, had to check if you were doing okay." She laughed, sounding strained and anxious. Natalie had a pug-like face, and she sniffled constantly in a way that seemed almost unnatural. Then again, not many things in Porthcrawl looked natural.

Joannie's muscles relaxed slightly. The fact that the customer was her co-worker, who knew how shit the place was and wouldn't blame her for it, was a relief. "Okay, cool. Let me know if you need anything, bud."

Natalie gave a thumbs-up before shuffling quickly to the back.

Joannie turned to look at the compass painted on the open window, the arrow pointed northward toward the black sky. Even when all the lights in town were dark, the sky was always empty. Almost like it wasn't sky at all, just some tar black roof covering the town and keeping something out. But that was crazy talk, the kind of thing her sister would spout after a couple of glasses of liquid confidence.

Natalie's throat cleared behind her and Joan turned on her heel, sea-green eyes squinting slightly behind her glasses as they adjusted to the brightness around her. The transition from looking outside to the jacked-up lights always made her wince slightly. "Sorry," She said and began scanning her stuff.

A bottle of iced tea, some chips, one of the few decent sandwiches they offered, and a pack of powdered donuts. Utterly mundane, but Natalie looked almost terrified. Her eyes darted back and forth like a cat's before a laser pointer.

"You good, buddy?" Joan asked, getting a little worried. "This doesn't look like stuff for a fancy dinner."

Natalie nodded. "Yeah, yeah, I'm fine. Just nervous about tonight. His parents are bringing food along. I don't know though, I didn't ask."

"I remember my last date." She chuckled, trying to ease the tension. "Her dad tried to make me try his venison jerky."

"How could he get venison all the way out here?" "He knew a guy. That'll be $13.85."

"I'll take a pack of cigarettes too. Marlboro Red," she said, her voice jittery as her fists squeezed and released in time with the overhead music. A weird sort of tension emanated from her as she waited there, a tension that no amount of Jimmy Buffett could cause. As Joan grabbed a pack of cigarettes, she finally noticed the white powder around her co-worker's nose, and more on the sleeve of her blazer.

"Oh Jesus fucking Christ." She sighed, putting down the pack in front of her. "Again, Natalie?"

"What do you mean 'again, Natalie?'"

"You know what I'm talking about," she told her, voice taking on an edge of warning as she gestured to the powder.

Natalie brushed a finger on her nose, eyes widening as it came back white. "Look, it was one time!" she insisted. "It takes the edge off when I'm gonna do big things, Joan, it's important!"

"Nat, I'm pretty sure your future in-laws don't want to see you on coke. No one does." She was almost done with her shift; she didn't need to deal with her co-worker being a cokehead.

"They're not coming."

A pause, then "I'm sorry, what?"

"They were never going to show up, Joan. I needed the night off for something else."

"For what then, genius?"

Slowly, Natalie removed a revolver from her pocket and pointed it between

Joan's eyes. "I'm going to see our boss, and you're going to help me."

* * * * *

"Look, Nat," Joan had said long ago, snuffing out the last of her cigarettes on the side of the building. "You have to let it go. I did, a long time ago, and look at me— I've been working here for ten years and I'm just fine."

Natalie wasn't convinced, however, swinging her arm back and throwing a beer can across the parking lot. The two had been drinking for a few hours now, sharing a day off for the Fourth of July, and most of their conversation had been dominated by

Nat's paranoia. "There's gotta be something there, Joan," she insisted. "No one just avoids their employees completely."

"Rich people do."

"I don't think there's any rich people in this town." Joan shrugged. She had her there.

"I need to talk to him, Joan," she repeated. "I just need a little courage."

"We've already had about four beers each. I think we've both had enough booze for the night." Joan climbed down from the picnic table she'd perched herself on. She was getting tired anyway. "Let's just get home. You want me to walk you back to your place?"

"I didn't mean beer," Natalie said, completely ignoring the offer. Digging both hands into the pockets of her shorts, stained with firecracker residue and ketchup, she pulled out a small plastic baggie filled with white powder.

It took a few moments for Joan's alcohol-pickled brain to figure out what was inside. "Natalie, no. We're in the parking lot. We could both get in massive trouble if you do that here." She reached for the baggie. "Just give it here and let me walk you home."

The speed with which Natalie turned away and snorted her supply straight from its bag was almost admirable. She turned to face Joan, wiping her wrist on her nose and jostling the little silver piercing there. "Have you ever seen him?"

"Look, we need to get you home." "Answer the question."

She sighed. "No, alright? I haven't, and I have no desire to see him." She grabbed Natalie's wrist. "You can't let this bullshit consume you, Nat. We've got things bigger than him to handle."

"I just want to see him, why are you acting like that's a huge crime?"

"Why are you hinging your sanity on some crazy old man who doesn't want to be seen?"

The two remained in a stand-off for a moment, glaring at each other until something seemed to come undone behind Nat's eyes. Hunching at the waist, she covered her mouth. "Oh God, I think I'm gonna be sick," she babbled, throat sounding thicker as she stumbled to the trash can.

Joan sighed, holding back the other girl's blonde hair. "This is why you don't get drunk and do coke at the same time, idiot." Affection poked through her icy words as she ran her fingers through Natalie's locks.

Natalie nodded, spitting one last time before standing on shaky legs. She looked like a deer, in truth, stumbling a little as she walked. With great care, she walked over to Joan and put an arm around her. She was much taller than her friend, lean and steel-eyed, but she held onto her tenderly. "Take me home, JJ," she murmured, leaning her head against her companion's.

If it was any other woman, Joan would feel flustered. With Natalie though, it felt right. "Just don't puke on me," she warned, patting her back and reveling in her laugh as they walked off. At least she'd helped to avoid a confrontation with the boss for now but, deep down, she knew it was inevitable.

* * * * *

The revolver didn't even shock her as she made eye contact with the barrel. The woman behind it was shaking violently now, and there was violence in those steely, terrified eyes. Something poked out of her sleeve, and Joan squinted to read it. The package read simply "Vanilla Sky," and she could see hints of the same white powder near its base.

"Bath salts? *Seriously?*"

"I needed something harder to get my courage up, Joan." Nat insisted, twitching a little now. "Listen to me, I don't want to hurt you. But I need you to take me to him."

"I'm not doing that, Natalie."

Nat clicked the safety off. "It wasn't a question, J."

Joannie watched her in silence for a moment, standing her ground. "Please, Nat," she whispered, now pleading with her. "I don't want to do this to you. You're my friend, and I love you, and I can't let you go in there—"

She was cut off by Natalie suddenly shooting into the ceiling. With an electronic hiss, the security camera system shut down completely. The little red lights of the Four Corners cameras flared brightly, then faded. No one could watch them now, save for the moon that shone high outside. "It. Wasn't. A. Question." Natalie repeated, aiming the gun back at Joannie's head.

The two stood there in silence before Joan hung her head and shook it sadly. "I'm so sorry, Nat," she murmured. Tears bubbled up in her eyes, and she breathed deep to try to stop them.

"You don't need to be sorry, J. Just take me to him. I know he's here. I can see his car."

Finally, Joan nodded and began leading the path they knew well past boxes of stock and down the hallway to the back office. She walked as though she was marching to the grave. Natalie's confused gaze, along with the point of the gun, followed her in silence. Eventually, they came to a heavy wooden door at the back of the hall. "Here."

Natalie lowered her gun and looked at the door. "Here?" Joan nodded.

"I don't understand, I don't recognize this door."

"It's probably because you're high off your ass," Joan said without humor. Her face was paler than usual, eyes clouded with an unspoken grief.

"Why do you look so depressed, Joan? We're gonna see our boss, aren't you happy? We can finally give him a piece of our minds!" Nat grinned, her own gaze hazy from her drug-induced stupor. She'd clearly dosed heavily for this, eager to a fault.

Joan just sighed. "I'm so sorry, Nat." "Sorry for *what*?"

She didn't answer, and Natalie scoffed. "Whatever." Still, her grin didn't fade as she knocked the door open with her shoulder. It swung wide, and she opened her mouth to speak only to close it slowly in disappointment.

The office, concrete walls blank and stark compared to the black desk in its center, was empty. No one at the 90s era computer, no one perched in the heavy leather chair, not a single soul in sight save for the faces in the forward-facing family photo at the front. Natalie's face dropped as she turned to face Joan. "You *lied* to me."

"I'm sorry, Nat."

Natalie swung the gun up and pointed it at her face again. *"Where the hell is he?"* she screamed, throat raw and eyes going wild. Her finger squeezed the trigger now, holding back just enough so it wouldn't fire. "Tell me where he is or I swear to *God*, Joannie."

In her rage, Natalie didn't notice the lightbulb slowly burning out above them — or the computer turning on all by itself. Wires began to snake out from its back, entangled and drenched in something that looked like oil but smelled like blood.

"He's in there," Joan repeated, voice trembling, raising her head to look at the looming electric beast. She was crying now, heavy tears leaking down her cheeks. "I'm *so sorry*, Natalie," she repeated.

Nat was about to speak when the wire-y creature leaped upon her and entangled her throat. Her scream of horror was cut off before it could even echo, wine red blood beginning to leak from her throat as bare wire curled and carved it. The wooden door shut, cutting off Joannie's view of her friend, but it didn't cut off her struggle or the attempts to scream. She knelt and dry-heaved in front of the door. This was the part she hated the most.

Joan stood, clutching the doorknob. Everything had gone silent. Swallowing down bile and tears, she unlocked the door and opened it to look inside. Everything was back to normal, not a sign of Natalie to be found save for her nametag on the desk's surface. The computer monitor was turned around, displaying a flesh-and- blood eye through the shattered glass.

She breathed deep, coughing again before speaking. "She was my friend, you son of a bitch."

The eye disappeared and words blinked across the screen: "THERE WILL BE OTHERS. THERE ARE ALWAYS OTHERS. YOU KNOW THIS. *NOW SLEEP.*" Then the eye returned, blinked once, and Joan's legs gave out from underneath her as she collapsed into dreamless oblivion.

When she woke up, it was with a grunt of pain and a violent set of coughs. She stood slowly, clutching the doorknob tightly. She spat onto the floor, recognizing that the monitor had turned back around. The boss was satisfied. For now, at least.

They'd transferred again, she could tell. The Carpenters crooned over the intercom and the smell of hot dog water still burned her nose as she took her place back behind the counter. An hour to go, then she could wander back to her trailer — if this new corner of the universe *had* it, sometimes she'd had to sleep in the spare room when their newest "stations" didn't have it — and drink until she forgot. It was tradition now, so much so that she kept extra money with her for the bottle. A natural cycle she despised.

As she gazed through the window at twin moons shrouded by falling and shrieking stars, the same old questions returned: *Where am I and where will I be tomorrow?* The questions still burned in her skull as she grabbed a pack of Marlboros, shoved three dollars into the cash register, and stepped outside for a smoke in this brave new world. A double-length break today, in memory of her friend.

Lady Killer
Melissa Ashley Hernandez

Emptiness. One would think that, for a place as populated as South Carolina, there wouldn't be an inch of land left untouched. Yet the expanse of abandoned fields dotted with trees and occasional abandoned buildings lining the highway had gone on with no end in sight.

John shifted in the driver's seat. How long had it been? An hour? Two hours? Three? If he had known he'd end up on this stretch of land without a gas station or welcome center for miles, he might have eaten something at the airport. Well, maybe. John's boss had delighted him with the promise of a private flight but forgot to mention that it was with some novice crackpot and her dinky plane.

She was nice enough, but John was relieved when they finally touched solid ground again. She took him inside the 'airport'—a little one-floor building—and offered to cook him up something to eat. Feeling a little queasy from the bumpy flight, John politely turned down the offer and instead asked for some water. She tossed him a bottle and the keys to the rental car his boss had promised; he somehow wasn't shocked that it was her brother's rickety pickup truck. With no other option, he thanked her, accepted the offer, and went on his way.

Now that the nausea had dissipated, he was fidgety, hungry, and maybe even a little lost. He had been dealing with spotty reception for a few miles now. He felt certain he had made a wrong turn somewhere, but his app wouldn't recalculate. He decided to pull over and throw curses at the sky for a little while.

About fifteen minutes later, John was highlighting a route on a paper map he found in the glove box, scarfing down an old granola bar he'd scrounged from his briefcase, and swearing he would only fly commercial for the rest of his life. With a new understanding of the road, and his belly somewhat sated, he turned the key to start the truck again, only to be met with a gut-wrenching grinding sound. In disbelief, he turned the key again and heard the same whiny sputter.

Taking a deep breath, he popped the hood, though he had no clue as to what he was looking at; his wife normally handled the mechanical stuff at home. He stared for a moment before pulling out his phone. He doubted the pilot would still be there, but there were a few emergency numbers written on the back of the owner's manual he discovered in the glove box. Looking at the lack of bars on his phone, John thought he might be better off if he tried to flag down a car.

He looked down the highway. No cars had come this way since he had pulled over. It soon dawned on him that he hadn't seen *any* cars since he turned onto this highway an hour ago. With that unsettling observation, he frantically dialed the number with *Mechanic* scribbled carelessly next to it. The phone struggled to maintain a connection before dropping the call. He redialed a few more times before he reached

a voicemail that said the mechanic shop was closed until the morning. He left a message explaining his situation and stating where the mechanic could find him if they couldn't reach him by phone.

It was almost seven PM. John had attempted to call his boss and use his navigation app to find a hotel nearby, but his phone had officially given up. He was in a dead zone; no calls in, no calls out, and no internet connection. The sun started to get low, and he was afraid of wild animals after dark. He was stuck in the truck until morning.

He rifled through the truck's contents: a small toolbox under the passenger seat, the map and manual from earlier, and a handful of brown napkins. John splayed himself across the front seats, a wrench from the toolbox in hand. Ignoring his fear of being the victim of a highway robbery, he tried to makeshift a pillow out of his travel bag. The sooner he could fall asleep, the faster morning would come.

He slept but stirred awake sometime later to distant clattering sounds. His eyes snapped open. Adrenaline coursed through him as he jumped out of the truck, white-knuckled grip on the wrench, prepared to fight for his life. He crept around and peered over the hood. What he saw almost made his knees buckle. He rubbed his eyes to make sure he was seeing properly. A short distance down the field was a building. He could have sworn the plot had been empty earlier today—was he hallucinating? He checked his phone.

3:00 AM.

Was he still asleep? As though in a trance, John found himself walking towards it. Lanterns burned and a soft glow emanated from the strange place. He pocketed the wrench as he approached a worn sign that read in faded letters, *The Six Mile Wayfarer House.* He wondered what this place was doing in the middle of nowhere.

"Can I help you, sir?" a syrupy voice cut through the air, sending a jolt through John's body.

"Oh! I didn't see you there—" His eyes met the speaker's and his words caught in his throat. Sitting on the steps was a gorgeous young woman. She was wearing one of those old-timey dresses, corset and all, but it didn't sit properly and revealed quite a bit of her pale skin. She giggled at John and though the air was sticky and warm, a chill ran up his spine; she had laughed, but her eyes were as cold as a starless night.

"That's quite alright, are you in need of assistance?" she asked again in that sweet voice. He silently reprimanded himself for thinking negatively about someone who seemd so kind.

"What is this place? Some sort of bed and breakfast?" he asked hopefully.

"You could say that, I suppose." She started inside. "Would you like to come in for a hot meal? A drink?" His stomach growled at the prospect of warm food, and after the day he'd just had, a stiff drink was too good to pass up.

John followed the beautiful woman inside and was greeted by a delicious scent coming from what he assumed to be the kitchen. The woman sat him down at a table and disappeared into the other room. She returned moments later with a cup of tea and a slice of some sort of meat pie. He used his fork to bring a piece close to his mouth, but something felt wrong.

The lady sat across the table, simply staring at him. He politely and carefully placed the food between his teeth and, once she seemed satisfied that he'd enjoyed it, discreetly spit it into his napkin.

"You know, I never got your name, Miss…?" She smiled.

"Our tea pairs quite nicely with your meal. Why not give it a try?"

He was taken aback by the odd response and looked towards the tea. The woman waited expectantly.

"I've, uh, never been a big fan of tea," John stammered. Her smile faltered, but only for a second. She stood up suddenly.

"You poor thing, out there all alone so late. You're probably exhausted. We have an open room tonight. Come with me."

Against his better judgment, he followed her. The promise of a bed sounded miles better than a rigid truck seat. Wired from exhaustion, he believed the apprehension in his bones would dissipate once he lay down in a nice, soft bed. As they walked down the hallway, the walls seemed to breathe with malice. Every step they took closer to the bedroom filled him with an intense uneasiness he couldn't quite shake.

After what felt like ages, the woman opened the door at the far end of the hall. He stuttered a thank you and walked inside. The woman closed the door with a loud click behind him and John surveyed the room. It was quaint. A full-sized bed, a dresser, a nightstand, a desk with a chair next to the door. There was a window off to his left that he thought he should open, just in case.

Locked.

There was a pit in John's stomach. He couldn't say why. Everything about the room seemed normal. He pulled out his cell phone to check the time.

3:33 AM.

It couldn't have only been 30 minutes since he woke up… walking through that hallway alone felt like it had taken at least fifteen. He finally had to admit it to himself; the place frightened him. He peered out the window to see that damned blue truck. He wouldn't have been in this freaky house if it weren't for his cheapskate boss cutting corners.

As he deliberated on how to leave, he heard a loud creak behind him. He whipped around right in time to see the bed he would be sleeping on fall through a trap door in the floor.

"Oh, to hell with this!" John sprinted to the door and wrenched it open, only to come face to face with the woman, who looked shocked to see him standing there. That surprise quickly morphed into rage as the woman's eyes flooded black. She pointed her bony finger at him.

"I WILL NOT LET YOU LEAVE THIS TIME, JOHN."

John slammed the door shut. The woman began to scream and pound on the door. He cursed at himself; he should have stayed in that stupid, rundown truck. As he pushed his hip into the door, he felt something hard digging into his thigh from his pocket.

The wrench.

His heart jumped with hope as he looked around the room. He reached for the chair and shoved it underneath the door handle. It wasn't much, and the woman was impossibly strong, but it would buy him enough time to carry out his plan.

The woman kicked through the door, splintering the frame and the chair like toothpicks. Her eyes were sunken black holes and her hands were dry and leathery, with long nails sharp as knives. She wore an old white wedding dress, rotted and torn, her breath strained and ragged. When she scanned the room for John, he had already escaped through the broken window.

As for John, he ran to the truck, which now seemed like a beacon of safety, only once turning around briefly to catch a glimpse of the ghastly woman in the window.

Once he was in the driver's seat again, he locked all the doors and turned to look in the direction of the inn.

It was gone.

He stared at the place where the building had stood mere seconds ago. And he stayed like that. Staring. Never moving, but gripping the wrench a little tighter. He wasn't sure when he fell asleep, but he woke up startled by a tap on his window.

"Hey, buddy, rough night?"

A portly man, roughly 50 years of age, stood at the driver's side window in all his overalled glory. It was the mechanic. John could have cried.

After he deemed the truck "too toasted to fix on the roadside," he offered to tow it to his shop and loan John a car that wasn't a bucket of bolts. After figuring out the logistics of returning the rental, John agreed, and they set out on the journey back.

As the mechanic navigated the highways with ease, John thought about everything he had experienced during the night. He realized he must have been dreaming, although the vividness of it all left him with gnawing uncertainty.

"*It's not real,*" he whispered to himself.

"What's not real?" replied the mechanic.

John burned with embarrassment and quickly explained that he'd had a terrible dream the night before. He described, at the nosy mechanic's request, everything he had gone through the night before, saying how real it felt and how scared he had been. After he had gotten it all off his chest, he had felt better, but a bit guilty at his oversharing.

"You've been reading too many ghost stories, kid," the scraggly man laughed. "No, they're not really my thing," John chuckled back.

"Really? Because what you described to me sounds exactly like the story of Lavinia Fisher. She's pretty famous around these parts! I'd be surprised if you've never heard of her."

John must have looked clueless, because he continued.

"She was America's First Female Serial Killer! We have a lot of ghost tours 'round these parts that love to talk about her. She apparently killed dozens of travelers by luring them in and drugging their meals. When they passed out in their beds, she and her husband would pull a lever, and a trap door underneath the sleeping men would drop them into the basement. Her husband would be waiting there to chop them up while Lavinia stole their belongings."

"How did she get caught?" John was in awe of this near replica of his dream.

"Oh well, that's my favorite part, now. A man stopped by and didn't trust her food and drink. She musta gotten cocky or something because he was mighty suspicious of her. When he went to sleep, he decided to sleep in a chair by the door, in case something happened. Then, later in the night, he was woken up by the bed dropping out from the floor, just like in your dream!"

John was pale.

"He opened the door and saw Miss Lavinia there, getting ready to rifle through his stuff, and she screamed for her husband to come up from the basement. Lucky for the traveler, he was a quick one, and he escaped and ran right to the police. Well, they hung Lavinia and her husband for their crimes.

"She tried so hard to save her own skin. Back then, they wouldn't hang you if you were a married woman, so she showed up to her own execution in her wedding dress! Can you believe the nerve? The cops hung her husband first, which solved that problem—she was no longer married. When they asked her if she had any last words, she said, '*If you have a message you want to send to hell, give it to me; I'll carry it.*' Spoken like a true sinner if you ask me."

"What was the name of the man who got away?" John felt the need to ask, although he felt as though he already knew what the answer would be.

"You know, it's funny," the mechanic said thoughtfully. "I'm pretty sure his name was John."

Subscribe For More!

Jessica Burgess

～～✦～～

I was your typical teenager, always with a phone glued to my face, countless hours spent lost in a rabbit hole of God knows what. I'd roll my eyes anytime my dad made those *'back in my day remarks.'* The ones about the good ol' days. 'We *didn't have cell phones and computers, back in my day we communicated like everyone should—face to face, having real conversations. We wrote letters and took pictures with a camera and had to wait two weeks to get the film developed. Meeting up with your friends on a Friday night and hanging out was never 'virtual'.* More eye rolls in three...two...one. Blah, blah, blah, the usual dad spiel. He would always end with: *Tills, one day you will get it, and you will say, dad was right.*

* * * * *

It was my junior year of high school. I was the loner kid, a self-proclaimed nerd. Not the loner nerd that gets picked on by the cool kids. I just liked to keep to myself. I wasn't what one would call a social butterfly. I mean, I had friends. They always sat with me at lunch, and we would have half-assed conversations about who was dating who, who was mad at who—average high school gossip. I never cared about any of that. I was glad when I could escape the never-ending banter.

We had a period after lunch that gave us the option to do a study hall class or spend that time in the library. Most of my friends went to study hall; I always made my way to the library. Our school was an older building with additions built on every few years. The library was in the oldest area and I loved it there. The smell of old books, the solitude—it was my happy place.

From a young age, I always had a love for reading and writing. My imagination was intense. I could find a story in anything. I had a taste for the macabre, the dark and twisted. I wanted to transform my love for such gruesome material into horror stories.

My seventeenth birthday arrived with a fresh blanket of snow. We were just about at the ten-inch mark that day; 2017 was cutting us no slack, and winter had not even officially begun. That crashed my plans of having the few friends I had over for my birthday. I wasn't sad about it; the gift of not having to endure the gossip at a slumber party was a relief. Mom cooked my favorite meal of lasagna, and then she made brownies for dessert. Once we had eaten and the dishes were cleared away, I asked if I could be excused to go to my room. I'd gotten a new R.L. Stine book I was dying to dive into.

I made my way upstairs to my bedroom. Opening the door, I saw a box wrapped in black paper with a big red bow sitting on my bed. Mom had told me that she and my dad would probably not be able to get me much for my birthday. Teary-eyed, I told her I understood. Money was tight. Mom had gotten laid off from her job, and Dad was barely keeping us afloat. I turned to find my parents and ask about the gift. To my surprise, they were already at my door, grins plastered to their faces.

"Well kiddo, open it already!" My dad was way too excited over this.

I tore into the gift. "Oh my fucking God! A laptop!" I said as I jumped off the bed.

"Tillie, watch your mouth! Geeze. Do you like it?" Mom asked as I hugged her. "Of course, I freaking love it! What's the catch?" I was suspicious.

"No catch, Tills. Me and your mom are very proud of how well you've been doing in school. We know you want to be a writer. We figured this could be something to help you start working on that dream."

I was one of the few kids my age that didn't have a computer of their own. It took a lot of persuasion on my part just to talk my parents into letting me have a cell phone.

I think I saw a tear in my dad's eye that day, but of course, in true Mom fashion, she abruptly ruined the moment.

"There are a few rules. You have to keep your grades up, and all your homework is to be done before you get on this thing. And please use your common sense about what is and isn't acceptable. The internet is a dangerous place. So many creepers out there. Got it? And if you don't like it…"

I guess my face was doing the talking for me. "Yes, Mom, I got it. I'm not ten.

I've had a cell phone for almost two years and haven't talked to any *creepers.*"

My dad broke the tension, "Happy birthday, kiddo. Enjoy your present and don't stay up too late." I hugged and thanked him and Mom.

Late that night I was still awake getting my new laptop set up, customizing and arranging everything on my home screen. I had a terrible case of OCD. Most kids might have been eagerly adding Facebook, Instagram, Twitter—all that social media crap. Me being the not-so-social type, I was more interested in researching ideas that would help me start my first story. Figuring out how I could even begin to get someone to notice me once it was finished.

I came upon a website that intrigued me: The Darkest Corner. The page was formatted to make it look like a dimly lit room. As I stared into what seemed like a never-ending abyss, something caught my eye. In the bottom right corner, a shadow appeared. It seemed to pulsate. Its red eyes burned brightly. I could've sworn I heard laughter. I should have just left it alone, but my curiosity got the best of me.

The only text on the page read 'SUBSCRIBE FOR MORE!' Under that was a small box to enter your email address. I thought, *what could it hurt for me to create an email account? People use email for a variety of things and if I want to be a writer, I surely need one. How else will publishers contact me?* I was pretty confident Mom wouldn't be mad if I did. If she found it, she would be able to see I was using it responsibly. I wouldn't be sharing anything personal, no harm done.

I created my email address and made my way back to The Darkest Corner website. This time when I looked over the page, the shadow was no longer in the bottom right corner. It had moved to the top left corner of the screen, still pulsating. The red eyes were more alive, with a seeming hunger deep inside them. *Weird. But a cool effect.* I thought *this must be normal, just something to spook people and keep the horror-loving fans coming back.* Something else that caught my eye was the shadow's smile. The first time I was here, I didn't recall seeing it. I'm sure I would've remembered it. It was sinister. A shiver ran down my spine as I looked at the two rows of tiny razor-sharp teeth grinning back at me. *Maybe I shouldn't do this,* I thought... *I want to be a horror writer for fucks sake. If I'm this scared to go through a website, I won't be able to write my own horror stories.* I entered my email address, hovering over the subscribe button for a few seconds. The shadow figure quivered more than ever. *Gross, that fucker is weird! Maybe it's a creeper.* I laughed as I remembered my mom's words of warning.

I held my breath and clicked the button. Nothing happened. It took me to a black screen. No words, no creepy ass shadow looking like it was about to orgasm, just darkness. *This is some bullshit, all worked up for nothing. I probably just got sucked into some spam scam and will have all kinds of stuff sent to my new email. Mom will freak. I better just go delete that email account and save myself the trouble.* I was getting ready to close out the screen when a sudden movement caught my attention. The shadow figure was back. This time it took up almost the entire screen. *What the actual fuck?* The crimson eyes, glowing like hot coals, leered at me. I couldn't look away.

Hours went by. Shortly after midnight, my laptop shut down, knocking me out of my stupor. *What in the hell?* Feeling confused and exhausted, I brushed my teeth, changed into my pj's, and climbed into bed. Watching the snow peacefully fall from the sky, I drifted off to sleep.

Nightmare after nightmare haunted me. I woke to the creaking of tree branches outside. The howling wind beat them against my window. The snow had stopped and the light from a full moon was illuminating the space. From the corner of my room, I heard my name being whispered. "Tillie, Tillie, TILLIE!" A floorboard creaked; I slowly sat up in bed.

"Hello?" Dead silence. A loud ping from my laptop cut my concentration. *No way! I'd shut it down before I went to bed.* The laptop had moved. I'd left it on my desk and it was now sitting on my nightstand.

I wanted to stay within the safety of my bed and hide there until daylight. An unseen force pulled me towards the laptop. I picked it up from the nightstand and opened it. The screen was on The Darkest Corner webpage. The shadow figure peered at me, its maniacal grin taunting me. I couldn't help but look over to the corner of my room where I'd heard the voice calling my name just moments ago. *I'm losing it, those nightmares have got me spooked, my crazy imagination is not helping me.* There was a notification box down in the right corner of the screen, it read: *NEW MESSAGE*. I clicked on it. Bringing up my email, I saw that it was a message from The Darkest Corner.

"*Dearest Tillie,*

Thank you for subscribing to The Darkest Corner. What a wise choice you have made. We hear you want to become a writer. A horror writer at that, even better. You came to the right place. Here we like to make your dreams a reality, your stories will come to life. You have some great ideas in that head of yours. We know everything about you. You would fit in perfectly with us. An offer such as the one we are about to give you, not many receive. This is just for a select few. The best of the best. To be accepted is very simple. A task that should come easy to you. This will be your first chance to be a writer, Tillie. We want you to write a story. Not just any story. A scary story. Something that you have thought a lot about over the last few years. Go into the darkest corners of your mind, bring those thoughts to light. Prove to our readers that you should be a part of The Darkest Corner. Get to work Tillie. We will be watching you."

-TDC

Faint laughter came from the corner of my room. Barely audible, but it carried a malicious tone. Movement from my laptop screen drew my eye. I looked down and there staring back at me, was the creepy, red-eyed, grinning shadow figure. It once again held my stare for what seemed like an eternity. The screen went black, the laughter stopped, it was unnaturally quiet in the room. The only noise was my uneven breathing. After a few moments, I heard the TV downstairs and felt a small comfort in that.

I did not go back to sleep that night. There was no way I could. To say I was scared shitless was an understatement. At the same time, there was a certain inexplicable calmness within me. I curled up in my comfy old reading chair. Wrapped up in my flannel blanket, staring into the dark snowy landscape of the cold winter night. As terrified as I was, I couldn't help but think this might be a chance that I shouldn't pass up. *The Darkest Corner believes in me. If they didn't see the potential I had, they surely wouldn't be giving me a chance. Could this be what helps start my writing career and only at seventeen?* I mean, I did find it odd that they knew so much about me. Even thinking and knowing that this wasn't right and I should have told my parents what was going on, I didn't. Something held me back from saying anything. I made up my mind that I wasn't going to let anyone know about that website, the email, or the story I planned to write. I would prove to The Darkest Corner that I was worthy. They would see it and help me show the rest of the world.

* * * * *

The following week, school had been shut down. We had gotten more snow and it seemed the world halted in our little town. I wrote from the time I got up until my mind was so exhausted that I'd fall asleep at my desk. I would get up, take a shower, grab some food then get back at it. This must be how authors whom I took inspiration from pumped out such great stories. Their sole focus is their writing. Nothing to distract them or get in the way. I ignored calls from my friends, gave excuses to my parents as to why I couldn't sit and eat dinner with them. I wanted to be alone, I *needed* to be alone. My parents didn't understand. This was my calling and nothing was going to stand in my way.

Thursday of that week, I was holed up in my room, feverishly working on my story when a knock came on my bedroom door.

"Tillie, honey are you awake?" My mom's voice was laced with concern.
"Yes, Mom. I am awake. I'm busy writing. What do you want?"
"Your father and I would like to speak to you, please come downstairs."
"Now is not a good time. I don't want to talk." I snapped.

"Tillie!" My doorknob rattled. "I don't care if this is not a good time for *you*! I said we want to talk to you *now*. You have five minutes to come downstairs or we are taking that stupid laptop away from you! Do you hear me?"

"Yes Mother, I hear you! How could I not, you're standing outside my door acting like a complete fool! I'm trying to do something here and you are fucking it up!" I roared.

"A fool, excuse me? Please tell me that is not what I heard come out of your mouth young lady! Unlock this damn door, right now!"

"NO! I won't unlock the door and yes, I said you are acting like a fool! I am a writer at work here!"

"Tillie Ann! I am going to get your dad! Grant, GRANT! Get up here NOW!" I could hear my dad's heavy footsteps as he raced up the stairs.

"What the hell is going on up here?" The anger in his tone was unmistakable.

"Ask your daughter—who refused to unlock her door and called me a fool. A fool!"

"Tills, come on, open the door, now." The doorknob rattled again.

"Jesus fucking Christ! What is wrong with you people? Let me be!" Rage coursed through my body.

"That's it, I'm getting the key! You are not going to disrespect me and your mom like this, Tillie!" I could hear Dad walk back downstairs.

I heard familiar laughter, then my email pinged. A message from *The Darkest Corner*:

"*Tillie,*

The Darkest Corner is the only family you need."

-TDC

My bedroom door burst open, both my parents were red-faced; Mom's was tear-streaked.

"What the hell is wrong with you, Tillie?" My dad screamed, out of breath.

"Nothing! Why are you guys yelling at me? I am an author at work! You don't get to interrupt me with your pointless bullshit!"

Mom laughed. "You have got to be kidding me? You are not an author, you are seventeen!"

"Are you making fun of me, Mother?

"Tills, please. Don't do this. Don't get your mom even more worked up."

"Ok! I'm sorry. I was really into this scene I'm writing. I just didn't want to be bothered. I have been cooped up in this house. I guess I just let it get the best of me. Mom, I am sorry, I didn't mean what I said."

Perfect, that should shut them up.

Dad sighed. "Tillie, that's no excuse for the way you just acted. Look at your mom, she's a wreck. You're seventeen, you know better. Maybe we should all just get some rest and talk in the morning. A family breakfast. I'll make my famous pancakes and we can talk all this out."

"Grant, you can't be serious. This needs to be dealt with now! She blatantly disrespected both of us, and her reasoning was because she was writing a *SCENE!* A scene, Grant!"

"Who is making a scene now, Maria? From the looks of it, she gets this from you! If you all want to duke it out, go for it. I am going to grab some beers and head down to the man cave. I'm not listening to this." Dad turned to leave.

"Fuck you, Grant! You always take Tillie's side, even when you know she's wrong!" Mom sobbed. She was defeated and she knew it.

The basement door slammed.

"I am so disappointed in you Tillie. Your dad finds this behavior excusable and without consequence. I, however, don't."

"I don't care what you think." I shot back at her.

"Give me the laptop Tillie." She held her hand out.

Another creepy laugh, this time from me. "No, Mom. That's not going to happen."

"This is your last chance. Hand over the laptop to me, *now*."

"This is *your* last chance. Get out of my room!" I made my way back to my desk. Before I knew what happened, Mom came around my bed and grabbed the laptop off of my desk. "You can have this stupid thing back once you think about your actions tonight and apologize."

She was headed out the bedroom door when I heard the voice, "Tillie, she is going to ruin your chance to be with us."

I jumped up and over my bed, knocking down the bedside table. "No! You are not going to ruin this for me! I am not going to let you!"

Mom was running out my bedroom door when I caught up to her. I grabbed her by her ponytail.

"Tillie! What the-"

Those were the last words she ever said. I took advantage of her shock. I snatched the laptop out of her hands. She stumbled forward. I rushed towards her and shoved her. A silent scream painted on her face as she tumbled down the wooden stairs. Her body made a soft thud as she landed at the bottom. Her legs and neck bent at an inhuman angle.

"Look, Mom! You don't have to be disappointed anymore!" I exclaimed as I stepped over her.

I went into the kitchen to grab a couple of slices of pizza and a Dr. Pepper. I had to get back to my writing. I was so close to finishing my work. One less distraction now. I made my way past my mother's corpse and back to my room. On my way up, I thought about how it must have hurt as her head banged off each step, and I loved it.

Back in my room, I sat down at my desk to pick back up where I was so rudely interrupted. About an hour later, I heard the basement door open and Dad stumbling around. *He must be good and drunk. How can I kill him? Maybe he'll spare me the mess and drop dead once he sees Mom laying at the bottom of the steps.*

"Maria! Oh God, MARIA, MARIA! Baby, what happened, talk to me love, please! Tillie, call 911, your mother has had a terrible accident. Hurry! No, no, no, please no. Tillie, call them!"

Slowly making my way out of my room, I stopped and peered over the banister. I stared down at my dad. "I'm not calling anyone, Dad. She got what was coming to her. I was a disappointment to her. Now, she doesn't have to worry about that anymore. She's DEAD."

I could see the horror in his eyes. "Tills please, please tell me this was an accident and you had nothing to do with it. I know you're in shock baby, but please. You couldn't have done this."

Letting out a frustrated sigh, "Dad, yes, I killed Mom. I pushed her down the steps. I watched her die, then went and grabbed some pizza and a soda and came back to my room to write. Now, *you* are here distracting me. I always liked you better than her, but you just won't leave me alone. You're going to have to die too, Dad."

"Tills, baby. It's ok, I'm here. You're talking crazy. Mom had a fall and you saw it. This is shock, just shock. We'll get you help, honey. Tills, please."

"Shut up! Listen to me, I killed mom!" "No, God no, no no!" Dad wailed.

"There is only one way you can help me, Dad. Let me kill you. If you don't die, then my story is going to flop. And we can't have that."

"Story? Tillie, you aren't making any sense. I'm going to make a couple of calls.

Just go back to your room, ok?"

I started down the stairs. "Oh Daddy, you poor thing. You just aren't listening to me. I guess I'm just going to have to show you."

"What is that in your hand?"

"Ah, this? I forgot to mention, when I was getting my pizza after Mommy Dearest took her nasty fall, I grabbed this butcher knife from the kitchen."

Dad began to sob. "Tillie, please, please. Stop."

He must have been frozen in fear. He hadn't moved away from Mom's dead body. I stood directly over him, he looked up at me, eyes pleading.

"I love you Tills, you don't have to do this."

"Yes, I do Daddy. If I don't, they won't accept my story." In one fluid motion, I slashed his throat.

I watched the life slowly drain from his eyes. Wet, gurgling sounds came from his wound. Blood bubbled up and pooled around him and Mom.

"Gross." I turned and walked back upstairs to my room. A new message was waiting.

"*Dearest Tillie,*

Marvelous! What an amazing story! What amazing talent for such a young writer. Your story has been accepted! All we need is for you to sign the contract that is attached and it will be a done deal! We hope that you will take us up on our offer."

-TDC

"Yes, I did it! Mom, Dad! I-oh wait, you're dead!"

I wasted no time in signing the contract with The Darkest Corner. Happy with the news I just received, I knew there was work that needed to be done. First, that mess at the bottom of the stairs had to be cleaned up. I was getting ready to head back down when the lights went out. A strong burst of wind rattled the side of the house. The lights flickered off then back on. Standing before me was the red-eyed, quivering shadow figure with its wicked grin.

"Hello, Tillie. Welcome to The Darkest Corner. We are thrilled to have you!"

The Trial of Jehenne de Brigue
C.C. Winchester

"I would rather have a lion or a dragon loose in my house than a woman... Feeble in mind and body, it is not surprising women so often become witches... A woman is carnal lust personified... if a woman cannot get a man, she will consort with the Devil himself."
- From Malleus Maleficarum

"Jehenne de Brigue, you stand before this court accused of witchcraft. How do you plead?"

Tapestries decorated the stone walls of the large, cold room. A group of men sat up high against one wall, garbed in the colorful robes of religious leaders. A man in a plain black robe sat at the center of a small stone desk below them. Two men sat elevated on either side of him, dressed in similar dark robes, with two high arched windows behind them. The sunlight shone through the bars in these windows.

The man at the center of the bench stood and stepped from behind it. He approached the woman who stood before them, her hands bound by rope. The man spoke to her.

"What say you, madam?"

"I have done nothing, sir," Jehenne answered. Her long, black hair was disheveled, her face streaked with filth after spending weeks in her cell.

Fourteenth-century France was a time of great persecution. The Inquisition was well underway. Pope Gregory IX had set up the first Papal

Inquisition in 1231. Gregory dispatched zealous, often fanatical inquisitors to gather evidence of witchcraft and sorcery. However, the pope never questioned the evidence brought forth from the often-sadistic inquisitors.

In the beginning, the Inquisition mainly targeted strange-looking or homely older women, people disfigured by disease or born with genetic defects. This made it easy to convince the general populace that the "ugly" were aligned with Satan.

In 1252, Pope Innocent IV made the act of torture official papal policy. Husbands suspected wives of being secret witches, even believing their children were the spawn of Satan. Friends, relatives, neighbors, and even passersby on the street scrutinized each other for eccentricities or strange behavior. This atmosphere of hysteria provided Hell and its demon spawn the opportunity to recruit human victims to their cause.

By the time of Jehenne's trial in 1390, the Roman Catholic Church was in the midst of the Great Schism. Pope Boniface IX held the official title in Rome, yet in Avignon, France resided a rival, Clement VII the anti-pope. Neither man seemed involved in the Inquisition, but it had taken on a life of its own.

"You claim you've done nothing? We have testimony from witnesses that say otherwise."

Jehenne stood motionless as the inquisitor continued. "How do you sustain yourself?"

"I make medicines from herbs and roots. I grow them in my garden and sell them."

"And the Evil One taught you this skill?" The inquisitor stepped closer to Jehenne.

"No, sir. I know nothing of the Evil One. I only love my lord, God."

"Did you use sorcery to cure Jehan de Ruilly of a spell that was placed on him by his lover, Gilette, as he claims?"

"I did not, sir. I merely provided him with herbs to help soothe his ailment." "And did the Evil One teach you how to do that?"

"I know not of which you speak. I love God."

"And when you fornicated with the Evil One, where did you do so, and how was the act performed?"

Jehenne had not responded to the last question. The inquisitor continued. "Bring forth he who accuses Jehenne de Brigue of the crime of witchcraft."

A man stepped forward, taking his place in front of Jehenne. It was customary in these trials for the accuser to face the accused while giving testimony. The sniveling little man prepared to speak. He was short, large of girth, and hairy. Long, black hairs protruded from his ears and nose. It didn't take much to be a ladies' man in fourteenth-century France, it seemed.

The inquisitor stood beside the accuser, and they both faced Jehenne. "Do you know this man?"

"I do."

The inquisitor now addressed the fat, little man. "Jehan de Ruilly, you may now testify before the accused. Repeat what you told the tribunal in your previous testimony."

"I was at death's door with an unknown affliction. There was no other explanation but witchcraft for my symptoms. My wife suggested we send for Jehenne de Brigue as she is skilled in handling such matters. The doctor had given up on my recovery. I had no choice but to follow my wife's instruction or die and leave her a widow.

That very day my wife fetched Miss de Brigue to our house. Miss de Brigue commenced to tell me that I was under a curse, and she believed it was my lover, Gilette, who had cast it. In my desperate state, I took her at her word. She helped me fashion a wax doll of Gilette and then suckle a pair of toads. I made a miraculous recovery, so I thanked Miss de Brigue with all my heart and paid her well.

Later I found Gilette had become gravely ill. Despite what I thought she had done to me, I did not wish her dead, as she is the mother of two of my children. She recovered, and I believe it was God's will as I finally learned the truth about everything that transpired. It was not Gilette who had cursed me, but Jehenne de Brigue herself.

It was all a ruse so Miss de Brigue could exact her revenge on Gilette for some imagined slight against her.

At great risk, I visited Jehenne de Brigue to confront her. She gleefully admitted everything and even told me she had a demon helping her—one who had taught her how to cast spells and work cures. It was after this encounter that I did my godly duty and reported her to the authorities."

The inquisitor faced the accused woman. "Jehenne de Brigue, what say you to these charges? Does Jehan de Ruilly speak the truth?"

"I know not of what he speaks."

"So, you deny the truth of his testimony?"

"I know nothing of witchcraft, demons, spells, and the like."

"Think carefully, girl. A full confession and coming forth with the names of all who are guilty would ease your punishment."

Jehenne continued to remain cold and unemotional as she answered, "I am innocent."

"The court here decrees that the prisoner, Jehenne de Brigue, who has previously denied all charges, will now be re-examined in praesentia carnificis, and with torture, through the power of the legal decision obtained."

* * * * *

The dungeon reeked of the residue of those who had died by the torture devices spread around the room. Jehenne was lying naked on her back, hands and feet extended at either end of her body, tightly bound. She was helpless and at the mercy of these madmen.

The inquisitor stood near the side of the device, known as the rack, and once again addressed Jehenne. "Under threat of torture, do you still deny the charges brought against you, Jehenne de Brigue?"

Jehenne was angry now and answered, "By the sacrament, what am I supposed to say? I have nothing to do with the Devil!"

The inquisitor nodded toward the executioner. It was the slightest of nods, but it was obvious they had repeated this performance many times. As the executioner turned the rollers, there was a sickening grinding sound as the chains tightened. Jehenne released a blood-curdling scream of pure agony. The executioner continued, oblivious to the woman's torment.

As Jehenne screamed, there arrived a new presence in the room. Standing next to her was Haus, a powerful demon in the hierarchy of Hell. Capable of taking many forms, he was now a horned figure complete with bat-like wings and a tail. Haus leaned down and whispered something to Jehenne. It was apparent neither the inquisitor nor the executioner could see him. The demon stood, smiling, and then vanished. Jehenne shouted, "I confess! I admit everything!"

With the slightest movement of his hand, the inquisitor ordered the executioner to stop the torture. Jehenne's chest heaved as she fought to catch her breath.

"Are you prepared to provide your entire testimony, Jehenne de Brigue?" asked the inquisitor.

"Yes, sir." "Please begin."

"Whilst it is true Jehan de Ruilly was dying because of a curse cast upon him, it is not true as to who did the casting. His wife, Macette de Ruilly, is the one who cursed him. She and I learned witchcraft together with the help of the demon Haussibut. We both learned how to cast spells and work cures by summoning this demon.

Macette cursed her husband because she was jealous of the time he was spending with Gilette. As Macette learned how to perform various magics, she became haughty and difficult to live with. Jehan had no idea why she had changed. He had no knowledge of her practice of sorcery. Macette had never provided her husband with children, so he assumed her unhappiness was because of her barren state. Jehan began to spend more time with Gilette and the two children he had fathered with her. This drove Macette into a frenzy. She cursed Jehan out of jealousy and anger, but when it became apparent that he might die, she realized she still loved him. She asked me to remove the curse from him and transfer it to Gilette. She planned to eliminate Gilette and use magic to make herself fertile so Jehan would want to be with her again.

I was not happy about this plan. I never wanted to cause anyone's death. But she was my sister in witchcraft. Bound by the honor among witches, I could not deny her request. I was the more powerful between us and the only one capable of performing such magic.

Jehan was in no state to question my actions since he was at death's door. It was easy to convince him Gilette was the culprit. So when I had him fashion a wax doll of Gilette before suckling the two toads, he merely thought the doll was made in the image of his mistress who had cursed him. In reality, I was simply carrying out the wishes of my sister Macette to transfer the curse to her rival."

* * * * *

Chatelet-Les Halles (the center of Paris):
Two women were bound to large stakes in the center of a large mound of wood. The Parisians mingled about talking among themselves. For the peasants of Paris, this was their only form of entertainment, it seemed. Watching people burned alive was a reason to celebrate. Jehenne appeared calm, remaining silent as if she accepted her fate, the other woman crying, insisting on her innocence between sobs.

"Stop crying," Jehenne cooed, smiling at the hysterical woman.

Haus then appeared between them just as the executioner began lighting the pyre. Macette screamed, Haus seeming to ignore her.

"But my lord, my love, why do you only take her? Why have you forsaken me?"

"She has proved her loyalty to me." "But she betrayed us by confessing!"

"No, you set the wheels in motion by betraying Jehenne to your husband! You sealed your fate!" And with that, Haus vanished, taking Jehenne with him as the pyre burned.

SEEDS
Marie McWilliams

Plant a seed and something grows. That's what my grandfather always taught me. Hours spent, trowel in hand, rain or sun. Muddy boots and sun-browned skin. We would finish, the scent of moss lingering on our skin, dirt ever-present beneath our nails, and reap our rewards. Home-cooked meals with homegrown vegetables. He even grew his own hops, an old copper water tank converted into a still hidden at the back of the shed. Keep hush, don't tell Grandma. I'll never forget that first taste of beer, musty but sweet, the amber colour of honey.

Everything changed when he died. Life darkened, ever in shadow, worsened when Grandma started to forget things, like the oven, the bath, me. Bounced from care home to foster family, concrete jungles, nothing green, nothing growing.

I got into trouble more and more, began moving with the 'wrong crowd.' That's what the judge called them. He used phrases like 'corrupted' and 'bad influence' to describe my rapid descent into juvenile delinquency. I was a sapling infected by the rot of an older tree. Infected with apathy. He declared I must be uprooted and relocated or risk decay. And so, I was sent to Pine Wood House.

Pine Wood was just another home under a different guise, wayward children sent to its remote location to learn discipline and essential life skills, at least, that's what the brochure said. It was run down and dingy and the staff showed all the enthusiasm of funeral directors but I didn't care. I had green again.

The home was named after the dense pine forest that skirted the edges of its border marked conveniently for all with a wire fence. It was so thick it felt like travelling in time when you passed beneath the canopy, an instant transportation to nightfall.

We weren't supposed to go into the forest. The staff said it was dangerous, full of wild Bobcats and other predators just itching to feast on a thirteen-year-old boy easily lost in the darkness. But there were rumours, stories being passed amongst the home's residents. Tales of children going missing, of ghostly voices, and a Native burial ground. Of a staff member driven mad by the woods, eventually hanging herself from one of the branches reaching over that wire fence, grasping at the children beyond.

Of course, I didn't listen. The call to be amongst nature was too strong. I was drawn to the trees. They pulled me in with the whispering of their branches and I gladly heeded their call. I walked the length of the fence, back and forth, staring into the shadows, head dizzy with the scent of pine needles and rotting leaves. It took four days to find it, a way out, an ugly gash torn through the metal border between my world and the woods. It was just big enough for a boy to slip through, and slip through it I did.

Things become hazy after that. I remember the feel of the dry pine needles underfoot, the sound of branches breaking as I walked ahead not knowing where I was going. But there was another sound there, quiet at first but growing louder the farther I wandered. A humming sound that vibrated in my chest, a whisper barely discernable to the ear but all around me as if the trees themselves were calling me, and then, nothing.

When I came to, I was back within the grounds of Pine Wood House, my clothes filthy and soaked with sweat. I had a cut on my arm that I could not recall getting, the blood long since having congealed, a newly formed scab sitting raised on the surface. It was night now, the sky a dark grey, the stars and moon hidden behind a thick wall of cloud. I had been gone eight hours and I had no memory of what had happened, but I remembered the sense of calm I'd felt in the woods.

The staff was furious. They had been frantically searching for me. The local Sheriff had been called and a search party was gathering when I wandered back inside. I was like a sleepwalker just awoken from a long, deep sleep, unaware of the trouble I had caused. There was yelling, a promise of punishment, and so many questions about where I had been, questions that remained unanswered for both them and me.

The second time it happened, I was supposed to be cleaning the toilets, penance for my previous exploration. I was on my knees, brush in hand, when I felt it again— that low humming emanating from the woods outside, the sweet beckoning call of a siren. I wasn't afraid. Perhaps I should have been after what happened before, but for some reason, I could not explain, I knew the forest meant me no harm. It sensed something in me, a special connection with nature that singled me out from the others. But more than that, I felt a sense of calm and contentment beneath those trees that I had not felt since my grandad died. It felt like I was finally home.

I recall the cool shade of the thick canopy, the feel of bark under my outstretched hand, the tickle of leaves on my cheek as I wandered deeper into the woods than before. But once again, I remembered little else other than the peace I'd felt as I rested among the trees. When I awoke, I was on the edge of the woods over four miles from Pine Wood House. My feet were sore and swollen and my head was spinning. It had been more than twelve hours since I abandoned my cleaning duties. This time, however, I had come out bearing a gift from the forest—a small oval locket, once silver, now tarnished with grime and mud. It had an initial on it, the letter C in a perfect cursive swirl.

It took over an hour before I saw torchlights in the distance and met with the mixture of staff and locals seeking me among the trees. I noticed they didn't wander far from the road, all remaining visible from the concrete strip that tore through the wilderness. They were afraid... I could feel it. There was an ambulance, an itchy foil blanket draped around my shoulders, and a stern Sherriff's Deputy pointing at me as he spoke in harsh, angry tones. I didn't listen. Nothing he said mattered. It was only when I saw his eyes widen as they fell upon the locket I held, a look of pain and fear washing over his face, that I began to pay attention to his words. Mike, his name badge said.

He had so many questions. They all did. Where did I find it? What else did I see? Where had I wandered to? But once again, no answers came from my lips. I could only tell them what I knew, and that was very little. I finally asked them why they were so interested in the locket. I was tired and hungry and sick of their questions, but mostly I was mad. Mad they had taken my gift from me and placed it carefully inside a plastic bag. It was mine, I said, why did they want it? The Deputy got down on his haunches to meet my eye. Grown-ups I've noticed always do this when they want you to take what they are saying very seriously.

He told me a story about two children. One was a kid like me, sent to Pine Wood House to learn some discipline. His name was Michael. The other, Clara, was a local girl whose mother worked at the home and brought Clara to work often because she couldn't afford a sitter. Clara and Michael became best friends. They played together and told each other secrets. Everything was fine... until one day it wasn't.

They decided to play a game. They would pretend to be explorers and venture into the forbidden woods to find adventure. After all, just like the staff room, any place marked as off-limits by the grown-ups must possess some amazing trait they wished to hoard for themselves and hide from the children. The two had only been walking a few minutes. They couldn't have travelled far, and yet they found themselves hopelessly lost, their home suddenly gone, replaced only with more trees. They grew scared and yelled for help, but none came. And then something terrible happened.

Two children had entered the forest, but only one, the boy, emerged many hours later, dirty and bloody and clearly in shock. He could not tell the grown-ups what had happened to Clara, just that something in the forest had taken her. He remembered blood and screaming but nothing more. Even when Clara's mother struck the young boy hard across the face, screaming questions, blaming him for her daughter's disappearance, Michael could provide no clarity. Clara was simply gone, swallowed by the woods.

There had been many versions of how Clara met her untimely death told in torchlight, under blankets, and beside campfires but no one ever truly knew. An official report had blamed a wildcat but the boy was never convinced and neither was Clara's mother. Distraught at her daughter's death, she hung herself on the edge of the forest that had taken her previous baby, perhaps hoping to find answers in death.

It took me a moment to understand the link between this tale and my own excursions into the woods. Then it dawned on me, *C for Clara*. The locket had belonged to her. I tried hard to remember where I had found it, what else I had seen, but there was just black, a vast hole where my memories should be. The adults questioned me some more before giving up again. I could see some of them thought I was lying, frustrated angry heads shaking disappointedly, but the Deputy believed me, I could tell.

What happened to the boy? I asked. Had he had a tragic end too? The Deputy looked at me then, tears in his eyes, and told me he had grown up determined to stop anything like Clara's disappearance from happening again. He became a police officer. Mike, his name badge said. Mike the Deputy.

I thought about the story a lot after that. Days passed without the forest calling me back, and in that time I searched for the memories hidden somewhere in my mind, but they never came. Something had made me forget, or perhaps I had chosen to forget. Sometimes it's better that way—better than remembering.

Eventually, I had a dream. It was strange and dark, but not unsettling. I was walking through the woods when I noticed a hand in mine. It was a girl, a little younger than me, with auburn hair and freckles on her pale skin. Her dress was a pale blue and I noticed when light penetrated the thick canopy, it changed to a dirty brown. Her skin would suddenly look grey, her eyes lifeless and glassy, but just as quickly as the sun revealed this change it was gone again as we walked hand in hand deeper into the woods. She took me to a fallen tree, its knotted root base the size of Pine Wood House. Her locket hung from one of these roots, swinging slightly despite the lack of any breeze. Slowly the girl pointed to the ground beneath it, and I realised that unlike the dry earth surrounding us, protected from the rain by the thick canopy above, this patch was wet and muddy. I moved to it and touched the raw earth, my hand coming back red with blood. I knew without her saying anything that this was her grave. I also understood why she had brought me there. The woods were telling me what they needed me to do.

I snuck into the staff office and used the phone to call the Sheriff's Department. I wasn't surprised when Deputy Mike picked up, despite the late hour. I had known he was working; the woods had told me. I told him I had been having flashbacks about the forest and the locket. I knew where I had found them and I wanted to take him there. I said I only wanted him to come because I was scared of the staff at the home and the other officers, but that I had liked him. He would have to come alone. It was only a half-lie, after all, a dream is a kind of flashback, and I had liked Deputy Mike. After all, any friend of the forest is a friend of mine.

I wasn't surprised when he came. These circumstances, meeting a young boy alone in the middle of the night, weren't normal. But decades of grief and guilt were blinding Deputy Mike, driving him forwards into danger. He looked different when he arrived. He hadn't shaved, brown stubble dotted with grey covering his chin. His eyes were red and tired, like he had been crying, and he smelled sour, a haze of body odour and stale alcohol emanating from his stained uniform. I realised he hadn't really slept since the night I found the locket.

We never spoke; we just walked in silence, me leading the way. I knew where I was going, the pull so strong I could have found my way blindfolded. It guided me and I in turn guided Deputy Mike. Time passed, but not as it should. Everything seemed too slow. Time, normally a straight and sure line, was now blurring at the edges, bleeding out. I can't say how long it took to find the spot but it felt like forever and just a moment all at once.

I stopped abruptly at the upturned tree and simply pointed at the spot beneath it. He looked confused but moved towards it anyway, kneeling to search the patch of earth for clues. It only took a small amount of movement to unearth the bones, mottled brown with age. He held the small skull in his shaking hands, tears snaking down his cheeks. He asked me something then, what exactly I can never be sure. Maybe what happened or how, but the words were drowned out by the vibration of the trees which coursed through me like a heartbeat. They had given me instructions and I gladly followed them.

One blue, two, three, four. The Deputy was distracted, exposed. He hadn't seen me as a threat. I was just a boy, after all, and I was helping him. By the time I stopped hitting him, the rock I held was slick with blood, and the spot where Deputy Mike's skull had once been was now just viscera and red, wet earth. I felt no remorse, although I did momentarily lament the fact that his skull would not match that of his childhood companion's. Never mind, these things cannot be helped.

I worked diligently, digging and clawing at the ground with my bare hands. As I unearthed more of young Clara, the hole grew deeper. There were more bones further down, more skulls, more souls. It needed them you see— It needed blood and bone to reform itself. Death was needed to bring life. I finished, panting and exhausted, sweat running down my back, and admired my handiwork. It wasn't huge but it was deep enough to push in what remained of Deputy Mike and cover him with a layer of topsoil. I felt the vibration strengthen, the forest around me singing with rapturous energy, building to a terrifying crescendo.

By the time I emerged from the forest, almost thirty-two hours had passed. No one knew that Deputy Mike had entered with me; they thought he was drowning his sorrows at the bottom of a whiskey bottle somewhere, dealing badly with long-suppressed childhood trauma suddenly brought to the fore. There were new officers, new people to be mad at me, to lecture me about safety and responsibility. I didn't listen, of course. None of it mattered. Nothing matters now except my friend in the heart of the forest.

I sit now inside an ambulance, waiting. Waiting for him to emerge, waiting for him to rise from a pit of mud and bones and take his true form. Waiting for him to lay this pathetic town to waste. Plant a seed and something grows, that's what my Grandad always said. I just have to wait now. It's only a matter of time.

Soul Grinder
Cecilia Kennedy

A thick trickle of blood stretches along a dirt track at the Breaker County Fairgrounds. In the moonlight, it gleams and pools into rivulets, mixing with motor oil. The engine of the modified tractor, outfitted with hungry turbo chargers, echoes into the night. A victim, bound and screaming, writhes at the other end of the track. Mitch Talon readies himself for a full pull before the empty stands. He presses down on the gas, pulling the sled, weighted with thousands of pounds. The front wheels kick up into the air, and a plume of heavy black smoke pours from the engine. The writhing victim's body bursts into gristly bits on impact. The larger pieces are fed into the turbo chargers, the heart of the beast. Flesh and bone break down into the essence of the victim's soul, which is what the Soul Grinder craves. It howls with satisfaction. The weighted sled is unhooked from the tractor and remains on the other side of the track, the lights in the cab still flashing electric green. Near the empty stands, a pink-laced tennis shoe has been carelessly tossed, the bloody stump of a foot still inside.

* * * * *

When the heel of my vintage Western boot hits the dirt path that leads to the Breaker County Fairgrounds entrance, a cloud of dust kicks up over my jean shorts. Sweet, freshly cut grass mixes with the smell of something fried, and my stomach lurches. The mask I've been wearing does nothing to take the edge off the smell or the heat. When I breathe in, the cotton fabric pulls tighter, but I don't take it off. The crowds are thick and loud. Out of the corner of my eye, I catch the leering smiles of men in broad-brimmed hats.

No one wears a mask. No one stays six feet away. In the distance, an engine revs, and an announcer's voice booms across the fairgrounds. I can hear the faint cheers of the crowd.

To shorten the distance from the entranceway to the youth barn on the other side, I cut through the baked goods exhibit hall. Display cases hold ribbons, rosettes, and cakes that reflect the theme of this year's fair: Burnin' it Out. One cake is covered in dancing flames made of fondant. On top, edible people-shaped figures link arms as if to state their purpose: to burn out the virus together. Breakers County is accountable to no one. No one will tell them what to do, and I'm just a visitor.

When I exit the baked goods exhibit hall, I wander past the animal barns. To the right of the goats is the youth barn, which is where individual fair booths are set up. On the first day of the fair, teens from various agricultural clubs decorate the booths and compete for a prize. The stakes are high: bragging rights and $300 for the club to spend on next year's booth. Often, clubs will hire outside consultants to do all the work, which is where I come in. It has been hard to get consulting jobs of any kind lately, but I've agreed to travel here to help the Strut and Stitch Club with the fair booth competition.

Joanna, the head advisor for this show horse and sewing club, meets me by the fair booth space she has bought, which is the largest that's allowed: a "triple space" that measures 18' wide x 5' long x 8' high. When she sees me coming closer, she looks me over from head to toe and frowns in disapproval.

"You must be Jesse. My goodness, gracious," she says as she looks down at my legs, then studies my mask. "In any case," Joanna continues, "This year's theme is Burnin' it Out, as you know, so we need something flashy—lots of bling and pop. We want to win this year."

"And it's in the contest rules that an outside consultant can be hired?" "Oh, honey! There aren't any rules. We just win."

The sudden sound of an engine revving up makes me jump. Though we're somewhat far from the main grandstand show arena, I think I can smell the scent of fuel.

"That's the tractor pull," Joanna says. "It's our main event here. Everyone comes to the tractor pull."

I've never understood the allure of the tractor pull. What makes contenders want to rig up a tractor engine, hook it up to a sled weighted with thousands of pounds, and pull it along a track?

"C'mon there, hot-to-trot," Joanna says. "I see that yearning look in your eyes. We'll watch one or two pulls. Maybe you'll meet a decent man who'll make you respectable."

"I'm taken," I say, showing her my ring. "My man's waiting for me at home." "Sure don't look like it. Does he know you're out here dressed like this?"

"Yeah, and he likes this outfit—especially the boots."

Joanna rolls her eyes and leads me over to her golf cart, which whisks us back to the tractor pull. It appears to be a never-ending event. There are lots of competitions, divisions, and classes.

Joanna and I stand near the bleachers, where the crowd is seated. We have a decent view of a shiny red tractor that's rigged with several turbo chargers. On the side of the tractor, the words, "Soul Grinder" are painted in bold letters. The man driving it is slim and tan. He sports shoulder-length, bleach-blond hair, and he kind of reminds me of all the guys I thought were out of my league in the '80s. The ones I'd long for. The ones that got away. I laugh at the thought because this is what probably became of them.

"That's Mitch Talon," Joanna says. "He wins every time. He's a real crowd- pleaser."

I watch as the Soul Grinder tractor comes flying down the track, the green lights flashing in the cab of the sled, which is hooked up to the back. The front wheels lift high off the ground, and Mitch's tractor makes it clear to the end. It's a full pull, and black smoke twists and turns above the engine. Joanna is thrilled, but now I'm done. I'm bored, hot, and tired—and I have a long night of decorating ahead of me.

On the way back, Joanna tells me more about Mitch Talon and the Soul Grinder.

"They say he wins because the engine's possessed by a spirit of a navy captain who drowned with his crew when it was hit by a torpedo, back in World War II. His last words showed concern about how many souls were still on board."

Joanna tosses her brown hair back over her shoulder with one hand as she drives the cart with the other. Leaning over the side, she spits on the ground and tells me there are also rumors that Mitch sacrifices people's souls to the engine, so that he'll continue his winning streak. She doesn't believe in any of the rumors, but every year, several people at the fair go missing.

"Does anyone ever investigate?" I ask. "Oh, heavens no!"

"What about the families left behind? What about the families of the missing people?"

"They're told to hush up, I guess. And they do. They always do. Someone goes missing and that's the end of the story. Nice little obituary in the paper—maybe a reception and a memorial service, but never, never an investigation."

"How many people go missing each year?"

"I don't know. Ten? Twenty? Probably brought it on themselves. They were probably drunk or something."

Joanna parks the golf cart in front of the junior fair building, and I get out. It's getting later, and the barn is practically empty. Kids and parents are wandering the midway and shoving pizza and fries down their throats until they have to go home at 10 p.m. I have a special pass, so I can stay longer. Some of the fair participants and their families camp out in designated spots around the perimeter of the fairgrounds. But late at night, when the doors are closed, I feel like I'm the only person awake on the planet—twisting sequined beads into flames and creating movable images on fabric and felt. The Strut and Stitch club will take home a prize, if I have anything to do with it.

Just as I'm about to hot glue more fabric onto the edges of the booth, the door of the barn opens with a loud bang. Two teenage girls are tearing through the place, laughing and carrying on. When they see me, they stop.

"You gonna tell on us?" one of the girls asks me.

"C'mon, Stephanie. Let's just go. No one cares," the other one says. "Mandy, I think this lady's gonna tell on us for being here."

"Why would I tell on you?"

"'Cause. You will!" Stephanie says. She comes closer and points her index finger at me. I can see that her steps are wobbly, and her breath smells like alcohol.

"Nah. I won't tell. I was once your age. But I do have a lot of work to do. You can help if you want."

But when Mandy throws up all over the floor, I can see that they won't be of much help. With the doors open, a light breeze enters, which takes the edge off the pungent smell that's beginning to overpower the room.

"Wait!" Stephanie says. "Oh, shit! Shit!" "What's wrong?" I ask.

"You don't hear that? Listen!" Stephanie says. I stop what I'm doing, and I listen carefully. I hear nothing, except maybe, in the distance— the sound of a motor.

"It's the Soul Grinder! It's coming!" Mandy says.

"Oh, come on. You don't believe that, do you?" I ask.

"It's totally true. My friend Susan—she went missing just last night. They found her shoe—with her foot still inside it—on the tractor pull track. But no one says or does anything about it. No one."

Stephanie erupts into uncontrollable screaming fits, throwing herself onto the ground. I have to cover my ears; the sound is so loud. Meanwhile, Mandy pulls at her shirt and tells her to stop, or else it'll find them.

"Hey! Hey!" I shout. "I don't hear the motor anymore. I think we're going to be okay. Everything will be fine. I'll help you sober up, and then I'll walk you back home. You're staying on the fairgrounds, right?"

"Yeah, we're in the Strut and Stitch club. Joanna's my mom," Stephanie says.

"I see. She probably wouldn't want you up too late—or drunk, I imagine. Look, I always keep some candy in my purse. It won't do much to soak up the alcohol or cover the smell, but it's something."

I hand each girl a packet of sour gummy candies and put them to work on the fair booth, hoping they'll burn off some of that alcohol. When they look like they're steadier on their feet, I offer to walk them back to their campers, so they can try to quietly sneak back in.

In the moonlight, we trace the paths past the goat barn; the animals seem to be stirring.

"Are the animals always this loud at night?"

"Yeah, it depends. Sometimes they're hungry. They're not always on their same feeding schedules while at the fair," Mandy says.

We start to cross the arena area just between the horse show barn and the main grandstand when Stephanie and Mandy stop still.

"I hear it again," Stephanie says.

When I listen, I think I can hear the engine as well.

"No! It can't be! We have to hide! We have to hide!" Stephanie says.

The two girls dart off towards a tree line, just behind the horse show barn, but I stay where I am. I honestly don't believe I'm in any danger, but the longer that I stay here, the louder the engine grows. The sound is unnerving, especially since nothing else, except for the animals, is awake. When I turn my gaze toward the grandstand, where they hold the tractor pull, I see a large, dark shape emerge from the shadows. The outline of a tire with a menacing tread stands out, and in the back, I see the glowing electric lights of the sled's cab. There's a driver in the tractor seat, but the cab for the sled is empty. No one is driving the sled; somehow, the tractor is pulling itself.

The tractor comes to a complete stop in front of me, and the driver climbs out of the cab. As he approaches, I realize that I'm looking right at Mitch Talon, the champion himself. In the moonlight, I can make out his face, and he's all smiles just for me.

"My, my, my," he says. "Don't you know what happens to pretty little ladies who wander the fairgrounds alone?"

"Really? Did you just call me a pretty little lady?"

"Would you rather me call you a little vixen? I have quite the reputation."

"I'm sure you do."

"I'll bet you'd like to know if it's true."

I'm about to tell him he shouldn't flatter himself when I happen to notice something odd about his shirt. It's white, so it glows in the moonlight, but it's spattered with something dark and thick. I tell myself it's just mud, though the weather has been dry, for days.

Behind me, the leaves rustle, and Mitch narrows his focus. The corners of his mouth turn up in a sinister smile.

"Looks like I've struck oil tonight," he says.

Mitch walks back to the tractor and pulls out a rope. Then, he heads for the trees, where I think Mandy and Stephanie are hiding.

"Wait! What're you doing?" I shout.

But he doesn't hear me; instead, he snatches Mandy from the bushes, dragging her out by her left foot. She writhes and screams, but in no time at all, he has her hands and feet bound. He tosses her over his shoulder and throws her into the back of the sled.

Mitch turns. "You're next. I can't be giving away my winning secrets. No one can know."

I really feel for Mandy. I want to save her, but the impulse to save myself is too strong, so I run, tripping over every uneven spot in the grass and dry path. When I think I hear the sound of the engine fading, I believe he's given up and is taking Mandy away—and I can escape.

I run for at least five or ten minutes. But when I get past the goat barn, I hear footsteps on my heels. My plan is to get back to the parking lot and drive away in my car, but my keys are back in the junior fair barn. I'll have to stop there first. I have no choice.

Near the poultry barn, I believe I can take a break because I can no longer hear footsteps behind me. I'm thirsty, my throat is dry, and my boots are digging into the backs of my heels. I'll have to ditch the shoes if I want to make it out of here alive. So I take a moment to breathe and hide behind the fencing near one of the stalls. I just want to get down as low to the ground as I can, but I hear muffled breathing, and I know I'm not alone. Over in the corner is a bale of hay, which is where I think I hear the breathing. The closest thing I have to a weapon right now is a metal bucket, but I'll take it. I'm not sure what I'll do with it, but I trust that I'll think of something. Slowly, I sneak up on the bale of hay and raise my bucket, but when I look down, I see a shoelace and follow it all the way back to discover that Stephanie has made it this far from Mitch as well.

"Stephanie! You're still alive!"

I hug her tightly and tell her that we'll get Mandy and that everything will be okay.

"We can't stay here, though. We have to go back to the junior fair barn. I've got to get my keys. I'll drive us somewhere safe, where we can get help."

Stephanie nods her head and wipes away her tears. Together, we decide to keep going as quickly as we can, but the lights in the barn suddenly turn on. Blinking back tears, we recognize the shape of the man who stands before us, and he has plenty of rope.

I pull Stephanie's hand hard and yank her up with me as we flee the poultry barn. Mitch's footsteps are close by, but I've got Stephanie's hand, and I won't let go. Just when I think we can make it, I feel the weight of Stephanie's body drop. She's on the ground, sobbing, and retching. The alcohol hasn't worn off. She is in no shape to keep running.

"Go! Just go! I can't make it!"

"Stephanie, come on! Stay with me. We'll get my keys—we'll get Mandy—and we'll get help. Just stay with me and pull it together."

Something looms in the shadows and rushes up behind Stephanie, pulling her back by the collar of her shirt. She's thrown down onto the ground, and Mitch towers over her. This time, in addition to the rope, Mitch has a hammer. He bludgeons her skull; I can hear it crack open.

"I love it when they're hammered," he says.

The impact of Stephanie's head with the hammer is sickening. I can't imagine that she has survived. With his right arm still raised, Mitch turns to look at me, his long hair waving wildly in the night air.

I toss both of my boots at him and run barefoot for the junior fair building. I'm not far now, and the hard, prickly earth on my feet makes me run faster, not to mention all the sharp objects carelessly thrown about. My guess is I've stepped on a nail or two as well. My feet are sticky with blood, but I don't feel any pain.

When I reach the junior fair building, I close the doors. They won't lock, but at least I'll buy myself some time if Mitch tries to enter. I find my purse and my keys as well. Throwing my bag to the floor, I hold tightly onto my keys and exit the building on the other side. Once outside, I start to run in the direction of the parking lot, but I think I hear footsteps again, so I turn and run the other way, hoping I can circle back at some point. Soon though, I realize I'm back near the arena, but on the other side, near an area of the fairgrounds I've not seen before. It's a more desolate place with a lake and a playground. The footsteps and the sound of the engine fade—and I believe I can rest for a moment.

* * * * *

A rush of air creeps up behind me, and when I turn around, Mitch is there, with the hammer and the rope. I have no choice but to dive into the lake and swim for the tree line on the other side. Under the water, I hold my breath, kicking hard and pulling with my hands—swimming as fast as I can, still clutching my keys. Nearing the other side, I reach up and kick toward the surface, fully expecting to take a breath and climb out, but something grabs me hard around the middle and pulls. The small space of air I've held in my chest grows tighter; my head spins, and I lose strength. The keys in my clutch drop to the bottom of the lake. Suddenly, the pressure around my middle weakens, but my scalp burns. When I finally surface, I realize that someone is pulling me out of the lake by my hair. Sputtering and coughing, I kick and scream, but Mitch, who has me in his grip, is determined to drag me back to the other side of the lake. Rocks and tree roots scrape against my back and tear at my clothes.

He finally lets me go and kicks me hard.

"You're coming with me. I have a feeling you'll bring tremendous luck."

Mitch ties my hands and feet with rope before picking me up and dropping me into Joanna's golf cart, which I guess is his new method for delivering victims to the racetrack.

In the back of the golf cart, my body rolls around as we hit each bump in the road. As we turn into the grandstand arena, I manage to pull myself upright so I can see. We pass several boxes of fireworks. I guess the Breakers County fair officials plan to put on one heck of a show.

When we get to the track, I see Stephanie and Mandy are still alive, barely. They're breathing, but they're slumped over and moaning. Their shirts and shorts are tattered and thick with blood. Mitch pulls me out of the cart, and I hit the dirt hard. I'm still soaking wet, so the dirt sticks to my face and hair. I can taste blood in my mouth as Mitch drags me one more time over to the empty bleachers, right next to the tractor pull finish line on the track.

It's hard to turn my neck, but I think Mitch is hitching the Soul Grinder to the weighted sled somehow, without the sled driver. He drags Mandy and Stephanie out to the finish line and ties them together. Their faces are bruised, and there's no light in their eyes. Over the loudspeaker, country rock music plays with a strong, thumping beat, and I wonder how no one hears this music? Why wouldn't families who are camped out on the fairgrounds hear the noise and come out here? Why are there no security guards anywhere? Competitors could poison each other's animals or destroy each other's cakes, for crying out loud.

My gaze turns to Stephanie and Mandy. They're just kids, with their whole lives ahead of them, so I try to wriggle out of my ropes. The palms of my hands are pressed up against each other tightly, but my elbows are free. I extend my hands in front of me and try to pull my elbows in at the same time. Just above the music, I hear the engine rev up. Mitch is in the driver's seat of the Soul Grinder, and he's driving full speed at the girls. Their heads have slumped over even more. I try to shimmy my hands from the rope. I even bite on the knot, but the rope is stubborn. A sickening, thumping sound turns my stomach. Mitch has hit the girls, the tires tearing over their bodies, crushing them and mutilating them. Spatters of blood and flesh spray up from under the tires and wash over me, pelting me like tiny bits of gravel. The tractor, on its own, lurches upwards and makes an otherworldly, howling sound, like it's absolutely satisfied with the sacrifice that Mitch has offered. Mitch feeds the larger body parts, heads and arms, into the turbo chargers, which make the entire machine respond with wicked laughter and groans of ecstasy. And that's when I realize that this is real—this is how Mitch wins—this is how people in Breakers County accept things as they are and sleep soundly at night. And I can't let that happen.

By this time, I've got both of my hands free, and I'm well on my way to getting the rope undone around my feet. It's not enough to just get away. I have to stop him. I have to stop the Soul Grinder.

"It's your turn, now. The Soul Grinder needs more souls, and I'll just bet you've got a feisty one, you little vixen," Mitch says as he comes towards me.

I try to push backward with my feet, but my backside collides with something hard and strong. When I look down, I realize that the tractor pull competitors are a messy bunch. They've left their tools all over the place, and the object that I've run into is a hammer. I'm staring up at the space between Mitch Talon's legs. I bring the hammer up hard. When he doubles over on the ground and retches, I drag him by his hair over to the track and use the hammer again to knock him out cold. Then, I climb into the driver's seat of the Soul Grinder, which is still revved up and ready to go. The entire cab smells like Calvin Klein Eternity cologne.

I push down hard on the gas and make perfect contact with Mitch's body, which gets destroyed under the tread of the tires. I feed what's left of him to the turbo chargers, which violently suck him in. The motor bangs, rattles, and explodes— burning itself out, just as the sun comes up, the music stops playing, the cars enter the fairgrounds, and the campers wake up to feed their animals.

Tired, sore, and caked in blood and dirt, I rip the charred grill from the Soul Grinder and put it in Joanna's golf cart—along with a box of Roman Candle fireworks and a lighter.

When I pull up to the junior fair barn, Joanna is there, along with all of the judges, competitors, and parents who are awaiting the results of the fair booth judging. My purse is still on the floor, so I pick it up. My keys are long gone, but my cell phone probably works, and I'll need my wallet, which, surprisingly, no one has stolen.

"What in the hell happened to you?" Joanna asks.

"Your daughter's dead—along with her friend, Mandy."

Joanna's eyes grow wide. In them, I can see that she knows what happened, but she presses her lips together in a hard line and takes a few shallow breaths.

"We don't talk about such things here. People go missing, that's all."

"Well, your daughter is missing and this whole county knows exactly why. You're all sick!"

"I hired you to do one single thing, and you didn't do it. The booth isn't finished. I see where you've started, and you might have helped us win, but there's no flash, no pop—nothing! It's not very... interactive."

"Oh, I'll make it pop," I say.

I walk back over to the golf cart, which is parked outside, and I drag the charred grill of the Soul Grinder over to the booth and toss it inside. Everywhere around me, I hear the low gasps of the crowd that has gathered. Then, I go back for the fireworks and the lighter.

"What are you doing? Stop!" Joanna yells, but I've already lit the fireworks—and I'm running like hell from the junior fair barn. Behind me, people scatter. It doesn't take long before I hear the first bang and whistle. One spark ignites another and the roof of the barn opens up in flames. The fireworks shoot off into the sky, and I can smell the sulfur in the air.

At the gate, the ride I've called is waiting for me. When the driver sees me, he's not sure if he should let me in his car, but I've already paid. As we pull away from the fairgrounds, I look behind me. Smoke billows out in thick clouds. A flashing sign near the gate pulses: Burnin' it out. . . Burnin' it out . . . Burnin'.

FLUID

R.A. Busby

It begins by slicing her open.

In the video, the doctor slides a scalpel from hip to hip across a woman's body, and since she is approximately my size, this process takes time. Below the surface, her skin is shock white. I always assumed the inside layer would be pinkish-red, but it is pale and rubbery like tofu and doesn't bleed much because the surgeon is using a tool that cauterizes as it cuts. When she does bleed, he singes her. I imagine a *bzzt, bzzt* sound as small plumes of smoke rise from her.

I wonder what she smells like.

Smiling, the doctor flips up her skin to show us the underside. Beneath the surface, her flesh is almost all fat. It hangs in dangling drips the color of mango, yellow and buttery. And because I see it during the pandemic, I think about her body open to all the microorganisms in the room.

One evening browsing YouTube to find new Photoshop techniques ("High-End Skin Retouching! Click the red button to subscribe!") I fell into an Internet rabbit hole and ended up on this video. Previously, I had imagined plastic surgery to be a painstaking process, delicate as Japanese art: a nip here, a poke there. This, though, is butchery, like work behind the meat counter at Albertson's, all slices and gristle.

Now, the doctor cuts a circle in the woman's belly and pulls her skin away. Beneath it, I see her navel is just a flaccid red tube in the dark world inside her, head drooping as if ashamed. When he stretches her skin back over it, he makes a slit and fishes the navel out again, a button to fit the brand-new buttonhole he's made. He tacks it to her abdomen with a staple so it will stay put, like an obedient tube.

Feeling sorry for the sad and stapled navel, I wonder why he went to such trouble. Do we even need a navel after we're born, really? Once, when I was still learning Photoshop, I accidentally blurred out a friend's belly button from her swimsuit picture, leaving her innocent as Eve. No one seemed to notice.

The doctor hacks away the skin the woman does not want. The flap, placemat- size, dangles with bits of bloody fat.

It occurs to me then that this rubbery discard was probably the most despised piece of skin this woman owned. She has, I imagine, run her hands over it ten thousand times, pinching the apron falling over her vulva, her upper thighs. In the shower, she has shoved it aside to shave, careful to work soap and washcloth into the valleys so she will not bear that waxy, heavy scent of folded flesh. She has gripped this unloved fold between her hands and wished she could rip it off. Did someone ever tell her, *I love your skin; I love the woman in it?* God, I hope so. But it was not enough.

I think I understand. Her body got away from her. She wasn't at home in her skin.

Her scar won't be wide, just a white line like a disapproving smile, but when her hands make their first tentative journey below her navel (recently relocated), they will clutch empty air. Perhaps tears will leak from her eyes as she lies on her bed and thinks, *I am free.*

But what will happen to her skin, I wonder? It all has to go somewhere. I know that now more than ever.

The nurse will put her pieces inside a red plastic bag embellished with interlocking crescents resembling tribal tattoos, but what then? In a landfill, something might find it. I imagine a coyote tugging until the skin comes away and dangles from his lips like an old red towel.

And because the woman despised this flesh so much she literally told a man to cut it off her, it will taste, I am sure, of bitterness.

* * * * *

The black Google Meet screen flickered at the corner of my eye.

"Thank God," came a voice. "I hate to ask you this, Ana, but can you do Mrs. Perrault today? The woman is up my ass, and I honestly don't have enough time. Or wine. She wants the last retouched prints today."

It was Kami, founder and lead photographer of Deliquesse, the all-female photography studio for which I work. Though we cover weddings and headshots, Deliquesse is mostly about boudoir. For a mere $800, we provide you with three looks and twelve images, or for $1500, unlimited looks and twenty-five images, with professional retouching, giving you an elegant and timeless set of personal photos available after about a week.

Yes, the price is outrageous, even when you throw in the makeover, free wine, and the loaner lingerie, but still, business has picked up. After all, Christmas is around the corner, despite the pandemic.

Normally at this hour, I would be at the studio. I work—well, *worked*—in the backroom behind racks holding intimate wear ranging from adorably virginal to somewhat sleazy. A perk of my job involved finding marabou feathers floating on the top of my coffee.

Since the virus hit, though, I've been locked inside like Rapunzel. Despite the noise, the interruptions, the phone, clients' chatter, the clacks of cameras, I found the studio comfortably reminiscent of my days working theatre tech. In many ways, the jobs are quite alike.

You see, I'm a photo editor. I'm here to make you perfect.

Although Deliquesse's motto is "Every Body is Beautiful," I've seen myself naked. Trust me, my body is not beautiful. To be honest, almost no one's is. The real problem isn't really hair or eyes or weight. It's skin.

The medieval monks wrote records on skin. So do you. Your skin is your record. On it is the story of your birthmarks, your illnesses, the Labrador bite when you were five, teenage acne, a college tattoo, your failure to use sunscreen. Oh, Kami and her makeup crew have a thousand ways to pose and dress and light it, but the rest is my job, so I know. I see it up close.

Kami's avatar flickered. "Ana? You still there?"

I cleared my throat. "Sorry. Of course, I'll help. What does Mrs. Perrault's brief say?"

"Not much." In the foreground, Kami balanced a tablet on her knee. A strand of her hair, a vivid purple, glowed richly on her warm, dark cheek. "She says, 'Don't retouch a lot. Only the basics.'"

"Do we understand what she means by 'the basics'?"

Kami took a breath. "I didn't do the shoot, so I missed a chance to talk to her beyond the intake form, but probably the usual. Spots and blots. You think you can do it before this afternoon?"

Clicking on the photos Kami attached, I nodded slowly. "Sure," I said. "I'll get right on it."

* * * * *

Soon after being hired by Deliquesse, I realized there was a fundamental contradiction between their slogan and their practice. If *every body is beautiful*, why did they need me?

When I first started mastering Photoshop, altering images was a game: Could I shift Tom Cruise's weird tooth to a proper alignment? Tinker with Angelina Jolie's back tattoos so they spelled out what our principal could do to himself with a carrot? Remake classmates into Victoria's Secret supermodels? Soon, I found myself trimming my friends' wiggly muffin tops, plastering pores, widening eyes. Everyone ended up looking like a Bratz doll.

After a while, I understood it's better to make a thousand tiny changes than three big ones. Nowadays, you can put your original next to my retouching, and it's hard to pinpoint why you're so much lovelier in my version. But you are. So much better.

But no. Every body is *not* beautiful. Including mine.

When quarantine hit, I stopped making those daily treks to the studio from the garage; I didn't walk around Smith's; I didn't go to the gym. I stayed trapped inside my apartment because whenever I worked up the guts to go outside, the sidewalks crawled with maskless morons who pretended the virus didn't exist. And I don't have healthcare. Gig economy, don'tcha know. I can't even afford to get a cold.

So sometime around May when I bent over to retrieve a dropped pencil, I sensed a bunching thickness around my waist and thought, *It's my sweatshirt*, but when I pushed it aside, I touched skin. My brand-new roll of skin.

I squeezed my flesh between my fingers till it stung.

The irony is, I agree with Deliquesse's slogan. I *believe* in body positivity, shape acceptance, treasuring your individual self and not some corporate cultural ideal, and loving the lush, luxurious skin you're in.

I'm just not feeling the love for myself.

With our clients, the issue is far simpler. They do not care that every modification, every adjustment, every correction I make is a silent judgment. *Every body is beautiful! But not this part. Or this one. Click. Click. Click.*

* * * * *

Over the next few hours, I learned the face and flesh of Mrs. Perrault as if I were her lover. There was not one inch I did not touch.

Her direct brown eyes stared out at me. I fixed points around her skull to anchor it, then tugged up her head to lengthen her neck. In the first photo Kami sent (*Look #1 of 3*), Mrs. Perrault sat on the edge of a rumpled bed, a purple silk bathrobe artfully draped on her shoulders. Her hair was quite thick, blonde with a few telltale gray streaks at the temples. *Catherine Deneuve*, I decide. *I will make her resemble Catherine Deneuve—well, at fifty—waking up en déshabillé inside a Parisian apartment after a night's vigorous coup.*

Face mode. I zoomed in. Most people's eyes are not equal in size, and Mrs. Perrault was no exception. Her left eye was slightly smaller; her right, a bit higher. I widened both, removing the slight eyelid slackness for which she would otherwise need blepharoplasty. Her nose bridge was wide; I shrank it to a more ideal proportion, 80% of her nostril width.

Below the rounded white expanse of her upper arm, from which I removed her old smallpox vaccination, I saw five thin lines, parallel scratches along the sides of her boob as if she'd been groped by Freddy Krueger. *Nursed a baby, probably*, I mused. With the smoothing tool, I gently pressed her breast until the scars disappeared.

She was not smiling. I added a smile.

* * * * *

"She wants a fucking redo," Kami explained later. "I went over your work with a fine-tooth comb, Ana, and it was goddamned amazing, like it always is. Low-key, very subtle. It's not you, baby. It's her."

Well. At least Kami's not throwing me under the bus. "What does Mrs. Perrault want? I mean, I could make her slimmer."

Kami paused, and in the background, I spotted the black-painted studio walls, the white umbrella edge of a reflector and seeing those familiar, ordinary things brought sudden tears to my eyes. I'd been crying at everything lately.

"No, Ana, it's actually—well, Mrs. Perrault thinks you made her look fake. Like melted wax, she said. Now, we both realize it's bullshit, but—"

Later, when Kami had clicked off, I stared a long time at Mrs. Perrault's prints. I opened a new file. As always, I start with the skin.

When I first retouched this photo, I'd begun by gently blurring her face, softening pores, smoothing scars, subtly swelling the trench along the nasolabial fold caused from age-related bone erosion. The usual.

Now, though, I took a new approach. Creating a black and white adjustment layer, I slid the bar for "reds" far over to minus-200, and on my screen, every single irregularity of Mrs. Perrault's skin burst out in stark relief like the pocked gray surface of the moon. With the tool radius shrunk to a pinpoint, I began to spot-eliminate the most prominent blemishes, the tiny whiteheads, the stray hairs. *Click.* I kept all freckles, the five moles, and even (after some internal debate) the chicken pox dent. I kept the left eye smaller than the right.

I took away the smile.

* * * * *

"Hey," said Kami about two weeks later. "You have a secret admirer."

I hadn't really left my bed yet, because when I woke up and stared at the blank beige walls, I found it wasn't worth the effort. Each day melted into the next, one interminable day since March.

"I haven't washed my hair in a week and I'm wearing old flannel pajamas," I said. "The only human beings I've had contact with in the last two weeks are the delivery driver from Foodz and a pizza guy. It was really erotic. He handed me a pizza and I gave him a five."

"Sounds totally hot," Kami grinned.

"The pizza? It was. No, seriously, what's the deal?"

"In the company inbox this morning was an e-card addressed to you. A gift certificate for a free year of Fluid."

I sat up and stared at the phone. "As in the photo editing program Fluid? As in the unaffordable-except-by-Bill Gates Fluid?"

"The same."

I snorted. "That's not a sugar daddy. That's the whole damn *cane*. What did they say?"

My phone gave a little ping. With a frown, I opened the email Kami forwarded.

"So…" I said. "This mysterious benefactor is literally shelling out for Fluid? As a thank-you? What's the catch?"

"Jesus, Ana, don't look a gift horse in the mouth," Kami chuckled. "And no, before you ask, I haven't the foggiest idea who it's from, but I've checked out the gift information and it seems pretty damn genuine. Order number, actual site, the whole deal."

"But why would…" I began, not sure what to say. "Why would someone send an anonymous gift? You've reviewed the address against our client files, right?"

Kami glanced at her screen. "Yep. No direct matches. I'm guessing it's basically the Gmail version of a 90's burner phone. It doesn't surprise me, though."

Then Kami explained something that I, who never dealt with billing, had never really realized. "Half the shit we do is under the table," she said. "Client comes by, puts the $800 package on Visa, right? But then they slip the photographer an extra hundred in cash to shoot some—well, let's call them 'after dark' shots not included with the set we send to their partner on

Valentine's Day, if you know what I mean. No one's the wiser. Hell, they probably want to thank you without leaving any traces."

"Like they've been Photoshopped out," I chuckle.

* * * * *

Before Fluid, nothing ever challenged the photo editing programs my college graphics design profs called the Big Three: InDesign, Illustrator, and Photoshop. When it appeared from some developer no one heard of, I shrugged and kept on Photoshopping, especially because Fluid cost an arm and a leg.

After Kami clicked off, I scrolled through the online reviews. "This program allows photo manipulation practically at the cellular level," gushed one. Another simply read, "WOW." There was a single two-star review complaining about an unexplained glitch or virus in the latest version, ending somewhat obscurely with the statement, "May cause personal image degradation issues." That was about all. It was astonishing. And besides, someone else was footing the bill.

"Let's do this," I said, my mouse hovering over the Fluid gift certificate. *Click.*

* * * * *

Five hours later, I understood the hype.

It was true.

On my screen was a selfie taken specifically for tinkering with the program, an unretouched and unsparing image of me nude with no makeup and my hair looking like I styled it with a Mixmaster. The usual.

At first, I wasn't impressed. Fluid seemed to boast essentially the same features as Photoshop—color correction, masking, smoothing, and so on. Big deal.

Then I found what Fluid did to skin.

You could get... so deep. It was like zooming into a fractal only to discover the tiniest part of the image was also a fractal, and each one had other fractals inside it, each layer smaller and smaller. *The cellular level indeed.*

When retouching my own photos, I start with the eyes. They are not the mirrors of my soul. They are hostile witnesses and victims of age, indifferent skin care, and squinting. For hours, I worked burning, dodging, pushing up by subtle micromillimeters the flaccid, crepey lids sagging to my lash line, filling tiny wrinkles deep as the Mariana Trench. I clicked into a deeper layer and saw each hair in perfect detail. I could name each separate pore. Then for fun n' games, I ventured lower on my body and played around awhile.

My phone chimed, and I stared at it. Five hours had passed.

Click.

* * * * *

"Damn, lady. You look good. Eyes all bright, cheeks kinda flushed," Kami winked from my screen the next morning. I'd forgotten to turn off my camera. "You finally swipe right on Tinder, or did you find out what else you could use your electric toothbrush for?"

The secret of Kami's success as a photographer was this freewheeling and generous sexuality encompassing everyone. Everything. Hell, she would flirt with the Boston fern shedding its leaves on the studio floor. *Undress,* her playful grin seemed to say. *You are not ugly to me nor unloved nor unwanted.* It worked. Even for the fern.

But for me, the possibility of actual human contact had become increasingly terrifying. These conversations were the closest I got to intimacy.

"Probably it's better coffee," I yawned. I didn't recall going to bed. "Gimme some then, next time you get a delivery."

Shoving the sheets away, I sat up, the light from the window hitting my face at an angle. On the screen, Kami tilted her head, sharp black eyes narrowing.

"Yeah, Ana," she said at last. "You sure that's not a filter? You seem…different." Here's a truth. Mirrors lie. They distort, sometimes by accident, sometimes on purpose, as every skinny-mirror gym owner can tell you. Lighting also lies. You might have three percent body fat but try on your bodycon dress under a single overhead changing-room bulb, and you'll look like you stuffed two pregnant bulldogs up there.

That's why, when I clicked off the meet and went to the bathroom, I didn't immediately believe the image I saw in the mirror because it was so familiar. At first, Kami might have joked I'd finally gotten laid, but her photographer's eyes, used to examining faces, had seen something.

So had I. I'd been staring over five hours at this version of my face yesterday on my monitor. *Click. Click. Click.* An image existing only in pixels. A fake face.

But now it was real.

My hands scrabbled around in my drawer for the compact I hadn't needed since April, and when I got it, I dashed outside. Under direct winter sunlight, I peered into the little round mirror.

Oh, Jesus. If I'd looked like this during high school, I might have gotten laid.

Yesterday, I used the contracting tool on the purplish puffs beneath my eyes and tapped the flesh there gently, shrinking it, smoothing it, watching my skin move and shift like water.

Like fluid.

Now, in the mirror, I saw the bags on my actual face had vanished. The wrinkles, gone.

The resting bitchface lines between my eyebrows. Gone.

The jagged scar from tripping into the whiteboard trough and almost losing an eye. Gone. The spiderweb veins from rosacea beside my nostrils. The chip in my lower front tooth.

Across the sidewalk, I caught sight of Mr. Charles, the apartment manager, taking his asthmatic cocker spaniel on his daily walk. "Come on, Bootsie," he growled, tugging on the dog's leash. His old blue eyes goggled with surprise as I yanked up my shirt to take a peek underneath.

My navel. Gone.

* * * * *

Just a little, I swore to myself upstairs as I opened the Fluid program and called up my picture. *Just a little more.*

* * * * *

The fairy tales told the truth. To get the prince, they said, we'd have to do some serious cutting. Snip our long hair, slice off our mermaid tails and sealskins. Lose our siren song. Cut off our human voices.

Cinderella's sisters, now. They hacked away their toes and heels to fit a see- through slipper, and not even that was enough. Still, you gotta give it to them: those bitches showed *commitment*. I'm named after one, so you can't say I wasn't warned.

Like most girls, though, I ignored the warnings and forgot about the fairy tales. Right about then, I lost control of my body. I'm not sure when it happened. Junior high, probably. Underwear ruined by a thick glut of menstrual blood. Craterous volcanoes from weeping pimples. Pinches of breast with nipples pointing everywhere.

All I remember is that I wished my flesh could be like a potato, all the same throughout no matter which way you cut it, not this loose mess rolling and sagging and bursting from every orifice as if I were a waterbed filled with spaghetti sauce.

Above all, it had seemed so fundamentally unfair. A betrayal. *Why can't our flesh just do what we want?*

"Oh, for God's sake, cut this shit out, Anastasia," my mother finally told me, slamming her saucepan down on the counter one evening. "You don't appreciate how lucky you are. You're healthy and able, to begin with. Other people have *real* issues with their bodies."

"That's even more unfair for *them*!" I shouted back.

And right before the pandemic, when some rogue cells hiding under the skin of my mother's breast came and killed her, I realized they must have been present during that very conversation, lurking beneath her worn-out bra from Sears.

Why can't our flesh just do what we want?

There's no answer.

I suppose it's one reason I became a retoucher: I wanted to restore that balance, to push the scales of justice one tiny bit closer to even.

Just a little.

With my photo on the monitor, I zoomed in, liquefying the awkward bulging plops above my hips, the two-inch strip between my thighs that rubbed itself to rawness when I walked. I evaporated the round skin bagel ringing my (now-absent) navel. Venturing lower, I cut and shrank a few specific items (*he hummed "Do Your Ears Hang Low?" when you took off your undies, you remember? And you let him do you anyway to prove you didn't care but you did you did*), and with my eyes narrowed to slits, made many other things disappear. *Click, click, click.*

It started to sound like the cauterizer in the video.

It hurt a little, too. Down at the deep levels of the program, I saw globules of my fat hanging like melted yellow wax.

Bzzt.

Did you ever pick at a scab, some itchy garnet lump on the bone of your elbow or knee? You start at the edges where it's rough-edged and grainy, and you scratch away a tiny pinhead's worth or two. Then soon, your fingernail works beneath the core, solid and thick, and rips it off to reveal a crater of wet, pink flesh. The pain is glassy and satisfying, isn't it?

Doesn't matter if it hurts. What's the old French saying? *Il faut souffrir pour être belle. One must suffer to be beautiful.*

I bet Catherine Deneuve knew that one.

Bzzt.

* * * * *

"Ana, what the fuck is going on?" Kami's voice had a worried note that made my heartache. "How's your temperature, lady? You're not sick, are you?"

I fumbled for the phone, but it was so dark I couldn't see my hand before my face, which seemed sticky. "I'm fine," I mumbled. "Everything's fine." With the hem of my shirt, I rubbed my eyes, but I still didn't turn on the camera.

You see, I didn't know exactly what I looked like.

"Listen, I'm worried about you lately. Like, ever since--well, your mom, and all the other stuff with the pandemic, and...' Kami broke off. "Where have you been? I've been calling you for *days*. I tried to contact your apartment manager and have him bust down your door or something, but he didn't pick up the phone."

"He's pretty old," I said. "I'm so sorry," I began. "No, Kami, it's—nothing. I've been busy." *And tired. So very tired.*

You see, the Fluid program had a way of wearing me out. The first time when I'd played around with it and erased my navel for the lulz, I'd ended up sleeping a solid eighteen hours after. This last time, I'd done… more.

"Anyway," said Kami, waving her hand, "we have a huge backup. I can handle some, but I need help. Besides, you're so *good*, girl. And fast. I was hoping you might take some overflow."

"Sure! Glad to," I said as brightly as I could, stumbling to the wall to find the light switch. It was sticky. I grimaced, wiping my hands on my shirt. The switch was already on.

"Okay," Kami said, and from her tone, I knew I hadn't convinced her, not entirely, but she changed the subject. "Hey, it'll be a chance to give the new program a try."

"Um…" I answered, scrubbing at my eyes again. "Maybe? But yeah, send over the files. I'll have it done today."

* * * * *

Even after I turned on the bathroom light, the room stayed dim, but I was still thick and heavy-headed, not myself. The skin stretched tightly across my forehead and eyes, and my arms and legs seemed to move in gawky, stuttering ways that rammed me into corners and doorjambs, and my vision was blurry. With a sigh, I drew a bath, letting the water surround me like a warm benediction as I scrubbed at my face with the slightly moldy loofah I'd meant to replace last March before the virus trapped me here at home between my four (rather sticky) walls.

Then something ripped free and dangled from my eyelid like a runner of spit. A membrane thin as sausage casing came away on the loofah, and the room became suddenly brighter. *Was this over my eyes?* With a grimace, I plucked up the white strip of skin and flung it toward the toilet, where it made a wet *smick* and clung to the seat like an old, used rubber. *What the fuck?*

As I scrubbed further, the water took on a dull yellow-pinkish cast, and on the surface floated a bubbling foam I took at first to be residue from my shampoo, but it wasn't. It had an iridescence. The steam was that same yellow-pink, rising with slow and lazy indifference.

When I got out, I stood before the mirror again and swiped the surface with my towel. Even through the smear, I saw the change. It was definitely my face. My body.

But so much better. In a thousand little ways. A hundred thousand. *Click.*

I glanced over at the toilet seat, but the little piece of membrane had vanished.

* * * * *

After this point, my memory became somewhat disconnected. How long did I sit there working with the Fluid program? Days flowed into days, the memory stiff and jangled like a half-remembered dream, but I realized I'd been sitting in this chair about a week and doing

Retouchings working on retouchings, touching everything, every surface must be touched

One must suffer to be beautiful.

When my fingers began leaking on the keyboard, I realized there might be a problem.

At first, I assumed it was blood. This was not entirely wrong. On the "Enter" key lay a fat round droplet, a flawless circle. The touchpad and chair arms were smeary, and the floor felt tacky and wet, the way lemonade does when you spill it on the kitchen floor and leave it to stick to your feet.

I spread my fingers wide and saw a thin amber liquid ooze from beneath my thumbnail. I stared at it, squeezed the tip, and watched as a bright yellowy stream squirted like an injection from a syringe and dribbled down the monitor. On the table edge, a golden droplet lingered a moment, then dropped with lazy indifference onto my sweatshirt where it left a little stain.

One by one, I squeezed my other fingers, swiping away the amber droplets from each one. It was like milking a cow.

I sat in darkness a moment before I thought of something. Opening the blinds, I let the sun stream inside.

The fluid was everywhere. On the walls, on the switch, and hanging over me in a hundred brown droplets like shower condensation. Yellowish tears oozed from the inner corners of my eyes and slipped down to my mouth.

The taste was buttery. A little coppery, too.

Later, staring into the mirror, my mind unable to process quite what had happened to my face, to my skin (*I'm mellllting I'm melllllting*), I recalled the reviews I'd read about Fluid, especially the one complaining about a virus causing "personal image degradation issues."

Yes.

I suppose you might call it that.

* * * * *

When you alter a picture, you're not changing anything. Not in reality, anyway. All you're really doing is shifting pixels. There's no fundamental unbalancing of the universal equation, the stoichiometry of matter. Yep, that's what matters about matter: Can't create it, can't destroy it, only change it.

But I'd done so much more to myself than alter pixels. So very much.

Let's start with fat. You know all those HIIT ab-blasting high-intensity workout videos on YouTube promising you'll "lose fat"? Ever wonder where it goes? Not to the landfill. Nope, we breathe it out. We piss it out. We sweat it out. Didn't some Shakespeare character wish his too-solid flesh would melt, thaw, and resolve itself into a dew? Guess what? We turn our flesh to liquid and to gas on a regular basis.

We make it fluid.

And it all has to go somewhere.

* * * * *

From beneath the sink, I took a stiff-bristled brush and a bucket with hot water and bleach. A thin film coated everything. The walls. The floors. The television remote control. Some string cheese I'd left on the counter.

My flesh. It's strung over the window like pink plastic. My skin. And oh, Jesus. When I peel it off, it stings.

Later, at my computer, I opened the Fluid file with my photo and hit *undo, undo, undo, undo,* my fingertips letting out high-pitched squelches at the tips each time I pressed them down.

It didn't undo.

* * * * *

"What do you mean you want Mrs. Perrault's number?" Kami stared out at me, perplexed. "Ana, please shut down the chat box and actually *talk* to me. Take yourself off mute, would you?"

I wanted to. I really did.

I'd awakened in darkness again Wednesday (?) morning from a dream I was drowning, and when I passed my hands over my eyes, my first thought was, *O God I have no face I have no face.* Below my bangs, my head seemed one featureless expanse of skin, smooth as a mannequin.

From the tiny remaining aperture of my mouth (*I still have a mouth o god*) came a whining, whistling sound as I scrabbled blindly for my blanket, scrubbing my eyes and scouring off rubbery pieces flapping on my cheeks like rumpled wads of half-chewed greyish gum. The skin below was pink. *The membrane. The membrane grew there on my face; it grew over my eyes and erased them, O GOD. Body by Jake; face by Slenderman. Whee!*

I typed some more in the chat box. My fingers were sticking to the keys, and I kept making errors and backspacing, but Kami was patient.

"What do you mean you've tried to email her and she won't respond?" There was an edge in Kami's voice now. "Come on, Ana. Talk to me, lady."

Ever since that bad Slenderman morning, I'd been taking precautions. I'd started covering my eyes with masking tape before I slept. When I woke up, I'd peel it away, and the overgrown membrane would peel away with it like the wax on a Babybel cheese.

Laboriously, I forced my fingers to squelch over the keyboard, trying to explain, ending with *it was her. It started with her SHEdidnfn like the pdxcture sd I made herlook likewax then the fluid prrgm came. It had a virus I caught a virus shes a wich a whitch*

Kami waited a long time before she responded. "Ana, I—"

I onlly wantttt it to stop, I wrote. *Shes a wictch i hope shecan stop it I don't, giveme the numberplease*

"Ana, you know I can't. It's not simply a client confidentiality issue, but it's what you're saying—honey, it doesn't make sense. Mrs. Perrault was perfectly happy with the revised—"

I typed, *Please ne thmemum mumber please*

"She's a working stiff like us, Ana. She works as a school secretary, and her husband owns an auto parts store. She couldn't afford Fluid, not as a joke, or whatever—" Kami shook her head. "Forget it. I'm sorry. What I'm saying is stupid. I'm concerned, hon. I'm coming over. We'll go to the QuickCare. We'll have a doc take a quick peek at you, okay?"

My fingers mashed into the keys. *Nnononoo noonno no*

The thing was, I couldn't afford it. Even if I could, I didn't want Kami to come over.

I think my skin wouldn't like it.

* * * * *

By now, I believe it has formed a neural network.

The other day, I reached for the hall light switch and sensed a tickling on my neck. I stood there, letting my fingers brush the rough apartment wall, victim of a million bad paint jobs, and I could feel the touch on my own skin above my collarbone. In the kitchen, the membrane had grown over the door to the refrigerator, and when I pulled it open, I felt a tugging rip somewhere in my esophagus. When I was done screaming, I shut the refrigerator door and haven't opened it since then.

It also itched. Just from scratching, I tore open the flesh underneath my left breast, which is (*melted warped hanging low*) not doing so very well. I've been howling a lot into my pillow. The neighbors complained, and there was an admonitory note from Mr. Charles the manager stuck to my window yesterday. I peeled open the door, wincing as the membrane made a little quiet *prrt* sound, and let Mr. Charles' memo drop to the ground after I read it.

And lately, I can sense it. A consciousness. A presence. When I sit at the computer staring at my blank monitor, I almost hear the membrane growing around me, persistent as Rapunzel's hair. There's too much to scrub off. It's on the walls, the ceiling, the vents, the apartment's air holes, a giant skin organism surrounding me. I'm never getting my security deposit back.

What's more, I am quite sure of this: It doesn't like me. I can hear it.

youtried to cut me you tried guess whos at home in their skin now ha

* * * * *

When Kami came, she picked up the dropped note and read it, then peered through the long vertical window beside my door, cupping her hand against the light. She rubbed the glass with the side of her fist, but I knew it wouldn't make a difference.

"Ana?" Kami called, her voice slightly muffled by her face mask. "Ana, I know you're in there. It's not like you've left this place since March. Come on, lady. I'm worried about you." She rapped on the door, then drew out her phone. My phone buzzed. I had to type the passcode. Face ID doesn't recognize me anymore.

I tried to say, "*Hey, Kami. I appreciate your coming over. It's so sweet. I'm not too well, so I don't want to make you sick. I'm fine. Everything is fine. Chicken soup, lots of fluids. Ha. Lots of fluids. Lots and lots. No problem,*" but I don't think I did it very well, and the words didn't sound right when I talked, and soon Kami was *hammering* at the gate, and I was afraid the neighbors would call the cops on her. I huddled beside the window and pleaded with Kami to go home, to leave while she was still safe because I loved her and I always had and there was nothing she could do anyway and please please leave. Her voice muffled and urgent, said things like *Listen, we need to get you to the doctor; I think you caught the virus. You look as if you have a fever. I'm going to find the manager's office and ask him if he'll open up your place, okay? Okay?*

With my face pressed to the window, I watched her as she walked toward the office, brave and bold, her purple hair gleaming. *Don't come back here, Kami. Please. Stay safe. Don't come back.*

When she gets there, I don't think she'll find Mr. Charles. All day, I've heard Bootsie barking, and all night long as well. Mr. Charles, wherever he is, isn't opening any doggie doors today. Not since he visited here. Not since he touched the window. The membrane grows on the outside now.

I think I know what happened to him. I think it got him. I can...feel it.

This morning, I awoke with the membrane fully covering my mouth. It had left me no little aperture this time. Worse, it had grown over the ends of the peel-away tape, and I had to scrub and scratch to find them. It took me longer than ever to free myself. A lot longer.

Humans can hold their breath about two minutes. I've been thinking about that quite a bit lately. How long will it be before the membrane figures out the purpose of my nostrils? Before I wake up gasping and purple, trying to claw a hole in my face so I can breathe? *Hey, kids! I've grown a permanent Covid mask! Fairytales can come true!*

I've set out a rough washcloth on the counter, and if it doesn't work, I've got my scissors. And a razor blade.

I think the skin I cut off will taste of bitterness.

Il faut souffrir pour être belle.

AUTHOR BIOGRAPHIES

~~~

Jessica Burgess spins tales of darkness from the deep woods of Kentucky, a place that shaped her love of the macabre. Her debut story "Cursed" from Kandisha Press is the world's first look into her craft. @msjessiebwrites (Twitter)

R.A. Busby - A member of the Horror Writers Association, R.A. Busby's story "Street View" (Collective Realms #2) was recently selected for inclusion on the Preliminary Ballot List for the Bram Stoker Awards for 2020, while two of her stories ("Not the Man I Married" and "Holes") were nominated for a 2020 Shirley Jackson Award.

R.A. Busby has several other published horror stories including "Bits" (Short Sharp Shocks #43), "Cactusland" (34 Orchard #2), "Kiss" (Women in Horror Anthology #3: The One That Got Away), "A Short, Happy Life" (Creepy Podcast 12/20), "Baby" (Good Southern Witches Anthology), and the recently-released "Cold" (What Remains Anthology.) In her spare time, she runs in the desert with her dog and looks for weird things to write about. @RAbusby1 (Twitter)

Holley Cornetto writes dark fantasy, horror, and weird fiction. To date, her writing appears in over a dozen magazines and anthologies. She serves as a reviewer and contributor for The Horror Tree, and can be found online at https://holleycornetto.com or lurking on Twitter @HLCornetto.

Tracy Cross – Tracy's forthcoming first book, "Rootwork" will be published by Omnium Gatherum Media in 2022. Her latest work, "Side Effects May

Vary" will appear in an anthology published by Skywatcher Press. She will also be featured in anthologies Don't Break the Oath by Kandisha Press and 99 Tiny Terrors published by Pulse Publishing. She was the recipient of the 2020 Ladies of Horror Fiction Grant. She has also been featured on the podcasts: "Black Women Are Scary," "Nightlight" and the forthcoming "Bane Podcast". A native of Cleveland, Ohio, Tracy lives in Washington, DC with her youngest daughter. You can find out about her at tracycrossonline.com or on Instagram at tracycrosswrites.

Cassie Daley is a writer and illustrator living in Northern California. Her first published short story, "Ready or Not", debuted as a part of Fright Girl Summer, and is available to read online. Her nonfiction has been published by Unnerving Magazine, and her short fiction has appeared in several horror anthologies. She is the creator of THE BIG BOOK OF HORROR AUTHORS: A Coloring & Activity Book and ROSIE PAINTS WITH GHOSTS, an illustrated spooky story for children. In addition to her writing, Cassie owns an online art shop and is also a contributing team member to the Ladies of Horror Fiction website, as well as a host on The PikeCast, a book podcast dedicated to reading and discussing the works of Christopher Pike. You can find Cassie on Twitter as @ctrlaltcassie, and you can find her artwork at shopletsgetgalactic.com.

Ariel Dodson is an author of fantasy novels for adults and teenagers. Ariel's novel, Blood Moon, was published on Smashwords and Amazon Kindle in 2013 and was inspired by a 16th century werewolf legend. She is currently working on the third instalment in a teen fantasy trilogy involving magic, jewels and an ancient family curse. The first two novels in the series, The Wind of Southmore and The Witch's Sister, were released in 2014.

Her work has been published in Ellery Queen Mystery Magazine, Dark Lane Anthology and, most recently, in the F is for Fear Anthology.

www.facebook.com/Ariel-Dodson-16116561190742321/

Alyson Faye - Alyson lives in West Yorkshire, UK with her husband, teen son and rescue animals. Her fiction and poetry has been published in a range of anthologies, (Diabolica Britannica/Daughters of Darkness) on the Horror Tree, several Siren's Call editions, in Page and Spine, by Demain Press (The Lost Girl/Night of the Rider), in Trickster's Treats 4, on Sylvia e zine and The World of Myth.

She has stories due out in Space and Time's July magazine and in October, in Brigid's Gate Press', Were-Tales anthology.

Her work has been read on BBC Radio, local radio, on several podcasts (Ladies of Horror and The Night's End) and placed in several competitions.

She works as an editor for a UK indie press and tutors. She co-runs the indie horror press, Black Angel, with Stephanie Ellis. Their aim is to publish and promote women horror writers, from new voices to more established ones.

She swims, sings and is often to be found roaming the moor with her Lab cross, Roxy.

Twitter @AlysonFaye2
www.amazon.co.uk/Alyson-Faye/e/B01NBYSLRT
blackangelpressblog.wordpress.com

Melissa Ashley Hernandez is a Latinx author working on her Creative Writing MFA from Fairleigh Dickinson University. Her poetry has featured in indie literary magazines, an anthology by Loft Publishing, and her chapbook, *The Love in*
Between; while her prose has been published in a quiet horror anthology, *Paranormal Contact*, by Cemetery Gates Media. You can keep up with her work on her website at https://melissaashleyhernandez.com.

Sheela Kean is the author of the paranormal suspense novella Sleep Wakers and short horror collect Night Frequencies. She lives in a small Michigan town with her husband and children. She has been an avid reader all her life, hoarding books all over her home. She loves being active in the bookish community, sharing her latest reads with everyone on social media. She enjoys camping with her family (which mostly just means reading in the woods) and painting (badly). As a mom to three young boys, she also values extreme amounts of coffee and silence. http://www.SheelaKean.com http://twitter.com/sheelakean http://instagram.com/sheelakean

---

Kirby Kellogg is a Maine-based horror writer and music journalist. Her work can be found on the pages of Black Rainbow Vol. 1, on the website Morbidly Beautiful, and in her own book Trampled Crown through Unnerving Press. Her twitter is @sugarbombstim.Kirby Kellogg is a Maine-based horror writer and music journalist. Her work can be found on the pages of Black Rainbow Vol. 1, on the website Morbidly Beautiful, and in her own book Trampled Crown through Unnerving Press. Her twitter is @sugarbombstim.

Cecilia Kennedy taught English composition and Spanish courses in Ohio before moving to Washington state with her family. Since 2017, she has published stories in literary journals, magazines, and anthologies. Her work has appeared in Maudlin House, Coffin Bell, Open Minds Quarterly, Headway Quarterly, Flash Fiction Magazine, and others. The Places We Haunt (2020) is her first short story collection. Additionally, she's a columnist for The Daily Drunk, an editor for Flash Fiction Magazine and Running Wild Press, and humor blogger: Fixin' Leaks and Leeks (https://fixinleaksnleeksdiy.blog/). Twitter: @ckennedyhola.

K.P. Kulski is the author of the novel Fairest Flesh, a gothic horror from Strangehouse Books. Her short fiction and poetry have appeared in various publications including Unnerving Magazine, the HWA's Poetry Showcase, and Not All Monsters. Born in Honolulu, Hawaii to a Korean mother and

American-military father, she spent her youth wandering and living in many places both inside and outside the United States. Now she resides in the woods of Northeast Ohio where she teaches college history. Check out her website, www.garnetonwinter.com or follow her on Twitter @garnetonwinter.

Caryn Larrinaga is a Basque-American mystery and horror author. Her award- winning fiction has been featured in The NoSleep Podcast, printed in multiple anthologies, and adapted for film. She is an active member of the Science Fiction and Fantasy Writers of America, the Horror Writers Association, the Cat Writers Association, and the League of Utah Writers. She lives near Salt Lake City, Utah, with her husband and their clowder of cats. Visit www.carynlarrinaga.com for free short stories and true tales of haunted places.

Marie McWilliams is a Horror and Crime writer from Northern Ireland. She has had short stories featured in several anthologies, magazines and book boxes. Her debut novel 'Broken Mirrors' is available on Amazon now and was short listed for the Book Blogger Novel of the Year Award 2020. When not writing, she is on social media sharing her love of horror books. Check her out on Instagram (@bookishmarie), Youtube (Marie McWilliams) and TikTok (@mariemcwilliams1) now.

Samantha Ortiz is a lover of psychological and paranormal horror. When she's not writing, she's making video games (some horror related, some not), watching obscure youtube videos, or hanging out with her pets. She has previously been published in 101 Proof Horror, an anthology by Haunted MTL. https://twitter.com/samloveskirby

---

Charlotte Platt is a young professional based in the far north of Scotland. She spent her teens on the Orkney Islands and studied in Glasgow before moving to the north Highlands. She lives off sarcasm and tea and can often be found walking near cliffs and rivers, looking for sea glass. Her short stories have also featured in Midnight in the Pentagram, The Infernal Clock: Inferno and The Future Looms. Her debut novel, A Stranger's Guide, is available via Silver Shamrock Publishing and she can be found on Twitter at @Chazzaroo.

Lydia Prime is a New Jersey born creature of the night. Her short story, Sadie, (published in Kandisha Press', Under Her Black Wings: 2020 Women in Horror Anthology) won the 23rd Critters Annual Readers Poll for Best Horror Short Story (2020). When Lydia isn't releasing monstrosities from her mind, she happily helps others work with their brain children through her custom editing services. On Fridays, she even offers free faulty advice to those in need. Charitable, and chilling—what a gal!

Socials:

Facebook: @AuthorLydiaPrime Instagram: @Helminthophobia
Author Blog: Lapsed Reality - lydiaprime.wordpress.com Twitter: @LydiaPrime - twitter.com/lydiaprime
Amazon Author Page: https://www.amazon.com/-/e/B083SSBQLG Fiverr: @Prime_Le

---

Jennifer Soucy is just a regular girl with an abiding love for the dark and twisty. Born and raised in New England, she left that all behind at nineteen to follow her family to Atlanta. She's spent nearly two decades in the South, delighting in how many people still call her a "Damn Yankee." She also lived in Las Vegas for two years, her home away from home. Just before turning forty, she started writing again to fulfill her childhood dreams.

Her novels include: DEMON IN ME, THE NIGHT SHE FELL, CLEMENTINE'S
AWAKENING (Silver Shamrock Publishing), and THE MOTHER WE SHARE (RhetAskew Publishing), and the upcoming SHE WHO DESTROYS.

She hopes to continue writing stories that occasionally make people sleep with the light on.

Learn more about Jennifer at her website, www.jenniferlsoucy.com/

Anna Taborska is a British filmmaker and horror writer. She has written and directed two short fiction films, two documentaries and an award-winning TV drama. She has also worked on twenty other films, and was involved in the making of two major BBC television series: Auschwitz: the Nazis and 'The Final Solution' and World War Two Behind Closed Doors – Stalin, the Nazis and the West. Anna's short stories have appeared in over thirty anthologies, and her debut short story collection, For Those who Dream Monsters, published by Mortbury Press in 2013, won the Dracula Society's Children of the Night Award and was nominated for a British Fantasy Award. Anna received a Bram Stoker Award nomination for her novelette The Cat Sitter, published in her feline-themed micro-collection Shadowcats, and also for her latest collection of novelettes and short stories, Bloody Britain (Shadow Publishing, 2020), which was also nominated for two British Fantasy Awards.

Sonora Taylor is the author of several short stories and novels, including *Seeing Things*, *Little Paranoias: Stories*, and *Without Condition*. In 2020, she won the Ladies of Horror Fiction awards for Best Collection (*Little Paranoias*) and Best Novel (*Without Condition*). Her short stories have been published by Camden Park Press, Burial Day Press, Kandisha Press, Cemetery Gates Media, Sirens Call Publications, Tales to Terrify, and others.

Along with V. Castro, Sonora co-manages Fright Girl Summer (frightgirlsummer.com), an online book festival promoting marginalized authors and voices. In 2022, Sonora and Nico Bell will edit an anthology of fat-positive horror called *Diet Riot: A Fatterpunk Anthology*.
Sonora's latest collection, *Someone to Share My Nightmares: Stories*, will be out in October 2021. She lives in Arlington, Virginia, with her husband and a rescue dog.
Visit Sonora online at sonorawrites.com.

Roxie Voorhees heard Rob Zombie's "Living Dead Girl" at 16-years-old and hasn't stopped striving to be an irresistible creature who has an insatiable love for the dead since. When she isn't reading, she is writing, and when she isn't writing she is creating something with her hands while binge-watching Buffy.

Originally from Central California, she now resides with her twins and mastador, Bellatrix, in NE Indiana, where she refuses to use the word pop, is hella progressive, and dreams of a proper taco. She is currently working on her first novel and a graphic novel series with her daughter.

Blog: www.confessionsofabookslayer.com Instagram: @the.book.slayer Twitter: @rvthebookslayer

---

C.C. Winchester believed that like many writers before her, her horror loving journey began with the works of Stephen King. After reading Salem's Lot as a teenager, she found it necessary to sleep with the light on for a week and she loved it! But upon reading said books, she was informed by her mother that around the age of five, she started sneaking into the living room late at night to watch zombie movies and such with her parents. Her mother said that though her infiltration was discovered and she was promptly removed from said living room, that she would return in what she thought was stealth mode, only to be removed again. She currently resides in Dallas, Texas with her daughter who also writes stories. Their home is full of four-legged loves; three dogs and four cats (all rescues), who love to help them write!

She is a member of the Horror Writers Association (HWA), and you can find her on the interwebs at:

Twitter: @MultiverseCC Website: multiversedream.com

Angela Yuriko Smith is an American poet, author, and publisher with over 20 years of experience in newspaper journalism. She is a Bram Stoker Awards® Finalist and HWA Mentor of the Year for 2020. She co-publishes Space and Time, a publication dedicated to fantasy, horror and science fiction since 1966. Join the community at spaceandtime.net or visit Angela at angelayurikosmith.com

About The Editors

Jill Girardi is the best-selling, award-nominated author of the Hantu Macabre series. A film based on the characters in the series is set to begin production in 2022, starring Malaysian MMA fighter Ann Osman. Jill has numerous short stories published, most of which feature her signature brand of dark humor and wicked little creatures. She is also the founder of Kandisha Press, an independent publisher supporting women horror authors around the world. Instagram/Twitter @jill_girardi

---

Janine Pipe is a Splatterpunk Award nominated author. Her debut short story collection TWISTED: TAINTED TALES was released in 2021 and she has contributed to many popular anthologies. She is a script editor for the Something Scary podcast and writes for Scream Magazine and Cemetery Dance. Coffee plays a very important part in her life. Twitter @janinepipe28

LIKE WHAT YOU READ HERE?
PLEASE CONSIDER SUPPORTING KANDISHA PRESS AND OUR AUTHORS BY GIVING US A REVIEW ON AMAZON, GOOD READS OR BOOK BUB!

ATTENTION ALL WOMEN HORROR AUTHORS:
If you are interested in submitting your work for consideration for a future Kandisha Press Women of Horror Anthology, please get in touch with us for submission guidelines and upcoming deadlines!

WOMEN OF HORROR VOLUME 5 COMING 2022

ALSO COMING SOON: SLASH-HER: ALL-WOMAN SLASHER ANTHOLOGY (CURATED BY JANINE PIPE) SPRING 2022

FACEBOOK: @KANDISHAPRESS TWITTER: @KANDISHAPRESS INSTAGRAM: @KANDISHAPRESS

WWW.KANDISHAPRESS.COM

AVAILABLE NOW:

UNDER HER BLACK WINGS
WOMEN OF HORROR ANTHOLOGY VOLUME ONE
KANDISHA PRESS JANUARY 2020
Available on Amazon Paperback, Kindle, and Kindle Unlimited

"What happens when eighteen women authors from around the world are tasked with creating their own Woman Monsters? This book! And your worst nightmares..."

Featuring stories from: Christy Aldridge, Carmen Baca, Somer Canon, Dawn DeBraal, Sharon Frame Gay, The Sisters of Slaughter : Michelle Garza and Melissa Lason, Jill Girardi, Alys Hobbs, Tina Isaacs, Stevie Kopas, Marie Lanza, Malena Salazar Maciá, Charlotte Munro, Lydia Prime, Paula R.C. Readman, Copper Rose and Yolanda Sfetsos

With cover art by Corinne Halbert (Hate Baby Comix) and Foreword by Brandon Scott (Author of Vodou and Sleight, Devil Dog Press)

GRAVEYARD SMASH
WOMEN OF HORROR ANTHOLOGY VOLUME TWO
KANDISHA PRESS JULY 2020
Available on Amazon Paperback, Kindle, and Kindle Unlimited

"Step through the prettiest cemetery gates you've ever seen and read through the night as the dead rise from boneyards all around the world!"

Featuring stories from: Christy Aldridge, Carmen Baca, Demi-Louise Blackburn, R.A. Busby, V. Castro, Dawn DeBraal, Ellie Douglas, Tracey Fahey, Dona Fox, Cassidy Frost, Michelle Renee Lane, Beverley Lee, J.A.W.

McCarthy, Susan McCauley, Ksenia Murray, Ally Peirse, Janine Pipe, Lydia Prime, Paula R.C. Readman, Yolanda Sfetsos and Sonora Taylor

With cover art by Ilusikanvas and Foreword by Doc Holocausto (Evilspeak Magazine, Harvest Ritual, Creepy Crawls)

THE ONE THAT GOT AWAY
WOMEN OF HORROR ANTHOLOGY VOLUME THREE
KANDISHA PRESS JANUARY 2021
Available on Amazon Paperback, Kindle, and Kindle Unlimited

"What doesn't kill me, might make me kill you!"

30 women authors from around the world were challenged to write about The One That Got Away. Here you'll find tales of unrequited love, blind dates gone wrong, stalkers and their prey, cursed guitars, alien symbiotes, sinister letters, and bitter acts of revenge. Dive into murky depths and discover what hides inside the minds of women scorned..

With Foreword by Gwendolyn Kiste (Bram Stoker Award Winning Author of The Rust Maidens) and cover art by Ilusikanvas.

Edited by Jill Girardi

Featuring stories from: Carmen Baca, Ushasi Sen Basu, Demi-Louise Blackburn, Ashley Burns, R.A. Busby, Amira Krista Calvo, Dawn DeBraal, Shawnna Deresch, Ellie Douglas, Amy Grech, KC Grifant, Meg Hafdahl, Rowan Hill, Stevie Kopas, Michelle Renee Lane, Catherine McCarthy, Villimey Mist, Mocha Pennington, Faith Pierce, Janine Pipe, Lydia Prime, Paula RC Readman, Marsheila Rockwell, Lucy Rose, Rebecca Rowland, Hadassah Shiradski, Yolanda Sfetsos, Barrington Smith-Seetachitt, J Snow and Sonora Taylor.

Printed in Great Britain
by Amazon